FAERIE RISING

The First Book of Binding

A. E. Lowan

Phoenix Quill Books

PITTSBURG, MISSOURI

Fic
Lowan

Phoenix Quill Books
24230 Deer Trl
Pittsburg, MO 65724

Visit the author's website: www.aelowan.com

Publisher's Note: This is a work of fiction. Names, characters, places, and incidents are a product of the author's imagination. Locales and public names are sometimes used for atmospheric purposes. Any resemblance to actual people, living or dead, or to businesses, companies, events, institutions, or locales is completely coincidental.

Book Layout © 2018 BookDesignTemplates.com
Cover design by Deranged Doctor Design
www.derangeddoctordesign.com

Faerie Rising: The First Book of Binding / A. E. Lowan -- 1st ed.
ISBN 978-1732316409

For our mothers, Peggy O'Rourke, Tammy Smith, and Theresa Vinck.

Thank you for teaching us that no dream — no matter how big — is out of reach.

ACKNOWLEDGEMENTS

No book is created in a vacuum. It has taken years and a small army of supporters to bring Seahaven and *The Books of Binding* to the world. A. E. Lowan would like to extend our humblest thanks to:

Deranged Doctor Design, for your amazing cover art. We are writers left without words.
(www.derangeddoctordesign.com)

Bradley Gunson, our dread alpha reader. This book wouldn't exist without you. We cower in fear of your red pen and marvel at your discerning intuition.

Our four Graces: Karen Jones, Keri-Dawn, Lacey Scott, and Marissa Southards, our infinitely patient beta readers. Dear ladies, we cannot thank you enough.

Tim and Peggy O'Rourke, for years of patience, encouragement, and keeping us going.

Robert and Theresa Vinck, for always believing we could do this.

Tammy Smith, for always encouraging us to do our best, and for all the sacrifices you have made to get us this far.

Seattle Public Schools, for an afternoon patiently answering a writer's questions.

George Cole with Alpha Omega Ink of Van Buren, Arkansas, for your invaluable advice in the creation of the Marks.

Dr. Christine Harker and Dr. Rebecca Harrison from Truman State University, for generously donating your time and knowledge.

The community at Mythic Scribes, for all your support and encouragement.
(www.mythicscribes.com)

Sam Giffen, for your paintball expertise and unending enthusiasm for the series.

Jonas Journey, for a thousand reasons. You are a blessing.

Judith Towse Roberts, for teaching us the rules and, more importantly, when to break them.

Shirley and Paula Schaaf, for lifetimes spent inspiring and fostering creativity.

Kyra Bergen, for lending a helpful ear.

Joseph Ingrassia, for offering support where it was sorely needed.

Mick Kasemeier, for reading work of early years and sticking through till the end, and now—new beginnings.

Nathan Matthews, for putting up with late nights and our obsession.

Ray Yettaw, for your encouragement and advice.

Robin Heather Owens Slicer, for being there for the terrible early stories and never wavering in your belief that the good ones would come.

Glenys McGhee, for teaching us how to collaborate.

How to Fight Write, for your technical advice.
(http://howtofightwrite.tumblr.com/)

Writing with Color, for answering honestly, thoughtfully, and quickly and for reminding us to always reach for more than the familiar.
(http://writingwithcolor.tumblr.com/)

The pioneers of urban fantasy who have gone before us, for boundless inspiration and leaving breadcrumbs for the tenacious to follow.

Chris Smith, for contributing business advice and being a typical brother.

Aidan Seek, for your sense of humor. Someday you will be the best office minion of them all.

A NOTE ON NAME PRONUNCIATION

The Books of Binding contain some names for which the pronunciations are not immediately obvious. Here is a guide to pronouncing those names which might prove tricky.

Aideen: Ay-DEEN
Anluan: AN-lawn
Anraí: AHN-rey
Aodhán: AY-awn
Bri: BREE
Ceallach: KAL-ukh
Chretien: CREH-tee-en
Cian: KEE-in
Ciarán: KEE-a-rawn
Dagda: DAW-daw
Deirdre: DAIR-dreh
Éibhleann: AYV-len
Eithne: EN-yuh
Eoin: OH-in
Etienne: EH-tee-in
Gaubert: Gow-BEAR
Lanadrielle: La-NOD-ree-el
Midir: Mid-HEER
Mulcahy: Mul-KAY-hee
Niamh: NEEV
Scoithín: SKUH-heen
Senán: SHAN-awn
Sorcha: SUR-a-ka

CHAPTER ONE

The little bell above the shop door preceded the desperate cry of, "Winter, we need you!" The urgency in her friend's voice tore the wizard's attention from her task. She dropped the open box of sterile surgical instruments on the long counter and rushed across the back-room clinic, passing the city map of Seahaven, Washington that took up one entire wall. On the map were red dots and a concise note for every violent incident this year. It was the end of October and the map was so covered in red that it looked like it was inflicted with a virulent rash. She pushed her way through the thickly-beaded curtain into the still-darkened storefront.

It was hours before the rest of the shops in the Historical District would open. The sun was just trembling on the mountain's lips and the deep shadows cast by the century-old buildings left the street so dark that the streetlights were still lit. Through the doorway walked Giovanni and Katherine, though 'walk' might have been too casual a description. He leaned heavily on her smaller frame, his dark skin ashen even in the dim light, but she bore his weight easily with her right arm about his lean waist, holding both his and her jackets in place against his back. Katherine kicked the door closed behind her and showed Winter her face, fair beneath the thick spray of blood that glittered on her skin and hair.

Winter swallowed down the rising bile of panic as the meat smell of heavy bleeding reached her. In her experience, that was the smell of a loved one's violent death.

She had seen a great deal of death.

"What happened?" she asked even as she quelled her trembling belly with a wash of icy professionalism and shoved a half-empty box aside with her foot to make a clear path. The shop was a disaster, thick with dust, boxes everywhere and the shelves half empty. But there was precious little she could do about it anytime soon.

Katherine carefully maneuvered Giovanni through the beaded curtain into the light as Winter held it open. While Winter slipped on surgical gloves and one of her white coats, Katherine lifted him up onto the sturdy old exam table.

"Sharks..." he began, his voice breathy with pain, but Katherine placed her blood-slick hand over his pale lips.

"Be still, Giovanni," she said.

He gave a small nod, his dark eyes glassy, and his tongue flickered out to taste the blood that gloved her arm to her elbow.

"Did he say sharks?" Winter raised a pale eyebrow in surprise, but her eyes were already focused on the soaked jackets that now clung in heavy folds to Giovanni's body, held in place by the sticky blood. She had to focus on the injury, not her friend, not his pain. Compartmentalize the current crisis so she could bring all her training to the forefront and take charge of the problem and not be lost in her fear and sympathy for him— or worse, be lost in the memories the overwhelming scent of his blood brought flooding back to her. The meat smell was coming from Giovanni, not Katherine, and Winter now strongly suspected that the blood covering Katherine's face was not her own. She took the edge of the makeshift bandage and began to peel it carefully away from his body.

"Four sharks at Twenty-seventh and Benton, looking for trouble." Katherine let her eyes close as Giovanni drew one of her fingers into his mouth and began to suck it clean. Her lips parted, her upper and lower fangs extending much like a snake to show startling white against the natural crimson of her mouth. She had licked her lips clean, but blood was drying in her hair, and completely coated her throat and chin. She wore a black t-shirt that was cropped too short for the late October chill, revealing a generous hand span of flat belly above her black jeans. Beneath another arching splash of blood across the shirt winked white letters, '*Strangers*

Have the Best Candy,' that did nothing to hide Katherine's hardening nipples.

Winter glanced at the city map, really more to have something else to look at than because she needed to, and then back at Giovanni's emerging wound. "That's outside their territory." She wished they would do that someplace... elsewhere. She knew the blood could keep Giovanni distracted from his pain, but it was a bit disconcerting. Both were becoming aroused, which only served to heighten the release of their pheromones. They were scenting at each other, but Winter was caught in the middle. She noticed that she had shifted her weight closer to the two of them, closer to their enticing scent, and consciously shifted away. They really needed to stop. She was in no mood for a cold shower.

"Are they pressing the lions again?" she continued, trying to distance herself from her own hormones. The two groups of therianthropes—shapeshifters bearing both human and animal forms—had experienced tensions ever since Corinne Lyons-de Vera, the Lion Queen, came to Seahaven. Their territories overlapped, the sharks being on the waterfront and in Eriksson Bay, and the lions holding the largest islands in the Bay. The lions had closely allied with the dolphins and selkies early on, which brought them into direct conflict with the sharks, the dolphins' natural enemies. And now there was this new alliance between the sharks and the orcas, pitting both groups against the dolphins and the lions... The factional fighting really would never end, would it?

Katherine opened her eyes with some small difficulty, their dove gray striking against the fine crimson spray that dappled her cheeks and eyelids, pupils dilated. This much blood... Winter could imagine it was intoxicating, even cold, but she really did not need to deal with a pair of blood-drunk vampires this morning, close friends or not. "It would seem so."

Giovanni was making small pain noises as Winter carefully tore loose half-formed clots that clung to the jacket fabric and Katherine slipped two other blood-covered fingers into the wounded vampire's mouth. "They had a couple of the younger lion boys cornered. I think they wanted to send Corinne a message."

Winter dropped the ruined jackets with a wet splat into her large metal sink and set to cutting away Giovanni's artistically faded t-shirt. With sharks, she expected to see a massive wound, as a therian shark would bite to remove flesh… but what had they been doing in the water, then? Twenty-seventh and Benton was not that close to the Bay. Therian sharks needed immersion to shift. But as she peeled the blood-soaked fabric away three parallel slices running from the point of his right shoulder blade to the lower edge of his ribs began to bleed with renewed vigor. Winter froze for a moment in surprise and then reached for a large sport bottle of sterile water. "Sharks don't have claws. Did the lions do this?" Sharks were one of the few predatory therian species to not be land mammals, and they also did not shift into half-form—the traditional 'wolf-man' often seen in movies. Like the other aquatic species, if they attacked on land, they attacked in human form. Even with a therian's strength and speed it gave them a considerable disadvantage against the fangs and claws of their more gifted rivals.

Giovanni moaned in pain as Winter began cleaning the wounds and grasped Katherine's hand in a white-knuckled grip. His full strength would have broken Winter's bones, but Katherine squeezed back, gently stroking the back of his hand and his wrist. "No, the sharks did it." She changed her grip on Giovanni's hand, so he could squeeze tight. "The fourth one snuck up behind him while we were dealing with his three friends."

As the water washed the clotting blood from the wounds, Winter noticed how very clean the edges were, no tearing at all, the slices driving deep through skin and fat and into the muscles of his shoulder. "This was done with three parallel blades."

Katherine nodded. "They have some new toys. Apparently, their King found a solution to his claw envy, and they've discovered the wide, wonderful world of fist weapons."

"Sharp, too," Giovanni rasped, pain and stress deepening the Eastern European tones of his Romani accent. "Didn't know how bad it was 'til my arm wasn't working right."

Wonderful. Because the factions in Seahaven needed more ways to kill each other. Winter checked the depths of the lacerations for debris, washing her friend's blood away and down to soak into the pile of towels tucked carefully against his side, and was grateful, not for the first time, that he was a vampire. It would take more than this to cause him to bleed his life away on her floor. It was painful, but it was already beginning to heal. "You're lucky he didn't bite you," she said as she set down the bottle and reached for a large jar of translucent green ointment. "You would be a while trying to grow back that much flesh." Now a wizard, on the other hand—wizards were much easier to kill. As much blood as there was here, there had been so much more when the twins... She shook her head, shoving the memories away. Kelley and Martina, her cousins, had only died six months before, but grief was an indulgence and she did not have time for it. The here and now was what mattered. Her gaze fell on Katherine, who watched her speculatively. "Are you hurt?"

Katherine shook her head and ran a finger across her chin and down her throat, scraping the caked blood coating her skin like thin icing. The grin she flashed at Winter was a savage thing, full of sharp teeth and fierce joy. "The one who sliced Giovanni was not so lucky."

Winter returned her friend's smile with a weak one of her own. At least someone was having a good time, here. John Donovan, the Shark King, was going to have things to say, later.

But so would she.

"Mulcahy?"

Again, the bell above the door jingled and an urgent voice, a stranger's, called, and Winter closed her eyes. Now what? "One moment, please," she replied toward the shop front. All she wanted was one single hour without a crisis, without someone bleeding. "Can you get him sitting up?" she asked Katherine as she reached into the jar and scooped out a generous handful of the ointment. Katherine took Giovanni's weight in her arms and easily lifted him upright.

Even so, Giovanni hissed with pain. "What is it with back injuries? Does *every* muscle in my body have to attach to my spine?"

"Mulcahy!" The man's voice was tainted with panic and only set Winter more on edge.

For crying out loud... but what if he was really hurt? Concern welled up in her chest, fighting with her rising agitation. "Are you bleeding?" Winter knew she was raising her voice higher than needed, but as the stress began to tremble in her belly again, she found she was caring less and less about propriety.

"What?" He sounded surprised by the question, and in a small part of her busy mind Winter acknowledged that it was an odd one.

"Are. You. Hurt?"

The man was quiet for a moment, then, "No."

Winter slathered the ointment into the first of the three slices, listening to Giovanni's labored breathing as cool medicine stroked heated flesh. "Then... *please*... sit down and wait!" Out of the corner of her eye she saw mild shock cross Katherine's pretty face, quickly replaced with concern. She did not have time to deal with it. She stroked the inner walls of the deep incision, feeling the warmth of the meat of him and the sharp edge of sliced skin against her gloved fingers as she made sure the ointment coated the entire wound. "This should take the pain away in a few sec..."

"Oh, my God..."

Winter looked over her shoulder. A middle-aged man with deep worry lines etched into his receding brow stood in the beaded doorway to the back-room clinic, his hands gripping a large bundle of towels, his eyes riveted on Katherine's face, covered in drying shark blood. Katherine drew her lips back off her extending fangs as she moved to put herself between her two companions and the stranger. Giovanni flung his hand over his nose and mouth as he muttered, "What is that smell?" in revulsion.

Somehow, something was very wrong about that bundle. Whatever it was, it was small. Winter felt herself beginning to tremble inside again, a memory of another small bloody bundle, a limp little hand... She shook her head again, crushing the images back down. Her usual two hours of sleep were not doing her any favors today, bringing the faces of her family to visit her. "If you would please wait a few minutes, I will be out to help you," she said, trying very hard to keep the grating tension out of her voice, when all she wanted to do was scream at him to go away. Scream at all of it to just *go away*. She turned her back on the man and her attention to Giovanni's second wound. The stranger wasn't bleeding. Why was he here?

"It's, uh, dark out there."

Winter continued to slather salve into the vampire's wounds and drew the numbness that let her keep working around her like a shawl. The tension still shivered in her shoulders, but the insane urge to scream and never stop began to trickle away. "Then, please, make yourself comfortable with us." She felt more than saw Giovanni look at Katherine over her head, and she ignored it. She was doing her best, holding Seahaven together by the skin of her teeth and the blood of her friends, but it was becoming increasingly obvious that her best was not nearly enough. How much more did she have? How much more did they want?

The Mulcahy wizards to come back, most likely. Twenty years ago, people would say you couldn't swing an arm in Seahaven without smacking a Mulcahy. But those twenty years had taken a harsh toll on the family. They had been the backbone of law and justice for the city of Seahaven, the force that held back the violence and factional chaos that a city so full of the preternatural would have long ago fallen into. Should have fallen into. Was still falling into. She removed the ointment-covered gloves and got out a roll of wide bandages. No, the Mulcahy wizards were not coming back, no matter how many people may wish for it.

Even if it was the only thing she ever wished for.

She drew the bandages gently around Giovanni's chest, and watched the pain leave his face as the magical ointment numbed his flesh and pulled the vicious lacerations closed. "Leave the bandages in place for the next few hours." She secured them with tape, and then retrieved a purple, soda-pop sized bottle from one of the many cabinets. "And, I want you to take a liberal spoonful of this, in your drink of choice, every two hours until it's gone."

Giovanni took the bottle, eyeing it suspiciously. "Hold on... is this the stuff Katherine gives the spawn?"

A smile tugged at Winter's lips, though it did not quite reach her eyes. The 'spawn' was little Mike, Katherine's thirteen-month-old son. Giovanni lived with them in Katherine's small vampire court next door. "It's a vitamin tonic. I don't recommend taking it straight. It tastes foul on its own." She turned away to toss the bloody towels and the remains of Giovanni's t-shirt into the sink with the jackets. She would have to get her apprentice, Jessie, to sort and wash everything salvageable later.

"You're giving me *children's* vitamins?"

"It's not just vitamins, and not just for children," she replied, giving him a tart expression as reward for his griping. "I want to make sure you heal properly and don't get an infection."

Giovanni dipped his chin slightly and gave her a sexy, arch smile. "Not likely." Neither vampires nor therian were prone to infections or diseases, but her philosophy was better to be safe than sorry. She wore surgical gloves both out of habit for those clients who needed them and for her own protection. He slid down from the exam table, cautious, anticipating pain, and breathed a sigh of relief. "Thank you, Winter..." he held his arms open to hug her, and she turned quickly, pretending she had not seen him do it, and went to wash her hands and arms. As she turned away she saw a look of hurt flash across his dark-skinned face.

Another memory, of being a little, little girl and Giovanni lifting her up, swinging her in circles by her fingers while she squealed with joy. The trembling threatened in her belly again, now prodded by guilt. She hadn't meant to hurt his feelings, and she wanted to be held, so much she ached with need—but she knew she would shatter, then, and never find all the pieces. Instead she said, "I want you to take it easy today. There's a lot of muscle damage, and I don't want you ripping anything open." She turned to face the vampires from the relative emotional safety of the sink area, but Katherine was already beside her. Even as used to a vampire's preternatural silence as growing up among them could make her, she almost threw up a hand to ward her off but forced her body to calm. Katherine was her life-long friend. She had to get this edginess under control. It was stress. Stress and the energy potions she took every morning and the gallons of coffee she drank during the day in a desperate attempt to keep up.

"Would you like me to stay?" Katherine asked quietly, her gaze sliding toward the man who was practically dancing in agitation.

Winter realized she was huddling, her back hunching and her shoulders drawing inward, so she drew herself upright and flashed her friend a small smile—a shadow of the bright confidence she might have had, were things different. "I'll be fine... you'll be wanting a shower, I imagine, and after all that blood loss I believe Giovanni is seriously considering eating my guest."

Katherine glanced back at the other vampire, who watched the nervous little man with intense eyes. "Yeah... the blood isn't nourishing unless it's straight from the vein." She turned back to Winter, her concern obvious even under the mask of blood. "If you're sure."

Winter forced a little more brightness into her smile. Inside all she felt was the horrible numbness warring with stress and trembling. "I'll be fine," she said, "But I think you better get him home and fed before he starts going after the neighborhood pets."

"Lies and prevarications. Only fictional vampires feed on animal blood, and you know it." For all her banter, Katherine clearly did not believe Winter's assurances, but moved back to Giovanni's side anyway. "Come on, you. Let's get you washed, fed, and put to bed."

Giovanni slipped his arm around Katherine's waist, but his dark eyes never left the human. They held hunger and warning. Katherine flashed the human a dark look of her own, one that said, *'This one is precious to us. Harm her at your peril.'* She paused and looked back to Winter, but spoke for the stranger's benefit, gray eyes glittering. "You need me, just call out. I'll be right next door." She turned to the man. "Vampires have very good hearing, you know," she said conspiratorially. And then they moved past him and out of the shop.

The man turned to face Winter, fear showing white all around his eyes, digging his eyebrows deep into his worry lines. She sighed softly. It was hard to remember, sometimes, that she was not the only one who hurt, who was afraid.

Because he was a stranger and she was alone with him, she opened herself up to see what she could see of his inner self. Winter was no seer to read the fates of others—that was her Grandmother Bridget's curse—but she was what was known in some circles as a soul reader, passed down from her great-grandmother, though the ability came and went. Sometimes she could look at people and see the source of their pain in vivid detail and full color as it left an impression on their soul. It was the gift that made her such an effective healer. Sometimes, look as hard as she may, she only read fractured impressions and had to rely on her medical experience to interpret what she saw.

She opened herself up and looked deep inside her visitor, and knew he was terrified and out of his depth. He had been told only to bring his burden to Olde Curiosity's Gift Shoppe, that the Mulcahy could be reached there, and that he could help him. He was so scared, scared of the vampires, scared of what he carried in the towels, scared that she would be useless to him. Winter knew why he was in doubt, knew as she looked into his wide eyes how he saw her. Tall and skinny to the point of illness, wearing an old-fashioned dress and a bloody lab coat over an oversized sweater that had seen better days. Pale skin, ice-blue eyes, and long hair white as snow pulled up in a matronly bun, a color and style completely at odds with her twenty-something face. Just a beanpole of a girl, not much older than his oldest daughter—how could she be the Mulcahy?

She had seen all of that in a few seconds, and the answer was that she wasn't. "I'm not the Mulcahy, but I do speak for him." Winter stepped closer to him, though not eager to get nearer to that smell. "Why don't you set that down?"

She cleared off her work table in a brisk fashion, not willing to have him lay the loathsome thing on her exam table, and the man deposited his bundle and then backed quickly away, eager to distance himself from it. His hands worked compulsively over his sleeves, scrubbing away at some lingering foulness. "I hit this with my riding mower yesterday. I was mulching, you know, lots of leaves this time of year... Karen, that's my wife, Karen, said I needed to tell the Mulcahy about it..." He looked a little lost, his nervous eyes moving from Winter to the bundle around the cluttered back room and back again. "Am... am I in the right place? My wife said the... um... Mulcahy..." He voiced the title with discomfort. He had no spark of magic in him, she could see that clearly enough. Normal human, married into the preternatural community, most likely. It did not happen often. Usually when a human got this close, they became one of them, one way or another. She looked him over, trying to see his Mark, the symbol that he would have been tattooed with when he was claimed by one of the courts or by a wizard family. At this distance and angle, she could not see behind his right ear, the traditional location for the vampire courts, and his jacket sleeves covered any regular tattoos a secondary Mark might have been hidden in. If he was not Marked, it meant he was not valued enough to keep, which did not bode well for his survival. But then why marry him? Why hadn't his wife brought the thing?

Winter slipped on new gloves, moved back to the bundle and began carefully peeling back the layers of towels, taking both custody and control. "Your wife was right. I'm Winter Mulcahy. The current Mulcahy is my father."

"Should I go see him?"

She shifted her gaze to meet his for a moment. "I'm sorry. He doesn't see anyone." Then she focused on the towels again.

"Why not?"

Winter responded with silence.

By the third towel she discovered the smell was rising from a viscous black fluid soaking slowly through the terrycloth. By the fifth towel, Winter decided he must have used every towel in the house. Finally, the contents were revealed, and Winter stepped back, thinking hard.

"Well... what is it?" The man was standing as far away as conversation and the limited space of the clinic would allow. Panic and fear leaked further into his voice.

Winter folded her hands together in front of her face and was about to press her index fingers lightly against her lips out of habit—then considered the nastiness covering the towels she had just been handling and thought better of it. "It certainly seems like you've found all the pieces." Bits of shredded flesh covered in matted, black fur were mashed into a gooey ball by the pressure from a linen closet full of towels... the shattered remains of a jaw studded with jagged teeth... perhaps six limbs... too many eyes... a cold chill ran through her as her mind struggled to process the grisly sight. She really did not need this today. "You only hit one creature?"

He nodded, a little too vigorously.

"Have you had any pets go missing in your neighborhood?"

The man looked a little startled by the question. "Yes, a couple. The homeowner's association thinks the coyotes are coming down from the mountain again, and they've hired trappers, but my wife..." he paused, hesitating.

"What is your wife?" Winter asked, keeping her tone conversational, light. Humans with preternatural partners had many secrets to keep. She did not want to pry, but the information could be helpful.

He hesitated a moment longer, then, "Cougar."

Winter nodded. Therian cougars, solitary by nature, did not often pair off with humans, but they were also as opportunistic in their choice of mates as any cats, therian or otherwise. It also explained why she could not find a Mark—there would be none to find.

Therian were not granted Marks. They were not considered important or powerful enough by the Council of the Eldest, the preternatural ruling body, to have them. So, they did not keep humans, as a general rule. She expected his marriage was probably fairly recent and would be short lived. Which could prove very unfortunate for him, but rescuing humans who played with fire was extremely low on her very long priority list. Hopefully his wife would turn him into a cougar, for his sake. "Your wife doesn't think it's coyotes because she doesn't smell them, therian or otherwise, she smells something much stranger... which, of course, she cannot tell your homeowner's association," she waited for the man to nod agreement. "And then you run over this with your mower and she recognizes the scent." Not that she could forget it... or smell anything else, for that matter. It was a putrid-sweet smell that clung to the nose and throat like rancid molasses. She was keeping her breathing as shallow as possible, but still the foulness invaded. Anyone who thought one could avoid smelling something by breathing through one's mouth had never been exposed to anything truly disgusting. People use their sense of taste as much as their sense of smell, and not for the first time Winter wished she could turn both senses off. At least she was not a dragon, who experienced smell and taste as a single sense. "But she still doesn't know what it is."

"Do you?" he asked, half hopeful, half defensive.

Winter looked back at him over the remains on the work table, numbness giving way to a trickle of irritation. "It's a goblin," she explained, hiding her emotion behind a scholar's reserve. Anger was another indulgence she could not afford. She had to remember that he needed her help, that he was simply scared and having a difficult time, and it did not matter one whit that she was, as well. "Some consider them a minor variety of pseudo-demon because they are often found among demon legions, but they are really more of a fae, actually. They average from sixteen to twenty pounds—I believe this one was on the small side—and are not known to be very dangerous to anything above their own size. They do tend to bite, however. I imagine you scared it out of its hiding place with your mower—"

"*I* scared *it*? It jumped right out in front of me! I didn't have a chance to stop!"

Winter drew back, startled by his vehemence. He was very tightly wound, perhaps even more so than she was, and it was suddenly very hard to stay in this room with this yelling man and his towel-wrapped problem. Maybe he had finally seen more of his wife's world than he could handle. She cleared her throat, swallowing down her sudden fearful tension. "If I could get your address, I'll need to check around your neighborhood."

"What for?" he asked, suspicion in his voice as if to ask what other strangeness she was about to shove into his life.

Winter drew her dignity about herself. Perhaps he had a right to be upset, but she refused to let this little man take his shaken worldview out on her. "Because goblins are not native to this realm, which means there is a rift in your area. I need to seal it."

The man looked skeptical. "What?"

"A rift. A rip in the veil between realms. The goblin came through it, and if it could come through, so could others."

His eyes widened, and he looked on the pile of fur and dark meat with new horror. "Oh, my God..."

Winter could almost watch the small army of goblins march across his imagination, and really could not disagree. She had similar visions of her own.

He gave her the address without further argument and left after securing her promise to come out as soon as possible.

Winter tossed her gloves into the trash as the bell above the door rang the man's exit and rubbed her hands over her face. If her day went the way it always did, as soon as possible would likely be well after dark. She did not like leaving a probable rift sitting open for hours and hours. Maybe she should head out right now, just turn off the clinic lights and lock the door, find the rift, and hunt down any other goblins there might be later tonight. She nodded to herself and turned, unbuttoning the top of her bloodied coat as she reached for her faded purple canvas hobo bag.

The bell rang. "Miss Mulcahy?"

Winter dropped the bag's strap and finished unbuttoning the coat. "Wait out there a moment. It's a bit nasty back here."

After this one, then.

CHAPTER TWO

"I don't know why I'm doing this." Etienne swirls the dark beer in his coarse, earthen mug, breathing in the yeasty aroma as he takes another deep drink. God, but he loves Bess's beer. She moves behind him and he feels her warmth against his back, her strong, calloused hands stroking his hair off his face, away from his neck. His hair is so much longer here, as it was then, when they were married.

"Because you love him." She speaks English, but strange to this modern time, her consonants more guttural, truer to their Germanic roots, each sound tongued in full. He loves the way she speaks. He has not spoken English like this in centuries.

"Love him?" Etienne snorts his denial. "I don't even know him."

"Not Senán."

Etienne falls into silence and lets it draw out. He can never lie to her. He can lie to himself just fine. After over a thousand years, he has gotten very good at lying to himself. But never to her. Not even when she had asked him if she was dying.

Bess's wonderful brown hands move from his hair to his neck, kneading his muscles until she draws a throaty groan of pleasure from him. "Because he needs to find his friend."

He remains silent under her hands.

"He can't do it alone."

He reaches back, slips his hands over hers. "Bess—"

Etienne awoke with her name still sounding in the thinning darkness and quickly closed his eyes again, struggling to hold on to that last wisp of dream. It slipped away like smoke through his fingers.

It had been a good one. He could feel her warm hands—she always had such warm hands—tucked away like little brown birds in his own. He could still smell her, the way she always smelled of smoke and babies and sweat and sunshine, of fresh-tilled earth and baking bread. Pain, sharp enough to steal breath, pierced his chest.

He could almost remember her face.

Etienne sat up, drew up his legs, and pressed his face against his knees, fighting down the burning in his throat. He missed her so much. It had been so long... so long, and he had been so young. He just wished... He drew a deep breath, and gently, but firmly, pushed it all aside. He could wish all he wanted. She was gone. Had been for six long, lonely mortal centuries.

He stood up, ignoring the old aches and pains brought on from sleeping on the ground with the patience of long practice. He picked up his clothes, stooped over in the dark of the tent, and the young man sleeping beside him sighed and snuffled for a moment before dropping deeper into his own dreams. Etienne listened to him sleep a moment, waiting for any telltale whimpers from the boy. Cian had more than enough reason for nightmares. Finally, content that his companion rested peacefully for once, he slipped outside leaving the boy to rest a little longer.

This close to Samhain the small campground was deserted, and Etienne had the quiet of the morning all to himself. He stretched his arms high above his head, body bare to the cold morning air, wincing slightly at the chorus of popping joints and complaining scars, and roughed his fingers through his dark-auburn hair. It was getting too long again, hanging in his face and curling against his shoulders. Not as long as in his dream, but maybe he should cut it short. On the farm in Kentucky, the home where they had been settled until a few days ago, they had been able to afford the luxury of letting their hair grow out. Cian's was even longer still, straight as falling water to just below his shoulder blades. Etienne hated to cut it, but he would.

Lacking entirely in human modesty—no one was nearby to shock, anyway—he dropped his pants and shirt on a log. He blew out a breath and braced himself for the freezing scrub down at the campsite's rusty spigot, trying desperately to pretend the October-chilled water was a hot shower and failing miserably. He wished for perhaps the millionth time that his mixed heritage had gifted him with the resistance to cold so common among his mother's people. He could abide it, but that was really more due to centuries of practice than innate immunity.

Etienne scrubbed his face and body red with the cold water and a bar of soap in a burlap pouch, dragging the abrasive fabric over the traceries of scars that covered his body. They were lividly pale against his work-tanned skin. He never had them in his dreams. Bess had never known them. His arms, his chest, his face… all covered with scrolling arcane glyphs, carved into his flesh as he lay at the mercy of his enemies. What they were for he would hopefully never know for certain. He was no magician and the markings held no more meaning for him than as a memory of agony and humiliation. As painful as the carving had been, the remedy had been worse. Dwarven runes, branded brown into his flesh, covered and negated the magic inherent in the glyph scars. Those he has endured willingly, silently, and paid a dear price for the bargain. He rinsed the soap from his marked skin and pulled his hair up into a ponytail, then quickly pulled on his jeans.

Next came his thread-bare t-shirt and the gun rig that he never went without. Embroidered leather nestled well-worn against his chest, covered in runes that gave him a sidhe's speed and strength. Some might call it cheating—Etienne called it making up for his mixed heritage. And in its underarm holster rested the venerable six-shooter, Agmundr. The Gift of Terror. Etienne had served a century among the dwarves in exchange for the rig and the named weapon that it carried. Agmundr and the enchanted bullets it used could bring true death to any sidhe dealt a mortal blow. Etienne had originally bargained for twelve bullets—he had seven remaining. Most sidhe now gave him a wide berth, just as he wanted.

A few minutes of quality time with the old sooty hearth and he had resurrected last night's fire, carefully tucking in just enough wood to see them through coffee and breakfast. It was quiet, here under the trees. As much as he would like to just spend a few days resting, they were getting very close to their destination and the urge to hit the road was stronger than the urge to linger.

Whimpers carried to Etienne's sensitive ears and he quickly ducked back into the low-ceilinged tent to check on his charge. Cian lay curled tight on his side, bedroll blankets shoved away, one long, slender arm thrown over his face as if to ward off a blow. The boy's fingers clenched into a fist as a low moan of pain and fear trickled from between his lips, and his breathing became more ragged.

Etienne knelt down beside the boy, and he firmly, but gently, pulled Cian's arm away from his face. "Cian," he called softly. "Cian, wake up."

Cian whimpered once more.

Etienne shook him. "Cian," he said more firmly.

Cian's eyes snapped open, terror showing white all around the brilliant green. "Please don't hurt me," he slurred, still seeing his nightmare.

Etienne caught the boy's face and turned his gaze toward him. "Look at me. Look at me, Cian."

Cian finally focused on Etienne's eyes, and confusion danced there for a moment, until, "Etienne?"

Etienne gave the boy a small smile. "Good boy. You're having a nightmare."

Cian rolled onto his back and rubbed at his face. A shudder racked his slender body and then he relaxed. "I just can't stop seeing him," he murmured from behind his hands.

Etienne pulled the boy's hands from his face and made him look up at him. "Then look at me, instead. You know I'd never hurt you, and I look nothing like him."

Cian looked a little confused. "But, you do…"

Etienne looked away, frowning, and then back at his young charge. "Not Senán." He did not like discussing his resemblance to Cian's friend. "Is that who you were dreaming about?"

Cian nodded, understanding dawning on his pretty face. He pushed himself into a sitting position. "I was dreaming that he was dead. That we found him, but… Midir…" his voice trembled as he hesitated over that feared name. "He'd seen us coming, and he killed him. And then he caught me again…"

Etienne tucked his hand around the back of the boy's neck and pulled him into a rough hug. "Shh," he murmured against the top of his head, trying to stop the tears before they started. It was a common nightmare for the boy in the days since starting this journey. "Put it behind you. It was just a dream." He was one to talk, of course, as tightly as he held his own dreams—but then, his nightmares did not feature the face of a murderous rapist. He rubbed Cian's back with one hand and then pulled away. Cian brushed moisture away from one eye and steadied his features until Etienne was satisfied that he had calmed. "I need to go make breakfast," he said before giving the boy's shoulder one last squeeze. "Take your time."

Cian nodded and gave the older man a small smile. It did not quite reach his eyes, but then Etienne did not expect it to so close to the nightmare. It was good enough. Etienne had learned from a lifetime of pain that good enough was usually as close to fine as could be hoped for.

Etienne emerged from the tent, opened his old rucksack, and started pulling out what he needed—aluminum frying pan, for Cian could not tolerate food cooked on Cold Iron, a couple of neatly wrapped little packets of food, and the last of his precious coffee. He pressed the soft leather pouch against his nose, taking a moment to breathe in the rich aroma.

It was the Americans who had introduced it to him, sitting around a fire in a bombed out French farm house, listening to the German bombardment pounding away less than a kilometer from their hiding place. He had been hungry and exhausted and the battered tin cup they handed to him had been hot and welcome. Coffee always reminded him pleasantly of the friendship he had forged over those long days, waiting for the chance to cross the German line and find his contact with the French Resistance. His American friend, a wizard, had been from Seahaven, Washington, USA, maybe still lived there, and Etienne had thought often of looking him up since they had first arrived on this continent. Maybe, when all this was over, he would take the opportunity. They would arrive in the city tomorrow.

The smell of coffee and sausages finally drew out Cian, who came shuffling out of the tent on bare feet, still scrubbing the sleep from his face. He'd pulled on his jeans and Etienne's old brown leather jacket, which hung short and loose on his shoulders. Even sleep-tousled and sloppy, he was exquisitely beautiful, but then his mother had been the most beautiful of their people and Cian took after her. He sat down on the split-log bench beside Etienne and laid his cheek against the older man's shoulder, displaying the casual physical affection of their kind. A full head taller than Etienne, but not nearly as broad, the boy had to bend to reach down that far. "That smells good," he murmured into the rumpled fabric of Etienne's sleeve.

Etienne mumbled acknowledgment and continued to prod the sausages into submission with his newish camp fork.

Cian rubbed his sleepy face into Etienne's shoulder. "Are we going to have tomatoes?" he asked, hopeful. He loved fried tomatoes. He loved everything that had anything to do with tomatoes.

"No, we ran out yesterday. We'll need to trade for some more."

"Oh." He was quiet for a moment and then he peered up at Etienne. "Is this the last of the sausages, too?"

Etienne nodded. They were running low on everything—food, gas, barter goods, money. But Cian did not need to worry about that. It was Etienne's responsibility, as it was his responsibility to care for the boy. "We're ok. There will be plenty of places to make money once we get to Seahaven. There always are in large cities. We'll get more tomatoes when we get there."

"And then we can have them for breakfast?" Those long-lashed eyes rolled up to gaze in plaintive anticipation.

Etienne smiled then. He couldn't help it. "Yes, then you can have as many tomatoes as you want."

He felt Cian grin against his shoulder, felt his complete trust and faith warm against his skin. Of course, Etienne said everything would be fine, so it would be. Etienne just wished he had the same amount of faith. They had been traveling together for somewhere near seven years. Etienne really did not know exactly how long. Seasons... time... ran differently from realm to realm and they had primarily wandered the borders of Faerie where all things were fluid. He looked down at the red-gold head pressed trustingly against his shoulder. Seven years with Cian, watching him grow from boy to young man. He had never failed to take care of him. He wasn't going to start failing now. Cian could play his guitar on a corner somewhere, which always brought in a little bit of cash, or maybe they could find a small casino with old-fashioned slot machines Etienne could use what little magic he had to trick into paying out. It didn't work as well in the larger casinos, anymore—with the passing years, newer machines had become what they called 'digital' and lacked the mechanical parts Etienne could manipulate.

Cian had no idea he was cheating. The boy honestly thought Etienne was just that lucky.

Without being asked, Cian got up and fished two tin plates out of Etienne's pack. While Etienne distributed sausages, Cian filled a chipped pottery mug with fresh coffee from the incongruously bright and shiny coffee press. Cian had bought it with the first money he had made on his own. It was glass and chrome and he had gotten it for Etienne. The shop girl had called it a French press and said that it was what the French used to make coffee, and since Etienne's father had been French... Etienne would never have bought the trinket for himself, but the boy was very proud of it, so Etienne used the silly thing. Besides, it really did make good coffee.

They sat in companionable silence, eating the last of the hot sausages with their fingers, Etienne sipping his black coffee, and watched the sun rise higher behind the trees. Birds chattered ceaselessly over their heads, and somewhere not too far in the distance their sharp hearing caught the rising murmur of early morning highway traffic.

Finally, breakfast was eaten and the last of the coffee was just a quickly drying stain in the bottom of the mug. Reluctant, Etienne sent Cian to the spigot to clean their dishes and he broke down the ancient leather tent. Since the start of his latest sojourn in this realm he was often asked what kind of hide the tent was fashioned from, and he had taken to telling people that it was made from buffalo hide, since 'fae leather' only got him strange looks. Of course, apparently having a leather tent at all was strange, anymore, so the looks continued.

While Cian's dish-washing abilities often left Etienne making another go at it before cooking the next meal, his previous attempts to put the old tent away bordered on tragedy, so Etienne was content to do it himself. By the time it was tucked away, Cian had finished up and returned, only marginally drier than the dishes. At least this time he had taken Etienne's coat off first. Etienne fished Cian's clean shirt and socks out of the leather back pack, and, sitting the boy on the bench, he took out an ornate wooden comb and brushed Cian's hair until it gleamed.

Considering the boy was pure-blooded sidhe, it didn't take much brushing. Cian had once been called The Glorious Dawn, a name he richly deserved. His hair was more than red-gold; it gleamed with all the colors of the first sunrise. Strands in shades of pale blonde, gold, crimson, rose, bronze, and honey spilled over and through Etienne's callused hands, exquisitely soft and much more evenly trimmed than his own. Etienne could cut hair on a straight line, unlike his young friend, as he had discovered the one, and only, time he had let Cian trim him.

With Cian emitting little sighs of pleasure, Etienne wove Cian's hair into a tight French braid with the deftness of long practice, smoothing every strand into place, and tucked the end up inside the body of the braid. No human had hair, or eyes, like his, and so no human could be allowed to see them. There were no formal rules forbidding it, of course, no matter what the vampire magicians of the Council of the Eldest might say—they only ruled the Mortal Realm. Humans had interacted with the sidhe off and on for centuries. But, since the fae had withdrawn from the Mortal Realm with the dawn of the Age of Iron, it was simply considered common sense to practice discretion as the better part of valor—plus, he had no intentions of letting his quarry know they were coming. Spies could be anywhere.

"All done?" There was a definite note of disappointment in Cian's voice.

Etienne patted him on his bare shoulder. "You're all set."

Cian's hands immediately went to his hair.

"No, don't fiddle with it."

Cian peered at Etienne through the crook of his own arm. His eyes were all the greens of Faerie in spring. Sidhe eyes. "I like how it feels." He lightly ran his fingertips over the smooth ridges of the braid.

Etienne shook his head, but he couldn't help the small smile that tugged at his mouth. "Go on, get dressed. No sword-work this morning. We need to get going."

Cian nodded obediently, disappointment showing on his face. Cian really enjoyed their morning sword lessons and after all these years was finally beginning to show promise of true skill.

Etienne filled the old pot from the spigot and made sure their campfire was completely extinguished while Cian finished dressing. The boy pulled on his socks and Etienne realized with a little start that, already much taller than Etienne, he was showing a couple inches of ankle below the jeans cuff, proof that he was still growing. The boots would prove to be a blessing, but he was going to need to find Cian some new jeans, and soon.

Etienne frowned. Their wandering through Faerie had been difficult. Etienne was not a popular man in the courts and was accustomed to scraping by as a day laborer or a sword for hire, or sometimes he could trade labor at a small smithy for forge time to create barter goods whenever he got his hands on any precious metal or sidhe steel. But he was a man full grown and hardened to hardship. Cian's life before had been soft, and he was growing, and would still be growing for many years, yet. He did not complain, but he had not been raised to scarcity.

And then Etienne had brought Cian to the Mortal Realm. Jumping realms was simply what Etienne did when he felt restless or unsafe, as was the case this time. But it had proven to be more difficult in this era even than during the last war. They had little money in this increasingly currency-centric world, and without it were forced to go without much of the time, to Cian's increasing detriment. When they had finally found themselves on the farm in Kentucky food had been plentiful, considering the way therian ate, but there had been few opportunities to make enough money to replace their clothing. Etienne pulled on his own thinning socks and sturdy, worn boots. He needed to find stable work somewhere.

But it would have to wait until after this business was finished.

Cian got his shirt on without fuss, and for once his special silk-lined riding chaps that protected him from the steel frame of the Harley, but as usual the laces on his boots gave him trouble. After a childhood of being dressed by servants, Cian was still slowly getting the hang of dressing himself. Etienne left him to it. This was a skill he had been working on since they met, and as long as the laces weren't in danger of getting caught in the spokes of the motorcycle, Etienne was happy to let him figure it out on his own. After some confusion, Cian yanked the laces into submission, and gave Etienne a dazzling smile of triumph. Etienne returned the smile with one of his own and nodded in acknowledgment. "Not bad."

He put away the kettle and the rest of their dishes, tucking everything into the backpack as he did a quick mental inventory. "Cian, where's the camp fork?"

Cian, shrugging into his heavy denim jacket, widened his eyes. "It's not there?"

"You washed it."

Those eyes shifted to the area around the spigot, and Cian jumped off the log and scampered over. Etienne shook his head and turned back to packing up their things. Their path across Faerie and North America could be traced by the trail of belongings that boy had left behind. This was camp fork number five.

By the time Cian returned with the fork, Etienne had pulled on his jacket and was waiting with their helmets. Cian pulled his on with no trouble, but Etienne caught him looking unhappy before his beautiful face disappeared behind the full-faced, mirrored visor. He knew Cian hated the visor, that he would far rather feel the wind on his face, but they were getting too close to civilization. With those inhumanly green eyes—while Etienne's human blood let him pass as mortal, it was clear to even the most casual observer that Cian was anything but. If half the rumors he had heard about Seahaven were true, he wanted to keep as low a profile as possible and parading around in the open with a sidhe prince was not keeping a low profile. Etienne swung his leg up over the old Harley Davidson Sportster and settled into the seat.

The plan was to get in, get what they came for, and get out. Of course, Etienne had never, ever, been that lucky.

Cian pulled on Etienne's back pack and climbed up behind him, wrapping his arms around Etienne's waist. "Etienne?" His voice, muffled by the helmet, was pitched high with tension.

Etienne paused, key in the ignition. "Yes?"

Cian was quiet a moment. "Do you really think we'll find Senán?"

Etienne kept his eyes forward. Before they came to the Mortal Realm, his answer would have been of course not. Cian had seen him die. But now... "I'm sure of it." The proof, ripped from a magazine, was folded neatly and tucked deep into an inner pocket of his old leather jacket. Senán was in Seahaven.

His kidnapper had taken him there.

CHAPTER THREE

Scrambling, Winter gave up a few more feet to the goblin's slashing claws and used the precious seconds she bought to frantically rummage in her faded purple hobo bag, murmuring the charm to bring a small parchment envelope to her hand while watching closely for its next move. She should have had the envelope out before this. She knew that, now.

She had started with a rake to defend herself, but then found out how well the nasty little thing could climb, as the incessant throbbing on the back of her right hand attested to. She had never actually been trained for this, unlike her cousins and two older sisters. She was supposed to be a teacher, a physician, and a potion master. She should be home, tucked away in her family's kitchen teaching a handful of little cousins to brew simple decoctions, not doing battle with a fae the size of a throw pillow in Karen's backyard.

And losing.

"Blast!" It darted to one side, trying to get past Winter and out into the night. She had to keep it boxed in, just for a few more moments. If it got loose into the neighborhood, she would be days finding it again, and by then it might have graduated to attacking children. Only luck, a couple hours of stressful patience and a trail of about two pounds of fresh chopped beef had gotten it into the shed. She kicked out, taking it in what passed for a midsection, and it bounced against the back of the shed like a large hairy soccer ball. Tools popped from their perches, and a pot was knocked off its shelf, all raining down on the neatly swept concrete floor.

A burning sensation flared up her right calf, and Winter knew the miniature monster had scored, too.

Keeping her eyes fixed on the ugly little hairball, Winter tore the top off the envelope. The goblin hunkered just out of reach, panting in a wheezy sort of way, slime dripping from its broken-bottle teeth, all its eyes glittering back and forth, searching for a way past her. Fear seemed to roll off it like a dark fog. Wherever it came from, it probably had no idea where it was now. It may have even seen what happened to its little friend. Winter knew how it felt, trapped and desperate to find a way out, bloody images of her loved ones tearing at her memories. For just a moment, she felt sorry for the evil little thing. No one would be coming to rescue the goblin, either.

Then again, she wasn't the one eating the neighborhood cats. She raised the envelope and—

With blinding speed, nearly twenty pounds of goblin impacted with her upper chest. Winter did not realize she was falling until the autumn-wet lawn struck her in the back, and she grabbed a fistful of greasy, matted fur with her left hand as it made to leap over her head to freedom.

It retaliated by sinking jagged teeth into her thin wrist, right through the sturdy fabric of her uncle's old Army jacket.

Winter let out a yelp of startled pain but did not release the frantically scratching beast. It flailed about, claws raking her chest, her neck, her face, digging bloody furrows into her pale skin wherever it could find purchase. She beat against its thick body in panic, the envelope almost forgotten in her clenched fist, and it worried at her wrist like a dog, the teeth digging deeper and deeper into flesh toward bone.

Rolling onto her side, she released her grip on the envelope a little, half dumping, half pounding the goblin with red, glittering dust, drew the magic from within herself and through gritted teeth released it in a resonating Word of Command. "*Bind!*" It was not needed, the spell in the powder was already primed, but she was in pain and wanted to be sure it worked.

The creature froze in place as the dust settled on it, her wrist still clamped between its jaws. Discolored teeth remained imbedded in fabric and flesh, but at least it had stopped chewing at the wound. Winter tried in vain to breathe without smelling. Wherever the little goblin had come from it stank and fear mixed with exertion did not help with the odor. Her own pain and adrenaline were not helping, and she fought down a wave of nausea. Grunting with hurt at the jostling, Winter jerked her lumpy bag out from beneath her hip and with one hand and her teeth uncorked a small blue bottle. The acrid smell made her nostrils sting. The goblin apparently smelled it, too, because it began to drool heavily in fear on Winter's hand and arm. She upended the bottle, the thick, bright blue liquid soaking into the beast's matted fur, and as it touched again produced a voice resonant with magical Command. *"Banish!"* Again, the magic in the potion was already primed, but sometimes a little overkill did not hurt.

With a shrill keen and a cloud of noxious smoke the goblin vanished, the release of its weight and jaws painful in itself. Winter rolled carefully up onto her knees, ignoring with limited success the way her torn cotton stockings neatly wicked up the freezing moisture from the lawn to chill her skin. Without teeth to block up the wound, blood welled up from the torn flesh, black in the suburban twilight, and began to run in rivulets down her hand.

She knelt there in silence, watching the first glittering drops fall onto the grass, and fought back the roaring rush of exhaustion in her ears with sluggish determination. Darkness crept along the edges of her vision, and she shrugged her injured arm carefully out of her coat sleeve and knelt in the October cold in just her long dress and her sweater, which she slipped off to bind about her hurt wrist. It felt so good, just being still. Just for a few more minutes.

She watched the cotton weave soak up blood and slime and found herself fighting back sudden frustrated tears as the pain wound its way to her brain past the kinder adrenaline. Her older sisters Sorcha and Mirilyn— even her younger cousins Kelley and Martina—they had been so much better at this than she was. They had been stronger, faster...

Her wrist throbbed with her pulse, still quick from exertion, and the smaller stinging scratches echoing across her face, chest, and arms made her wish she could kick the evil little thing just a few more times. Sorcha had once taken on an entire pack of hell-hounds that threatened her day camp, for heaven's sake. Granted, Grandfather and Mirilyn had had to rescue her, but they had all three come home in triumph. A single, nasty little goblin would have been no match. What was she doing wrong?

"Mulcahy?" a woman's voice called out.

Winter twisted to peer over her shoulder as a chill breeze rose to tease a few more white strands of hair free from her loosely coiled bun. She had no time for self-pity. Crossing the lawn on bare feet was a pretty brunette, her hair bobbed above her shoulders, her pink sweater a nice contrast to her well-fitted jeans. At a glance she looked like every other soccer mom on her block and her bright, healthy face was suffused with concern and curiosity. But Winter noticed that she moved in utter silence across the grass with a predator's grace and, backlit by the porch light, her eyes glowed gold-green in the shadows, reflecting the spare glow of the street-lights. She knew without looking that Karen would have manicured and painted her fingernails to conceal their unusual thickness, and that her hands and feet would be heavily calloused. Winter rose with care, both to avoid startling the therian and to attempt to hide her weakness and exhaustion. "Are you Karen?"

The woman smiled, teeth too white in the gloom. "You've got it." She stopped, just out of arm's reach. "That's a nasty bite you've got there." Her nostrils flared delicately, catching the scent, and her lips parted just a little, and Winter saw into her soul, like she had her husband. When she was a child, she always saw people just like that—saw their souls behind politeness and decorum and the masks adulthood makes one wear. Now, though, she could control it, shield herself from prying into strangers' hearts, unless Fate opened her to it—or unless she was too tired to protect herself, as she was now. Karen breathed her in, and Winter knew she felt hunger. She saw herself, wounded and bleeding on the grass, and knew Karen smelled her weakness and found it good. A human might have actually felt the concern Karen mimicked, but the predator knew only eat and being eaten. Concern was for cubs and kin. Karen was therian. She had either never been human or was human no longer.

Anger leeched new strength into Winter's body, and a polite smile stretched her mouth, a slight bearing of teeth. Like Seahaven itself, Karen's civilization was just a thin veneer for the neighbors, with the monster lurking just below the surface. Winter accepted that. But then, she had never been human, either. She was a wizard. Not a predator, *per se*—but not a meal, either. "Thank you, but I'll be fine," she demurred, giving off a soft flash of power in warning. Karen started and took a step back, a cross look on her face. The tiny burst of magic was akin to squirting the cat on the nose and looked to be having the same effect. It was rude, but so was considering nibbling on the guests. Winter felt an abrupt change in subject was in order. "Can you track it?"

Karen blinked. "Pardon?"

"The creature. Can you track it?"

Karen crossed her arms in irritation and her face drew down into a full scowl. "I am no dog."

Winter fought the urge to roll her eyes in annoyance. The felines could be the most difficult of the therian. "But you can scent prey, can you not?"

Karen's gaze flickered to Winter's bleeding wrist, and then away to the woods. "Of course."

The wizard forced more warmth into her smile, hoping it rose close to her eyes. "Then, please, help me find where it came from. Those goblins came through the veil somewhere, and we need to seal it."

Karen did not look fooled, but she did look slightly more cooperative. "You mean there's a rift out there."

Winter's smile broadened, relaxed into something a little more genuine. "Exactly." She moved forward with determination, trusting that Karen would follow her across the backyard and into the wilder area beyond. It wasn't possible to live in Seahaven, to walk in the shadows of the preternatural community, without knowing about the rifts. Of course, that was about the limit of what most people knew. There were rifts between the worlds, because the area around Seahaven was massively unstable. That instability, in fact, was what drew most of the preternatural community to this area in the first place.

Her father had been fond of explaining that once upon a time the different realms had been separated by the thinnest of veils, and even mortals—humans and those others native to the Mortal Realm—could move between them with relative ease... or by accident. But something had happened, some said war, some said the advent of human obsession with Cold Iron, though no one really knew, and the veils became walls impenetrable as stone. There still existed gateways, though, rifts and holes and thin places where passage was difficult, but possible. But around Seahaven the barriers were not so much like stone walls as lover's hands, palms pressed close and fingers entwined. Power fluxed and shifted between the realms like tidal waters, attracting the magical and magically inclined to Seahaven like a lodestone. In the unrest, cracks and fissures opened, allowing relatively free passage.

And that was why wizards were needed here.

Karen's tart voice tugged her from her reverie. "So, Mulcahy, why do you need my help? Shouldn't you just... I don't know..." Karen held out her hands and wiggled her fingers, "...use magic to find it?"

They were crossing into the land of crazy mixed up ferns, and Winter frowned at the cougar's tone. "I'm not the Mulcahy," she said, her voice cool. And if she was... what could she do about a rude cougar? Her grandfather Dermot would have probably had her hide for his wall... but Winter was very young, wizard or no, and not a particularly commanding presence to boot.

"What?"

"My father is still the Mulcahy," Winter turned back to mind her footing in the dark. "I only speak for him. And to answer your question," she hurried on, cutting off the cougar, "I can sense rifts with no problem. I just want to make sure I get the right one, or we'll be here all night."

"Oh my god! You mean they're all over the place?"

Winter felt a smirk draw at her lips, the sudden image of Karen up on a chair in her kitchen leaping to mind, and quickly squelched the thought. It just wasn't nice to enjoy the other woman's panic. "Not really. Think about it like this. Opening a rift in a stable area is basically poking a hole in the fabric of reality. It alters the structure of the universe, changes the magical balance irrevocably, even if in a small way. That takes a great deal of power. However, in an area like Seahaven," and thank the powers that be that there were few enough of them, "which is already incredibly unstable, rifts tend to manifest on their own, and often are too tiny for anything to pass through and fairly harmless—hardly worth calling a rift at all. Obviously, you've got one around here that isn't so tiny or harmless, but I can take care of it."

Karen gently laid a hand on Winter's shoulder and moved ahead, dropping slowly until her fingertips brushed the forest floor, head bent low to the scent. Winter felt the feverish heat the therian's body produced as she passed. She did not seem to notice Winter's flinch at being touched. "This way," Karen murmured, half to herself. She led the way a short way off the path and leapt silently down into a shallow ravine, turning to help the wounded wizard descend. Winter ended up sliding on one hip and pine needles, fragrant and sticky, clung to her long dress, her stockings, and caught in the weave of the ruined sweater. Brushing at the mess just made it worse, smearing sticky pitch across her abraded skin.

"Here it is." Karen's nose was wrinkled in distaste. "Foul smelling things, aren't they?"

Winter looked up from her futile attempts to pick the needles free, her gaze drawn to the rift in the low retaining wall. The hole was innocuous, just looking like the cement had given away, revealing a hollow place behind it. Only there was no dirt behind the cement, simply blackness edged in licking orange flames visible only to Winter's magical sight. The hole was small, little larger than Winter's closed fist, a dainty fracture in the world. How in the universe the little goblins had squeezed through was beyond Winter's understanding, but it could not have been a pleasant experience. Winter slung her large hobo bag around from behind her back and rummaged one-handed.

"Are you going to close it?"

Winter shook her hand. "I can't close it... no wizard can, really. It takes too much power." Winter pulled out a large, misshapen lump of green-flecked chalk. "But, we really don't want anything to come through it, either, so I'm going to seal it."

"Seal it?" Karen crouched down beside the wizard and reached a tentative finger toward the hole. Winter pushed her hand aside. "Isn't that the same thing?"

"Not really... and stop that," Winter repelled another attempt to touch the rift. Cats and curiosity... The flames would not burn the cougar, they were heatless, but still, there was no telling what might be ready to come out. "When I'm finished, the rift will still be here, but nothing will be able to pass through it, in either direction."

Karen sat back on her heals. "Could the seal be broken?"

Winter opened her mouth to deny it, but then decided there was no need to lie. "Yes... but the amount of power required would be..." Winter spent a moment as she traced the first circle around the hole. "...probably enough to set off Sarah."

Karen craned her neck to look up the mountain and gave off a low whistle of appreciation. Seahaven nestled comfortably in the shadow of what was often described as the 'most inactive active volcano in North America.' Originally called Tamarawas, Mount Sarah rumbled, she grumbled, and occasionally let out a lady-like belch, but she never was rude enough to blow her top. Geologists at the University of Washington, Seahaven said she had not done so in ten thousand years.

"Eventually, it might even close on its own." Winter neatly completed the second circle, warming up to her subject. She loved teaching, and Karen seemed to be interested. "See, the rift and the hole aren't actually connected. This wall could be knocked down, but the rift would remain. Now, the rift caused some of the erosion to the hole, but it isn't dependent on it... it's just that the Universe as a rule likes a bit of order, so rifts and gateways will form in conjunction with an existing structure or opening. There are some theories that..."

Karen jumped away so high and far that she landed on the far lip of the ravine. "What's that?" Fear lent a tremble to her voice.

The world shifted sideways. Winter braced herself against the wall with her one good hand, the chalk grinding against the concrete as she fought the initial wave of disorientation. Something was horribly wrong. Within the rift, power was building up, as if someone had just crimped a running hose.

And she was holding the nozzle.

Nine glyphs in the seal, each unique, complex, and time consuming. Each must be drawn with precision, or the whole seal would fail. Winter had never drawn glyphs so fast in her life, her hand frantically scraping the chalk against the wall in her desperate race against... against what? It felt like a tidal wave, rushing implacably toward her. Somehow, something was affecting the balance of power.

"What's happening?" Karen's voice had taken on the plaintive cry of a child. As a preternatural, she could sense the maelstrom building, but had no way of understanding or affecting what was happening.

Winter had no answer for her. She spoke each glyph as she drew it, magic resonating in her voice with each syllable. Six glyphs to go. Its name spoken, the glyph would take on a glow, casting the hole in sharp relief, bringing out each line of exhaustion on Winter's face.

Highlighting the growing cracks in the cement around the rift.

After the seal went up, the cement became irrelevant. It could be ground to dust and the seal would hold. Before then, however... the seal needed a matrix, something solid to hold the lines she drew with the en-spelled chalk. Before then, the seal was all too fragile.

When the surge hit, it would blow the rift wide open. Those two little goblins would only be the beginning... and there would be precious little left of Karen and Winter, and probably the surrounding square acre or so.

Five glyphs.

She wasn't going to make it. Winter's shoulders were burning, her hand beginning to cramp and shake, her hurt wrist felt like it was on fire. The glow of the seal began to fade as her magic was drained by pain and panic and exhaustion. She needed more power. She did not have time to ground and pull power from the earth... leaving only one choice. "*Karen!*"

There is power to control in a name. She spoke the name with resonant Command and suddenly the cougar was there, terrified eyes wide on the wizard beside her. Ruthless, she pushed aside the older woman's flimsy natural protections and pulled what power there was into herself. It was wild, and tasted of dark places, pain-filled joy, and kittens warm in the den. This was not a wizard's gift she used but came of her mixed blood. A full-blooded wizard would not have deigned to use the therian like this, would not have been able to pull power like this from outside their body even if they wanted to. The spell flared back to life, and Winter redoubled her efforts.

Four glyphs.

The hole began collapsing inward, little chunks of cement falling into the flame-wreathed darkness.

Three glyphs.

The chunks were getting larger, the cracks creeping closer to her fragile chalk lines.

Two glyphs.

The surge was now audible, a tsunami rushing toward them.

One glyph.

The ground beneath her knees was quivering with the building pressure.

The seal blazed just as the tidal wave of magic rammed it from the other side, the whole ravine shuddering from the impact, then the lettering settled into the cement, leaving the two women alone in the quiet night. Winter slumped with relief as the seal held, her forehead pressed to the unyielding wall. "Karen, thank—"

The cougar's scream slashed through the calm and Winter snapped her head to the side just in time to see her fur form disappear through the trees, leaving her clothes behind. The stab of remorse cut deep. "I'm sorry," she murmured. But there was no one to hear her.

Winter rose to her feet and went in search of a gentler incline, so she could climb out of the ravine alone, her shoulders slumped with the burden of guilt. She had broken a sacred trust tonight. This was the reason wizards were respected and feared—mostly feared. Therian could sense magic but could not wield it, and only rarely did a wizard choose to become vampire. That meant the vast majority of the two largest groups of preternaturals were defenseless against magicians. Wizards on the whole were arrogant and capable of some very unpleasant acts toward those they saw as inferior. It was a reputation her family had worked hard for generations to live down, to gain the trust of their community so they could keep the peace without resorting to terrorizing the preternatural groups in their care. Even though what she had done to Karen was not wizard magic, even though it had saved their lives, it did not matter. She had used magic to abuse the cougar and once word spread Winter would have to work even harder to get the factions to trust her again.

She finally found a break in the ravine wall where pine needles and earth had filled in to make a ramp of sorts. Glancing back at the glittering track of blood drops she had trailed, she fought down the return of her exhaustion, now coupled with blood loss, and began to squirm her painful way up the pine litter-slick incline. First, find her way through the woods back to her Volkswagen Bug. Next, dig out that restorative potion from the box in the trunk. Finally, make it back home.

Why did three little steps sound so impossible? She made it to level ground and struggled to her feet. Putting one foot in front of the other, she did not so much walk through the woods as maintain a controlled fall forward. Always forward.

As she did every single day.

CHAPTER FOUR

Winter rested her head on the massive oak door, letting the elaborate carving leave impressions on her skin, taking just a moment to make the world stop swaying so much. The cream-colored sweater still wrapped around her arm had soaked completely through and the stain was seeping through the sleeve of her old Army jacket.

So, the restorative potion had not lasted all the way home, but made it home she had. She had never been hurt this badly before. She wished she could have gone to the hospital, though what exactly they could do for her that she could not do better herself, she had no idea. Then there was the issue of her blood. A full-blooded wizard could pass for human, but Winter's mother had been fae and Winter's bloodwork would reflect that. It wasn't worth her life to threaten the Veil of Secrecy that protected the preternatural world from human knowledge by letting humans draw her blood.

Her sister Mirilyn had once lost her left hand to the snapping jaws of a hydra. Their grandfather had been there to get her home safely, however, and through the family's combined efforts within a few weeks the hand had grown back. It never was exactly the same, of course... the skin was new as a child's and did not match the rest of her arm. Mirilyn had been sensitive about that. Winter suppressed a shudder of exhaustion as she pushed the door open. This was not that bad.

Soft lights came up and the great entry hall of Mulcahy House was revealed. Two graceful, sweeping staircases arched down from the second level on either side of the massive room, like warm, carven-wood arms open wide for an embrace. From the dark-stained chair rail nearly to the century-old oak ceiling beams, the pale cream walls were covered with hundreds of framed pictures. Some were paintings, more than a few damaged by fire and time, but most were photographs, formal and casual, the frames themselves as mismatched and eclectic as the people grinning and laughing out from them.

Her family.

Winter smiled at them, a sad, tired smile that did not reach her eyes, but a smile all the same. "I'm home, Papa." She said it quietly, on the very outside chance her father was sleeping. If he wasn't, it really didn't matter, for he would not answer, anyway. As she made her slow way down the dimly lit hallway, she saw the lights in the Library were not on, but then she really had not expected them to be. He would not have turned them on. She would check on him before she went to bed, but first she had to take care of herself.

The soft sounds of her footfalls sank into the darkness of open doorways as she passed, concentrating on putting one foot in front of the other, and it seemed an eternity before she entered the cavernous kitchen toward the back of the great house. The middle sink was filling with warm water as she arrived, and the doors to the massive medicine cabinets were open and waiting. "Thank you," she said aloud, knowing she would be heard. After five generations of caring for Mulcahy wizards, the House was quite adept at anticipating their needs.

She unwrapped the blood-soaked sweater and dropped it into the depths of the outer sink where it hit the bottom with a wet slap. For a brief moment, Winter considered running cold water over it, but she knew the goblin drool and pine pitch would not come out as easily as wizard blood. Exhaustion struggled fleetingly with thrift, and she spun the cold tap on that sink's faucet, hoping morning would find it improved. She had no energy left for stain removal, but nor did she want to needlessly replace the sweater. Even with holes in the sleeve, it could still be wearable.

Taking a moment, Winter rotated her wrist, watching for the tell-tale pulsing in the flow of blood that meant she was in real trouble. Of course, it had been so long that if an artery had been severed she would have never made it home, and she should have done this in Karen's yard... but better late than, well, late. Rivulets of blood rose and trailed lazily down to drip chrysanthemums into the clear water, but the ooze remained steady. The goblin had missed her arteries.

She was procrastinating, and she knew it, but after another moment's hesitation she slipped her bitten arm into the warm water, carefully rubbing it with her free hand to loosen the blood clots and dried slime. When the water invaded the depths of the worst punctures she spent another few minutes fighting back dry heaves from the deep, nauseating pain which shot up her arm and caused the muscles in her shoulder to spasm, but she refused to stop rubbing until she was certain the wounds were completely cleaned out. She cried out once and it echoed throughout the kitchen. It was met by silence.

By the time Winter was satisfied, her throat was burning tight with suppressed sobs and she was barely able to clumsily wrap her arm in a clean towel before her knees gave out and she slid to a heap on the floor. It *hurt*. She held her wrist to her chest with her right hand, the claw marks there smearing the nice white towel with renewed blood, and bit by bit folded her tall body around the pain until her forehead touched her knees. "Papa..." Her throat was raw, and she gave a little choking cough. He was up. She knew he was up because he never slept. "Papa, please help me."

Silence answered her.

Winter raised her head, and tears spilled down her flushed cheeks. "Papa! Please!" she called louder. The sound echoed like a mad thing up and down the hall, perhaps the loudest sound heard here in months.

Still nothing. No footsteps, no pale figure emerging from the dark.

"*Papa!*" This time she screamed, shouted her pain and frustration into the empty kitchen. Her throat buzzed from the sound of it. Surely, he heard her that time...

She caught movement at the kitchen door, and her heart jumped with excitement. "Papa!" But a sharp gray face with lapis lazuli eyes peered at her around the corner, and the rest of the large cat followed. The disappointment was like a blow, and Winter dropped her face to hide her pain.

The greymalkin simply sat there, expectant.

Winter wiped her eyes with the bloody towel and raised her gaze to face the faerie cat. "I'm sorry. Did I wake you?"

The cat blinked, then walked over to the right medicine cupboard and washed her face.

Taking a deep, shivering breath, Winter gathered up her pain and frustration and stuffed it firmly back down into the pit of her soul where she kept her grief, her anger... everything else she did not have the time to indulge in. And a fit of temper was an indulgence, indeed. The cat paused her washing to look impatiently over her shoulder at Winter and then resumed with the other side of her face.

As sitting and bleeding were doing her no good, Winter clutched the lip of the sink with her good hand and dragged herself to her feet. There was no one to help her but the faerie cat... and she would do nothing but sit there and scorn her frailty. The greymalkin was, after all, immortal and tended to hold all others to her high standards. Her knees did not want to cooperate, but Winter was able to stagger over to join the cat.

She found the jar she needed in the well-organized, if depleted, cupboards with ease, and simply let herself sink again to the kitchen floor and pried the top off with the jar held between her scraped knees. The scent of the contents rose spicy into the air, and she scooped out a generous handful of the thick, translucent green ointment with her right hand while carefully shaking the towel off the other.

The bite was an ugly thing; all ripped skin and exposed flesh, pink and white from the water and crimson smears of fresh blood. Cool air seeped into the open wounds, breathing on places never meant to be touched. The sensation brought back the nausea, and she set to applying the ointment. It took three handfuls before she was satisfied, carefully filling in each puncture before pressing the flesh back into place. Her arm went blessedly, wonderfully numb, as did the scratches as she dabbed at her face, chest, legs, and right hand. A dressing of clean bandages followed, as neat as could be done with one hand, and she just sat there on the floor with her legs stretched out before her for a few long minutes, enjoying not being in pain. She reached up blindly, her hand finding a long red bottle, and drank it all down, screwing her face up as she spat the dregs back out. Her great-grandma Maria had created the best potion to treat blood loss, but there had to be something she could do to improve the taste. Honeysuckle, maybe, or another sugar? Or a couple of shots of whiskey beforehand, just so she wouldn't care so much.

Even with the healing warmth pulsing through her body, Winter caught herself nodding off on the kitchen floor. That would make for an unpleasant morning, and she desperately wanted a shower, although that would have to wait until the scratches healed. In the absence of pain, she could feel her scalp and skin crawling with dirt from rolling around on the ground with the filthy little goblin and then her later adventure in the ravine.

What, exactly, had happened in the ravine? She rolled the long neck of the bottle between the fingers of her good hand, frowning a little in thought. Instability was one thing. The entire area around Seahaven was massively unstable and things came through the larger rifts with frequency. But what happened tonight—she had never experienced or even heard of such a thing. What caused it? Could it happen again? There were so many questions that she just did not have answers to.

Enough was enough. She did not have time to sit on the kitchen floor fussing about this all night. She needed to check on her father, then get clean and find her bed for what precious little sleep she could get. She stood, still a bit shaky, but she was able to keep her feet, and she made her careful way down the wide hall to the Library. She would check on her father, and then find a shower and her bed.

Mulcahy House was famous throughout the magical world for its two great treasures—the Mulcahy Gardens, first planted in the 1860s when the House was created and then taken up by generations of Mulcahy wizards, most notably Maria Stetson-Mulcahy, who made it into one of the most remarkable magical gardens in the world. The other was the Mulcahy Library. Other Great Houses could boast impressive libraries dedicated to one or two schools of magic, but only the Mulcahys had such a vast and wide-ranging collection, with copies of thousands of rare books and hundreds of volumes that were unique. The Mulcahys were known for their eclectic tastes.

Among wizards, perhaps only the library collection of the Wizard Council itself was as broad in material, although she had heard that the

Servants of the Eldest possessed a library that surpassed it. Her father, Colin, would know for certain. He was the keeper of the Mulcahy Library.

Winter found him exactly where she expected to find him, in his worn green leather chair in the deepest corner of the stacks. Piles of books surrounded him, buried the table beside him, and littered the floor about his feet. A wooden tray was balanced on top of one of the piles, a full bowl of soup and a small plate of toast untouched. "I'm home, Papa." She checked the cup—at least he had drunk his water. She had dosed it liberally with her vitamin tonic, so it was better than nothing, but still... "I wish you would eat." The food she had laced with anti-depressant potions. He refused to take them on his own. She would have put them in the water, as well, but unlike the vitamin tonic they both colored and flavored whatever they were added to and he knew whenever it was in there.

Unfortunately, like conventional anti-depressants, her potions needed time and consistency to build up in the system and affect the brain chemistry of her patient to be effective. Her father wanted no part of that. He ate so infrequently that what little medication she could get into him was ineffective, and he knew it. So, she had a medical practitioner's greatest frustration and greatest grief—a treatable patient who was non-compliant. And worse, it was her parent.

He did not look at her. Colin's head rested against one wing of the old chair, his dull eyes staring fixedly at the nothing beside her. He wore a dirty brown robe, threadbare at the neck and the elbows, the cuffs nearly black with accumulated grime. His dark hair hung stringy and limp to his shoulders, his face covered with a scraggly beard. White streaks marked his thin cheeks from where tears had fallen and been allowed to dry.

Winter pushed the books away from his feet, noting that they had not changed position or order in weeks. He was not reading them anymore. "Can you hear me, Papa?"

She watched his hands, rather than his face, for his response, but his fingers did not so much as twitch. Colin had been born mute. When they were children, she and her sisters would try to ignore their gentle father by simply not looking at him—it was a good way to get something thrown at them, though. And heaven help them if their mother caught them doing it.

Winter barely remembered her, but she did know that Tersa would abide no one, not even her own daughters, mistreating her sweet Colin.

Winter picked up the blanket that had pooled around her father's bare feet and tucked it back over his thin legs. Her mother had disappeared nearly twenty years ago, and her father had not left the house since. However, the depression had not consumed him, not entirely, until the deaths of her older twin sisters, Sorcha at twenty-two, Mirilyn along with her husband and little daughter the year after that. When her cousins died six months ago, leaving the two of them alone, he had simply stopped leaving the Library.

Winter knelt and laid her head against his bony knees. He had always been shy, always been gentle, while her mother had been fierce and proud, the face of their marriage. Her mother would know how to fix this. Winter didn't. "I wish you would eat, Papa." She closed her eyes a moment, grief tugging at her, but no tears came. She had no more, tonight. "I miss you." She whispered it against the blanket, a bare breath of sound.

Something moved against her hair, and she felt the warmth of her father's fingers against her neck. She pressed her face harder against his knees.

They sat in the dark, in silence.

CHAPTER FIVE

The alarm went off, piercing Winter's drugged sleep, and she burst from uneasy dreams like a popped balloon. She slapped at the button and rolled up onto her elbows, pressing her eyes into the heels of her hands as she fought down the nausea brought on by too little rest. The long, frayed weight of her sleeping braid slid down over her shoulder, coiling on the sheet beside her...

She jerked herself back awake, her breath coming in short gasps, her bandaged wrist aching dully from the weight of her head, and she looked at the clock. 4:43 a.m. Almost forty-five minutes lost to weakness. Winter grimaced with irritation as she flipped on the harsh light and reached down to rummage in the covered basket tucked away between her bed and her nightstand. She didn't have time for that sort of self-indulgence.

Her groggy fingers roamed over night-cool glass, picking up first one bottle, and then another. Empty... empty... empty... please, surely one was left? She could have sworn... Empty... empty... she began to feel the tide of desperation rising and shifted her body half off the bed, the better to see... She just needed one! Finally, her shaking hand closed on the cool weight of an unopened bottle, and she pulled the long green glass into the glow from her bedside lamp.

The taste was foul, medicinal, and she shuddered in distaste even as energy flowed hot and harsh from her belly out, forcing back the floatiness of the sleeping draught she had taken only a few hours before. Nasty way to wake up in the morning, but it was awfully effective.

Winter carried the potion bottle across the hall into the bathroom with her. She closed and latched the door behind her, entirely out of habit. Her father would not venture up the stairs on his own and there was no one else to bang on the door and howl that she was hogging the shower. Kelley and Martina were always terrible about that. They insisted on using the bathroom across the hall from Winter's room, because they said it had the best bathtub. It had been the most annoying thing about her young cousins. Pain, knife-edged under her sternum, caught her breath. What wouldn't she give to have that back?

Winter took another pull from the bottle, swallowing down her pain, her loneliness, and caught her reflection in the mirror as she brought it down from her lips. She was getting even thinner. Her cheeks had sunken in more, the shadows under her eyes deepening. The corners of her mouth were becoming pinched. When was the last time she had really smiled? Smiled with her eyes and her soul? Had it been so long since she had been happy? She closed her eyes and tried to remember when her family had been around her and their warmth had filled her more surely than the bottle she nursed... but it had been so long. So very long. She was only twenty-four and already she felt like an old woman.

Winter opened her eyes and faced her harsh reflection, her gaze clinical. It was stress wearing her down. That and the poison-green potion she drank. She was too well-trained a physician to deny it. The stimulant was stealing from her even as it gave her the energy she so desperately needed to keep working. She was overwhelmed and self-medicating; dosing herself at night to sleep through the stress and nightmares, dosing herself in the mornings to claw out of bed and face another painfully long day, dosing herself during the day with enough caffeine to make her heart race right up until late into the night when she again fell to bed with the sleeping draught. Soon would come the day when she would not know if she was up or down, when it would all catch up with her.

She knew it, knew that for anyone else she would warn them that they were traveling a dangerous path, that it was a danger for any medical practitioner to practice on themselves in such a reckless fashion—but what choice did she have? Find her rest while the city burned around her? She was the lone Mulcahy wizard remaining functioning in Seahaven, where once there had been dozens. She held the reins on a wild horse, barely under her control. Trying to hold against the power vacuum left by her family's demise was eating her alive, but she alone held the ability to maintain the tattered remnants of the City of Peace founded by her great-great-great-great grandfather and Erik Eriksson, the King of the Seahaven vampires. The vampires had her back—she knew the city would have exploded into factional wars months, even years ago, without them—but she was the wizard here, the ultimate authority and neutral negotiator for Seahaven. With the newest Mulcahy brought low by his crushing depression, Winter had no illusions how alone she truly was.

She could not afford to give the vampires, her closest allies, too much power. The other groups would riot in protest—were already grumbling that the Mulcahys favored the vampires over the other groups. Seahaven had been founded on a balance of alliances, where no one group had power over the others, where all could live in harmony and peace, unlike other cities of the world which were ruled by one powerful group to the detriment and subjugation of the others. Erik Eriksson had had an egalitarian dream, born from his Viking heritage and centuries of living through power struggles and the machinations of vampire politics in Europe, of founding a city ruled not by vampires as would be expected of him, but of power shared.

Mahon Mulcahy had similarly sought peace from a world of strife but understood that there must be at least some authority to rule that peace, to maintain the balance and protect it from those who might take advantage of the unique political experiment he and Erik proposed. And so, the family of wizards ultimately ruled Seahaven, taking the reins of power here where wizards in the rest of the world preferred to remain aloof and above what they considered to be the petty squabbles of the masses. It was a responsibility the Mulcahy family took very seriously, acting as the peacekeepers of Seahaven. A responsibility that had slowly, inexorably, come to rest fully on her thin shoulders.

Winter held her own gaze in the mirror and drained the potion bottle slowly, defiantly. She would not let them down. No matter the cost to her. Her family before her had made a promise and she owned fifty-four black dresses that still hung in a room in this house, a testament of their sacrifice to this city. Fifty-four funerals over twenty years, the measure of Mulcahy blood spilled for the sake of peace in Seahaven.

And when she, too, was gone…

Winter dropped her eyes from her reflection's, as the false energy from the potion filled her belly and spread out to her slender limbs, burning just a little more of her away. The emptiness of the house stretched around her. No one banged on the door to rescue her from her dark thoughts. She had no one to rescue her but herself.

She scowled and set down the bottle, picking up her sturdy brush and set to work on her hip-length hair. She would die, sooner than later—but today was not that day. Today, she would stand between the factions of Seahaven and act as the buffer that held chaos back. Just for one more day. It was all she could do. One day at a time.

Winter bound her long hair up into her customary bun and pinned the wavy, curly mass into some semblance of order, brushed on a little light brown mascara to darken her white brows and lashes, and then unwound the bandage from her left arm. It stuck to the skin where blood and oint-ment had dried, and the flesh remained sore, but she was satisfied that the deep wounds had been reduced to a tracery of pink lines. Long sleeves would be the order of the day, then. In the late October chill, she preferred it that way, anyway. She tossed the bandage into the laundry chute and crossed back to her room to dress for the day.

Before five fifteen Winter was carrying the basket of empty bottles down the chilly back stairs to the massive kitchen, her steps quiet in her well-cushioned flats. She knew where each squeaky spot was from years of early mornings in a house of late sleepers and avoided them out of hab-it. All three greymalkin greeted her as she emerged into the relative warmth of the kitchen, kept that way by the English stove's constant heat. Freya, her companion from the night before, was the smallest of the faerie cats and the quickest to scorn. Freya's two companions topped out at over twenty-five pounds of sleekly furred muscle each, their green-and-lapis miss-matched eyes fixed on her. Frick and Frack were twins, as far as Winter knew, and probably Freya's mates as well, though they had not once produced a litter in the hundred and fifty years since they had ap-peared with Winter's sidhe ancestress, Eithne.

Eithne and her sister, Aideen Laughing Waters, had appeared to Mahon Mulcahy when he reached this shore, and Eithne had chosen him for her husband. Shocking, for wizards fanatically guarded their lineages and never sought spouses outside the Wizard Houses, Mahon and Eithne's marriage set a precedent for the Mulcahys to seek mates outside the established Bloodlines. Though their marriage was short-lived as many fae/mortal matches were, Eithne gifted Mahon with three powerful sons as well as the greymalkin, and, with her sister's assistance, Mulcahy House.

Winter smiled a little to see her medium cauldron already out on the custom-built casting stove, the House again anticipating her needs. "Thank you," she said politely into the quiet of the kitchen. Though the House had quieted slowly over the years as the family died, the figures in the densely-carved woodwork ceasing their dance, the many rooms no longer changing to meet the needs of owners no longer there, the kitchen remained the heart of the House and the last stronghold of faerie magic. Only one other building in the city was remotely like it, the smaller version Aideen and Eithne built when Aideen eventually married, but the carved figures there had not moved in well over a century, the magic not surviving the death of its original mistress. Mulcahy House still lived, but it, too, would probably become still when the last of the Mulcahys were gone.

Winter set the basket of bottles near the washer and started stacking them inside to be cleaned. "Maria's Great Book, please," she said aloud. This particular washer had been designed strictly for bottle washing, its two wide racks filled with upright posts for holding the potion bottles in place, and Winter filled it to capacity. She closed the door and slid the latch home, started the fill cycle, and turned to find her great-grandmother's immense tome perched on its big book rest on the casting counter.

The book lived in the library, where it would be kept safe from everyday kitchen messes, but held court here when in use, in the casting section of the kitchen. She brushed her fingers over the soft, scrolled-leather cover, then deftly opened the book to the recipe she needed. It was quickly becoming a worn place in the book, Winter noted with chagrin, one of those places the book would open to naturally, like the 'good parts' of a well-loved romance novel, and just as embarrassing. Any other potion master who found how easily the book opened to this one page would know in a moment exactly what Winter had been doing.

Well, 'other' was probably a strong word to use. Winter caught up her favorite basket and carried it to the enormous glass-fronted cabinets that held her spell ingredients. Winter was only twenty-four—extremely young as wizards went, who could easily live to see thirteen or fifteen decades— and talented as she might be she had never been formally trained outside the family, as most wizards were. Technically, she was no potion master and there would be few among the wizards who would consider her such.

She went from door to door, deftly plucking up bottles, boxes and jars, noting which were getting low and needed to be replenished, which was a lot. She needed to spend time in the garden and the House's huge conservatory gathering ingredients, she needed to spend time processing those ingredients for storage... she just needed time! Winter set the basket down on the low counter a bit harder than she intended to, frustration welling inside her again. She needed the time to do the work of five wizards and did not even have enough time to brew herself morning coffee. The Daily Grind, the coffee shop near her store in the Historical District, got a great deal of business from her.

Standing in her echoing kitchen, the Great Book open before her, Winter found herself feeling a little like a fraud, even as she set to filling her cauldron with purified water. Everyone said that she had learned at Maria's knee, and she let them because that much was true. She had been knee-high to Maria when she taught her, a tender four-year-old, the most basic tenants of potion-making, all with the promise that Winter would in time become her official apprentice and take her place at Maria's side.

But then Maria had died, of food poisoning of all the damn things, at barely sixty-eight. And Winter had been left alone with the Great Book, the culmination of Maria's life's work, all painstakingly recorded, annotated, and indexed. It was a brilliant work of incredible value and only in the past year had Winter begun to feel confident enough to add her own notes, to begin filling the blank pages that comprised the last quarter of the book. Pages Maria herself should have filled. Losing her at such a young age was a tragedy for both the family and wizards at large, for hers had been a once-in-a-generation mind. Maria's death also seemed to be the great ill omen that doomed the Mulcahys, for after that they began to die more and more often, singly, in groups, even whole families, taken by death in the twenty years since.

And the wizards of the world had watched... and done nothing. The Mulcahys were cursed, it was whispered. They brought this on themselves by breeding outside the Bloodlines. But the truth was no one knew the reason why. Many accomplished, experienced Mulcahy wizards had spent what would prove to be their last days desperately searching for a curse that they would never find. And the idea that it was their mixed blood was ludicrous. For Winter, who had grown up with her family dying all around her, it was simply, tragically, horrifyingly normal. It was only when she realized that her friends did not go to so many funerals that she began to ask '*why*,' as well. But there were no answers for her, either.

The Mulcahys had once been powerful, and even now held claim to a seat on the Wizard Council, the governing body wizards answered to among themselves, after the Servants of the Eldest. But Mahon Mulcahy had lost a power struggle in Ireland that cost him the original Mulcahy House as well as his first family and drove him underground and across the Atlantic for fear of his life—until he met a Viking vampire in New York who wanted to found his own city. Mahon found running until he hit water again to be a tempting thought and ended up with Seahaven.

Over the next few decades he managed to return his family to its position as a Great House, even with his scandalous marriage—it was amazing what forgiveness could be earned by raw power among the wizards, and Eithne's sons had raw power to spare—but they never rose as high as they had once been. Even then, most of their marriages were made within the other Great Houses, both in Europe and the United States, and Winter's sister Mirilyn had married the scion of an Arabian Great House. But the deaths quickly ground them down. Houses once considered good friends and allies stopped coming to the funerals, stopped courting the Mulcahy Bloodline, powerful though it may be, especially after Dermot died. The remaining Mulcahys, bitter and increasingly isolated, were happy to see the door hit the other wizard families on the way out. Not one Mulcahy had sat on the Council seat since Dermot, and he had only rarely traveled to London to attend. Even he had finally taken his ball and gone home.

The Mulcahys, long considered eccentric, were now pariahs.

Winter's hands moved automatically, her eyes flickering to the page but more out of practical caution than real need. She could make this potion in her sleep—had made it before under the influence of her sleeping draught—but all potions had the potential for dangerous mistakes and today her mind was simply not on her task. She rubbed her eyes and pushed herself to focus more. The line between potion and poison was very thin and screwing up this brew would result in wasted time and ingredients at the very least. Should the mistake go unnoticed until it was too late, the results could be tragic.

Some said that that was what had happened to Maria, that an experiment had killed her. Winter did not believe it, but she had had enough of her own close calls over years of trial and error to urge caution.

Winter added the last of the ingredients, a tufty herb she needed to re-order from Nepal much sooner than later and gave the brew the prescribed number of precise stirs from right to left, then left to right, to ensure even mixing. Now she had come to the part that separated an herbal stew from a magical potion. Pulling power, she focused on her glyph-scribed spoon, large and heavily carved of oak for its durability. It had once belonged to Maria. All wizards had focus objects related to their magical specialty, and they ranged from the expected wand or staff to spoons, looms, and brooms, as her grandmother Bridget had liked to explain. Bridget had not been a wizard herself—she had been a seer—but she figured being Irish and over a hundred years old—somewhat immortal—when she married an eighteen-year-old Dermot Mulcahy gave her enough credit to lecture on the subject. And of course, no one was lacking enough in sense to try to argue with her about it.

Winter's father's focus object, as Keeper of the Library, was a blank leather journal, heavily tooled on the outside. Since he could not speak, he would write his spells and Commands in the journal, and the Library obeyed. He also used it as a regular journal, though Winter had not seen him simply write in it to record his thoughts in years. He had lost the heart for it.

Pulling and moving power was one of Winter's primary gifts, derived from her mixed heritage. While all wizards could draw on the power within their bodies, and there was quite a bit to draw on, Winter could pull from outside herself and actually act as a conduit for the magical energy. It was what let her seal the rift in the face of that strange surge the night before, by pulling additional power from the therian's body—she winced from the guilt that memory prodded within her—and what gave her greater endurance while casting potions. Winter's sisters had been able to do it, too, but then the infusion of sidhe blood was even more recent for their line than for their various cousins'.

Winter's own mother, Tersa, had been a sidhe mix, though of what exactly was never known, but it was theorized to be some sort of greater fae. Tersa forbade the family from asking as one of the conditions of her staying among mortals, and Colin obeyed her wishes. He had no desire to leave his family for Faerie, but he loved Tersa with his whole heart, so when she laid down her conditions to stay he had agreed readily. Such arrangements were common enough when the fae married mortals, and since neither condition was onerous they were never questioned too closely. That Winter and her sisters all developed somewhat normally was frankly all that the Mulcahys hoped for.

Power was not even a requirement. Dermot's marriage with the seer, Bridget, had produced one son of their four children with no magical ability what-so-ever. He was accepted and loved with or without magic. Her Uncle Mark ended up being a high school teacher and had had a perfectly normal life with his husband Steve—until they died in a car accident. He was not the only Mulcahy to be born as something other than a wizard, just the only one in her direct line. Winter even had had therian bears in the family in Colorado and one Mulcahy wizard had married a naiad in San Francisco when he could not find a wizard bride… but it seemed that even mixed marriage and distance could not save them from death.

Winter swallowed and swallowed again. She was getting thirsty, and it was the vaguely nauseating smell coming from the cauldron that was setting her off. She wanted more potion. She should not have more—one was more than plenty and she shouldn't be taking them every day like she was, but she was catching herself sneaking a second sometimes.

When would come the day it would be a third? When would she skip the frappes and stick to the much harder potion to get through her day?

Sooner than later, most likely. She set thoughts of her addiction aside—looked at it as an addiction, accepted it, and moved on. She needed the potion, and she needed to be able to focus to get it. She could not dwell on the complications right now. Maybe later, maybe if the pressure would lighten up a little, she could direct energy to clearing herself of the sticky mess of self-medicating she had gotten herself into. Later, in private, where no one would know of her shame. Her weakness.

She just needed it a while more.

She trickled magic down the oaken spoon as she slowly stirred the simmering green liquid, easing the power into the potion. Forcing it would do no good. Potion-making and cooking had many parallels, and among them was the rule that good cooking can never be rushed. There were potions in the Great Book that took days of constant attention, and Winter knew of other, legendary potions that had taken years to brew. She was grateful that she could cast up this particular potion in just a couple of hours. But even though it was one of the quicker brews did not mean she could rush things along. So, she coaxed magic into the cooling cauldron, watching the color slowly take on a more vibrant hue, all the while getting thirstier.

But it wasn't just about raw power, it was about focus. Determination. With each rotation around the cauldron, Winter focused her will into the magic, infusing it with what she wanted from the potion. Energy, focus, mental agility, alertness. She chanted each word under her breath, sharpening her focus with her voice. Words held power, for wizards even more so than other preternaturals. They used symbolism to focus their magical wills, and words were simply very powerful symbols. Language did not matter. Winter preferred to cast in English, but it was only individual taste. Many wizards cast their magic by using glyphs and charts and weaving symbols together to bring about arcane meaning from ancient languages, but the power was not just in the drawing, in the speaking. It was in the will, and the magical attunement to impose that will on the universe. A human with no magical spark could do exactly the same thing she was doing but would only end up with a warm cauldron of wasted ingredients. It was that spark, that connection to the power flows of the Universe, that made a wizard, and the depths of their connection determined how much potential for power they possessed.

Winter's connection, through her sidhe blood, was deep indeed.

Finally, the potion reached the color and temperature she sought, at just the perfect time. It would be a good batch, and her mouth was watering. Her hands trembled as she carefully cleaned her spoon, washing all remnants of the potion off so as to not taint the next brew. It took all her control to get out the ladle and funnel, to set them down gently by the cauldron and not just ladle the potion directly into her mouth. It was an addiction, but Winter would keep a reign on it. She opened the washer and pulled out the now warm and dry bottles, setting them in rows on the counter. Some potions required a precise temperature for the bottle, some even required a particular color or quality of glass, but this potion was not so exacting. Winter used the tall green bottles because the potion itself was green, and because she had a lot of them, so they would all match. Winter had picked up the habit of using bottle shape and color to identify her potions from Maria, and often only labeled those potions she intended for public consumption. She also tended to cast a small return charm on each bottle to encourage those to whom she gave them to turn them back in. She had a local glass blower that she gave frequent business to, who made to her specifications and did not ask too many questions about her stranger orders, but she was pricey, and Mulcahys tended to be frugal.

Winter took the funnel and the ladle and carefully filled the first bottle with just the right amount of potion… and then set the ladle down, feeling the bottle warm in her hand.

This was stupid.

She brought the potion to her lips, feeling the heat spread through her core even as it travelled to her belly. If she tried to fill all the bottles without drinking, she would be either a shaking mess of cravings by the end or racing through the process and getting the dosages wrong. That was what she told herself as she spun about and leaned her backside against the low counter, throat working as she tipped the bottle higher and higher, filling her body with false warmth. Her free hand worked in the air as she swallowed, her fingers clenching spasmodically with each convulsion of her throat.

Winter finished drinking, gasping for breath, and rested the bottle against her forehead. There was no strength to be found in the glass against her brow. She closed her eyes and fought to not cry.

She had no time for tears. The city was burning, and she would have fires to put out today.

CHAPTER SIX

October twenty-seventh decided to dawn chilly and rainy as Winter pulled into her parking space in the small merchant and resident only lot behind Olde Curiosity's Gift Shoppe. Founded by her Great-Aunt Curiosity Mulcahy-Reynolds in a bid to keep herself occupied when her husband Arthur went to fight for the U.S. during World War Two, Curiosity's was a fixture of the Historical District... for those who knew to look for it. The mundane eye would usually slip from Sweet Treats on the corner of Old Main Street and Pacifica to Katherine's Retreat on the left, skimming over the small store with its backroom-clinic and upstairs apartment. But those with a magical spark, or those guided in by them, would notice the painted metal sign hanging over the red door, and the small display framed by lacey curtains in the window. Over the years, Winter often found herself surprised by those who could find their way to the tiny shop.

Winter could see none of this as she opened the back door centered on the windowless brick wall and was surprised when she reached to turn on the back-room light, only to find it already on. Music was playing—too loud. "Hello?" she called nervously, knowing only three other people had keys to her store, and none of them should be here at just before eight in the morning.

"We're in front!" came the call back. Winter rolled her eyes in relieved exasperation. And there was one of them. The very one who should not be in here on a Friday morning. Well, that explained the music, at any rate. She crossed the back room, dropping her canvas bag in the desk chair and hanging up the old Army coat where she would remember to drop it off at the cleaners later. Blood still darkened the olive-green fabric of the left sleeve, and as the coat had once belonged to Uncle Arthur, Winter did not trust it to her home washing machine. Katherine's usual cleaner was accustomed to getting blood out of older fabrics—surely, they could handle the bloody old coat.

"Who's 'we'?" she asked, passing through the thickly beaded curtain to find two teenagers bustling about the front of her store.

The boxes that had littered the floor were mostly gone, what little they had in them tucked neatly away on the store shelves. A pleasantly plump brunette girl of about sixteen tossed a broken-down box onto a pile of its mates and flashed Winter a bright smile. "Just Brian and me," she said, her voice raised up above the electric guitar and not-unpleasant male singer and pushed her glasses up her nose. "We were hoping to get this done before you got here... so, surprise!"

Winter reached over to where Jessie had plugged her MP3 player into her speakers and turned the volume down to something more conducive to conversation. It sounded like they were listening to Johnny Smith again, Jessie's favorite. Winter did not listen to a lot of music, but what she had heard of the rock star through Jessie she liked.

The young black man rested his hands on his broom and smiled warmly at Winter in greeting. "Jessie said you needed some help, so we came over." His long, thin dreadlocks fell just a little into his dark eyes to brush below his collarbones, and his gloriously broad shoulders and defined chest strained the fabric of his bright white t-shirt when he moved, neatly framed by the baby backpack he wore. Dangling from it was Justin, Brian's two-year-old brother, busily chewing wetly on a toy that he occasionally rubbed against the back of Brian's head. Brian did not give it much notice and let the toddler muss him at will.

Winter glanced around the much-tidier store, appreciating what looked like a couple hours-worth of work. Fixtures were straightened and dusted, what stock she had left was put out on display, even the cash wrap was organized and cleaned. She wanted to defend her ability to handle it herself but squelched the impulse in favor of a politer response. "Thank you! But, Jessie, you shouldn't have skipped school to do this..."

"What school?" interrupted Jessie. She walked around to the cash wrap and made to grab up another box.

"The school you have every Friday. I don't want your parents—"

Jessie rolled her caramel eyes and set the box down on the counter. "Don't get me started on them, please. It's too early. Besides," she said, picking up a large take-out coffee cup and handing it to Winter, "Frappe!"

"What?"

"Now, here's your caffeine hit. You need it. Mocha frappe with espresso." Jessie screwed up her pert little nose with distaste. She was not a coffee drinker.

Winter took her coffee, her mascara-darkened brows pulling inward in a small scowl.

"Drink," the teenage girl ordered.

Winter drank deeply of cold mocha and whipped cream with chocolate syrup. She didn't care about the calories, empty though they may be. The way the energy potion burned through her, she needed all she could get. Besides, she *really* liked the way The Daily Grind made their frappes. "How did you pay for this?" she asked as thought followed enjoyment. She did not pay Jessie enough to be buying her frappes. Jessie was supposed to be saving for college. It was why Winter paid for her cell phone and martial arts classes and had given her one of her family's old cars for her birthday. She would have bought her a new car, but in Jessie's neighborhood that would not have been safe or sensible. Jessie's parents had already declared that Jessie was on her own for college.

"I took the money from the register and just rung it as petty cash," Jessie replied, picking up her box again and heading off toward the store shelves.

Winter nodded. That was fine. Something nagged at Winter's mind, and she took another drink from her coffee, feeling the caffeine seep into her system and chasing the brain lag the energy potion left in its wake. Register... And it clicked. Today was Friday, bookkeeping day. Bookkeeping was not something she had the time, or the talent, for. On Fridays she always sent it out to a freelancer who was retired and doing a little bookkeeping for some of the Historical District stores part-time. "You derailed me!" she accused, turning on Jessie in exasperation.

Jessie turned from the shelves, and Brian gave her an I-told-you-so look. She bent and set the box on the floor, then stood, hands on her ample hips. "Yeah, I did. I'll own it."

Winter glanced at Brian and gave him a small smile. "Excuse us, please."

Brian nodded. "You need me to go?"

"Oh, no, please. We'll just take this to the back." She looked at Jessie and motioned to the back room. Jessie admirably refrained from rolling her eyes and preceded her through the beaded doorway.

Jessie leaned her backside against Winter's large work table and looked unrepentant. "I'm sorry I played you," she began.

Winter waved away her apology. "That's not the issue, Jessie. You knew you were in trouble and you were putting off me being upset at you about it. You're sixteen. I expect some trouble evasion."

Jessie opened her mouth to defend her honor.

Winter continued. "You're also very honest and own up to your mistakes. So, no, I'm not mad at you for derailing me. I am, however, concerned about you skipping school."

Now Jessie did roll her eyes. "Yes, because the educational standards at South City High School are so high that missing one day to help a friend in need will prove detrimental to my permanent record."

Winter's raised her right eyebrow. "Your vocabulary hasn't suffered."

"I picked up my vocabulary from you, Miss Mulcahy."

Winter thinned her lips and started again. "I know that South City is not the best school in the city—"

"Best?" Jessie squawked. "They won't let my sketchbooks through the metal detectors. You know why? Because I might assault another student with the metal wire binding!"

Winter watched the younger woman flail her arms and jump around as she vented her frustrations. This was a common conversation.

"I wanted to go to Seahaven Academy of the Arts! But, no, my parents wouldn't fill out the transfer paperwork." She shoved her long brown hair out of her face in irritation. "And when I filled it out, they refused to sign it. Said they weren't paying for me to be an art fag. It was free! I'd passed the fucking audition!" She paced back and forth, and finally flopped her backside back against the heavy work table again, dejected. "I'm only allowed two units of art at South City. You know what we do in art class? Everyone sketches the same wooden model that's missing an arm, over and over, while the teacher gets progressively more wasted as the hour goes by because, you know, the next period is his planning period. Usually, by the bell he's pretty close to passed out. If he passes out *before* the bell, the asshats in the back who never do anything anyway start throwing what little art supplies we have."

Winter did not bother to correct her for cursing when she was venting like this. She sighed and reached out to rub Jessie's arm in sympathy. "You can major in art when you get to UWSH."

Jessie shrugged off her hand and Winter let her. Sometimes Jessie would let her touch her, sometimes not. Winter accepted it and moved on. "How? I have to audition to get into the program, and with only two units of art in four years on my transcript they'll just laugh at my application."

"You know I won't let that happen."

Jessie shook her head and looked mulishly away. "No. No string pulling. If I can't earn my way in, then I don't belong there."

Winter fought for her own calm. She was just as frustrated with the situation as Jessie, and even more powerless to change it. "I know this is hard on you, sweetie, but you have to go to school. I don't want you declared truant."

"I could go to Seahaven Arts if I was homeless."

Winter's eyebrows shot up as Jessie dropped that conversation bomb. "Pardon?"

Jessie turned back to face her. "I talked to the district enrollment office. I can present as an unaccompanied student if I'm homeless and escaping a bad home situation."

"A runaway?"

Jessie nodded.

Winter shook her head. "Oh no, honey, we are not talking about you becoming homeless just so you can change schools."

The teenager shrugged. "Why not? I spend half my time couch surfing anyway. If I'm not here, I'm elsewhere avoiding my psycho 'rents.' The main reason Jessie had a key to the store was because she sometimes slept in the upstairs apartment to escape her parents' drunken tirades. It was simply furnished and empty, Winter not having the time or inclination to deal with renters. Winter also did not have the time or inclination to deal with Jessie's parents, who had developed a hatred of Winter over the years, so the apartment was a secret and Jessie tried to use it as little as she could. At least until Jessie turned eighteen and would legally be her own person.

"Because living here counts as a residence, and I won't let you couch surf full time. It's not safe." Fear filled Winter's belly. She should drag Jessie back out to the front of the store and have her ask Brian about exactly how dangerous living homeless could be for a teen, but not only would that be callous to Brian's memories of what she was sure was a bad past, if Brian had not already told Jessie about it then it was not her place to make him. So, she skated past it all together. "And if you're not in school full time you can be arrested for truancy. Jessie, if they put you in foster care or detention, I may not see you again until you turn eighteen."

"Well, if they did that, then you can pull your magic strings and I could move in with you."

Winter gave the girl a sad smile. "If only I could," she said softly. She had that kind of power, but they both knew why Jessie could not stay at Mulcahy House.

Jessie nodded. "Yeah," she said, just as softly. "Me, too. That was dumb."

"There is never anything dumb about wishing."

"All I ever wanted to be was an artist."

"Then an artist is what you are. Jessie, you're the most talented illustrator I know, and you know how much Katherine loves the character portraits you draw for her books. Whether or not you go to an arts school has no bearing on that. I believe in you, and so does she."

Jessie's eyes burned with a hopeful light. "Really?"

"Oh, yes." Winter shifted toward the beaded curtain. "Do you want to go get us some breakfast? If you're here, you may as well stay the day."

A smile blossomed on Jessie's face.

Winter held up a stern finger. "But, school on Monday. I'm going to have a phone message from your parents at some point this weekend to look forward to. I'd just as soon not have two within a week."

Jessie passed through the beaded curtain and picked up the bank bag from beside the register. "And," she added, "I'll go drop this off with Muriel, so she can do the bookkeeping."

Winter gave her a grateful little smile. "When did you pick up mind reading as a talent, young lady?" she asked quietly.

Jessie rolled her eyes again and snorted. "Yeah, like I need to add that to blowing random stuff up." Jessie was not so quiet.

Winter widened her eyes slightly in warning and glanced pointedly at Brian, who was sweeping over near the shop door.

Jessie blushed and lowered her voice. "He's gonna find out some time, you know. How can he not, living in the Historical District?"

Winter had to give her apprentice that. He lived at Otherworld Books, directly across the street from this store and a building full of vampires, and he and Jessie were text-all-the-time close. Winter hoped that they would start dating someday. Jessie was sixteen-years-old, she should be dating, not living like a hopeless nun like Winter. But on the other hand, both teens were fated to do great things in their lives and Winter worried about the burden that such fates could bring. Brian had been born more different than he could ever dream of, and it worried Winter even as she readied quietly for his future. And Jessie St. James was a wizard.

But not the usual sort.

"He'll find out someday, but today is not that day," said Winter, firmly closing the book on that. Jessie did not know it, but someday, hopefully far, far in the future, they would all see the quality of Brian MacDowell.

Jessie crossed her arms with characteristic stubbornness but kept quiet. Winter had sympathy. It was not easy, being so gifted but not able to tell the people you were closest to your secret. Winter had grown up with that secret, too. But she had had family to support her. "Do your parents suspect you're here?" The very thought made her mentally cringe.

Jessie snorted hard, blowing a long lock of straight hair off her face. "Hello, it's Friday morning. They're probably still drunk from last night."

Winter nodded. It could be Tuesday morning and they would still be drunk, but Winter did not say it out loud. She let Jessie vent her frustrations but did not participate in disparaging her parents—at least outside her own head. "Did you sleep here last night?"

Jessie shook her head, looking up toward the little apartment wistfully. "Naw. I stayed somewhere else last night… but I may come back here tonight, depending. If they noticed I was gone, probably not." As often as they failed to notice their only child's absences, Jessie's parents got very upset when they came out of their alcoholic fog long enough to take note. Winter never knew if it was out of concern, or a desire to control. Jessie gave a philosophical little shrug. "We'll see."

Winter wanted to hold her, to give her the affection that was so lacking in her life. She always had. But, ever since Winter caught a twelve-year-old Jessie using magic to shoplift in her store, Jessie had shown distinct discomfort with being hugged or even complimented. Besides, Winter wasn't sure who she was seeking to comfort, Jessie or herself. So, Winter simply nodded, accepting Jessie as she was, and took another long swallow of her frappe.

Jessie looked at Winter, her face becoming serious, and lowered her voice. "Look, we need to talk."

Movement stirred in the corner of Winter's eyes, and she turned her head to see Brian making his way back to them. She held up a long-fingered hand to quiet her apprentice.

Brian wandered close, his dustpan full, Justin's legs kicking idly at his sides. Winter gave him a small smile. "How's your mother doing, Brian?" It had been a few weeks since she had touched base with the MacDowell family, technically her distant cousins. It had been the settler Thomas MacDowell that Aideen Laughing Waters, Eithne's sister, had chosen as husband.

Brian emptied his pan into the trash. Unlike Winter, Brian's smile always went to his eyes. She remembered a time, when they were both much younger, when it had not. "Norah's pretty good, actually. Her depression is lifting a little bit every day, and she's taken over a few more of her old chores at the bookstore." His smile broadened, showing straight white teeth against terracotta skin. "I told her to take it easy, and she told me that she's spent the last year 'taking it easy.'"

Justin held out his toy to Winter, and she gave his little wet hand a squeeze. Norah MacDowell, Brian's adopted mother, had lost her husband over a year before to a workplace shooting. Winter often found herself wondering if violently was the only way people died in Seahaven. Jake had been a good man, well liked in the Historical District. Norah had been destroyed and after the funeral fell into a severe depression, often refusing to come out of her bedroom for weeks at a stretch. Even with the help of his neighbors in the Historical District, Brian had been forced to step into the role of single father and provider to his mother and little brother, running the store and taking care of them both. It was a secret kept by the entire community, for fear that the boys would be taken from their mother's custody. But even though it caused him to fall behind on his home-school studies and put off college for a while, Brian bore the burden gracefully and without complaint, holding to the faith that Norah would recover. And a couple months ago that recovery had begun.

It gave Winter some small hope for her father. If only she could find a way to get his medications into him.

Brian's phone gave a discrete buzz, a far cry from the range of obnoxious noises that regularly rang from Jessie's, and he dug it out of his pocket. "It's Norah," he said, looking at the text screen, and his thick brows rose slightly. "She made breakfast from scratch," he said in pleased surprise, and with Norah's reputation for cooking from boxes it was a surprise indeed. "We've got to get going... do you want me back later?"

Winter gave him a grateful smile. It almost reached her eyes. But, Brian did bring that out in people. "No, you've done so much already. Thank you."

Jessie walked Brian to the door and let him out, locking it behind him. They would not officially open until ten. She turned away, missing Brian's gaze linger over her before he, too, turned away and headed across the cobble-paved, pedestrian-only street to the bookstore. Winter watched him, feeling a little sad for him. He was eighteen and Jessie just sixteen. Two years was a long time to wait when you are young, but it seemed to be what he wanted to do.

Winter gave her head a little shake. When had she gotten so old?

"Earth to Winter."

Winter turned her attention back to Jessie, who was standing before her with her hands on her hips. "What?"

"We need to talk." Jessie leaned forward, determination etched into her young face.

Winter took a last drink of her coffee and set it down. This could not be good. Jessie had her bulldog look. She sat on the stool behind the register and gave her apprentice her full attention. "Okay. What do we need to talk about?"

Jessie took a second to gather her words. Her brown eyes softened, and she said, "Look, I miss your family, too. I've known you for four years, and I've watched them die all around us. And when Kelley and Martina died in April you got left all alone. You need help."

Winter shook her head. "I'm okay, sweetie. I can handle it."

Jessie shook her head. "No, you can't! I know how sick your dad is, even if you won't let me come out to the House anymore. I used to be out there all the time, I saw how he was before and I know he's got to be worse by now." She paced away and paced back, her agitation building. "People talk to me, you know. They remember when this town was full of Mulcahy wizards, and now it's just you two."

Winter slid off the stool and headed into the back room. "I can handle it, Jessie. You have other things to worry about." She should have seen this coming. Jessie was passionate and loyal. And young. Very young.

Jessie followed her, relentless as a terrier. "What 'other things?' School? My psycho parents? How about the city burning down around our ears?" She waved her hand at the map taking up one wall of the back room. "Don't think I don't know what that's all about. The factions are going ape-shit—"

"Language."

Jessie blew her off. "—and they're all leaning on you to make it right. It's not fair!"

Winter turned to her. "It's the way it's always been. The wizards keep the balance, so everyone else in Seahaven can live in peace."

"Erik says that's not the way it was supposed to be."

Winter's eyes narrowed. "When have you been talking to the Vampire King?" Behind her back, none-the-less.

Jessie paused, then gathered her courage and forged ahead. "We talk. He's got my number. Winter, he's worried about you. We're *all* worried about you. The vampires, more than anybody, but yeah, all the groups are worried about you. They're not blind, and they're not stupid. You give everybody the 'I'm fine' line, but we can all see the strain." She took a breath. "Erik says that the city was supposed to be run by a coalition of the preternatural groups, that that was what he and Mahon talked about before he went back east to gather settlers. And then Mahon pulled his little land-grab and homesteaded or purchased most of the land here while Erik was away."

"That's not the whole story…" Winter began, a little uncomfortable.

"Erik was there. He remembers how it went down."

Winter did not respond. Yes, Mahon had gone behind Erik's back to acquire the land around what would become Seahaven. But he did it to secure peace. The preternatural groups needed someone to lead, to maintain the balance of power, and Erik was not willing to do that. Erik had never complained before. Ok, she had to be honest—had never complained that she knew of. He wouldn't have complained to her. He'd changed her diapers and still saw her in pigtails.

A small voice in her head reminded her that the city had never been so close to chaos, either. Maybe he'd never had reason before to complain.

Jessie shook her hand to wave her own words away. "But that's beside the point. The point is you're getting thin, and sick, and you need help."

Winter opened her mouth to object, and Jessie scowled at her until she shut it again. The girl drew a quick glyph on her palm with her finger and summoned a six-inch ball of fire to her hand. "Look," she said, her eyes on the fire. "It's stable." She passed it from hand to hand, and then rolled it over her knuckles to her palm again.

Winter watched with her. Just six months ago, Jessie could summon the fire, but had been barely able to control it. It would explode or fizzle out as Jessie struggled with it. No matter how often Martina had worked with her, it was one of Jessie's most difficult spells. Now it sat tamely in Jessie's hand, putting out heat and light as hypnotic patterns danced through it in yellows and oranges, just waiting for Jessie's will as it reflected those patterns on her glasses. But how? Winter pulled her gaze from the fireball and caught her apprentice's eyes. "Have you been practicing magic at home?" she asked with dawning apprehension.

Jessie shook her head in denial, closing her hand and extinguishing the ball. "Of course not!" She paused, smooshed her lips a little, and added, "I've been practicing at the Theatre."

Winter closed her eyes in a combination of relief and annoyance. Of course. With the vampires. The Seahaven Opera House was the biggest building in the Historical District, and one of the oldest, housing Erik's entire court. "Jessie—"

"I can't do magic like you do it, and since Kelley and Martina are gone there isn't anyone to teach me magic my way. I can't come over to your house to use the casting tower anymore, so I need to practice somewhere…" It all tumbled out in a nervous rush, making Winter wonder exactly how long Jessie had been doing this. How long she had been saving up those words.

Winter held out both her hands. "Please stop interrupting me. I was going to say, that's a very good idea. Just don't burn Erik's Theatre down. He likes it."

Jessie blinked, and smiled. "Really?"

Winter rubbed her tired eyes and stifled a yawn. "Yes, really. The vampires have watched little wizards learn for over a century. I don't think you could be in better hands." And it was true. Without access to the casting tower at Mulcahy House, Jessie had precious few places to practice what Kelley and Martina had taught her before they died.

Jessie screwed her face up at the mention of 'little wizards,' but continued to plow ahead with her argument. "So, my control has really improved. I can help you!"

Winter's face closed down, and she turned away again. "No."

"But Winter…"

"Under no circumstances. Did Erik give you this idea?" She would have words with the Vampire King, 'Uncle' Erik or no.

"No, this is all me. Why not?"

Because she didn't want her to die, too! Fear danced through her eyes, but Winter kept her face turned away from her apprentice—really more Kelley and Martina's apprentice, but as they were barely out of girlhood themselves, only twenty when they died... Dammit! "You're too young. It's out of the question."

"Winter..."

"No," she repeated, putting a little resonant Command in her voice to close the book. It would have little effect on Jessie—it was not a compulsion, after all, and she could not do those, anyway—but it would hopefully serve for emphasis.

She could hear Jessie breathing behind her, getting control over her frustration. "Fine," she said at length. "But if you won't let me help, at least get other wizards to come to the city."

Winter's eyes widened with horror at the thought. She shook her head. That was the one thing she could never, ever do. Not if she wanted to keep Jessie safe. "No."

She heard Jessie mutter, "Oh for fuck's sake," under her breath. "You need somebody, Winter. Why not?"

How could she tell her? The Mulcahys were the only wizards Jessie had ever met. Her family, iconoclasts that they were, welcomed and accepted Jessie with open arms. Other wizards would not. Jessie had been born to human parents, and to the Bloodlines that was a crime.

Before it had always seemed like one of those issues that could be addressed later. Jessie was young, maybe when she got older... but here she was getting older, and it was up to Winter to explain to her that she was called a 'sport' by other wizards, who considered the very fact of her birth to be a threat to their pure lines of descent. As if it was her fault that, once upon a time, some wizard had not been too picky about his lovers and had left a child behind to carry magic into the world. It happened all the time, it was just that wizards refused to acknowledge their fault in it. Instead, whenever a sport was found, they were either forcibly sterilized and taken into the 'refuge' of a House as an indentured servant or killed outright. It was a tradition practiced over centuries to protect the sanctity of the Bloodlines.

How could she tell Jessie that she was an outcast, and that Winter was quickly losing her ability to protect her? That Winter should have her tattooed in magical ink under her left collarbone with the Mulcahy Mark, two interlocking spirals branding her as wizard property. Chattel. "They won't come," she said quietly, once again putting off the inevitable. She turned and lied to her apprentice's face, feeling like a coward. "The wizards won't come, Jessie." Not as long as Winter was there to stop them.

Jessie's eyes narrowed as she looked over Winter's shoulder, and as Winter turned to see the Army coat hanging behind her Jessie's hand shot out to grab Winter's left wrist. Before she could stop the girl, Jessie jerked up her sweater sleeve. The healed bite was etched in livid pink lines into her pale skin. "Really?" she asked, incredulous.

Winter snatched her wrist back, pulling the sleeve down over the marks. "I'm fine," she said, moving around her apprentice to return to the front of the store.

Jessie was close behind her. "And how long were you going to not tell me that you got hurt last night?" she accused.

Winter picked up her empty frappe cup and threw it into the trash. "You didn't need to know. I handled it."

"I should have been with you."

Winter's mind flashed back to the mysterious power surge. What if Jessie had been with her and it blew? "No." Her chest clenched at the very thought of Jessie being in danger. She could not bear to lose her, too.

Jessie practically hopped with frustration and opened her mouth to continue arguing.

Winter's head swiveled to face the shop door, and she held up her hand to silence her apprentice. Someone was outside. "Hold that thought. I'm sure you'll remember to scold me later. Now, get the door and then take the bank bag and on your way back fetch us breakfast."

Jessie rolled her eyes at being thwarted but obeyed.

Winter sighed, then mentally braced herself. Her long day was beginning. "Jessie, also fetch two more frappes, please."

CHAPTER SEVEN

It was a goddamn fortress. Etienne stood on the sidewalk and scowled at the tall stone wall studded along the top with twining Art Deco rose vines and 'decorative' iron thorns. The thorns were each as long as his hand from middle fingertip to heel and came to lethal-looking points. A few feet to his left, the iron vines swarmed to form a gate that stood open as tall as the wall and wide enough to march ten men abreast through without bumping elbows—the work of a skilled blacksmith. In one corner was a half-decorative wrought iron web, complete with wrought iron spider.

It was mocking him.

The gate guard wasn't mocking him. He was downright threatening—glowering from behind the glass of the small guardhouse, making it very clear that Etienne, in his ponytail, worn jeans, and brown leather jacket was not the sort of person who he would let pass. Etienne squelched the urge to throw an obscene gesture.

Two lanes passed in and out of the iron gates and the occasional car rolled slowly by, the mortal driver handing the glowering guard a white rectangle, and the guard opening the white barricade and letting them roll through. Bisecting the lanes was a large, black, stone obelisk with water running down the sides, and 'Moore Investments' in raised silver lettering down the front. Etienne knew he was in the right place. The magazine picture in his pocket, taken from inside the walls, showed two men, one young and one older, standing in front of a glittering, black-glass tower. And there it was. Rising high into the sky, far enough from the wall to be in easy view, was the tower itself, sleek and gleaming smugly in the autumn sunshine. Of course, somehow it hadn't looked quite so huge in the picture. Somewhere in that tower, he hoped, was Cian's friend Senán.

He needed more information.

He turned and walked down the glittering wet sidewalk, the stone wall keeping up with him until he got to the corner and a busy intersection. On all sides buildings rose, most no taller than a handful of stories, none as magnificent as the gleaming black tower. It was one of those faux-forest corporate reserves, an island of enterprise surrounded by a sea of over-priced, cookie-cutter houses, with trees and walking paths and tiny shopping centers serving fast lunches and trendy beverages, all catering to the needs of the neatly dressed men and women who rushed about with cell phones in hand, ignoring it all.

Etienne crossed the busy street with a tide of about a dozen suits, all talking—none to each other—and found Cian sitting on the motorcycle in the coffee shop parking lot where he had left him, helmeted face turned toward the black tower. Even under the jacket, Etienne could tell the boy's shoulders were tight with tension. "What do you see?" he asked Cian.

"Glamour."

Etienne turned and faced the tower himself. The members of his mother's court had been fond of saying that his human blood was a contamination that muddied the pure, clear spring of his sidhe magic—poetically cruel, but basically correct. Etienne could not see through faerie glamour at all. Because of the glamour he couldn't even see magic was in use here. What magics he could wield were weak and limited. Cian, on the other hand, had no such contagion. "How much?"

Cian turned the visor toward Etienne. "The whole thing. There's nothing on this side of the wall, but the gates and grounds and tower are all warded, and the glamour covers the entire thing. It conceals the wards." He turned back toward the tower. "There's another layer of glamour on the tower, beneath the wards... but I can't see what it's covering."

Etienne let out a low whistle. "That's a hell of a glamour." In all his years wandering across lands both faerie and mortal, he had never heard of such an extensive glamourie, especially one cast over Cold Iron. It spoke of an incredible amount of power. And it also begged questions. Was the glamour to hide Senán? If so, why? He was widely rumored to have died years ago. But, if the glamour was not being used to conceal a supposedly dead sidhe prince, what was it hiding?

"It looks like it's dormant."

Etienne raised his brows. "How so?"

Cian pointed at the cars moving through the gate. "They're not setting anything off. I can see them moving through both glamour and wards, but nothing is happening. It's like…" he groped for an explanation.

Etienne understood. "Like they've been turned off for the day." With so many mortals moving in and out, even as powerful a magician as Midir the Proud could not key active wards to such a number without revealing himself for what he was—and secrecy was much too important to all the fae for him to do such a thing. The most efficient method would be to simply have guards watching the grounds during the day when the mortal workers were about and activate the wards at night.

Guards Etienne could deal with. A small, hard smile tugged at his mouth. "Stay here," he told Cian.

He felt Cian tense even more. "Where are you going?" the boy asked.

"Just to get more information. Stay put and keep your eyes open." Maybe he would get lucky and they could end this right here.

Etienne crossed back to the wall, excitement quickening his steps, and continued to follow it down and away from the main gate. He wanted to be as far from that gate guard as possible. He had no white rectangle, so he had to make his own, less obvious, way inside.

The wall led him several hundred paces away, around another corner, until it jogged inward suddenly to make way for a large tree with a small sign. He tucked himself into the alcove formed between the tree and the wall, then looked up and around. The wall rose at his side, the tree towering above it. People moved about up and down the sidewalk on the other side of the tree, going about their business, but none turned to look at him with any curiosity. He ran one hand down the bark and tucked his body as far behind the tree as he could. While he may only be half sidhe, he was still half sidhe… He crouched and waited for a lull in the foot traffic, then sprang nearly to the top of the wall, catching his weight with one hand on the iron vines, the other hand braced against the tree trunk. Mindful of those vicious thorns, he pulled himself up until his boots were secure on top of the wall, and then eased himself over the rose vines, dropping silently to the soft ground on the other side.

The cry of alarm did not rise from the sidewalk, but from the other side of the bush he landed beside. Etienne snapped out an arm and reeled in a man in a brown canvas jacket and hat, an MI logo printed on both, and tightened his grip on the man's throat. The human struggled under his strength, hands clawing at Etienne's wrist while Etienne looked carefully around to make sure the human had been alone.

After a moment, confident that they would not be disturbed, Etienne spun the man about and caught him firmly in a sleeper hold. "Sorry about this," he said softly in his accented English and squeezed down, cutting off blood flow to the man's brain. Within moments the human hung limp in Etienne's grasp and he released him gently to the ground. Satisfied the human was still breathing—it had been a while since Etienne had been forced to incapacitate a mortal and they were more fragile than the fae—he checked him over for anything useful. Immediately, he found one of the white rectangles and grinned. He turned it over in his hand, wondering what magic it held. Featureless, it seemed to be made of this 'plastic' that was new since he had last spent time in the Mortal Realm. It was only a few inches wide and about the thickness of a quarter. Fascinating.

He pulled off the man's logoed clothing, pulling the jacket on over his own and tucking his ponytail up under the hat. The man should be unconscious for a while—long enough for him to get a good look around, and maybe even find Senán.

Etienne slipped out from behind the bushes and strode boldly across the open grass toward the gleaming black tower. Nothing drew a guard's eye like skulking, but few and far between were the ones who questioned a confident man who looked like he knew what he was doing and belonged where he was doing it.

He just hoped he could figure out exactly what he was doing by the time he reached the tower. Few things inspired less confidence than floundering around looking lost.

Finally, he spotted a small party of people entering the tower via a side door and watched them brush their rectangles against a black box that stuck out at about waist level. A tiny light turned from red to green and his sharp hearing picked up the click even this far away as the door unlocked itself as each person was admitted. Red and green made sense—he was long accustomed to traffic lights. He made his way toward the door.

Acting as if he did this every day, he pulled out the white card and brushed it against the black box.

The red light gleamed steadily.

Etienne paused in consternation. This was supposed to work. He glanced at the white rectangle and brushed it against the black box. Again, the red light refused to change. His jaw clenched.

Did everything in this place mock him?

He was about to try a third time when he heard, "You new?" from behind him. He turned to face a middle-aged woman with a friendly face, the stench of cigarettes wafting heavily from her. He nodded, not trusting his voice to not choke on the sudden assault on his sensitive sense of smell. She returned the nod in understanding and pulled out her own card. "So many new people lately, huh? Security really needs to get on the ball about the pass keys." She swiped, and the door clicked to green. Etienne held it open for her. She smiled at his courtesy and stepped inside. "So... rumor mill has it we're having a major expansion. What have you heard?" she asked in that quick fashion as he followed her into a hallway, dark after the bright sunshine, and she looked back at him with curiosity. English only being one of Etienne's languages, he heard several terms he did not understand and so replied with a shrug. She waved negligently in his direction, turning away again. "Well, I guess Grounds Management wouldn't hear too much, huh?" she said with very mild disappointment.

Etienne gave her back an apologetic smile. "Sorry, I guess not."

She turned back, plucked brows lifted. "Oh, wow... great accent. Where are you from?"

Etienne fell back on his usual explanation. "Ireland, but my father was French." There, no one could complain about how muddy his accent was to humans. Besides, it was basically true. His birth language was Faerie Gaelic, and his father had been a medieval French troubadour. His old friend Arthur Reynolds was to thank for that explanation. He warmed, remembering the young wizard he had met in that bombed-out farm house on the front, how they had shared the camaraderie of being other than human, of keeping their secrets from the other soldiers. Arthur had been an easy man to like and he had shown him his picture of his pretty wife back home in Seahaven. He was, what, in his eighties now? Nineties? Not grievously old for a wizard. When this was all over, he would look him up. It would be criminal to be this close and not.

They emerged from the windowless hallway into a massive central lobby. Etienne extended what senses he had to their limit, listening and looking for any direct threat, any sign of Senán. In the center of the room was a large round desk with framed pictures that moved all in a line below the counter. A man in the same guard uniform as the one at the gate sat within, watching a certain frame closely and talking to a small black box in his hand. His back was to them as they entered the lobby. Etienne waved his thanks to the woman and set off in a random direction away from her. The building was huge, how was he...

"Hey," the woman said.

He turned and looked back, hiding his irritation. He needed to lose her.

She tapped her white rectangle. "Don't forget to get this fixed before you get locked out again." She pointed to the round desk. "Just go talk to Gary. He'll get you another temp key while Security gets yours sorted out."

Etienne smiled at her and nodded his thanks. He turned to make his way in the direction of the round desk, all the while listening for her footsteps to take the cigarette smell with her. Finally, he heard her brisk steps carry her away from him and he changed his course to pass the round desk and head deeper into the building. He did not want to talk to 'Gary' about getting a 'temp key.'

"What's he doing?"

Etienne kept walking, just in case they weren't talking about him, but perked his ears to the new voices. He slid his eyes toward the round desk. Gary had a companion, now.

"He's just sitting there, watching the building."

Etienne's chest squeezed tight. He changed direction, moving closer to the desk, and saw that both men watched the one frame now. He shifted to get a better view.

Somehow, there was Cian, sitting on the back of the motorcycle where he had left him. He was watching the building, just like he'd told him to. His helmet rested against one thigh and his face was in full view to the world.

Etienne clenched his jaw, biting back a curse, and his heart hammered in its now tightened cage. Gary held up a finger to his ear and talked into the small black box again. "Yeah, go ahead and see what this joker's up to. I don't like the looks of him."

Etienne turned and made his way back toward the windowless hallway as calmly as he could manage. Adrenaline pumped, urging him to run, to save Cian from capture, but he kept his steps steady. He could not afford to alert the building's master of their presence. He did not know what it meant for the guards to have spotted Cian with their picture frames, but he did know he could not let them take him at any cost.

Once he made it to the hallway and heard no footsteps, Etienne allowed himself to open up and run. The spells on the gun rig granted him the full speed and strength of a sidhe, so he covered the distance within mere seconds. In the open, he would need to be much more circumspect—mortals might be watching. Breaking out into the sunlight, he crossed the grass in a brisk walk, heading back toward the tree alcove where he had come over the wall. It put him further from Cian but gave him a secure place to cross where he would not come into direct confrontation with the guards before he absolutely had to. He passed the still-unconscious form of the human grounds keeper, checking his breathing as he passed, and leapt to the top of the wall.

This time he was not as delicate getting over the rose vines and in his haste, he tore his jeans and lacerated his hands. Cursing softly, he dropped to the dirt behind the tree and shot out from behind into foot traffic, eliciting a startled cry from a woman on a phone. He immediately settled into a ground-eating lope, keeping close to the wall to bypass the denser sections of people, and raced the wall back to where Cian waited unaware that Midir's guards were about to descend on his position. Each rushed breath repeated the boy's name in his head. Cian... Cian... Cian...

As he rounded the corner and came within sight of the coffee shop parking lot, Etienne spotted several guards emerging from the Moore Investments gate and head across the street toward Cian. The boy had slipped off the back of the bike and stood, helmet in hand, eyes turned up—he did not see them. Throwing caution to the wind, Etienne leaned into the rig's magic to push just a little more than human speed to get to Cian's side. The quick movement drew Cian's eyes to him and the boy smiled.

"Helmet!"

Cian tilted his head to the side. The guards saw Etienne running and began to run themselves to intercept.

Etienne pointed as he ran. "Helmet! Now!"

Cian's eyes widened with understanding, and he pulled his helmet on just as Etienne reached him and leapt onto the driver's seat, rocking the bike off its kickstand with his hands and magically tripping the ignition as he let gravity take him down. The engine roared to life as he shifted, the bike bucking under him as it objected to Etienne's unorthodox start. Cian jumped back on the bike behind Etienne and threw his arms around his waist, finally realizing they had company. Etienne ignored the Harley's protests and gunned the bike, eliciting a small squeal from Cian as the bike kicked up a bit and forcing the guards to scatter out of his way as he tore out of the rain-slick parking lot. The wind of their sudden acceleration whipped off his stolen hat and his short ponytail fluttered behind him as he wove through traffic, putting the gleaming black tower and Midir the Proud behind them.

Far away from the corporate forest, Etienne finally felt comfortable enough to slow down and pulled into a small neighborhood park. The close call with Cian had left him shaking, and he sat still for several moments, the engine running, both to get control and to cover his reaction.

"Etienne?"

Etienne took in a deep breath and let it out, then turned off the engine. The park was quiet, no children played. "Yeah?"

"What happened?"

He rocked himself out of the seat and turned to face Cian's visor. "The guards saw you," he said, never being one to coddle. "I don't know if they recognized you... I don't think so... hell, I have no idea." He sighed, looking back in the direction they had come. He stayed quiet for a long moment, going over the morning's brief events. He sighed again and surrendered. "But I do think that this is bigger than I can handle alone."

"We can't give up…" Cian began.

Etienne cut him off. "I never said that. But, your safety is paramount to me. I won't risk you in exchange for Senán."

"But he's more important…"

"Bullshit!" Etienne put so much force in that one word that Cian rocked back slightly on the motorcycle seat. "Never, ever, say that to me. Even if your father never became a king, he was a prince, as are you, and most important to me he was the only person who gave two shits for me in the courts." It was Prince Eoin, Cian's father, who had helped him escape from those who had carved the spell scars into his flesh. He who had taken him to the dwarves. Who had been, in the end, his one true friend in the courts. "Your father was a man of honor. Senán's father is a backstabbing lickspittle—"

"He's your king, too."

Etienne snorted. "He was never my king. And he's only one king. One king among dozens. Don't let his fat head fool you, Cian." He paced away and then paced back. "But all that is neither here nor there. I'm not giving up, yet, but I do need help."

Cian straightened. "I'll do anything," he said, eagerness making him breathless.

Etienne waved dismissively. "Not you. You're still a child." Besides, after what Midir the Proud had done to him… getting him directly involved would be cruel. No matter how eager to help the boy might be. Fear churned in his belly at the very thought.

Cian practically deflated.

"I need to look up my old friend. Arthur said you couldn't swing an arm in his hometown without hitting one of his family members. I'm hoping he wasn't exaggerating."

Cian made a visible attempt at mopping up his sulk. "So, we're going looking for your friend, then?"

Etienne took the brown canvas jacket off and dropped it to the ground. "What's that movie line?" He pulled his helmet off the back of the Harley and tugged it securely over his head. "'We're off to see the wizard.'"

CHAPTER EIGHT

Jeremy sat on the edge of his large mahogany desk and watched her struggle to get back into her panties without raising her skirt. She looked confused. Less than a week on the job and already on her back on her boss's couch. Must be tough. Jeremy smirked and lit up a clove cigarette.

The snip of the lighter made her jump a little and she turned toward him, pale green eyes wide and startled. She blinked several times and raised a hand to touch her pretty face. "Mr. Moore...?"

Jeremy leaned forward, taking a deep drag on the skinny little cigarette. "Is there a problem, Miss Johnston?" He exhaled the question in a stream of white smoke.

She looked down at herself; one shoe kicked aside, silky panties around her thighs. "I'm just..." her disheveled blonde curls danced as she took in her surroundings with more urgency "...not sure what just happened."

Jeremy rolled his eyes. Not again... He just didn't get women. One moment they couldn't get enough of you, the next they were pretending they didn't mean to do any of it. Like they accidentally had sex. How do you accidentally have sex? Why couldn't they just admit they enjoyed a good screw and leave it? Now his girlfriend, Lana, knew how to party. The woman had no shame. "Well, you seemed pretty sure while you were giving me head."

She blanched, then flushed hard enough to make her neatly sculpted and, he knew for certain now, dyed eyebrows stand out in pale relief. "Oh, my god," she breathed, her eyes getting even wider as panic began to set in. She grabbed her panties, and then froze, obviously torn between the need to pull them back on and a desperate reluctance to stand up and risk exposing herself.

"Oh, please. I've seen it already." Jeremy was beginning to get pissed and disgusted and he let all of it leech into his voice. "Just pull them on and get out." If she hadn't wanted to have sex she could have said something. It wasn't like he'd raped her or anything.

That would have pissed off his father for sure.

As if on cue, his office door swung open and in walked the great man himself. Terrific. Jonathan Moore, founder of Moore Investments, and his boss, strode into his office like he owned it. And he did. Jeremy groaned, but did not move from his perch on the desk.

"Oh my god... Mr. Moore...!" If Miss Johnston blushed any harder, she would begin to bleed from her ears. Her eyes began to glimmer with unshed tears. Jeremy looked away, sick envy welling up in his throat. No one at MI called *him* 'Mr. Moore' like that—awe and reverence and respect mingled with her embarrassment. They called him 'Junior' when they thought he couldn't hear.

Jonathan's ice-blue eyes swept the room and took in the whole scene—disheveled secretary, tousle-haired son with his shirt unbuttoned and untucked, languid smoke rising from the smoldering tip of the cigarette—and fixed Jeremy with a look of cold rage. A little spring of fear bubbled in Jeremy's belly, but he clenched his jaw in defiance and took another drag.

His father turned to Miss Johnston and like a light his eyes brightened, the look in them warm with sympathy and concern. He slipped a silk handkerchief from his pocket and offered it. "It's alright, young lady. Please, take a moment to put yourself together." He then stepped in between Jeremy and his secretary, his back to the trembling girl, using his own body as a dressing screen.

Jeremy avoided his father's cool gaze. He finished his cigarette and lit another, promising himself some quality time with his stash after this was all done. Behind Jonathan the girl dried her eyes and slipped her panties back on and he turned back at just the right moment, as she finished straightening her stylish little suit. "If I may have a moment, Miss Johnston?" His father gently laid his hand on her arm and led her from Jeremy's office.

Jeremy sat on his desk, smoking the skinny little cigarette, wishing it was something stronger, and watched the master at work. He couldn't hear what his father was saying, but she hung on his every word, eyes wide with fervent attention while he spoke in quiet tones and stroked her cheek. She nodded several times, and finally a smile broke like sunlight over her face. His father finally slipped his handkerchief from her fingers as she thanked him profusely enough for Jeremy to hear, and then practically skipped away. A moment later she ran back for her purse, laughing lightly at her forgetfulness, and left again, brimful of smiles.

It was always amazing. Jeremy had no idea how his father did it, but he could charm anyone into doing anything. He'd once seen Jonathan walk into a rival company's board room and announce his intent for a hostile takeover, then leave with them cheerfully signing the papers and offering to break out champagne. Jeremy grimaced. He admired his father's incredible charisma and hated himself for it.

Jonathan walked calmly back into Jeremy's office, closed the door behind him with exaggerated care, and strode toward his son. Jeremy took one more drag on his cigarette and rested it on the edge of his desk. "So, to what do I owe the hon—" Stars burst behind Jeremy's eyes as his father's backhand took him across his right cheek, rocking his head to the side. Blood blossomed against his teeth in a hot, coppery burst, and Jeremy spat it out onto the lush white carpet. He had learned early that swallowing would only make him sick.

"What the hell do you think you're doing?" The cold rage was back, joined by seething contempt.

Jeremy slipped off the desk and sneered, baring blood-rimmed teeth. "What? Develop chivalry since this morning?" He spat out more blood. His face throbbed and he could feel his cheek beginning to swell. "I screwed my new secretary. Isn't it executive privilege or something?" Jonathan reached out to grab his son, but Jeremy danced out of his reach, laughing, and put the leather couch between his father and himself.

"While I care very little what you amuse yourself with on your own time," his father began, his cold, cultured voice leaving no doubt in Jeremy's mind of how very little his father cared—and thought—about his amusements, "you cannot help yourself to the staff. It is inappropriate."

"Oh, please. Don't try to tell me you don't. You've never brought the same piece of ass home twice."

"It's called discretion, and I believe it is time you learned it. None of my interests work here." Jonathan looked carefully at the back of his hand and pulled his handkerchief again from his breast pocket. Some blood spatter had speckled his perfect skin. "It would put undue pressure on our business relationship."

Jeremy snorted. "What? Some social climbing slut has second thoughts about spreading her legs, so I should...what? Feel bad?"

His father's eyes narrowed, the blue darkening with his anger. "Surely you have heard of a sexual harassment suit, you idiot." He began to stalk slowly toward his son, and Jeremy moved away from him, the two circling around the couch.

"She's just an admin. What's she gonna to do?"

"All it takes is one complaint to the right ears."

Jeremy retrieved his cigarette and took a long, thoughtful drag. His eyes never left his father. "She can't. She jumped me, not the other way around."

"Oh, and now you are a lawyer?" Jonathan's voice dripped with scorn. Jeremy flinched a little around the eyes, and his father smiled. "But, no, she won't sue. She is going downstairs to work with Sales." He moved away from his son and looked around the office. "She won't mention it and you will not seek her out again."

Jeremy let out a long breath of exhaled smoke, not quite in his father's direction. "Why would I want to? She wasn't that good." He watched Jonathan idly examine the lavish decorations, the paintings and sculptures tastefully displayed in lit niches and on pedestals. As richly decorated as the office was Jeremy kept nothing personal in it, nothing that made it his own space. It was just a hole his father shoved him into during the day. It was supposed to help 'build his character.' Instead, he passed the time listening to his music and screwing his way through the secretarial pool.

His father turned his back, taking a moment to admire the sensuous lines of an abstract sculpture near the door. It wasn't Jeremy's style. The decorator hadn't cared. "You disappoint me, Jeremy."

Jeremy rolled his eyes. "There's a big surprise."

"So like your mother." He reached out and stroked his long fingers over the cool, smooth stone. "She was a great disappointment, too." He looked casually over his shoulder, to where Jeremy had frozen in the middle of raising his cigarette to his lips. His dark-blonde hair had fallen over his eyes, but Jeremy knew it could not hide his burning rage. Jonathan gave his son a cruel, little smile. "But, I have mentioned that before."

"Leave her out of it." Jeremy's voice shook, the cigarette forgotten between his fingers. He could not remember his mother, could not remember many things, but there was a flickering image of her in his head, like a glorious angel. He was very possessive of it, even as his father loved tearing at it with his years of insults.

Jonathan's smile grew wider, mockery glittering in his eyes. He let the moment stretch, and then released it. "As you wish." He turned away again and rubbed his thumb thoughtfully against the underside of a sculpted curve. "I don't know what disappoints me the most about you, Jeremy. Is it that you sit up here all day and do absolutely nothing productive? No, I expect that of you, now. I had hoped you would find yourself here... but I know now that there is nothing to find."

Jeremy's cigarette had extinguished from neglect, and he relit it, hands shaking with impotent anger. He said nothing.

"Perhaps it's that you host illegal activities on my company's servers, hoping to destroy everything I've built here?"

Jeremy took an angry gasp and choked on sweet smoke. How the hell had he known? The guy who set it up said he was the best...

"But, no, if it had been well done, at least I could be proud of your cleverness and initiative. But it wasn't. It was sloppy and stupid, and you didn't even have the skills to do it yourself, so now your little friends are being arrested as we speak." Jonathan twisted and looked directly at his son. "No, I know what it is." Faster than thought, his father flung the sculpture through the air, striking Jeremy in the chest and knocking the breath out of him in a sudden cloud of expelled smoke. He was always so damned fast! Jonathan was right behind it, left hand catching his son by his hair, the right deftly snatching the lit cigarette from Jeremy's suddenly slack fingers. He dragged his son to the ground, one knee digging into his stomach. Jeremy writhed as he fought his spasming diaphragm for breath. Jonathan leaned forward and said in that calm, reasonable voice, "It's your complete lack of self-control."

Jeremy managed a gurgling inhale, followed by a retching cough as his diaphragm found its rhythm again.

"I have told you, repeatedly, to keep your hands to yourself, but no. It seems you must continue to take so much after your faithless slut of a mother that you will rut with anything that crosses your shadow."

Jeremy struggled against Jonathan, who only ground his knee in harder, until he collapsed back down to the floor from pain and exhaustion. Jeremy felt his mouth stretch into a defiant grin, felt himself begin to slip into the quiet place where he went when his father hurt him. When he wanted his father to hurt him. "What? Can I help it if the ladies can't get enough of me?"

Jonathan bounced Jeremy's head once on the thickly carpeted floor and Jeremy saw him frown. He really needed a harder surface to do it right. He laughed at the thought, the sound a little too high. His breath rattled a bit on the inhale.

Jonathan leaned back a little, and Jeremy felt, more than heard, a creaking in his chest. A broken rib, maybe? It wouldn't be the first time. His father fiddled with the clove cigarette, smoke still rising from the tip like a delicate white exclamation. "Between the sex, the drugs—the blatant stupidity—one lawsuit, one news story, and all I have built will be destroyed." His father looked down at him, eyes dark with carefully controlled rage. "I am too close, now, to risk you destroying all with your antics. I have worked too hard, for too long..."

Jeremy narrowed his half-mad eyes. Close? "Close to what?"

Jonathan smiled, and it was humorless. "Oh, no, my boy. You're not in a position to question me." He tightened his grip on Jeremy's hair and pressed the side of his face to the carpet. "All I want from you are promises, and apologies." Jonathan took the little cigarette between his lips. The scent of burning cloves grew stronger as his breath coaxed the ember hotter and brighter. "And this time, you will mean every… single… word."

Jeremy's eyes widened with the first blossoming of true fear.

Aodhán heard a scream as he touched the office door and looked behind him to the cube farm. No heads popped up over the fabric walls in fear and curiosity, which was a good thing. Apparently, the boy had angered his father again. He waited patiently until the sound died away and slipped quickly into the office, shutting the door quietly before another scream escaped into the open behind him. No need to frighten the employees on a Friday. He stepped closer and watched Jonathan press the branding tip of a tiny cigarette into his son's cheek. Jeremy let out another shriek and writhed in pain against his father's hold, to no avail. Aodhán waited for the noise to dissipate before he cleared his throat. "Excuse me, Jonathan?"

Jonathan shifted his weight to settle it all onto his son's chest and looked up at Aodhán. "Good morning, Aodhán," he said pleasantly as Jeremy struggled to breathe beneath him. "How are you today?"

Aodhán thought a moment and gave him a small smile. "Intrigued, actually."

"Oh, really?"

"We have something downstairs you'll want to see."

Jonathan looked down at his son and sighed. "I suppose I can put off the rest of our conversation until later, then." He ground his knee viciously into Jeremy's chest and pushed up to his feet. Jeremy rolled to his side with a groan. Jonathan stepped over his son and joined Aodhán. "Shall we?"

Aodhán waved courteously for Jonathan to precede him and the two men left Jeremy's office.

Aodhán leaned in slightly as they made their way to the elevators. "Out of curiosity, what did he do this time?"

Jonathan frowned tightly. "His new secretary."

Aodhán twisted his lips in mild disgust. "Is he ever going to get control over that?"

"Apparently not."

The elevator opened obediently—Jonathan Moore did not wait for elevators in his own building—and they headed down. "So," said Jonathan, "where downstairs are we headed?"

"Security. We had some interesting visitors to the building this morning."

Jonathan frowned again. "It's too damn close to Samhain for 'interesting,' Aodhán."

Aodhán slid his eyes toward Jonathan. "'Interesting' is why I am here, if you recall."

The doors opened, and Jonathan headed briskly toward his Security Department. His security chief, a hulking behemoth of a man, waited just inside for him. "Right this way, sir," he said with a reverent nod, bowing him past the receptionist and into the viewing room. Jonathan followed. He hired the best and trusted them to do their jobs, but he was also a micro-manager at heart. Aodhán followed behind, watching people instantly look busier as Jonathan approached, and hid his amusement.

The viewing room had a single image on the large central monitor—a breathtaking young man sitting astride the back seat of a motorcycle in the coffee shop parking lot across the street. Aodhán let the security chief pull out two chairs for them and then waved the man out. The chief closed the door behind him.

Aodhán noted that Jonathan remained standing, transfixed by the monitor, and kept his feet. "My question is," he said, watching Jonathan's profile, "since when did sidhe we did not recruit start coming to Seahaven?"

Jonathan kept staring, eyes wide. He remained silent.

Aodhán watched him for several long minutes. Finally, he could no longer stand the silence. "My lord Midir," he probed. In private he could be more formal with the great prince. "What is attracting them? Do you think they sense the—"

Midir turned his face toward Aodhán, but his eyes stayed on the image. "Is the boy alone?"

Aodhán's eyes narrowed slightly with suspicion. What did Prince Midir know that he did not? Volumes, he was certain. "No." He took up the remote and hit fast forward on the video, until a man in a groundskeeper's uniform came running up to the bike. The hat obscured his features, given the high angle of the camera, even as he drove toward the guards rushing toward them, and by the time it was blown off he was at such an angle the camera could not get a good visual of his face. "The boy's rescuer. The license plate came back registered to a man in Kentucky. Security is looking into it as we speak. We have video of him inside the building as well," he said as he brought up a second monitor and showed Jonathan a back hallway. "Here we get a much better look at him." The man walked across the monitor following a woman from Accounts Receivable. Aodhán had already contacted her supervisor about disciplining her. He let the video play until it reached the clearest view of the man's face, and then paused to watch Midir's reaction.

The great prince leaned forward, peering closely at the still, his face quizzical. "Now who do we have here?" he said quietly.

"And why does he look like Senán?" Aodhán asked in return.

Midir's eyes widened in recognition and he jerked back, features twisted in rage. He shook for a moment, and finally spat viciously, "Summer's Get."

Who? "I beg your pardon, my lord?" Aodhán asked quietly.

Midir looked at him, turned back to the monitors, and sneered. He then turned back to Aodhán, shook his head, and stalked out of the viewing room.

Aodhán watched him leave, questions tumbling in his mind. Summer's Get? Who was that? He had been five centuries exiled from Faerie—the name meant nothing to him. But, watching the way Midir reacted, it made him wonder…

How could this Summer's Get be put to use?

CHAPTER NINE

Etienne paid for their lunch with the last of their cash and joined Cian at the picnic table he held in reserve for them. The boy's eyes lit up when he saw the flash of red peeking out from the sides of their generously piled sandwiches. "A BLT?" he asked with delight. He sat with his face in full view, the helmet back with the Harley. Etienne had given up, much to Cian's relief. The boy had been seen so what was the point in making him wear it now?

Etienne smiled and pushed Cian's plate toward him. "Just for you." Which was not entirely true. Even though it had become Cian's favorite, Etienne had been thrilled with his own first discovery of the BLT, which had not been around during his last sojourn in the Mortal Realm. He took a drink of water and bit into his own sandwich, relishing the mingled flavors of thick bacon, fresh tomato, and mayonnaise on excellent toasted bread. The lettuce added a nice crunch, but you could not call it flavorful. He looked around as he chewed, trying to plan their next move. They had ended up in a large public market that looked like it took up at least two city blocks. On one side was a tourist area zoned for pedestrians only that extended several more cobble-paved blocks over. It bustled with young shoppers looking in windows and slipping in and out of store fronts. A few more blocks to the west was the waterfront.

Etienne sighed in frustration. He had spent the morning wandering the city, racking his brain to try and remember any details from three weeks of conversations with Arthur that might help him locate the wizard. He could remember he had said he lived in Seahaven, and that his wife had opened a shop to keep herself busy. He said his family was huge and everyone had heard of them. Etienne had asked in several places if anyone knew the Reynolds family, only to receive reactions ranging from politely blank stares to the very suspicious, before he remembered that Arthur once mentioned that he had married into his wife's family instead of going the other way around. That name he could not remember—it had not been important at the time. Just that it was Irish... or Scottish, maybe? He was just not that familiar with mortal names.

He ground his teeth and pulled out the street map again. He had no idea why. It had gotten him to Moore Investments, but that was a new structure. Mortals had an unnerving habit of rearranging their architecture every few decades or so. The city probably looked dramatically different now than it had looked during the war. He looked over the map, tracing the morning's route in his mind, and pinpointed their current location—the Seahaven Public Market in the Historical District.

Yeah, that was a big help. He took another bite of his sandwich.

"Where are we going next?" Cian asked before taking a drink of his water. He craned his neck, curious about all the colors and lines, but Etienne knew the boy could not read most of it, especially upside down. He simply was too new to English to decipher it.

Etienne swallowed his food and pointed to the map. "I can see where we are and where we've been." He ran his finger up the illustrated waterfront slowly. "What I can't see is where we need to be." He sat back and looked around them again. During the war, he remembered that the London phone boxes would often have books of names and numbers in them. That would have proven useful today. But since coming to the New World last year he had seen precious few of them and never with a book inside. There was a phone box within sight of their picnic table, but it contained neither book nor phone. Instead, it was decorated with flowers and filled with some sort of sculpture. He shook his head at the strangeness of mortals and looked back down at the map.

Just above his resting fingertips, a spit of land was depicted stretching and forming the northern edge of Eriksson Bay. It was a slender arm extending out about a mile and flaring at the end of the point. Etienne's eyes widened slightly as he remembered. '*You should see the House someday, my friend. It sits on the tip of the Point, with Eriksson Bay on one side and the Pacific on the other. Glorious!*' He looked over the map again, trying to be certain. There were a couple other smaller points jutting into the Bay, and several large islands, but only one that straddled the boundary between bay and ocean. "I think I found him," Etienne said at last, and grinned up at Cian over the map.

Cian returned his grin with a bright smile of his own and popped the last of his sandwich into his mouth, chewing happily.

Etienne rushed through the rest of his lunch, eager to head out to the Point and find Arthur. He then washed it down with the last of his water and gathered up their paper plates. "Let's go." Cian followed him to dispose of them, where Etienne had reason to pause. There were two containers, side by side. The wire one he recognized as a trash bin, its open mouth nearly full from the remains of the lunch crowd. But the other was green and had a covered lid with two large holes in it. In relief on the top was a strange triangle formed of arrows and lettering that distinctly said, '*No Trash.*' How very odd. Wondering what he was expected to put in it, he tossed their plates and water bottles into the trash bin and turned away.

"Hey! I saw that!"

Etienne and Cian turned back to find a scowling woman with very colorful hair approaching them. "Pardon?" asked Etienne.

She reached into the trash bin and pulled out the two water bottles. "The recycling is right here. Geez!" She then stuffed the bottles into the holes in the green bin.

Etienne was baffled but decided that apology would be the better part of valor. "Um… Sorry," he said, but the colorful little woman was already moving away in a flutter of skirts, muttering under her breath about ecosenseless jackasses and saving the Earth. That made him pause again. Saving the Earth from what? He remembered occasional mentions along those lines when they lived on the therians' farm in Kentucky, but he had chalked it up to strangeness on the part of their hosts.

To be honest, no matter how much the Mortal Realm changed each time he sojourned here, a pack of therian wolves living on a farm in the middle of nowhere and trying to pretend it was still the Middle Ages was pretty damn strange. But they were good people and Etienne missed them. In his pocket was the number of the pack's only phone, a reminder of the promise he made to their Wolf King, Kendrick, that he would call to let them know they had made it to Seahaven. A call which would be easier of he could find a working phone box.

Etienne and Cian passed out of the Market and wove their way through the lunch time crowd back in the direction of the parking lot. A group of young women caught sight of Cian and fell to blushing twitters and giggles as they craned around each other to get a better view of him. Etienne released a long-suffering sigh. "And that, right there, is another reason I wanted you to stay in your helmet," he scowled at Cian.

Cian rolled his eyes. When had he started rolling his eyes? "I just don't see what the problem is. I have two eyes, two ears, one nose and one mouth. How is that so different from human?"

Etienne scowled harder. "Your hair, to start. No human has hair like that. It's not normal for them."

Cian waved his hand toward a young man with green spikes standing straight up from his head. "And that is?"

Etienne opened his mouth to reply and closed it again. He had to admit there was no arguing with that.

Guitar music filtered through the foot traffic and he looked around, finally finding a young man with an instrument that saw more love and attention than his clothing, sitting on the sidewalk between two storefront windows. His head was lowered over his guitar, eyes closed, and long brown curls hiding much of his face as he gave himself over to his music. Etienne tapped Cian on the elbow to keep him from wandering on ahead without him and made his way toward the street musician, feeling the music pulling at him like a gentle hand. It was beautiful, even more beautiful than the music played in his mother's court. The boy was better than Cian, who Etienne loved to listen to play.

His music reminded him—Etienne stopped short, eyes wide—reminded him of his father. Chretien de Aquitaine had been a magnificent musician. His music and his beauty had drawn Etienne's mother's attention, much to the troubadour's misfortune.

He remembered sitting at his father's knee as a child, learning to play. He wasn't a quarter the musician his father was, but Chretien had never faulted him.

He remembered his father's suicide, when he lost his mother's favor. He could never remember the good without remembering the bad.

The street musician's hands stilled on his strings, stroked the wood of the guitar, and finally looked up at Etienne through his long curls. A small, gentle smile brushed over his lips.

Etienne was frozen, still struck by his memories. "Who...?"

The young man shook his head. "The question you need to ask is 'Where?'"

Etienne's brows drew in.

The street musician stretched his thin arm and pointed down the block, deeper into the Historical District. "What you want is that way. Across the street and next door to the cupcake place. Olde Curiosity's Gift Shoppe."

Etienne craned his neck to look down the sidewalk, and then snapped back to look down at the boy. "Did you say 'Curiosity's'?" Arthur's wife had been a physician named Curiosity! He remembered!

The boy's gentle smile widened, and he nodded once. "Now you understand me."

Etienne dug into his jeans pocket and dropped the last of his change into the boy's guitar case. He turned, eager to pursue this new lead, and then turned back to thank him. But what came out of his mouth was, "Who are you?"

The boy swung his long hair back behind his shoulder, revealing more of his face. Pretty, but well within human normal. "I'm just Stephen. Welcome to Seahaven."

Etienne looked more closely at Stephen, and he was indeed as he appeared. Simply human. But then how was he able to do what he'd done? Clearing his throat to cover his confusion he said, "Well, thank you, Stephen."

The boy smiled and inclined his head with grace. "Anytime." He then set to playing again.

Recognizing a dismissal for what it was, Etienne turned away and headed down the sidewalk in the direction Stephen had indicated, Cian following close behind. Finally finding space to pull up alongside Etienne, Cian glanced back at the musician. "What happened?"

Etienne gave a small frown, and then an even smaller shrug. "Not sure," he said. "But, I think he's sending us in the right direction." And if they didn't find Arthur or his wife here, it would cost them no gas, and he could always go back and ask this Stephen if there were any open street corners nearby for Cian to play on. So, there was no real harm in trusting the musician. Though what he really needed was to find a small casino. Cian's playing was good, but Stephen was better. Busking anywhere near him would guarantee Cian would not earn as much as usual.

They came to the corner with the Public Market on their right and wonderful smells wafting from some sort of East Asian restaurant, East Meets West, just to their left. Across the street facing them was the cupcake place, Sweet Treats, with its little bistro tables lined up under a brightly striped awning. He was familiar with pastry shops from his last several sojourns, but a shop that sold only cupcakes was very strange.

Beside Sweet Treats, pressed in between the confectionary and a large building with 'Katherine's Retreat' scrawled artistically over the open entryway was a small shop with a red door. The black sign that hung above the doorway was painted in flaking gold lettering in a style he recognized from a couple mortal centuries ago and which read, 'Olde Curiosity's Gift Shoppe.' He gave Cian's coat sleeve a small tug to make sure the boy followed him as he set out across the pedestrian-only cobble-paved street.

Beside the red door was a display window framed with cream-colored lace curtains, creating a picture out of a small wooden table and two cushioned chairs. The display on the table top had been completely picked over, leaving only the stands behind. Etienne leaned in to look deeper inside the store. The storefront was tiny, just some shelves built into the walls, some more shelves taking up floor space, and the counter that held the register behind which was a thickly beaded curtain he could not see through. The shelves were notably poorly stocked, and—he looked around the space again to make sure—the shop was empty. He stepped back, unsure of how to proceed. There was no open or closed sign visible. Should they just go in? Maybe Arthur's wife—or even Arthur himself—was behind that beaded curtain?

"What should we do?" asked Cian, still peering into the empty store.

Etienne shrugged and opened his mouth to reply but was cut off by a quiet voice breathy in reverence, "Hot damn." He looked to his left to see a plump girl in glasses dressed in a wildly embroidered and beaded shirt and jeans, carrying a small cardboard box full of lunch sacks. She stood frozen on the sidewalk, lips parted slightly, and brows raised for a long moment as she looked at Cian. Pretty little thing, she couldn't be much older than his Bess when they married. She blinked, gave herself a small shake and looked away, cheeks flushing. "Um, yeah… right," she muttered, keeping her eyes averted, she moved with purpose toward the red door.

This caught Etienne's full attention. "Miss, do you work here?" he asked.

The girl turned back to face him, box balanced on one arm as she grasped the doorknob with her now free hand and presented him with a pert smirk. "Nope. I just like to break in, leave lunch, and skip off merrily into the sunset." She paused. "Except it's too early. That won't work." She turned and pushed open the door. "Never mind."

Etienne crossed his arms and watched her move through the door. What exactly had that been all about?

The girl turned and craned her head back through the open door, straight brown hair swinging in a curtain. "So, you guys coming in, or what?"

Etienne raised an eyebrow. "Can we look forward to more sass once we enter?"

She grinned. "I like that. You do the eyebrow thing just like my boss." She stepped further into the store, holding the door open with her backside. "You may enter, good sirs."

Cian laughed softly behind him, and Etienne shook his head, stepping past the girl into the little shop. Cheeky wench.

She released the door when both men passed through and bellowed, "We got company!" as she set down her box on the counter. The sound echoed in the sparsely stocked store, and Etienne and Cian both cringed slightly at the effect the volume had on their sensitive ears.

A moment later a young woman pushed the beaded curtain aside, a cross expression on her thin face. Etienne's breath caught for an instant in shock. It was a sidhe woman, her white hair caught up in a loose bun, iridescent tendrils curled about her shoulders and catching the sunlight from the front window. "For pity's sake, Jessie, don't do that. The whole District now knows we have company."

The girl, plainly ignoring her, dug into her back pocket and pulled out a plastic card. "Here."

"What?" The woman took the card, looked puzzled a moment, and then handed it back to the girl. "Please put that back in my wallet and put the punch card in the register."

Jessie nodded, moving to obey as the woman turned to face them. She seemed to try to focus on them, but she flickered her light-blue eyes back and forth to the box and back to them. Without being asked the girl fished in the box and pulled out a large cup which she held out to the woman. Etienne noticed how the woman's hand trembled delicately as she took it and he glanced to Cian beside him, who watched her hand with concern. He looked back at the sidhe woman. *"Please excuse our intrusion, Mistress, but we seek Arthur Reynolds. Do you know of him?"*

The woman looked confused for a moment, her gaze moving from him to Cian and back again. The girl looked to her employer and whispered, "That was so cool! What was it?"

The woman's eyes widened with understanding and she shook her head. "I'm sorry. I never learned Faerie Gaelic. Do you speak English?" She spoke slowly to make her words easily understood, her voice low and melodic. Etienne liked it.

"Oh, he speaks English just fine," Jessie interjected.

The woman turned to the girl with a raised eyebrow and the girl flushed. She then turned back to face Etienne. "I'm sorry about that."

Etienne gave his head a little shake. "Please, I'm the one who should apologize for assuming. You just look so much like one of our kind."

The woman gave a small smile. It did not reach her eyes. What was making her so sad? "I do, I suppose. I favor my mother. She was a sidhe mix."

"A what?" Jessie cut in. "I thought you said she was fae."

The woman turned to the girl, glanced back at Etienne and Cian, and then replied, "She was, like they are. The sidhe are greater fae, though from what I've been told they don't like to admit it. They consider themselves above all other fae." She gave Etienne and Cian an apologetic look.

Etienne waved it off. "Don't worry about me. I think they could use being taken down a peg or two." He just wanted her to keep talking. Lovely voice. But—he glanced at Cian, who continued to look a little concerned—was she sick? Her hand still trembled on the cup.

Jessie looked Etienne up and down. "I still don't get it. She's a she? So… she's a woman, right?" Jessie looked back to her boss. "Dude, it's the twenty-first century. If she wants to use female pronouns, that's her right."

Etienne blinked. Was the girl talking about *him*?

The woman's blue eyes widened in annoyance and she shook her head and reached for a pen and paper, murmuring, "I could have sworn you'd have picked this up from somewhere by now." She began writing, and in a louder voice said, "Using your proper pronouns is fine, but that's not what we mean. Not 'she' like this. 'Sidhe' like this, Irish Gaelic for the Shining Ones, the Fair Folk."

Etienne frowned as understanding dawned. "I'm a faerie knight. A male one." English was a stupid language.

"Oh!" Jessie said, brows raised. Her cheeks flushed, but she plowed ahead. "Well, then… we all pick our identities. If you want to call yourself a fairy, that's also your right."

The woman covered her face with her hands. "No… no. Jessie, no…"

The girl erupted in giggles. "I can't take it anymore. That one was too good to pass up!"

The woman looked thoroughly exasperated. "For pity's sake! Go in the back and organize something—right now."

The girl tried to hold back a chuckle, snorted as it escaped, and gave her employer a salute before disappearing behind the curtain carried on a current of laughter. The beads did nothing to dampen the sound.

The woman turned back, cheeks bright pink to her ears. "I am so sorry. She's been acting like a teenager all morning."

Etienne looked away from the curtain and back to the woman. He had no idea what the girl was laughing at or why she should find it so funny.

"Don't worry about it." He motioned to Cian at his side. "This one's start-ed rolling his eyes at me."

Cian looked affronted and rolled his eyes.

"See? There he goes again."

Cian stuck his tongue out at Etienne and then moved toward the curtain himself. "Fine. I'll go organize something with the other kid, then." His spoken English was much better than his written, though more heavily ac-cented than Etienne's.

The woman gave him one of those sad smiles. "You go right ahead," she said, reaching back to part the strings of beads.

Cian reached the beads and froze. "What was that?"

Etienne was at his side instantly. "What was what?" He looked around, suspicious.

The woman gasped. "You felt that?"

Etienne narrowed his eyes at her. It would not be the first time a sidhe woman betrayed him. "Felt what?" he asked, warning in his tone.

Her jaw clenched at the change in his voice, the woman edged herself closer to the curtained door, putting herself between them and her girl. "I'm sorry. No one outside my family has ever felt that before. I—"

"What was it?" Etienne cut her off, not trusting any unknown magic. The fact that it had been used on Cian made him burn. He slipped his right hand under his jacket, fingers brushing against Agmundr.

She raised her chin and straightened her back to her full height—taller than Etienne by a few inches, though not nearly as broad. She looked as if she could blow away even as she pulled dignity about her shoulders. "I am a soul reader," she said, "and you are strangers to me." She looked at Cian. "I just gave you, a powerful young male, permission to be alone with my teenage apprentice. There was no way I would let you through that door without taking a closer look at you."

Etienne had never heard of a 'soul reader.' "What sort of magic is this?"

For just the briefest of moments she looked uncomfortable. Then, "I in-herited the gift from my grandmother."

Etienne frowned, unsatisfied with the answer. He crossed his arms, the brown leather of his jacket too worn to creak. "Okay, so what did you see when you looked at him?"

Her blue eyes flickered from man to man and she began to relax. "I saw great power and potential, both untapped. I saw a gentle heart and terrible pain." She looked back to Cian, and he raised his hand to his chest, but did not look distressed. "I see... searching." She blinked a few times and looked back to Etienne. "It's not a very reliable or precise gift, or even a good parlor trick, I'm afraid."

Cian's eyes were a little wide, and Etienne slowly uncrossed his arms. "What about me?" he asked, because he had to. What secrets had she seen? How bare had she laid his soul?

Again, she gave him that strange, sad smile. "I read you first. It was obvious you were in charge." She paused, eyes turned away, fingers trembling around the cup in her hand as she chose her words. She looked back to him. "I saw that I needed to trust you."

Etienne's brows rose. "Just that?"

She nodded as she stepped aside. "Just that. I am an excellent judge of character, and it was the strongest feeling I've had in a long time." She turned to Cian. "Why don't you go on back and be a good influence on my troublemaker?"

Cian looked to Etienne in confusion.

Etienne returned his look with a small shrug and motioned for him to go ahead. The boy shrugged off the backpack, setting it down on the floor at the end of the counter with a soft creak of ancient floorboards. Etienne turned and watched the woman make her way to a stool behind the counter, where she pulled a second stool around for him. He still felt a little wary but sat.

Jessie exploded from behind the curtain. "'Scuse me. Hungry woman, coming through." She pushed herself between Etienne and her employer and rummaged in the box. "You," she declared in a dictatorial fashion as she pulled out a bag and pushed it toward her employer, "eat this. All of it. Here's your next coffee." She looked over her shoulder to Etienne and said conspiratorially, "I'm waiting for her to vibrate to the center of the Earth. This is, like, her tenth coffee today," before she grabbed the cup in the woman's hand and tested the weight. "Drink this before it gets colder." She made to hand the cup back and then snatched it back. "Why are your hands shaking again?"

"I'm fine."

"Uh-huh. I'm telling Erik and Katherine."

The woman's voice sharpened. "That's enough. Now go eat your lunch and let me speak with this gentleman, please."

Jessie hesitated, worry playing across her face, and then she picked up the box. "Fine. For now." She moved to the curtain and then spun back. "Hey, you guys hungry?" she asked Etienne.

Etienne's head was spinning a bit from the whirlwind that was Jessie. "No," he managed, "No, we just ate, but thank you for offering."

She looked at him, head tipped to the side, her expression measuring. After a moment she chirped, "'Kay," and bounced back through the curtains.

Etienne shook his head, amused and confused in turns by this place. "She's quite something." The woman was taking deep swallows from the cup, her long throat working.

Finally, she set the cup down and tucked one trembling hand in the other, her face turned toward the back room. "She is, indeed," she said quietly. The smallest of smiles pulled at her lips, but her love and affection for the girl were plain to see. She turned back to him. "Now, where were we?"

Etienne's smile did reach his eyes. "Introducing ourselves, I believe." He sat up straighter and gave her a small bow in his seat. "I am Etienne Knight, my lady, and my companion's name is Cian."

Her eyes lit up with recognition at his name. "You *did* say Arthur Reynolds," she said, her voice breathy with wonder. "I'm Winter Mulcahy. Arthur was one of my uncles. He used to tell us stories about you from the war. I think we even have a picture of you at the House."

Etienne's heart jumped. Yes! Mulcahy was the name he had forgotten. "Do you know how I..." he trailed off, thinking over what she had just said. "Did you say 'was?'"

The sadness returned to her face, and she turned to look behind her at the various bric-a-brac hanging on the wall. Etienne followed her gaze and saw an old photograph in a scrolled frame. It was Arthur and his pretty wife, just as he had been during the war. "Arthur and Curiosity passed away a few years ago. I'm terribly sorry."

A burn started in Etienne's throat and he swallowed past it. How? "I don't understand. They weren't that old."

Winter faced him again. "It was a car accident." Her voice sounded hollow. She picked up her coffee and took another long swallow.

He was quiet for several moments, taking time to mourn, letting her finish her coffee. She still had not touched the lunch bag. Finally, he had to gently let Arthur go and focus on the present. Cian needed him to find help. "Then maybe the rest of your family can help us?"

Her mouth twisted as she looked away quickly, then back at him. "I can make no promises, but I'll do what I can."

Etienne reached into his breast pocket. "No, if you're unavailable, then surely someone else can do it."

"There is no one else." She spoke so quietly even his sensitive ears barely heard her.

"What?" Etienne leaned in closer. She had folded her hands in her lap and lowered her gaze. "Arthur said there were so many, and that was decades ago. Where did they go?"

"They died," she replied in that hollow voice, still so quiet as if by saying it out loud she would no longer be able to hide behind silence. "We don't know why, and for some we don't even know how. But, my father and I, we're all that remain. Anywhere."

He wanted to soothe her pain, to make it right somehow. "My lady…" he began, reaching out to touch her face.

Winter flinched away from him, slipping off the stool and around the counter to put it between them. She cleared her throat and straightened her shoulders. "My father is the Mulcahy, the head of the family and neutral arbiter of this city. I speak for him."

Etienne sat back, accepting her rebuff. He barely knew the woman, after all. "Do I need to talk to him, then?"

"No, he sees no one. I speak for him."

"Why?"

Her lips tightened, and she shook her head, answering him with silence as she turned away, but not before he saw the depth of the pain in her eyes. She turned back after a moment. "Tell me what you need." She was cool, professional, reserved. Etienne glanced down. Her fingers still shook.

He reached again into his jacket's breast pocket and pulled out the page ripped from a business magazine in Kentucky. "I hunt a fugitive. Several years ago, he violated two sidhe courts, one Seelie and one Unseelie, murdering their princes before disappearing." He opened the folded page and handed it to Winter. "Nine days ago, Cian and I found this. We've been in the Mortal Realm just over a year. Judging by this, I'd say they've been here longer. The younger one is one of the princes, apparently alive, and the older one is the fugitive."

Winter looked the picture over. "If this prince is alive, might the other—others—also be alive?"

Etienne lowered his voice. "Cian was one of them, yes. The other one, the Unseelie one, definitely not. From what I've heard, his skull was fashioned into a chalice and presented as a gift to his parents. It drove his mother mad."

She looked at the picture with revulsion. "That's horrible." She tapped the bottom edge of it with one short nail. "I think I know these men, but I haven't met them personally." She glanced over the text at the bottom and nodded. "Yes. I was right. They've been here for about four years with my family's full permission, keep largely to themselves, never a day of trouble out of them." She turned the picture around. "This is Jonathan and Jeremy Moore."

Etienne reached out to take the picture back, but she frowned slightly and turned it back to face her. "To you, perhaps. To me they are Midir the Proud and Prince Senán."

"Why do you look so much like Jeremy?" she murmured, blue eyes flickering from him to the picture and back again.

Etienne took the picture from her and folded it back up. "It's Senán, and it's not important. He's Cian's friend and kinsman. Cian is desperate to rescue him. Can you help us?"

Winter opened her mouth to reply, closed it again, looked perturbed. "I... I don't know." Etienne opened his mouth and she raised her hand.

"We must maintain a balance among the different preternatural groups in the city."

"What is 'preternatural?'" That was a new word for him.

She tipped her head to the side. "Well… it's us. You, me, vampires, therian, witches, dragons; everything else that really does go bump in the night. If it's not human, not entirely, it's probably one of us."

He nodded. "Thank you. Please continue."

"As I was saying, we maintain a balance, which means I can't just go to Moore Investments, bang on the door, demand he turn this Senán over. They haven't done anything to warrant that kind of action on my part." Etienne slid off the stool and began to pace. "Honestly, I've heard no reports of any issues over there, and they looked fine in the picture…"

Etienne turned to face her. "There is glamour all over the building. Wards like nothing Cian has ever seen, and even more glamour beneath hiding I have no idea what."

He watched her press her fingers together and touch them to her lower lip, her brows drawn in slightly in thought. After a long moment she said, "I need my father's permission before I move forward, but I would like to at least get a look at that myself. I will talk to him tonight."

Etienne gave her a small bow. "Thank you, my lady."

She lowered her hands and her eyes brightened a little. "In the meantime, where are you and Cian staying?"

Etienne froze a moment. Empty pockets, mostly empty gas tank—he had no idea where they were staying tonight. Finally, he made up something plausible. "One of the motels on the interstate. We'll be back in the morning."

She raised her eyebrow just as she had with her apprentice.

"What?"

She sighed. "You're old enough to take care of yourself, but I'm not sending that boy to sleep on the street," she said as she moved past him toward the beaded curtain.

"Wait—"

"Jessie, can you run next door and ask Katherine or Giovanni if they have extra room for the next few days?"

"What for?"

"My lady, please—"

"Call me Winter."

Etienne growled softly under his breath as she turned away from him again. Damn stubborn woman.

"It's for our guests. They need somewhere to stay."

"My—Winter, we can't pay."

She looked back at him, her expression arch. "Family friends don't need to. Besides, if you paid then you wouldn't be guests."

"Why don't they just crash upstairs?" Jessie asked, poking her head through the curtain and looking from adult to adult like it was the most obvious solution in the world.

"Are you sure, sweetheart? That's your space."

She blew hair off her face. "Oh, yeah. I can always crash at the Theatre or someplace. No worries."

Winter turned to face Etienne again. "There's a small furnished apartment upstairs, but it does only have one bed. There is a couch…"

Jessie came out from behind the curtain, Cian following close behind. "Totally recommend sleeping friendly. The couch is okay for sitting, blows for sleeping. Here, let me get your bag." Before Etienne could do more than lift his hand in protest she bent, grabbed the backpack strap, lifted, and dropped to her knees. "Holy fuck!"

"Language, and are you alright?" Winter knelt beside her felled apprentice, face filled with concern.

Jessie cradled her right shoulder with her left hand, grimacing in pain. "Jesus, what do you guys have in there, anyway?"

Etienne crouched on her other side. "I tried to stop you. You're quick."

Cian dropped down behind her and rubbed her back, worried for his new friend. Winter looked from his hand to Jessie's face, but said nothing. After a few moments Jessie's grip on her shoulder relaxed and she began to roll it. "Guess it wasn't that bad, after all," she said at last. "But seriously, that thing weighs a ton. What's in it?"

Etienne took the bag by the strap and lifted it off the floor, then handed it to Cian who swung it up on his shoulder. "A lifetime," he said. "It may be close to a ton, I'm not sure. There's a lot in it."

"Seriously?" Her brown eyes widened.

Etienne smirked at her. "Don't I look serious?"

Her look turned skeptical. "C'mon, Cian. I'll show you upstairs."

Winter stood with him, close enough that he could feel the warmth radiating from her body as they watched the kids make their way up the stairs. Her delicate scent reached him—herbs and flowers. "I take it the bag is enchanted to borrow space, but not enchanted to adjust its weight. Does it really weigh a ton?"

He glanced up at her. "I was serious. I've never weighed it. And it takes more weight than that to be of issue for a sidhe."

Winter was quiet for several moments. Finally, she said in a soft voice, "I don't turn my back on friends, and you have been a friend to this family. I'll find a way to help you."

Etienne nodded in gratitude. "Thank you. That's all I ask." But as he glanced at her by his side he caught a look of apprehension.

What was she afraid of?

CHAPTER TEN

Lana wet her tongue and ran it across the edge of the paper before finishing the joint with a roll and two practiced twists of her dry fingers. She added it to the others on the tray beside her on the window seat. That should be enough to keep the idiot good and mellow for a while.

"Lana, I need more burn cream."

She rolled her eyes, knowing he wouldn't be paying close attention to her face. "Whining isn't sexy, babe," she muttered as she stood, her movements languid, her body on display.

"What?"

"I'll go get it, babe," she said, and turned to pick up the tray. Something caught her eye outside the window and she looked out past the striped awning below her. Red-gold hair flashed in the sunlight. Pretty. But it was the auburn-haired man striding beside that froze her in place. "Holy shit," she breathed. It couldn't be. She looked back to the man lying on her bed and then to the one crossing the street below her. Shit-shit-shit-shit-shit-shit... It was, but how? Where was he going? Her hand flew up over her throat as she watched his progress. Not here, not here, not here... Dammit, not now! It was too soon! But the man continued walking and after a moment of interacting with the fat girl stepped inside the wizard's little clinic.

"Lana, what are you looking at?"

She covered calming herself by picking up the tray and giving Senán a generous view of her dainty black panties as her mind churned. Summer's

Get, here? And why? He had gone next door, but it was still too close for comfort. It had something to do with her resident headache, she was certain—but then why go to the wizard?

She let a smile take her mouth as she turned, tossing her curtain of black hair off her bare breasts. Because Summer's Get did not know Senán was right here. She relaxed and moved toward the bed, making sure to put a slow swing into her stride. She may be running out of time, but it was not gone, yet. "What was I looking at?" she repeated, her low voice both mocking and seductive. Senán raised himself up on his elbow, the better to watch her approach, and nodded. The burns on his face and neck were swollen angry and red, but already looking better than they had when he'd arrived. She slid the tray onto the bed and crawled after it, her breasts high and tight enough that they barely swung. He liked them that way. "Maybe I saw a hot piece of man-candy and was thinking about trading up."

Senán snorted his disbelief and reached down to catch her around the waist. "You can't do any better than me, baby," he said as he hauled her up beside him.

Lana took one of the joints and held it up to his lips, keeping hidden behind lowered lashes and a coy smile. Senán couldn't hold a candle to what she'd had before. She fished up a matchbook from her strip club and struck one as Senán took the joint between his fingers. "Maybe I saw a beautiful girl and I'm going down there to invite her to play with us."

Senán took a lungful of smoke, held it a moment, then expelled it. "Fuck yeah! Bring her up. But first, go get the burn cream." He slapped her hard on the ass. It stung. She had the sudden urge to stuff the lit joint up his nose but refrained.

She needed him trusting and complacent.

So instead she laughed and slid off her bed and into the bathroom. The 'burn cream' sat on the vanity, just a little used up makeup jar filled with triple antibiotic ointment. Senán actually thought he was human and she somehow had the hookup on high grade pharmaceuticals. Moron. He would be healed and unblemished within a couple hours all on his own.

Lana paused, looking over her reflection in the mirror. Not bad, not bad at all, but as screwed up as the idiot was it was difficult for her to read what his ideal woman looked like. It was a constant game of hot or cold and it annoyed her to no end. She enlarged her breasts just a little, maintaining their firmness. Pinched in her waist a little more and added red highlights to her dark hair. She nodded, pleased with what she saw. This look would work well at the club, too. Senán wouldn't notice any changes—no man in the thrall of a succubus ever noticed. They only found her more desirable.

Her mind wandered back to Summer's Get as she carried the jar back to bed. What was he doing visiting that strung-out wizard? She hadn't used to be so bad, but up until a few months ago there had also been a few more of them running around. Lana had heard though the rumor mill that the other two had been torn apart by something.

Oh well. Not her town, not her problem.

Her problem was working on his second joint, his eyes half-lidded. Maybe it was his third. It took a lot to mellow out a sidhe as strong as him.

She did not believe in coincidence. If Summer's Get was next door, it involved Senán. Of that she was certain. What she was not certain of was how much time it left her. She had screwed around with this twit for far too long, but she had had to be so careful, and she was dancing on this wire with no net. One misstep and the fall would kill her.

"Close to what?"

Even with her acute hearing, Lana barely heard his slurred words. Instincts honed by years of court intrigues riveted on those three syllables and she slid up beside him on the bed. "What do you mean?" she asked softly, tracing her nails over his skin.

Senán closed his eyes in pleasure and exhaled smoke. He slurred something incoherent. His eyes did not reopen.

Lana rocked herself up on one knee and straddled his waist, nails digging in harder. "Jeremy, baby. Talk to me."

The hand with the smoking joint lowered to the bed and a small snore trickled from his lips. Shit. Ordinarily this would be her cue to put out the joint, pick up her paperback, and order sushi in. In the morning she would gush about what fantastic sex they'd had. Since she couldn't feed on him without Prince Midir sensing it she preferred it this way. Imagine, a succubus choosing fiction over fornication, but he just sucked that much in bed.

She frowned down at his pretty, snoring face, hands on hips, and considered her options. On one hand, her book was getting to a good part. On the other hand… Screw it, something told her she really needed to know what the idiot was talking about. She knew from months of dating that Senán plus pot equaled taking forever to wake back up and she so did not feel like spending the next forty-five minutes coaxing him to alertness. There were much more direct approaches. A smile stretched her mouth and she knew it was neither sweet nor inviting. After all, a rare opportunity to mess with the idiot was really not something she wanted to pass up.

She plucked the joint from his slack fingers, set it in the ash tray before it burnt a hole in her bedspread, and then bit his nipple just this side of bleeding.

Senán woke up with a scream like a stepped-on cat. "Jesus, bitch!" His voice was still slurred, but he was definitely awake. He clasped both hands protectively over his left pectoral, propped up awkwardly on one elbow.

Lana tossed her hair and laughed. "Aw! Did I bite too hard, baby?"

He tried to squirm out from under her. "Why'd you bite at all?" The whine was back in his voice.

"You fell asleep on me." She nuzzled the backs of his hands. "I'll kiss it better for you."

"It's gonna bruise. You're not getting anywhere near it."

She flickered her tongue over the backs of his fingers and put heat into her gaze. Senán's pupils dilated, his wriggles of protest stilled. She held him with her eyes alone for one heartbeat… two… three… He was hers again. She slid her palms up the heated skin of his ribs, beneath his shielding hands and pushed them aside to reveal the wreath of small marks her teeth had left behind. "Poor Jeremy," she crooned, lips ever so close to the wound. He made a hissing noise as the warm air of her breath brought his nipple to a hardened peak. "So very abused." She stroked the peak with the heat of her tongue, making him writhe beneath her again. This time he was not trying to get away.

Lana sat upright, still straddling his belly, and picked up the half-smoked joint to relight it. Senán ran his hands up her thighs and she felt his glamour coiling around her, enticing her back to him. It was strong—he was a prince, after all—but he was also a fraction of her age and she was used to older and stronger princes than he trying to seduce and control her with their glamour. She blew it off with no effort. Had he been aware he was doing it she may have had to work harder. Had she been mortal her panties would have been on the floor, aware or not. It was how the idiot usually got laid.

She pretended to take a hit on the joint and passed it back to Senán. "You said something before you crashed out on me," she said, watching him take a deep drag. She tickled her nails with seeming idyll over his chest, but she remained attuned to the slightest clue he could offer her.

Senán released the smoke and shrugged. "Don't remember." He ran his free hand up her ribs and over her breast. "Does it matter?"

She stroked her fingers through his blonde hair. "Everything you say matters to me, baby." And it did. He was her one keyhole into Midir's world. He may not have his master's confidence, but he was the blind spot that lived in his pocket, and while those clueless gray eyes saw things that may make no sense to him, to her they were pearls beyond price.

Pearls that would buy her vengeance.

His eyes were glazing over, and she took the joint back, pretending to smoke it again. "Something about being close," she coaxed, letting his hand wander. If he fell asleep on her again it would not be his nipple she'd bite.

Senán's eyelids began to droop, then snapped back open. "Oh yeah!" He let his hand fall to her waist. "Dad said something about, 'I'm too close.'" His brows knitted together, the little three-legged hamster working the wheel in his brain. "He wouldn't tell me what, though. Fucker."

Lana slid off of his belly to sit beside him on the bed and had to admit her own hamster was getting a workout. Close? If he was close to something she really was running out of time, becoming pressured from more than one side. A chill swept over her that had nothing to do with the October afternoon. She was going to have to start taking risks or face failure. And failure was the one thing she could not face. Only success now stood between her and the things that made death a luxury.

She needed more information than Senán alone could provide. She needed inside the glamour and iron that cloaked Moore Investments.

She was terrified.

She stretched out beside Senán and reached over him to drop the roach into the ashtray. She laid a kiss on his bare shoulder. "Don't you want to know?" she whispered against his neck.

"Know what?" he murmured back.

"What your father is up to." She went up on one elbow, her hair cascading down over his arm. He had turned his head to face her. "What he's close to."

Senán's eyes widened and he turned his whole body to her, rising up above her on the bed. "If I know, what if I can bring the whole thing down around him?" His breath came shallow and fast.

Lana's smile stretched into a grin. "Imagine what that would do to him."

"He'd go fucking insane." Anticipation and terror danced in his eyes.

"Jonathan Moore, not so perfect after all. It could get in the news."

He looked off into space. "How, though…"

She touched his cheek and brought his attention back to her. "I'll help you."

His look turned skeptical. "Lana, seriously, what can you do?"

She savagely squelched the urge to twist his bitten nipple and instead let a dangerous smile pull at the corner of her mouth. "Trust me, baby. Get me into that building, and we'll find out what your father's planning." She twined her fingers through the short hair at the nape of his neck. "You know I have my ways."

He began to look thoughtful and hopeful. "Tomorrow's Saturday. He's going to be in the building… I mean, we live in the damn building… but if we go in tomorrow night there'll hardly be anyone around at all. We'll have the whole place to ourselves."

Good boy. Lana pulled Senán down and kissed him. "And then your father goes down," she whispered against his lips. She had one card. One single, solitary card.

And she meant to play it.

CHAPTER ELEVEN

"Hold still. You see the redness here? You're becoming infected."

"That stuff's cold. And I know what an infection looks like."

Winter held Etienne's large, warm hand cradled in her gloved palm as she applied green ointment. "It's not hurting you. You did this on iron spikes?"

"Rose thorns. Moore Investments's wall is topped by them."

Winter frowned. "That's rather a lot of iron for a sidhe to surround himself with." Very strange. She looked closely at his gray eyes. They were clear, no indication of burst blood vessels and the skin around them was smooth and unblemished. "You're not feeling ill?" The wounds didn't show any signs of burning, either, which she would have expected from Cold Iron breaking the skin.

Etienne shook his head, a smile tugging at one corner of his mouth. "Thanks to my human father, iron has no effect on me. I'm a blacksmith by trade."

"Oh?" That sounded very interesting. She set the ointment jar down and wiped her fingers off on a towel before picking up the roll of bandages.

"They're just scratches. I don't need bandages." He started drawing his hands away from her.

She reached out and caught his wrist again, giving him an exasperated look. "It's not for your hands, it's to protect my furniture. The green stains. Now stop pulling. The ointment will have your scratches healed within an hour or so, and you can take off the bandages then." Why did men—no matter the species—have to be such big babies? She looked up at his face as she wrapped his hand, again examining the scrollwork and brands that covered his cheeks. Who had done such a thing? She was half mortal also but had never born a scar in her life. How much cutting and branding had it taken? She ached for him.

"What?" he asked in a gruff tone. Not aggressive, only like a man not used to being taken care of.

"You scar," she replied softly.

Etienne looked down at the scarred back of his free hand and frowned. "Yeah, I do. I also ache from old injuries in the morning and get infections and illnesses. I'm faster and stronger than a human, but not as fast and strong as a sidhe... not anymore, anyway. And while I'm immortal I think I'm easier to kill than my fully sidhe kinsmen."

"You think?"

His expression turned wry. "As I am still alive I have obviously never tested the theory."

Winter smiled a little at his humor and nodded, finishing the bandaging and turned to the other hand. "Why do you say not anymore?"

"I developed a serious infection from the cutting and I've never been the same since." He shrugged. "It left me crippled."

She wrapped the other palm with gentle hands, his fingers rough and calloused. She felt his eyes on her as she worked.

"You're a wizard. Do you know what the glyphs are?" His voice was quiet now, a little lost. She knew that feeling intimately.

She pushed up the sleeve of his red flannel shirt, careful to not overly stress the worn fabric. He had left his jacket upstairs and wore only the unbuttoned over-shirt over his gun rig and a plain gray t-shirt that had also seen better days. There had to be some way to get this proud man and his young companion into newer clothes... She would figure something out. "I wish I did." She traced her fingers over one of the glyphs, raising the fine hairs on his skin. He stepped back a little then pulled his sleeve back down, and she gave him a quizzical look. He was looking away from her, his expression stoic. What was that about? "I didn't know my mother long enough for her to teach me much of anything, and my sidhe ancestress left nothing written behind," she explained. "What are the runes?"

Etienne cleared his throat and looked back up at her. "Dwarven. The friend who brought me to them thought the glyphs might be used for compulsion and control." The smile tugged at his lips again as he remembered. "Eoin was a better knight than a magician, by a long shot, so it was really more a best guess from knowing those who had attacked me. The runes negate those types of spells."

A thought tickled the back of her mind. Maybe… "I might have a resource, but I'll have to ask for an introduction. We'll see how far that road takes us."

He inclined his head to her. "I'm most grateful for any information, but there's no rush. I've worn these for six mortal centuries and they're not going anywhere."

Winter finished the bandage. "But now I'm curious." She twisted around to put away the remaining wrappings and a thought occurred to her. "On the topic of curiosity…" she said as she turned back to him, "If you were looking for Arthur Reynolds, how did you know to come here?"

"We ran into a street musician not far from here, and he told us that what we were looking for was here," Etienne replied.

Only in Seahaven would that make sense. "Average height, long, curly, brown hair?"

"I don't know what's average height these days, but the hair sounds right."

She smiled. "You met Stephen."

Etienne nodded. "Yes, that was his name."

Winter considered her audience, then asked, "Do you know what he is?" It was a fairly rude question to ask in Seahaven, with its general 'live and let live' philosophy, but her new guests did not know that yet, and curiosity had been eating at her for years. Stephen was the first person she had ever tried purposely to soul read—and the only one she had never succeeded with. Fate had always interceded. Someone would need her, or the crowd would thicken, and he would wander off. Once she had almost had him, and someone bumped into a flower stand and dumped it on her. She reasoned now as the wizard of the city if anyone besides Stephen had a right to know, it would be her.

Etienne knitted his brows slightly in confusion. "I'm not sure what you mean," he replied. "Do you?"

She shook her head. "He's been around as long as anyone can remember. At least a century, though he did not arrive with the settlers. The vampires say that one day he had just been here for a while, but no one knew how long it had been." She gave a small shrug. "He's never hurt anything. We assume he's some sort of fae, but we've never known what kind. I was hoping you might."

"Fae?" Etienne glanced back in the direction they had come, and then turned his eyes again to Winter. "He seemed quite human to me, if a bit... strange."

Winter tipped her head slightly to one side, and it was her turn to look confused. "How odd." What then was he, besides a homeless musician?

Footsteps came rattling down the stairs, carrying words that she did not understand. The sound was liquid, but not liquid like still water. It was the tumbling brook, sliding seamlessly over rocks and falls in tone. Jessie emerged from the stairwell, followed by Cian. "That was awesome! Ok, so how do you say—?"

"Jessie?" While she was on the subject...

Jessie turned her attention to Winter. "Yeah, boss lady?"

"Would you please take my card and go get Stephen something to eat?"

"Yeah, sure. Come on, Cian. Stephen's pretty cool." She rifled through Winter's wallet with practiced ease and disappeared with the young prince through the store front.

Etienne raised an eyebrow slightly as he watched the two leave. "Stephen seemed to be making good money out there. Why feed him?"

Winter began pulling off her surgical gloves and smiled. "All the shop owners in the Historical District take turns feeding him, some of us more often than others. We know he passes the money he makes from playing on to those who are even worse off than himself and works with the street kids to better their lives. He lives somewhere under the docks at the waterfront. So, he goes hungry a lot, but it's because he sacrifices for others.

He…" a glove slipped from her fingers and she bent at the knees to pick it up. "Your jeans are freshly ripped. Did you do this on the fence?"

"Yes, but I'm not scratched."

She shifted down to one knee and pulled at the larger rip, exposing a line of scarred skin to her examination. "Are you sure? These tears are bad." On the other hand, she did not smell blood or infection.

Etienne tried pulling away, but she had a tight grip on his pants. "No, really, I'm—"

"Little girl, what the hell are you doing?!"

Winter jerked back at the bellow, nearly falling on her backside. She felt Etienne spin around above her, hand sliding back underneath his flannel shirt, which only served to make her balance more precarious, and she fell forward onto both knees. Suddenly, she realized exactly what it had looked like and frowned. She rose to standing and placed a gentle hand on Etienne's wrist under his shirt tail to reassure him. "I'm doing my job, Erik."

Braced in the doorway, beaded curtains held aside by either hand, stood the Vampire King of Seahaven. Well over six feet tall and nearly half that as broad, the ancient Viking glowered at her and Etienne equally, his sea-blue eyes dark. "Since when is *that* your job?" he growled in his resonant bass.

Winter's back stiffened and her cheeks flushed with anger, but before she could defend her honor a graceful young man ducked underneath Erik's arm and gave him a reproving smack on his war-hardened belly. His other hand was emerging from beneath the breast of his jacket. "Stop it. Winter would never have sex with a stranger." Michael smiled a warm greeting at Winter and then looked up at his King. "Unlike you."

Erik scowled for another full second and then broke into a belly laugh before bending to kiss him. "You're not wrong." Winter rolled her eyes. So, Erik was having one of *those* days, was he? She stepped forward, sniffing delicately. No, the smell of mead was no stronger than usual. He was just being his mercurial self. Suddenly, Erik looked up from his favorite and took a strong sniff of his own. "I smell gun oil." His suspicious gaze landed firmly on Etienne.

"So do I," Winter sighed. "I'm standing right next to him. I can also smell Michael's gun."

Etienne glanced up at her. "I didn't think wizards could scent that well," he murmured.

She smiled back at him. "No need to keep your voice down. They're vampires; they can hear you around the block. And no, there is nothing special about wizard senses. I'm just a potion-maker and a physician. I need a finely-honed sense of smell to do my job safely and effectively."

Erik stepped further into the room, his personality taking up more space than even his large body could muster. "Who cares about that? I want to know why you're letting an armed stranger be alone with you."

"He's not going to shoot me."

"How do you know that?"

She thinned her lips at his high-handed tone. "You know I'm an excellent judge of character." She should have just told him Etienne was a family friend. Of course, Erik had never met him, he might not have believed her— but that was not the point. He was treating her like a child.

Erik's eyes slid to Etienne and back to her. "What if you're wrong?"

Winter shook her head. "I'm never wrong."

"Dammit, it just takes once!"

"And what could you do?" she snapped and slapped her hand over her mouth in a desperate attempt to take it back. A look of helpless grief flashed across the Vampire King's face and shame burned at her core. She had wounded another friend. "Oh, Erik," she whispered. "I am so sorry. You... you deserve better than that." He had known her family since before the city's founding, had watched them all die just as she had watched, only without the insulation of childhood.

Erik roughed his hand over his short, black hair and cleared his throat. "I need to talk to you. Sit."

Everyone wanted to talk to her today. "I'll stand, but Michael, if you would like to sit, please feel free."

Michael squeezed Erik's hand and moved to lean against the desk. "Thank you, but I think I'll just keep my feet. No telling when I may need to jump in and referee."

She sighed. Michael was showing tension, which meant he was expecting more outbursts from Erik. Excellent. Being yelled at by the Vampire King was her favorite activity. She looked toward Etienne. "You don't need to be here for this."

He leaned back and rested a hip against the work table, his eyes still on Erik. "I'm fine as I am."

Winter blinked once. Was he being protective? "Erik would never hurt me."

Etienne cocked his eyebrow. "I'm not such a good judge of character as you."

She sighed. Please don't let this become a penis measuring contest. Wizards were not, as a rule, religious, but sometimes a little wishful thinking couldn't hurt. Not that it had ever done her any good in the past, mind. She stepped away from him and toward Erik. "Here I am. What do you need?" She raised her hands and spread them slightly, presenting herself as the target she felt like.

Erik pointed at her red-spotted city map. "This crap has to stop."

Winter flushed, opened her mouth to snap again—then snapped it shut. She counted to three, and still ended up replying, "I'm sorry, but as you can see there is rather a large amount of 'crap.' To which are you referring today?" Her tone was arid, not as diplomatic as she could have been had circumstances—had life—been different.

"Don't sass me, miss. I know Giovanni was torn up the other night. My vampires don't need to—"

She set her hands on her hips. "'Your' vampires? Giovanni is Katherine's, unless you're laying claim to the other two vampire courts in this city?" She knew where he was going with this and was not in the mood for it. If she could derail him…

"Three."

Erik was not the only one who could be derailed. Both she and the Vampire King turned to Michael. "What?" she asked.

"Three others, four total," he responded, his voice a flavor of bland that only a stage actor like him could achieve. "Us, Katherine, the Servants' lawyer Raphael, and now we have Erik's Aunt, the Eldest Himiko." Vampires traced linages like families. Erik's vampire father, Marcus of Rome, shared a progenitor with Himiko, meaning Erik owed her filial hospitality in his city, which she had only taken advantage of the previous year. Raphael was a Servant of the Eldest, a senior lawyer to the vampire courts, and had settled in Seahaven at Erik's invitation a century before.

Erik would not be distracted and waved off Michael's aside. "As far as this goes, yes, I'm still calling Giovanni mine, just like he was before little Mike was born. And I'm sure as hell calling Katherine mine—she's still my queen and the mother of my son. Same goes for any vampire you want to throw in the middle of this new dispute between the lions and the sharks because you can't keep the factions under control. Only mine and Katherine's are foolish enough to get involved, anyway."

Winter's cheeks burned bright under Erik's direct accusation. He was right, of course. But admitting it out loud was another matter entirely. If she confessed he was right, that she had no real control here—then what? The cavalry came? There was no one. She could have promised to talk to the lions and sharks—again. She could have asked for more time—again. But that would change nothing. So, she kept her spine straight, stared the Vampire King down, and said the only thing that would bring about the change Erik wanted. "Then pull your vampires," she said quietly, evenly. "I can handle it on my own."

"What? Wait a minute…"

Etienne had moved closer to the map, reading the notes and dates—factional conflicts, injuries and deaths. Rifts sealed. The map was covered with those annotations. He turned back to face Winter, a frown etched into his face. "Are you at war?"

Winter glanced at the map and a wave of exhaustion washed over her at the sheer volume of red. She wanted more caffeine, wanted to let herself sag with weariness, to even fall onto the dubious comfort of the exam table and sleep until the world ended, but she stood straight and tall before these men and held her crumbling ground. "That depends on your definition of 'war,'" she replied, expression wry.

Etienne waved his hand across the map. "War wears many faces." His eyes found Erik before returning to her. "I would not let you face this alone."

"Dammit, that's not what I said," Erik grated between his teeth. He glared at Etienne. "Who the hell are you, anyway?"

Etienne faced down the much larger man. "Etienne, Knight of Seelie." He did not offer his hand.

Erik noticed and did not extend his own. He crossed his battle-scarred arms, taking his time assessing Etienne. At length he finally said in an aside to Michael, "Well either he'll be damn useful or a right pain in the ass."

Winter thinned her lips in irritation. "And he's still standing right here."

Erik stepped toward her. "And you, young lady, knock it off with the dramatics. You know I'd sooner set my Theatre on fire than pull my support for you."

Winter fought the urge to roll her eyes. Erik always did this to her—suddenly she was twelve-years-old again, a little girl and not the wizard of the city. But the irritation remained clear on her face. "And is that what talking to Jessie behind my back is? Support? Don't think I don't know half the groups call you my 'Uncle' Erik and they're not being flattering."

"Who the hell cares? I don't. You know as far as I'm concerned, I *am* your uncle."

"You wouldn't care. It just makes you look good. You're not the one hearing the complaints from everyone that I'm giving the vampires too much power, too much favor."

"And I say you're not giving us enough."

Winter turned away, crossing her arms. "I can't do that."

"Yes. Yes, you can."

"It would upset the balance."

Erik pointed over her head at the map. "Does that look balanced to you?" He reached out to take her shoulders and she moved out of his grasp. She couldn't do this with him. Not today. Maybe not ever again. She utterly lacked the emotional resilience.

Erik gritted his teeth in frustration and followed her. "Dammit, little girl, how many months do you think we have left before groups break out into open warfare? This skirmishing crap will lead right into it and when it gets out of hand the Eldest will get involved, and you know it." The Eldest, who would think nothing of leveling the city if it kept the Veil of Secrecy intact.

Winter felt her backside run up against the wall counter. "So, you think I should unbalance the city now, rather than later? Is that it?" She craned her neck to meet his frustrated gaze.

"What I think is that you can't do this alone!"

"I have to."

"Bullshit!"

Halfcocked's version of 'Bad Reputation' suddenly erupted into the small break following Erik's exclamation. Michael pulled his phone from his pocket and bent his head to read the text message. Again, he was bland. "Erik, Katherine says if you don't stop bellowing at Winter and interrupting her writing while she's on deadline she's going to kick your ass back to the Middle Ages."

Erik turned to face the wall separating Curiosity's from Katherine's Retreat. "Dammit, woman, I'm making a point here!" he roared in a voice once meant to be heard over battle screams and swollen seas.

Michael's eyes never lifted from his phone. "'And this point needs obscenities? BTW, you're waking the spawn from his nap.'"

"Stop calling him that!"

One of Michael's brows twitched, and he put his phone back in his pocket. He glanced at his lover. "She said, 'Whatever.'"

Erik scowled. "No, she didn't."

A small smile tugged at Michael's mouth, but he said nothing.

Erik turned back and looked down at Winter. The volume of his voice had dropped dramatically. "Winter," he began again.

"Wait," she said. Winter planted both hands on the Vampire King's chest and pushed him away. He let her. She would never have had the strength to move him had he not. "You're looming."

Erik scowled. "I do not loom."

Michael smiled up at him. "You loom."

He turned his scowl on Michael, whose smile did not dim in the slightest. "Well, I wasn't looming then."

Michael rubbed a thumb over one of his eyebrows. "Yeah. You were."

Erik looked skyward and muttered in Norse. Winter recognized it as a prayer to Odin. He once had reserved it for conversations with her grandfather Dermot, but now she was hearing it directed about her. She waited until he was done. "I believe you were swearing at me," she prompted him to continue.

The Vampire King nodded, not bothering to look abashed at his behavior. "The point I was making before my woman interrupted me," he said, raising his voice slightly in the direction of the wall again before continuing in a gentler tone to Winter, "is that you need to let me help you. Officially."

"The Mulcahys have always been the law in Seahaven." Always. She could feel their eyes on her, watching her fail. "That's not going to change now."

His jaw clenched, but he took a deep breath. "Winter, you may be the law, but you have no threat."

She narrowed her eyes. "A wizard is capable of some very unpleasant things," she reminded him.

Erik looked grim. "Yes, but *you* are not."

Winter felt a trickle of fear for her vulnerability. Because he was right—she was simply not that kind of wizard. And she needed the fear of things in this city that could tear her flesh from bone without dropping their triple caramel macchiato. "No one needs to know that," she said, ever so quietly.

He reached and gripped her by her shoulders and she stiffened under his large hands. Not because she feared the Vampire King would hurt her, but because she wanted him to hold her and make all the bad things go away, just as he had when she was a little girl, with a desperation that tasted like pennies in her mouth. He gave her a little shake, not hard, and she saw Etienne move protectively to her side out of the corner of her eye. "Let me help you before they figure it out on their own," Erik said, his voice gruff with fear. "Good God, little girl, let *someone* help you. If you don't trust me enough," his voice faltered just a beat and it brought the burn of tears to her eyes, "trust the lions. Corinne is your friend; you know she'll bring her pride to back your threat in a heartbeat."

She shrugged gently from under Erik's hands. "I'll always trust you," she said, quietly. She could not accept his offer of help, but she could not stand to hurt him again.

He stepped away from her, and the frustration had returned. "But you'd rather die than let me help you," he growled out.

Winter replied with silence.

Erik turned to Etienne. He looked the faerie knight up and down again. "You hurt her, boy, there's no hole in the realms deep enough to hide you."

Etienne merely nodded.

Erik considered the faerie knight's response. "But Godspeed if she actually lets you help her." He turned away to head out, his hand moving possessively to Michael's shoulder.

"Erik," Winter called after him on impulse. "I'll speak to my father about it tonight."

The Vampire King turned back and gave her a small nod, but it was his turn to respond with helpless silence.

They both knew what Colin would have to say.

CHAPTER TWELVE

"Sure, ask him for an intro. Just do it in front of me. I want to see his head split open." Katherine grinned in amusement.

Winter placed a fresh jar of translucent, green healing ointment into her storage cabinet and stretched yet again. Her joints would not stop complaining about rising at three in the morning to brew more and there was a small persistent buzzing noise in her left ear from drinking that third energy potion. She had been up late trying to get any response from her father, but to no avail. Erik wanted an alliance she could not give, and now she was going to have to ask him for another favor to help the sidhe lords. It was shaping up to be another red-letter day. She turned her full attention back to Katherine. "Surely it wouldn't be that bad. He invited her here, after all."

The vampire queen rubbed little Mike's back in circles as she breastfed him and grimaced. The music of steel kissing steel filled the early morning silence as the two sidhe lords practiced their blade work in the small grassy area outside.

"Oh, now what?" Winter put her hands on her hips and tried to not look too irritated at her friend.

Katherine shook her head. "I told him to tell you," she muttered, and then said full voice, "Himiko invited herself and Erik couldn't tell her no."

Winter waited for Katherine to elaborate. When she did not, she tilted her head to the side. "I don't see what's so dire about that. If I had an aunt who wanted to move to my city, she would be more than welcome." What would she give to have an aunt living?

Mike fussed some and Katherine caught his cheek to keep him from worrying at her breast. She tucked her finger into the corner of his mouth to get him to unlatch and when he let go she shifted him to her shoulder. The four small puncture wounds surrounding her nipple closed within seconds, just before she got herself deftly tucked away. "If that was all there was to it, you would have met her months ago." Katherine turned her son around to stand on her knees facing Winter. He smiled and shook his fists at her, then began his campaign for freedom. Both women ignored his entreaties. "But she's... well..." Katherine stopped, groping for words.

Winter smiled. "I know Himiko's reputation as a loose cannon. I know she's one of the Eldest, and that she's eccentric, and I appreciate you not wanting to alarm me. But she has two babies of her own and Erik said she wanted to come raise them here because we're considered fairly neutral territory—granted that's by people who don't actually live here." Her eyes flickered to the map. "How terrible can someone like that be?"

"She's a sorcerer."

Winter's smile vanished. Technically, wizards did not judge sorcerers and in fact some wizard families had become sorcerers themselves, regardless of what must be great risks and sacrifices. Wizards prized power as the greatest virtue. But the Mulcahys prided themselves on being defenders of the innocent and traditionally did not move in the same circles as those who dealt with greater demons—and demons consumed mortal souls. She herself knew very little about sorcery. It was one subject the Mulcahy Library did not cover in depth. "Is she bringing demons into the city?" Winter would have liked to think she would be somehow aware of such a thing, but the truth was she was just one small wizard and Seahaven was a big place.

Katherine bounced the baby on her knee. "Not from what I've heard. But, historically Himiko keeps to herself until she's ready not to, so who the hell knows?"

Mike arched his back to look at Winter upside down and she tickled his neck. "What does that mean, exactly?"

"She refuses to associate with the other queens, for one." There were many, many female vampires in the world, but of them all only a tiny percentage 'rose upon making' as powerful breeding queens. In all the world there were only thirty-two. Winter did not know if that number included Himiko or not. What she did know, growing up under Katherine's watchful eye, was that the queens had formed a tight-knit unit for mutual friendship and protection. Their motto for the last eight centuries glittered on the bracelet on Katherine's wrist: *Universae Stamus*. We Stand Together.

At a little over three-thousand-years-old, Himiko predated the sentiment by a considerable margin.

"Why? Is it just that she's so old?"

The baby began kicking his legs and squealing in earnest to be let down, and Katherine gave in, holding on to the back of his shirt to keep him somewhat corralled. "Partially. She's always done her own thing. And, honestly, at this point who's going to tell her she can't? But the new thing that's got her nose out of joint is her twins. She wants the queens to acknowledge them as princes and we won't."

"You won't?" That seemed strange. If this Himiko was a queen, and she would have to be if she'd borne children, then of course her children should be princes, just like Mike. Just like the sons of all vampire queens.

Katherine gave a small shrug. "It's really weird—I mean, of course it's weird, it's Himiko. She's the only vampire to have ever held Kingship over a city and just walked away. And she's done it more than once. But in all these centuries she's never borne a prince, never allowed a male near her during her heat. And all of a sudden, wham! Last year she shows up here, estate already purchased, and gives birth to dhampyr twins, fathered by a sidhe."

That brought Winter up short. Her sidhe consort was who she wanted to talk to about Etienne's scars, but she had not heard that he was the father of Himiko's children. Male vampires could father the rare dhampyr on a human woman, but they were widely considered to be frail, tragic creatures too weak to forge their own way in the courts, who had their fathers' need for blood but their mothers' human lifespans.

Winter had never heard of a queen accepting any but the most powerful of male vampires to attend her heat. And she had never heard of a vampire mixing with anything but a human. What would these children turn out like? Both parents were immortal, powerful... it was amazing. "How is that possible?"

Katherine shook her head in wonder. "That's what we've been trying to figure—"

Winter's world slid sideways. Memory forced her back to the rift in the ravine, only this time she did not stand a chance of holding back the tsunami. This time there was no build up—the wave crested, the floor seeming to rise and buckle beneath her legs, and she was under. She felt the reverberation of impacts resonate through her bones, over and over again as rift after rift blew wide open against the pressure of power behind the tattered fabric of the veil. What was happening?

Somewhere Katherine was calling her name, the baby wailing, but she could not see, could barely hear, and could not draw breath to reply. The buzzing in her ear was overwhelmed by ringing. She was drowning in wild magic. It swirled around, battering against her shields as colors danced behind her blind eyes. She had to get out, somehow, before she passed out.

Panic tried to claw its frantic way up her throat and she brutally forced it back into the pit of her belly. It would kill her even more surely than magical suffocation. She released what little breath she had left with a broken promise of more, stilled her mind, and drew on her surgeon's focus that let her face down shredded flesh and shattered bone and still hold body bound to soul. Power flowed all around her, but with her newfound calm she could sense it abating. The natural balance realigning on its own. She tried to follow it, to track it to its source, but the currents ran in too many different directions as it trickled away, running in rivulets through the hundreds of minuscule rifts that perforated the veil around Seahaven. She found her way to what passed for a surface as the flood subsided.

Winter's first inhalation tore through her chest and left her racked with coughing as sight returned. She found herself on her knees and would have collapsed forward but for the vise-like grip on her biceps cutting off the circulation to her hands. Katherine knelt before her, the other woman's lips white with fear. Winter tried to speak but her greedy lungs were only interested in more air. Little Mike sat on the floor beside her, howling inconsolably as he clung to his mother's hip.

The back door swung open and a grim-faced Etienne pulled Cian bodily through, both silvery-gold swords gripped in his other hand. The boy was pale and shivering with fear. "Are you ladies alright?" he asked, raising his voice over the baby's cries.

Winter nodded. "Fine," she managed to croak. She shrugged her shoulders to encourage Katherine to release her panicked grip on her arms and tried not to hiss as blood rushed back into her hands. The vampire queen gathered up her frightened son and Winter stroked his back, unable to resist taking a moment to help soothe him. Though not magicians themselves and thus not as vulnerable to the chaos the flood of wild magic had caused, Katherine and Mike were still preternaturals and that made them more sensitive than an average human. She bent and kissed the baby's soft dark hair, breathing in his warm, milky scent as he fussed. She tried to ignore the quaking fright in her own belly. She felt Katherine's hand brush her shoulder in the first motion of an embrace and forced herself to stand, fixing what she hoped was a confident smile on her face and moved to the map on her wall. She had work to do.

In the distance a siren sounded. Winter paused to listen. Fire truck. If the humans were involved her life became more complicated.

Complications in her life were hardly new. A city full of open rifts, though...

"What was that all about?"

She jumped a little at his voice close to her shoulder. Etienne was warm beside her, smelling good of herbal shampoo and exertion and male, and she moved away from him, just a shifting of weight. The fading adrenaline was making her jittery and she wanted coffee. "I don't know. There was a smaller one a few days ago that seemed to only have affected one rift. This one covered a much larger area, though. I felt several rifts tear wide and I need to find and seal them."

Etienne looked over the map with her. "So, what now?"

"First things first, I have a Gate to check."

He did a double take. "A Gate? Where?"

A real smile tugged at her lips. "Across the street."

Etienne looked impressed.

When her sidhe ancestress Eithne and her sister Aideen came through to the Mortal Realm, they arrived via a Gate, a stable crossing between the realms. Most of the Gates that Winter had ever heard of connected the Mortal Realm to Faerie, but theoretically she supposed they could connect anywhere. It was just that these two realms, in particular, were very closely bound and had even once overlapped in many places. Aideen had eventually fallen in love with one of the human settlers who had come with Erik—Thomas MacDowell—and it was decided that to help conceal and control the Gate that they would build their dry-goods store right on top of it. Over the generations the MacDowells forgot their true heritage and the building changed uses until it, ironically, became Otherworld Books. There the Gate sat snug in the building's large basement, secure behind a gate of scrolled Cold Iron. With the hammering the veil around Seahaven had just taken, the Gate suddenly became Winter's first priority.

She closed her eyes and relaxed, reaching her senses out the short distance toward the Gate. There was Brian, moving around the apartment above the bookstore where his family lived. He glowed against her magical sight like a candle's flame. She could not see his mother and brother, or any other human for that matter—they simply did not have the spark of the preternatural. She looked down below the bookstore to where the Gate sat. It looked to her mind's eye not like a jagged tear ringed in orange flames, as a rift would appear to be, but as a smooth-sided aperture in the veil, opening into darkness and bounded by layers of wards.

"How does it look?" Etienne asked. The baby had stopped crying.

"It's fine, for the most part," she replied. "The tsunami, or whatever that was, did have an effect and appears to have..." She paused, thinking of a way to describe what she was seeing. "It looks like the Gate is rather stretched a bit. I can see more space between the misdirection wards than I could before. It's very odd."

"'Stretched?' Is that bad?"

"It's not good," she said quietly, "but it's also not an immediate danger. The Gate is fine. They're natural phenomena and as such are quite sturdy." But sturdy did not mean indestructible and the power release from a Gate collapse had the potential to level the Historical District. Maybe even The

Waterfront and Signal Hill with it. The first instability she could have chalked up to Seahaven strangeness. This second one indicated a dangerous pattern forming. Fleetingly her thoughts shifted to Mount Sarah. Now there was a nightmare scenario, but it would take much, much more power to tip a dormant volcano into an eruption than to blow the Gate, so she let the thought go. She opened her eyes, releasing her magical sight. She had to figure out what was causing the tsunamis—fast.

But, again, first things first—her life was eternal triage. She had rifts to seal. Her plate was overflowing, and it was not yet nine.

She pulled a pen and pad of paper close and focused on the city map, using it for its intended purpose—scrying rifts. She poised the pen in her hand and released a cleansing breath to concentrate.

"What are you doing, now?"

Katherine answered for her. "With the crap we just went through, rifts would have blown like tires across the city. She's scrying for them using the map, so she can go out and seal them before anything comes through."

Winter brushed her fingers over the map, connecting to the glyphs drawn in patterns all over the back. Images swam in her mind, overlapping dizzily as they fought for her attention. So many! She was used to only one at a time, two at the most. How...? She felt a large, rough-skinned hand close over her own and her eyes flew open, startled. Etienne was pulling the pen from her fingers.

"Here, let me help."

Her lips parted and, "I'm fine," nearly escaped, but she stopped. It was such a small thing, and it really would help if she could just say the addresses out loud instead of breaking trance to write them down. She had never seen so many before, and time mattered. So, she nodded, let him take the paper as well, and closed her eyes again.

This time she placed both hands on the map and the images leapt to her mind with startling clarity. With each image the magic of the scrying brought letters and numbers that formed themselves into locations she could understand. She spoke them to Etienne, her voice toning in her ears as if spoken from far away. She knew where each one was, even without the addresses. This was her city, brick by brick. She opened her eyes, drawing herself out of the trance with a slow molasses feeling.

Her need for coffee was growing desperate.

She turned to grab her purple canvas bag off the desk. "Katherine, this is going to take me several hours at least. Could you call Corinne and ask her to please open her clinic to the public for the day? I'll offer her a favor." The large and wealthy preternatural groups often had their own medical care and the lions were among the largest and the wealthiest. They only called on Winter in the direst of circumstances. She opened a drawer and grabbed a handful of banishing potions, spilling them into the depths of her bag.

"I could, but she's going to want to talk to you about it, anyway, to be official."

"Blast!" Winter thinned her lips and tossed a couple of lumps of spell chalk into her bag with more force than was needed. "When is someone going to make making my life a little easier official?" she muttered.

"Winter..."

She sighed. "I'm sorry, you're helping too much as it is. I'll call her on my way. Could you just catch Jessie when she gets here and have her direct patients to Xanadu?" The lion pride's home and primary source of income was the destination hotel and resort sprawled over Sibbett Island and the other large islands in the Bay. Coincidentally, this was also the source of their conflict with the sharks, who had wanted use of the islands themselves. Corinne had won the development bid and the rest was faction war history. "Corinne won't say no. She just wants to go through the motions."

Katherine nodded. "Yeah, no worries." She came and looked over Etienne's shoulder at the list of addresses, little Mike resting on her hip. She let out a low whistle. "Wait up a minute and I'll get Giovanni to go with you."

Winter came and tore the list from the pad. "I'm fine. Erik's still angry with me for dragging you two into my problems, and I'm not looking for another reason for a shouting match."

"Erik would shout at the tide. Winter, you can't go alone."

She hitched her bag higher on her shoulder and kept her face neutral. "You know the factional politics just as well as I do. I have to." She brushed her fingers through the baby's black hair and went out the back door, pulling her phone from her bag's exterior pocket as she walked.

The call picked up on the third ring, just as she reached her yellow VW Bug. "*Buenos días*, Winter."

She frowned a little as his warm Spanish accent filled her ear and then she pulled her car door open. "Good morning, Santiago. Is Corinne alright?" Corinne's Lion King did not often answer her personal cell phone. Winter did not have the private numbers of all the preternatural leaders, but Erik had been right; Corinne was her good friend and tended to treat her more like a younger sister than the city's wizard. Corinne was eight weeks away from the end of her five-and-a-half-month pregnancy and Winter would be her midwife. The pride doctor was a gifted trauma specialist, as a therian physician had to be, and had taught Winter quite a bit over the years, but Winter had much more experience with obstetrics.

"Little Bella kept her up most of the night using her bladder as a trampoline, but she's fine. She's in the shower now. We're just getting a slow start."

Winter raised her brows, even though he could not see her. "Both of you?" Corinne was the CEO of Xanadu Entertainment Limited as well as being Lion Queen. Her husband, Santiago, oversaw all security operations. Their mornings routinely began almost as early as hers.

His chuckle rolled over her like soft fur. "You know Corinne. She refuses to suffer alone."

Winter found her ignition key by touch and slid into the driver's seat. She faintly heard Cian's voice raised in protest and glanced briefly in the direction of the shop's back door. "I actually have a reason for calling."

"Was it about that… magic thing?" Tension leaked into his rich voice.

"Yes. I've got to deal with fallout from that, so I can't man the shop clinic this morning… maybe for the rest of the day, I'm not sure. Would Doc be willing to take patients today?"

"*Sí*, I'll talk to her, but I'm sure she'll be fine with it."

"I'll owe you—" Her passenger side door swung open and Winter gasped in alarm, then saw it was Etienne swinging in to sit beside her, belted sword in hand.

"Winter, you all right?"

She widened her eyes at Etienne in exasperation. He grinned in reply. "I'm fine. I'm fine. I'll call you guys later." She exchanged goodbyes with the Lion King and hung up before turning her full attention to the faerie knight. "What are you doing?"

"Going with you." He snapped his seatbelt home with a definitive click.

She sighed, rested her forehead on the steering wheel, and wished it would rain coffee. "No, you can't. Go back to the store." She was wasting time.

"Because the factions will object to you showing too much favor to anyone?"

"Yes," she said to the dashboard.

"My lady… Winter, what faction do I belong to?"

She paused, then sat up and really looked at him. He was looking back at her with half a smile tugging one corner of his mouth. It pushed against the spell scar on his cheek.

He continued. "Since I am not of this city, and will depart when my business is concluded, consider me your mercenary."

Her eyebrows shot nearly to her hairline. "My what?"

Both corners of his mouth became involved. "Mercenary. Sell sword. It's my usual line of work, as forges are often in short supply, and I'll accept my usual rate of pay."

She looked at him askance. "Which is?"

"Room and board for Cian and myself. Of course, that's just for lending you my sword arm. For your help in rescuing Prince Senán, I suppose I'll have to put in extra effort."

Something about the way he said that in the close confines of her car made her heart beat faster. "I'm…" she began.

He reached up and placed his fingertips on her lips. She could feel the hardened edges of his calluses, breathe the hot metallic scent the sword hilt had left behind. "Don't say 'fine.'" He brushed the backs of his fingers across her cheek before pulling his hand away. "You are very far from 'fine.'"

Winter's lip quivered, and her eyes began to burn. She twisted away from him, her face turned toward the driver's side window and the blank brick wall beyond. Etienne was a silent presence beside her as she bound her emotions back under control and for that alone she was deeply grateful. Finally, she inserted the key into the ignition without looking at him. If she saw the pity in his gray eyes again she might not be able to keep herself together. "All right." She pulled out of her space and looked over the list of addresses at the same time, all the while managing to avoid hitting other cars in the lot. Which one first? Biggest? Closest? Again, her life was a matter of triage.

But how to perform triage when you were one of the bodies on the ground?

CHAPTER THIRTEEN

When it came to rifts, Winter had decided that size mattered.

She parked on the South City side street and downed the last of her burned-bitter fast-food coffee in one large swallow, attention riveted several blocks away on the smoking textile factory swarming with emergency workers. It would not be the first time she had had to evade human eyes as she worked—that was a skill every preternatural had to acquire, or else they would be killed by the Servants of the Eldest before they could reveal their true natures to the world at large. It would, however, be her first time working in such a busy accident site.

"I take it our rift is there." Etienne watched the firefighters. Winter could see no flames, only the smoke, and wondered where it was coming from. It was a big building. If the rift site was actively burning she was not sure she would be able to get close enough to seal it. On the other hand, maybe nothing would be able to come through until after the fire was put out, either.

She made a soft, rude noise to herself and began to dig in her bag. This was Seahaven. She knew better than to hope for things like that.

"The power release that tore the rift open is what caused the damage," she explained as she sifted through her bag. She pulled out a felt tip marker. "On the positive side, the explosion would have occurred on both sides of the rift, giving us time."

"And on the negative, whatever is on the other side is going to be pissed as hell."

She pointed the pen at Etienne to acknowledge his point. "So, what I need to do is get in there and seal the rift before anything on the other side notices it's there and gets curious enough to pass through." She rested her left hand on the steering wheel and began drawing on the back of it.

Etienne leaned forward, drew his handgun, a Glock if she was not mistaken, from the holster at the small of his back and checked the slide to make sure he had a round chambered. "I've seen my share of rifts, jumping between the realms as often as I do." He holstered the gun again and straightened his leather jacket back down over it. "I can feel the pull from here. That's why things cross over. Did you know that?"

She did know that and felt the pull of the rift herself. What she did not know was if she felt it because she was part fae, or all preternatural. She had asked her cousins and her sisters, rifts being a common subject of conversation among the wizards of Seahaven, but as all were part fae in some way or another none could come to an agreement, and Winter was reluctant to bring young Jessie, with her pure wizard blood, out into the field. She finished the design on her hand and blew on the ink out of habit to hurry the drying.

"Pretty. What is it?"

"It's a misdirection ward." She spoke the Words of Command and the ward glowed bright even in the morning light before settling into her skin. Now if the ink was smeared all to heck the ward would remain stable until she removed it. If her hand was removed she had bigger problems than losing the ward.

"Does it make you invisible?" He reached for her hand to take a closer look, and she moved it closer to him, angling her wrist to better show the design.

"Not exactly. It encourages human eyes to skip over whoever or whatever it's cast on, and whatever I'm engaged with, to technically see what's warded but not be able to consciously acknowledge it. It makes working near humans easier and safer." She took her hand back and opened the car door. Etienne followed suit.

"Just humans?" he asked over the roof.

She hitched her bag over her shoulder and locked her door with the key. The yellow Bug was a '69 and had no power anything. "Yes. Anyone preternatural will see right through it, like you're doing now. Curiosity's is covered with them. It's why only those with a strong magical spark can find it." She came around to lock his door and found his head bent down to the task of fastening his sword belt around his hips. The hilt was very simple, lacking entirely in ornamentation and the cross guard was a little imperfect. She tilted her head to the side, curious. "If you have a gun, why the sword?" She knew why vampires carried both, at least within their courts. The surest way to kill another vampire was decapitation and vampire politics could be lethal. It was only in recent decades that guns had become powerful enough to do any real damage to them.

Etienne shifted the sword hilt around until he was satisfied with the position. The wry twist of his mouth had returned. "I'm cheap."

That was a new answer. She had expected a short lecture on effective killing methods of various fae and other preternaturals, the sort of information that had been poured into her ears since she was a child. She locked his door, then pulled a piece of spell chalk from her bag and motioned for Etienne to turn around, giving her his back. "Cheap?"

He twisted his head to the side, peering at her over his shoulder as she smoothed the back of his jacket, fingers pressing against the outlines of the gun rig he wore underneath as she made herself an even work surface to draw the ward. The handgun at the small of his back stood out in sharp relief against the brown leather. His muscles moved smoothly under her palms as he gave a small shrug. "Used to be with flintlocks that I could make my own bullets from lead. And if I could retrieve them I could melt down the lead and re-use it. I didn't like them very much, though—damn slow to reload and pretty useless against anything not human, and humans mostly leave me alone."

Winter was having a hard time with a tricky curl and bent at the knees to grind the chalk against the pavement to sharpen her edge. The pen would have been easier, but she hated to mark up the soft, worn leather. "What about iron shot?"

"Not as easy to forge as you might think. No, I was much more impressed the next time I came to the Mortal Realm and revolvers had taken over everything. They were more powerful, did a lot more damage, but the bullets blew themselves to hell. Still do. So, every time I use the Glock, I have to bear in mind the cost of buying more ammunition."

Winter smiled as she drew. She understood that, being frugal herself. "What about the gun under your arm? I've seen you go for the one at your back, but not that one."

His good humor disappeared, replaced by something darker. He hesitated, then, "That's Agmundr. It's only for killing sidhe."

And she remembered; she *had* seen him reach for it—when Cian had felt her soul read him and Etienne had been angry. She knew, then, he had slipped his hand under his jacket with killing her in his thoughts. The October morning was suddenly much colder even under her felted coat, a shiver taking her smile away. She had not been wrong, he had not hurt her, and she was right to trust him... but still. She swallowed and finished the ward in silence.

Winter set other wards to protect them from the smoke and to give them some resistance to heat. Making them fireproof was beyond her talents. Only a wizard with a specialty in ward magic could do that. As they approached the smoking factory she scanned the faces of the busy firefighters, looking for flickers of notice and recognition. There would be no vampires among them, she was relatively certain. It was unusual for a vampire to take work outside of a court and she knew all of both Erik's and Katherine's vampires and court therian. But there could very well be free therian or witches or other preternaturals on the fire crew.

She bypassed a water-filled pothole and stepped over a large hose, watching men and women move briskly back and forth without so much as a glance in their direction. A large man, listening to his radio, spun on his heel and changed paths, forcing Winter to dance out of his way and bump hard into Etienne's chest. Even still, the stiff fabric of his gear brushed against her hand as he passed.

"What was that all about?" Etienne asked, letting his hands drop away from their steadying grip on her elbows.

She blew out a determined breath and kept moving toward the large set of open doors. She would have preferred a more out-of-the-way side entrance, but experience told her that in South City neglect ran rampant and even the best unlocking cantrip meant nothing to a rusted-out padlock. She simply lacked the upper body strength to contend with time-frozen steel. "The misdirection wards keep the humans from noticing us as long as we don't do anything to overtly draw their attention, like bumping against them or making a lot of noise nearby." The open doorway looked like an anthill some child had jiggled a stick in. She could feel the worry lines crease her brow.

Etienne watched with her. "And tell me why we're going in this way?"

She glanced wistfully at the side of the building. "The side doors are rusted shut."

She heard a sigh behind her, and his large hand caught her by the upper arm and steered her in that direction. "Etienne..." she began, her voice rising to an indignant pitch as he pulled her further from the busy front. Even through her coat and sweater she could feel each finger against her skin and it... wasn't unpleasant. He pulled his hand away a moment later and she surprised herself by fleetingly wishing for its return.

"Let your mercenary earn his keep, my lady," he replied, a hint of amusement coloring his voice.

They moved far away from the bustling fire crew across cracked pavement where dried weeds as tall as Winter's thighs crowded against her long skirt and stockings, leaving little barbed seeds as souvenirs. A steel door with lines of rust weeping tears of age down its face came into view, its padlock the size of her open hand, frozen into place by years of neglect. "I don't see what you think you can do to get that open," she said. "I've tried others like it before. Even the tumblers in the lock are rusted solid."

His eyes twinkled with amusement. "If I wanted to unlock it, I would be concerned." He grasped the padlock with one hand and she felt a magical pull between him and the leather gun rig he wore. He gave one swift twist and with a sudden, painful shriek the lock snapped off. Winter spun around to look behind, but no alarmed, uniformed faces looked their way. She opened her mouth to ask how, and then remembered the ease with which he carried that backpack. Sidhe strength, something she had never inherited. Something about the rig combined with his heritage granted him the full strength of a sidhe warrior. Etienne eyed the neglect-encrusted door. "This is going to make considerably more noise. Is there anything you can do?"

Winter pulled out her secondary focus from under the collar of her dress, a ring on a silver chain. The ring was a simple, slender, golden band with an oval opal stone set between two small diamonds. When she moved the ring, the sunlight played across intricate engravings on the inside of the band. It was Maria's wedding ring, once her great-grandmother's secondary focus, and now it answered to Winter. She quickly sketched out a simple sound-baffling spell. It would not cover up the percussion of a bomb blast, but the screech of a rusty door it could handle. She needed to conserve as much power as possible, as it took her time to renew her magic by drawing from the earth. This was only rift number one.

Etienne looked around until he found an old length of rebar lying in the weeds and then used it to pry up enough of the door to give himself finger holds. That did not make too much noise and Winter began to relax, to stop flipping her attention from the faerie knight to the firefighters and back again. The buzz from the fast-food coffee was fading into memory and weariness was creeping into her joints.

Then he dug his fingers into the divots he had made, and the rusted-out door screamed like a thousand tortured angels. Her hands flew up to cover her ears even as she spun about, expecting firemen to come running, wards or no. But as he dragged the door open just enough for them to slip through into the smoky darkness, no one came.

Etienne did not wave gallantly for her to precede him. His face grew serious, eyes wary of danger, determined to put himself between her and whatever lay beyond. He drew his blade and waited in the doorway, listening. The scabbard coiled itself up tight, removing itself as an obstacle for his legs. Winter noticed that while the sword's cross guard was unpretentiously imperfect, the blade itself was a work of art, the pattern welded steel rippled like water over stones—the smith who forged it placed his priorities on function over form. She had grown up around those whose lives depended on the weapons they bore, even though she herself went unarmed, and could view Etienne's blade with an educated eye. She knew from lessons learned at Erik's knee that the carbon beaten into the pattern welded steel made it not only durable but wickedly sharp.

The metal down the middle of the blade was like the swords he had practiced with only an hour ago. It was a pale silvery gold color with an iridescent quality, very beautiful, and the rippling of the pattern welding only enhanced its beauty. But the welded edges were darker, also pattern welded to a rippled beauty, though this beauty spoke to her of death, somehow. With a start, Winter realized why the edges were so much darker.

They were forged of mortal steel. Cold Iron with carbon beaten into it. Etienne was brandishing a killing blade, completely unlike the swords she had seen him use this morning while teaching Cian, something capable of delivering death to a lesser fae even without a mortal wound. He was prepared to slay other fae.

What was he expecting to come through the rifts? She knew from long experience it could be anything, from anywhere. What did Etienne know that she did not?

"I can't hear anything over the fire crew," he said evenly, and his words sank into the empty space beyond. Voices rang distantly to them, firefighters calling to each other in the gloom. She could smell the chemical nature of the smoke, but it did not burn her lungs. The wards were working.

"It's in there. Let's go before one of them finds it," Winter urged, hitching her bag higher on her shoulder and waited for him to move forward. She knew better than to put herself in front of an armed escort.

Etienne slipped through the doorway and after an uneventful moment Winter followed. Morning sunlight speared from the entry through the smoke into the vast space cluttered with rows and rows of dust and filth-shrouded machines, marching in ranks into the dark depths of the factory floor. Tall patchwork windows let in a grimy species of light, shot through with the occasional brightness of a vandal-broken pane. To their right and several hundred yards away the main doorway was a hive of light and activity and a roof of smoke hung low over their heads, undulating like a living thing as it made its constant escape through every opening it could find. Finally, Winter saw the flames, licking their way in a sulky fashion down at the far end of the factory and seeming to send up more smoke than actual heat—not even hot enough to attract salamanders or any other of the common fire elementals. Maybe something was actually going her way for a change.

She grimaced and nearly clapped her hand over her face. She just had to think that, didn't she?

Etienne's head turned left, the same direction Winter felt the pull of the rift. "That way," she confirmed, refocusing on the task at hand. "I think it's toward the back." They made their way in the dim light around the outer wall, avoiding the fire teams making their way deeper into the factory, until at last they came to a line of doors along what looked to be the back wall. They stopped at one with a partial sign that read, "—age Room 3." Winter could feel the rift beyond, a steady call of emptiness where the barrier between the realms had been ripped.

She brushed the backs of her fingers against the doorknob, tapping gingerly to gauge the temperature without committing to fully grasping what could be searing hot metal. "Blast," she whispered as she snatched her hand back. The ward that provided protection from heat left her with no difficulties determining temperature. The doorknob was hot, but not branding.

Etienne pulled his hand back from testing the door itself, apparently coming to the same conclusion. "What now?" he asked.

Winter gave a small frown as she considered their options. It did not take her long; they really did not have any. The rift had to be sealed as soon as possible. With firefighters in the building the chances of one of them stumbling across it rose dramatically. While she had little sympathy for those humans who played with preternatural fire and got burned—she considered their present circumstances and took a second to appreciate the irony of that thought—she could not in good conscience allow the innocent to come to harm through her own inaction. Especially since these innocents were protectors of the innocent, themselves. "We go in," she replied.

She dropped into a crouch, folding down as far as she could. Usually thoughtless about her nearly six feet of height, today was a day she wished for her sisters' smaller frames. Both of them had inherited their Grandmother Bridget's stocky Irish figure, neither being over five three, while she took after their tall, fae mother. Etienne watched her with curiosity and then understanding lit his face. He shifted his sword to his left hand as he dropped down beside her. He pushed aside her hand as she reached forward with it insulated by her black-felt coat sleeve. "Let me. I'm first in."

She nodded and ducked her head down even further as he gripped the doorknob and twisted it open.

Heat and smoke came roaring out of the room, loosening curls from Winter's bun as it blew them back and made the skin of her forehead feel desiccated even with the protection ward. She threw her arm over her face to protect it as the blast of hot wind whipped past, escaping into the cooler air of the factory, and then it was gone, the temperature and air pressure equalized between the two rooms. She rubbed her dry eyes and looked at Etienne, who was lowering his own arm and rising cautiously to meet whatever challenge waited in the storage room.

At some point the large room had been filled with racks. Winter could see the indentations on the concrete floor where they had been and drag marks gouged out from their removal, to whatever repurpose she could not guess. Now only a handful stood side by side at the far end of the room and that was where the heart of the fire blazed. Bolts of rotting fabric were stacked tight as cordwood, flames licking up the sides and roaring high, billowing smoke roiling in a low ceiling a few yards above their heads. Winter could see salamanders, their sinuous, flickering bodies winding in and out of gaps in the bolts. They were beautiful elementals, appearing as if all the colors flame could take swirled beneath their glassy hides; oranges and reds predominant, blues and whites and greens like ticking on fur. But she knew the lovely things would only be too happy to burn her to the bone and dance in her ashes. They were not malevolent; it was simply their nature. The only thing they feared was water, and they would flee to their native plane as soon as the firefighters arrived with their hoses.

"What caused the fire?" Etienne asked, raising his voice over the roar of the flames. Within the confines of the storage room the noise was constant and loud. His eyes were also on the twining salamanders and his sword was back in his right hand, but it was not pointed at them. He apparently knew better than to threaten an elemental with a weapon.

Winter moved further into the dry, heated air of the room, sweating under her felt coat but keeping it on to protect her skin. "There must have been a gas line running under the building. The power surge both ruptured it and sparked the explosion. Something similar happened during the San Francisco earthquake in 1906."

Etienne nodded, his face grave. "I remember. The whole city burned down."

Toward the back of the storage room it looked like someone had given up on order and simply threw random junk into the corner, maybe around the time the factory closed down. Shelving units rested on their sides and at angles against each other and a stack of crates that towered up into the undulating ceiling of smoke had partially collapsed, leaving shattered wood and machine parts scattered across the floor. Winter looked over the chaos and then gave out a small cry of shock. There was the rift, so large her eyes had wandered over it twice before seeing it for what it was.

She was used to seeing natural rifts as cracks or holes in walls, never more than a foot or two in diameter. She knew that theoretically they could be bigger. The Gate in the basement of Otherworld Books, while not a rift, stretched to the ceiling and was wide enough for two people to walk through side by side. But rifts were just tears in the fabric between worlds.

This was one heck of a tear.

The storage locker was taller than Winter and tilted at an angle, its one door swinging wide open. Beyond lay a chasm of darkness ringed by cold orange flames. With all the fire she had at first taken it for yet another burning.

Etienne let out a low whistle of appreciation. "It's been a while since I've seen one that big."

She turned to face him. "That's the largest I've ever seen."

He shook his head. "They've gotten smaller with the Age of Iron, but there was once a time when Faerie and the Mortal Realm actually overlapped in places. This is nothing, just a rift filling an opening. The first one I passed through when I was very young filled a valley; I came to the Mortal Realm by accident in my wandering." He shrugged. "Decided to stay a while."

She heard an echo of something in his voice, but it was too faint to identify. "How long ago was that?"

He hesitated a moment. "Six hundred mortal years."

The echo was pain and Winter felt the part of herself that could read the soul instinctively try to open, to want to find the source of the pain so she could soothe it, but she willed it closed. If he wanted to share it with her, she would listen, but his hesitation told her that it was private, and she did not know him well enough to pry. She had seen enough on her first search of his soul to know he hurt, but it was not a hurt for her to heal. That was sufficient. So, she moved the conversation along and stepped forward, picking her way through the debris to the locker. "So, I know this was caused by the surge we felt earlier and it's not the only one," she cringed internally at how her day was shaping up, "even if it is the biggest. Why now? After six hundred years, why do we have surges and a monster rift?" Sweat ran in a stinging line into her eyes and she wiped it away with her coat sleeve. Her skin felt tight in the heat and she began to worry a little about the wards. They could be overwhelmed by too much of whatever they protected against if they weren't strong enough, and her specialty was potions, not wards.

She looked back to see Etienne moving away from her, using his left hand to move shelving units aside so he could search behind them. Moisture beaded up and ran down his face, but he seemed to ignore it. "Wild magic is common in Faerie," he replied, and bent to poke the tip of his sword under a tipped shelf. "And it's my experience that rifts in the Mortal Realm connect with Faerie in some way or another."

Winter stood before the utter darkness of a rift between the realms that rose above her head and swallowed down a fleeting sense of vertigo. She was not going to fall forward and through it. Resolute, she dug into her bag and pulled out the spell chalk. Nine glyphs in the seal. "Actually, rifts can and do open up to anywhere." She looked the locker up and down, planning out the positioning of the glyphs as she took on her teaching tone.

He gave a small snort. "Does all of your experience tell you that?"

She snapped to attention and turned to where he continued his search. "Well, that was patronizing," she said, her voice tart.

He glanced back at her and gave her that twist of his mouth. "I do have a thousand years on you, and every rift I've ever passed through has either taken me here or back to Faerie."

She narrowed her eyes, face flushed with more than the heat, and turned back to her task, but kept talking. "I'm a wizard with access to the largest House Library in the world and I've done a little reading. I've also been sealing rifts since I was twelve and began my apprenticeship working in the clinic with Aunt Curiosity saving lives when I was fourteen, because all other hands were needed to keep this city together." She finished the first glyph and shot over her shoulder, "I may be only twenty-four, but I seal at least one, sometimes three or four, rifts a week and then clean up the mess. Many of those messes are not caused by fae. If you do the math, Etienne Knight, that means I've seen, sealed, and banished the results of more rifts in twelve years than you could have possibly hopped through in your lauded thousand."

Etienne raised his free hand in surrender. "You're right. I shouldn't have said that."

Winter turned back to the locker and began drawing the second glyph, cold orange flames licking at her hand. Sweat was running down her spine and she could feel the fabric of her dress cling to her skin. "Erik already treats me like a child. I don't need you to start, too." She loved the vampires like family, but a drawback to loving immortals, in her mind, was that they, especially Erik, would always see her in pigtails. In the end, if she had a mortal lifespan she would be a mere episode in theirs. It made earning their respect that much more difficult.

She heard his voice behind her. "I'm sorry. Bess always said I'm an ass when I'm edgy."

Grateful for a change in subject, she asked, "Bess?"

The silence thickened with the smoke above their heads, until she finally named the glyph to set it and turned to face the faerie knight. He was not looking around anymore. Instead he watched the smoke at the top of the tower of crates.

"What's wrong?"

He held up two fingers on his free hand for silence and strode over to the tower, tension singing through his body. He pressed his shoulder to the tower and shoved, and Winter could feel him pulling at the magic in his gun rig again. The crates groaned, tilted, and over the crackling of burning fabric and cracking wood she heard gibbering cries of panic.

They weren't alone in the room.

Etienne backed up and rammed his shoulder against the teetering tower, causing it to rock violently, and three bodies were launched from the concealment of the smoke-shrouded top crate to the concrete floor. Etienne put himself between them and Winter, concealing her and leading with his sword, and spoke to them in lilting Faerie Gaelic as they scrambled to their feet.

They were all three thick-bodied in a uniform way that made determining gender impossible, a little over five feet tall, and so filthy that the rags they dressed in were the same patchy gray tones as their lumpy skin. All three bore blackened axes with viciously jagged edges, as if their smith had forged them with sadism in his heart. The only color they wore were their floppy, slightly pointed hats, dyed in uneven shades of deep rusty brown.

Memory tugged at her for a moment and it was the color that dragged it to the surface. She knew that color well—it was dried blood. These were redcaps, a particularly violent breed of fae that was known to dye their hats in the spilled blood of their enemies. One pulled his soot-blackened rags down from where they had covered his nose and mouth in the smoke and replied to Etienne in a voice like grinding gravel, using his axe to gesture at the crates and the locker. How they could be the same language, Winter did not know. There was no lilt, no grace to his words, only aggression.

Etienne spoke again, gesturing with his free hand toward the locker and stepping aside to give them a free path while keeping his sword up in a defensive posture. Winter moved with him and the three snapped their attention to her, black eyes glittering as they wandered over how the sweat made her dress cling to her thighs in a way that made her think automatically of all three as male. The one on the right elbowed the speaker and rumbled something and the speaker made a noise that may have been a laugh. Whatever it was it made Winter pull her coat closer about herself in the heat of the room, feeling suddenly unclean. The exchange was not lost on Etienne, who spoke sharply and gestured this time with a sweep of his steel-edged sword. Winter made out a single word: "Unseelie."

Again, memory from long hours of childhood study in her family library surfaced and she knew why the redcaps looked at her with such predatory speculation. In the Unseelie Courts, the courts of the dark fae, the strong ruled while the weak sought protection or were preyed upon. She had read rumors of gangs of fae wandering the halls of the subterranean courts, looking for victims with no patrons to protect them. It did not matter that she was a woman—the redcaps would have given her the exact same regard if she had been a young man. They may even have looked at Etienne that way, had he been less forceful. It was that she was unarmed and looked weak, sick—like easy meat. She looked like a sidhe woman, vulnerable and tempting. And they thought Etienne was her patron. This was nothing about desire and everything about power. The look in their eyes clearly said, *'We could rape what is yours and there is nothing you could do about it.'*

The three redcaps leaned into each other, rumbling, eyes moving from her to Etienne and back again. She knew that look, that blossoming confidence, had seen it many times from the edges of therian gatherings just before the explosion of a dominance fight. They thought they could take Etienne. If they could, she was easy game for them. She might be able to surprise one with a banishing potion, but all three... Her heart began to race, and she backed away from all four males as she heard Etienne grind out, "*Merde,*" through gritted teeth and then blow out a steadying breath. She kept moving the short distance until stopped by the back wall. She was a noncombatant and had no business being in the field of battle. She felt Etienne pull on the magic of the gun rig and he was no longer standing there.

Winter had grown up preternatural and as such had seen more violence, or the results of it, in her life than most humans. On TV and in the movies fights were long, lasting several minutes and often covering a great deal of ground as choreographers and directors drew out as much drama from their storytelling as they could. But in reality, fights could be as short as a matter of seconds and as simple as the first one to make a mistake was the one bleeding their life out on the floor. That was when humans fought. Vampires moved faster than her wizard eyes could track, and therian, while stronger, were not much slower. She had never seen a sidhe fight; she had been inside that morning talking with Katherine instead of watching Etienne with Cian, and Cian had only been learning for six years—he could be expected to be slower. Before her now she could see what a millennium of experience looked like up against three vicious opponents.

Redcaps were foot soldiers and mercenaries and when not kept busy they turned to raiding. These three moved as a unit, converging on Etienne as he drove into them in a blur of speed and violence, and just that fast their attempt at unity exploded into chaos. Forced to slow to meet the three counter attacks, Winter could actually see his movements. Etienne met the leader's axe with a parry of his sword, the sound of the two very different metals clanging with strange dissonance. His left foot connected with the thick body of one and he let the motion of both the parry and the kick carry him around, grabbing up the third redcap by a fistful of rags with his left hand and propelling him with his full sidhe strength into the piles of burning fabric.

The redcap began screaming his horror even before the salamanders set on him.

Etienne was moving again before the redcap ignited, not even bothering to look back, and brought the mortal steel edge of his blade down in a vicious arc meant to split the redcap leader's head in two. It was barely parried in time and fresh blood soaked his cap and ran in a rivulet into one of his eyes.

Slapping wildly at the salamanders writhing over his charred body, the screaming redcap behind Etienne pulled himself from the fallen bolts and flames. Winter's skin tightened at how much agony he must be in, or perhaps redcaps were made of tougher fiber than others. She reached into her bag and pulled out one of the bright blue banishing potions. Whether she was trying to get it away from Etienne before it brought its flaming horror of a body into the fight, or trying to save herself from watching it struggle, she was not sure. Either way, she moved into a good position to throw the small glass bottle and tried something she had never done before. She threw the potion bottle with all the strength she had.

It reached the redcap's burning body and bounced off soft fabric and flesh.

Winter gasped in alarm and choked on smoke as the small bottle rolled across the concrete floor. So much for television. Jessie owed her a frappe if they made it out of here. She coughed again and heard Etienne cough, as well. The wards! She looked up at the smoke ceiling, now brushing the top of her hair. The wards were becoming overwhelmed. She shook her head and looked for the bottle. The fight had to end quickly, and they had to get that rift closed, but first she had to get that blasted bottle back. If one of the redcaps stepped on and shattered it, great; that would be one banished redcap. But if Etienne stepped on it, she had no idea what would happen. And she really did not want to find out in a burning room full of rapacious Unseelie fae.

Etienne was driving back the redcap leader and the unburned one and she spotted the bottle behind them, and behind it was the burning one, limping up behind Etienne with his axe dragging. Winter darted forward into the fray, hoping the burned one's eyesight had been damaged, and dove down just as she slid in between them, snatching up the bottle and rolling against the redcap's legs at the same time. Heavy and with a low center of gravity, this did not trip up the fae as she had hoped. It merely made it grunt and notice it had a closer target. It raised its jagged axe, and Winter uncorked the bottle with her sweat slicked hand even as she cried out in fear.

Metal flashed, and the redcap's head toppled off in a fountain of blood, his body collapsing downwards and back as lifeless meat. She looked to Etienne, but he had already turned back to his other two opponents. She coughed and dumped the potion on the new corpse, eliminating the evidence, and scrambled away until she found herself back against her safe spot at the back wall.

The redcap leader evidently decided they needed a change in tactics, because he barked an order to his fellow as he made a mad drive at Etienne. The other redcap broke away and ran at Winter. She grabbed at her bag, scrambling for a banishing—

"Down!" Etienne roared, kicking the leader back, and Winter was belly to the concrete before his echo died, her right elbow jarred numb from impact. She heard several sharp cracks, concrete chips scattered on the floor, and she smelled blood like a fine metallic mist. Momentum carried the redcap forward, and it came crashing to a stop up against her side. There was little left of its face from the chin up, and Winter scrambled back from the blood that poured from the devastating wounds to pool on the floor.

Where had its face gone? Winter turned her head to look at the wall behind her, where there were now large chips missing, but then her eyes widened as she felt a spreading warmth down her neck and across her scalp as it soaked into her hair…

She knew where the missing pieces were.

Her gaze moved to Etienne, fighting with the gun in his left hand. The voice of her sister Sorcha, who had been a police detective and died in the line of duty, kept running through her head, '*In like a penny, out like a pizza,*' over and over. Suddenly the shock and horror of it rose in heat from her belly and Winter threw up the cheap fast-food coffee.

She backed away from the mess she had made and glanced away just in time to see Etienne cut down the redcap leader. She gave a heavy cough and spat out soot. The wards were weakening by the second and they did not have long left, at all. Her eyes wandered back to the one Etienne had shot. She had not thrown up in the face of carnage since she had been sixteen. She had to admit, she was a little embarrassed, especially since as nightmarish as the gunshot wounds were, it was not the worst she had ever seen. Her hand found its way up into her hair, and her fingers brushed up against hard bits. She shuddered, and her stomach threatened to dry heave. That had to be it. She had been at hundreds of aftermaths, and on the fringes of violence, but never before so close as to have brain and bone and gore in her hair.

And then she saw movement and froze like a rabbit. The shot redcap's fingers were flexing. Etienne was coming her way, coughing and winded, and she looked up at him, her breath coming too fast.

Etienne simply nodded to her, and reached down, grabbed the redcap by its matted hair, and sliced its throat to the spine with his steel-edged sword. A fine line of smoke rose as the steel, mostly composed of iron, passed through fae flesh. "Bullets are still usually lead," he said, his voice gruff. "They won't kill a fae outright." And in the quiet after, Winter had the time to realize that until he had ordered her to drop, he had been utterly silent the entire fight. She was so accustomed to therian fights, which were half call-outs and taunting, or the duels she had seen her Grandfather Dermot and Erik or her many other friends engaged in, with all the banter and carrying on. She realized, watching Etienne clean his blade on the redcap's rags with a perfectly unexpressive face, that Etienne was not a cheerful duelist. He did not do this for fun or honor. He was a killer.

It made her feel both a little disquiet... and safer.

She gave him banishing potions to dispose of the two bodies while she sealed the massive rift, and they cleared out of the factory just minutes before the firefighters worked their way back to their storage room. Winter sat on the sidewalk in the morning sunlight and kept her arms wrapped tightly about herself while Etienne picked bone and brains from her hair, but there was only so much he could do short of a shower. With his help they dried as much blood up as they could, and she spent the rest of the day wearing a head scarf. Fortunately, most people were accustomed to Winter's eccentric mode of dress, so it earned her few stares.

Another sixteen rifts later and exhaustion ground through Winter's bones long after the sun had lowered below the Pacific. But at each site where they had encountered creatures, they had all been fae. Thank little green apples not all those encounters had been violent, though Winter had feared Etienne was going to strike the drunken dwarf who had patted her on the behind. In the end, though, all that one wanted was a little dance with a sidhe woman and he was content to be escorted back through his rift. Winter thought Etienne may have escorted him a little more firmly than was strictly needed.

All the creatures present were fae, and the magic emanating from each rift had an unmistakable flavor of Faerie to it. Winter was beginning to strongly suspect the surge of wild magic from that morning was also of Faerie origin—there was just a taste to it, that after running across it again and again over the course of the day she knew it was the same.

All the rifts finally closed, Winter left Etienne and Cian to Katherine's capable hospitality and set out for home. Part of her wished she could stay and enjoy an evening with Katherine's small court, but her night was far from over.

She stood under the pounding heat of her shower back at the House, uncoiling her long, blood-caked hair, and tried to work out her next move even as she worked out the smoke, gore, and chaos from her body. Ordinarily she would turn her suspicion on the newest fae in town, but Etienne was not only not a magician, he had been with her the whole time, and

Cian was an untrained adolescent. Granted, the faerie knight had been out-side when the initial tsunami had hit, but if the origin had been that close, she would have felt it, no question. That left Jonathan Moore and Himiko's mysterious sidhe consort, both supposedly powerful magicians, and though neither had given her any trouble before, there was a first time for every-thing. Her instincts were pulling her toward Jonathan. While she did not like having a sorcerer in the city, that was Himiko, not her consort, and it still left open the question of Jonathan's son Jeremy being this Prince Senán.

Her sister Sorcha had liked to say a good cop came equipped with what she called a 'bullshit detector,' and as much as they had not always gotten along, she had thought that Winter had one of the best she had ever seen. Most of it was her soul reading, but a lot of it had to do with the fact that as wizard of the city she was lied to a lot, so picking up lies in body lan-guage was second nature. Conveniently, a full-blooded sidhe, and most fae, could not lie. If they did, they would risk becoming foresworn and would lose not only status and honor but their ability to wield magic. However, they did engage in creative truth telling and could let you be-lieve whatever you liked. Lies of omission did not count.

Winter scrubbed at a particularly dense clot and shuddered when it turned out to not be a clot at all, letting the mass fall to join the small pile clustered around her pale feet in the swirling pink water. She compart-mentalized it with every other horror that battered at her increasingly fragile health and blew out a determined breath. Just one more of so many.

She needed to talk to Jonathan Moore, then, and she needed to do it be-fore the next tsunami. One more powerful than that last could rupture the Gate under Otherworld Books and she could not conceive of what sort of magical fallout would result from a disaster of that proportion. Since she had no idea when that might be, that meant she had to do it tonight. She ruthlessly stuffed down the small part of herself that whimpered for her bed, which was oh, so very close.

Tonight.

CHAPTER FOURTEEN

Winter was used to a certain degree of deference from the preternatural leaders, not just because she was a wizard, but because they knew her well enough to know she would not interfere unless it was important. If she called, they took her calls because there was an emergency. If she showed up, they cleared space in their schedules for her. They might fight with each other over pittances, but they gave her respect—by habit so far, though she knew habits could be broken.

So, when she had called to let Jonathan Moore know she needed to speak with him and his secretary replied in her cool, beautifully professional voice, "Mr. Moore is quite busy until after the first. Would you like me to pencil you in for a date in November?" Winter had stood there in her towel, unsure of how to respond. She had never met the sidhe lord personally. He had not been one of her problem children, not until yesterday. Like the principal of a troubled school, she had not needed to. Finally, she had told the woman, firmly, that he could expect her within the hour.

So, there she was. The chairs outside of Jonathan Moore's office were quite comfortable, which was a good thing, because Winter had been sitting in one for verging on an hour and a half. Apparently, her firmness had been less than impressive. The secretary in her smart suit was clicking away at her keyboard, her eyes occasionally flicking over in Winter's direction. She had tried three times to get her to schedule an appointment, but Winter could feel what must be him just beyond those double doors to her left. She told the woman she would wait.

Besides the clicking, the office was quiet enough for Winter to hear the roar of her own exhaustion in her ears. She sat up straighter in the chair, trying to not look too much like she was stretching her stiff muscles. Her eyes burned, her blinks becoming longer as the warmth and stillness sank further into her bones. She twisted, re-crossing her ankles and tucking her feet beneath her, and she caught her reflection in the night-black window behind her. It had to be an effect of the glass, because surely, she didn't actually look that ghastly? She had showered away the gore and the reek of smoke and chaos that the day had left behind, but soap and water could do nothing for her hollow cheeks and the rings under her eyes like domestic abuse bruises. She looked undead—fitting, this close to Halloween, but not appropriate for a meeting with a corporate CEO. Of course, neither was her choice of apparel—she did not own any little suits—but she cared much less for that. She looked back to the doors, willing them to open.

They didn't.

Her big canvas bag shifted when she repositioned, pressing the cool, hard weight within against her ankle. Sitting on the side of her bed at home, she had grabbed an energy potion out of the basket on impulse and shoved it into the depths. Why had she done that? Four of them in one day was insane. She had never had three in one day before today. It sat with a tangible presence at her feet and she wanted it. With every quiver of exhaustion, with every click of the secretary's keyboard, her fingers twitched to reach into the bag and wrap around the cool green glass. She swallowed convulsively. Maybe... just to get through this meeting...

The door to her right swung open and she snatched her guilty hand away from her bag strap. A tall man stepped into the outer office casually but neatly dressed for the weekend in a button-down shirt and jeans. His wavy, black hair was pulled back into a long ponytail, and as he passed he looked her up and down with curiosity in his cornflower-blue eyes, beautifully flecked with gold. Winter could see the softening about the edges of her perception of him that told her he was glamoured, mostly about his lower body suggesting he was hiding a weapon. Shifting to her magical sight for a moment she could see the matrix of the spell itself floating about him like a crystalline wireframe of deceptive simplicity. This was how wizards saw spellwork. She thought perhaps that it was how all magicians saw it, but she had only known wizards, so she did not want to assume. She raised her chin slightly and returned his regard with a small nod as she tasted his power. He was a sidhe, full-blooded, but younger than Etienne by her estimation. For a race that rarely crossed into the Mortal Realm, Seahaven was getting crowded with them.

Interesting.

Aodhán pulled his eyes away from the thin, young woman and made his way past the secretary into Midir's office. He pulled the door closed behind him and turned to face the great prince, who sat at his mahogany desk, ice-blue eyes riveted to his monitor. "Do you know you have a wizard in your antechamber, my lord?" he asked, crossing the large office.

Midir shifted his mouse and clicked, then made a noise of displeasure. "I am aware."

Aodhán moved so he could see the monitor and paused a moment to study the display. "Your Knave of Hearts is free."

"Ah! Thank you."

Aodhán took one of the comfortable chairs in front of Midir's desk and stretched his long legs out in front of him. He watched the other man play his game, his mind working. His employer was a puzzle box he had yet to solve and he was running out of time to tease him out. But, the question was, how much did he really need to unravel? He did not want to completely undo Midir—no, that would not suit his purposes at all. But he did need to find out more about the players in this game and Midir had been tight-lipped about that since this 'Summer's Get' had shown up. Aodhán had to step carefully. Midir was no stranger to the game and due to long history was cautious to the point of paranoia about being screwed over.

Considering that was exactly what Aodhán was going to do to him, he had every reason to be paranoid.

"So," he said, deciding to prod at this new angle, "is there a particular reason we're keeping a wizard waiting?" He thought there was a saying about doing that that involved ketchup… or maybe that was dragons…

Midir did not look up from his card game. "To start, I think calling her a 'wizard' is a bit of a stretch. She's little more than a child. But, to answer your question, she invited herself here and won't leave or make an appointment. I see no reason to reward her ill manners."

Aodhán turned this answer over in his mind. Midir, like himself, could not outright lie, but that did not mean he had to be completely truthful, either. And the great prince had millennia of experience at dancing around the truth. "How long has she been out there?"

The other man sighed and sat back, turning his attention to Aodhán. "Long enough for me to become bored watching cat videos. This is the third computer game I've played." He tapped his elegant fingers lightly across his keys and glanced at the office door with a small look of longing. "And I'm getting hungry."

A candid answer? He must have been holed up in here for quite a while. The obvious question, of course, was why he didn't just leave, but Aodhán held it back behind his teeth. For one, he did not want to hint to Midir that he was being so transparent—it would encourage him to fog the glass, and it was too important to Aodhán to be able to catch these few clear glimpses. Plus, as interesting as his potential range of waffling answers might be, the fact that Midir had let the presence of a wizard child tie him up in his office was itself the telling piece. Talk her down all he liked, the prince far preferred to evade her than confront her. Samhain was nearly upon them and Midir wanted to avoid anything that might even resemble a complication. So, he put on his most helpful smile and said, "Well, let's figure this out…"

Midir straightened in his seat, blond brows furrowing. "What is she doing out there?"

In the outer office, Winter struggled in a losing battle between the opposing tidal pulls of sleep and the energy potion. Exhaustion grinding in her bones, her eyes closing in ever-lengthening blinks, she kept sensing flickers of movement at the corners of her sight that proved to be nothing when she turned. And there was… there was a smell. Winter did not want to say it reminded her of her mother, but… she would have thought that Etienne or Cian would have smelled of Faerie, but they did not. She supposed they had been too long in the Mortal Realm. This, though… her mother had had this scent about her, her mother who had been half-wild and who her grandparents had needed to bind to the Mortal Realm with conditions, so she could not spirit away their son.

Her mother who had fled the moment those conditions were broken. Winter felt the edge of her old anger and pushed it aside. Now was not the time. It was never the time.

The secretary had now taken to giving her strange looks. Winter refused to pull out the green bottle and drink it down while the human woman looked at her like that. Her pride would not stand for it, no matter what the cravings begged... demanded... screamed for her to do. She tried pulling out her e-reader again. Katherine's newest vampire romance from her *Love Bites* series was on there and had been for months. Winter really wanted to read it, but so rarely got a chance to just sit still—now that she was being forced to, she couldn't concentrate on the words in front of her. She scanned the same paragraph six times without registering anything before she put the reader back in her bag.

Desperate to focus on anything else, Winter shifted to her magical sight again. Etienne was right. The glamour on the outside of the building was amazing, the structure like nothing she had ever seen before. She had not been able to spend much time outside studying it, remembering Etienne's story about Cian and the security guards and not wanting to repeat the experience for herself. But, if Jonathan Moore—or whatever he wanted to be called—was going to be rude enough to leave her out here, she would take advantage of his breach of the usual protocol in Seahaven as well as plain bad manners and take a good look at his glamour from the inside.

The secretary immediately disappeared from her sight, confirming Winter's belief that she was human. The walls and floor and ceiling around her took on the crystalline wireframe structure and opened to show her the layout of the floors and building around her—*that* she was not expecting. Digging her fingers with her short surgeon's nails into her now-invisible chair to fight the sudden sensation of being suspended high in the air, Winter looked around examining the layers of spellwork. Much of it was glamour, she could see that well enough, layers and layers of it, but the glamour rested on a base of magic. She saw the whole building in glowing outline around her and came to a stunning realization that stilled her breath for a moment—the black-glass tower was a faerie building, just like Mulcahy House only so much more massive.

How had he done it? She had signed in at the front desk and been escorted by a security guard who had swiped a card to give her clearance for the elevator to reach this level. She had felt no pulse of magic then, nor when the elevator had operated—nothing but the usual underlying buzz she normally associated with human electricity. Mulcahy House did not run on electricity, it never had. Power lines running out to the Point were a fairly recent phenomenon, mostly because they accompanied phone, cable and internet. The House did not like the electricity and had rejected it. Only a long series of negotiations and pleas with the House had resulted in working television and lines of communication, and even now those could be spotty.

Had Jonathan Moore somehow been able to integrate the magic of the faerie tower with human technology? And where had he gotten the sheer volume of power to build it in the first place? The implications made her head spin.

Mind churning, she saw out of the corner of her magical eye a blister in the glamour in the vicinity of the basement, far, far below. To an ordinary wizard, this would be a mere curiosity, something to observe and remember, but not really anything they could take advantage of. Wizards required counter spells to remove glamour, and there was not a counter spell in the world powerful enough to tackle what Jonathan Moore had laid down here. But Winter was at least a quarter sidhe, and while she was not able to cast glamour herself, that was limited to the Fair Folk alone, she could move and manipulate power. Without thinking, she reached out and probed at the blister, curiosity overriding caution.

The blister shifted, magic moving beneath it.

The door to Jonathan Moore's office opened and the beautiful-eyed sidhe stepped through. He glowed under her magical sight in the moment before she snapped back to normal. "Mr. Moore will see you, now," he said, looking at her with even more interest than before.

Winter pulled back from the blister and stood, hitching her bag strap over her shoulder. She gave a small nod to the secretary before slipping through the opening the man provided her as he stepped aside.

Jonathan Moore's office was spacious, with one wall entirely dedicated to windows. During the day it must have been filled with light. This late she could see the city laid out in lights stretching below them and skirting Mount Sarah, and it caught her eye for a moment. Not many buildings in Seahaven were this tall, so seeing her city like this was a treat she did not get often.

"Beautiful, isn't it?"

She turned to face the man who had spoken. He sat behind a large desk with a gleaming piano finish, his ice-blond hair trimmed short and neatly combed back from his face, his ice-blue eyes, so like her own, regarding her intently. She wondered fleetingly if they could be related. It had been one of the two conditions holding her mother in the Mortal Realm, that no one ask after her lineage, and surely that was the one which had been broken. It was impossible for any present at the binding, her grandparents and her father, to have broken the other one. She suspected it had been her father who had done it, in a moment without thinking, and that was why he never spoke of it, why his grief was so great. Even so, it was frustrating to not know half of her own bloodline.

Winter jerked her wandering thoughts back to the present. Her fatigue was getting the better of her. "Yes, you have a wonderful view." She noted he had remained seated when she entered and stepped up to his desk to hold out her hand to shake. "It's a pleasure to finally meet you, Mr. Moore." She kept her spine straight as she held out her arm, positioning herself in a way to force him up to his feet to meet her half way across his desk.

Let the games begin.

Jonathan Moore looked at her hand and then slowly raised his cold eyes to her face, letting the moment draw out. "Been a while since you met another magician?" he asked, dry amusement twisting the corner of his mouth.

Winter blinked once, and then felt heat creep into her cheeks as she pulled her hand back, cursing her fair Irish complexion for putting her embarrassment on such obvious display. Wizards did not casually shake hands with other magicians, or each other—skin on skin contact breached personal shields, making them vulnerable. But she had not met a strange wizard in years and had never met another breed of magician strong enough to be paranoid about touching. Winter was American and accustomed to being the only powerful magician in the room. She shook hands. Her gaze flickered over to the other sidhe, where he stood just behind Mr. Moore's desk. Those lovely eyes danced with mirth.

She was glad she could be so entertaining.

With a small noise she cleared her throat and tried to get her footing back. "Yes," she said quietly, "it has been some time. I am Winter Mulcahy."

"So my secretary informs me."

She ignored his rudeness and his dismissive tone. "Do you prefer to be called Mr. Moore or Midir?"

The cold pleasure still played at the corners of his lips. "If we're speaking of preferences, I prefer 'my lord.'"

Winter returned his amusement with her own arid humor. "This is America. We stopped using titles a while ago."

"And we are... what is that new word?" He looked back to his associate, who gave him an amused quirk of his brow, and then back to her. "Preternatural? It's one thing to play human, but among ourselves we don't care about such polite fictions as democracy and equality, now do we, Miss Mulcahy?"

Her jaw tightened, but she had to give him the point. Immortals, in her admittedly limited experience, did tend to get hung up on titles. Erik and Katherine ran their courts very informally compared to other vampires, but she had heard even them occasionally addressed as 'my lord' and 'my lady.' Raphael, the vampire lawyer based in Seahaven, and the Eldest Himiko held their courts to much stricter standards. "As you like, my lord." He had not offered her a seat, but after sitting for so long in his outer office she really would rather stand. It was very rude of him, all the same, and effectively showed his continued contempt of her authority. She needed to get some traction here, and fast. "What about your son? Does he answer to Jeremy or Senán?" She only had one piece in this game, so far—may as well play it.

The amusement flashed from the sidhe lord's face. If Winter had not been watching so closely she might have missed it. "I see that Summer's Get found his way to you, then." His lip seemed to curl up at the name.

"Do you mean Etienne Knight?" Even as tired as she was, she hesitated to mention Cian. Her frayed instincts told her not to. She did not have the energy to wonder why.

"He is also known by that name."

"Then, yes. He and his are under my protection." It was important to state that very clearly. If he wanted to get at Etienne and Cian, he would have to go through her—and to do that would be to challenge the balance in Seahaven. "Why call him 'Summer's Get?'" She had heard that some fae were often known by multiple names, earning them over their long lives, but that one did not sound complimentary.

Midir leaned forward in his beautiful chair and tented his fingers on his desk. This time his lip really did curl with the force of his disgust. "Because his mother is a whore whose passions burn as hot and as brief as summer itself."

Winter mentally rocked back at his vehemence. "I didn't think the fae judged based on love and sexuality."

He averted his eyes for a moment as they glittered with some emotion she could not decipher. "That is because you've never met the bitch."

She took in a breath to keep talking, and Midir was out of his chair and at her side, in her personal space, as fast as any vampire. She choked on her gasp and reeled back a step.

"What do you want, Miss Mulcahy? You wear my patience thin." He stepped forward into her, looming inches above even her height, the heat of his body radiating against her. She felt her pulse speed up with the threat of his sudden aggression, and her eyes flickered to his companion. The other man looked... intrigued?

Winter felt cold anger rise and used it to brace her spine, to set her feet on the thick carpet. She was a Mulcahy. She would not be intimidated. "I want to talk to your 'son.'" She emphasized her doubt of his relation to the missing prince. "I also want to talk to you about the magical instabilities lately." She waved her arm, purposely stirring an eddy of power, shifting it to taste.

"Talk to Jeremy all you want." The amusement returned, but he did not back up. "He won't thank you for sharing your 'crazy,' and he won't thank me for sending a skinny, badly dressed, busy-body his way."

Winter heard his words but was not really listening. She had been so tired… the familiar flavor of the magic in this building, the scents—they weren't familiar just because they reminded her of her mother. She had spent the whole day immersed in it. She raised her head from her thoughts and looked Midir in the eyes. "What are you doing?" she asked, her voice even. "What are you hiding in the basement?" Whatever was beneath that blister nearly filled the building's footprint.

He crossed his arms. "What do you mean?"

"You're causing the instability. The rifts leading to Faerie I've seen all over town today, the wild magic that nearly drowned me this morning, that blew them open in the first place, they all possessed a magical signature that underlay everything—and it's present here, as well. That cannot be a coincidence."

"And I suppose you'll tell me that it's too strong to be a residual trace. That instability washed over everything, you know."

She shook her head. "No. I don't have to. If it wasn't true, you would have said so." Midir's face clouded with anger, and behind him his associate put his hand over his eyes. What had she said?

Midir paced away from her, toward the window, and stood there for a moment looking out at the lights as if he was king of all he surveyed. He then turned back, the smile again on his face, now razor-edged and ruthless, his ice-blue eyes glittering. "And what of it, young lady?" He gave a small shrug and an even smaller laugh. "Are you going to wiggle your spoon at me? Don't look surprised, I know exactly what sort of wizard child you are—and what your specialty is capable of." He looked at the other man. "Perhaps she'll give me a rash with one of her decoctions."

The man with the beautiful eyes laughed.

Midir crossed the room back toward Winter, his steps slow, menacing. "You see, Miss Mulcahy, it doesn't matter what I'm doing. There is nothing you can do about it." He stopped, again standing within her personal space. "You have no power here."

She swallowed down her fear and refused to back down. She knew she was alone here with these men and terribly vulnerable, but she had to know what was going on, what he was doing to her city. She reached down and opened herself. After what had happened with Cian she knew Midir would be able to feel her reading his soul, so she knew she would only have a moment.

"What...?"

She saw... fragments of images that flitted about the edges of her vision, like puzzle pieces long lost from the set. No! The fragments skittered about, giving her little more than nonsense—rage, heartbreak, betrayal... oh, so much betrayal. But only hints, only vague impressions, nothing new and nothing tangible. She was having one of her off days. And then Midir's hand fastened around her arm, pain lancing up through her shoulder as he bruised her flesh in his grip. She could not catch the small cry of pain before it escaped her lips.

"This meeting is over. I need to speak with people who actually matter, now," he said, his voice sharp with anger as he jerked her toward his office door. He pulled it open and shoved her through, pushing her with enough force to knock her to the floor. She landed hard on her hip and bruised elbow, the carpet providing only so much cushioning. The secretary paused her incessant clicking. He turned to address her. "If she's not in that elevator in thirty seconds, I want Security to escort her bodily from the building."

Aodhán heard the secretary's muted affirmative through the door. That had been fairly productive. The identity of Summer's Get still meant nothing to him, but five centuries was a long time to be away from Faerie—to say he was out of the loop would be a gross understatement. That Midir seemed to know the man's mother was interesting, but who she was exactly and why she elicited such a strong response in him was now a new mystery, one he would tuck into his mental pocket and see if it would prove useful.

However, what seemed to be the most intriguing was the wizard child. He had been five centuries in the Mortal Realm, squiring his lady through her magical circles. He was a magician himself and knew intimately what wizards were able to do and not able to do, and interacting with power like it was sticky taffy was not a wizard ability. Just looking at her, even as sick as she appeared, he could tell she was not pure-blooded. The corner of his mouth twitched. So, the wild rumors they had heard about the Mulcahy wizards breeding with anything that crossed their paths were panning out. If she was not at least half fae, then neither were his twin babies.

But that flare of magic at the end…

Midir crossed to his bar and poured himself a finger of bourbon. He stood, sipping the drink, his eyes distant.

Aodhán came and stood at the other end of the bar. "What magic was that, my lord?" he asked the great prince. Something had been… familiar about it.

Midir was quiet for a few minutes before responding with, "I've never seen the like."

"What was she doing?"

He took another sip. "It was as if she opened me like a box and was rummaging around inside." He looked into the amber liquid as if he could scry the answers within. Finally, he said, "I need to know more about this wizard child. This close to Samhain I cannot afford any complications."

Aodhán wanted to know more, too. "Rumor has it she runs a clinic out of a shop in the Historical District. I'll get the address and we can go look into it after we grab a bite to eat."

Midir raised his eyes and regarded him for a moment. Aodhán kept himself relaxed, helpful, until the other man nodded. "Yes, let's do that."

Aodhán gave Midir a small bow and headed out of his office.

Winter was on her feet and in the elevator under the secretary's haughty glare—she was sure the woman was counting—in well under thirty seconds, but her hands were shaking so badly she had to push the button to the lobby with the knuckles of her clenched fist. The doors closed with a whisper, and she wrapped her arms around her quaking core, fighting the burning humiliation that made her eyes swim with unshed tears. Her lip quivered, and she clamped her hands over her mouth, stifling her traitorous weeping. If she started now she would never get herself back together and she refused to flee the building sobbing.

The doors opened at the lobby and she stepped out, her soft-soled shoes surprisingly loud against the gleaming floor in the silence. The guards at the round desk in the center all looked at her and one spoke to the mic on his shoulder, too quietly for her to make out the words, but his eyes never left her. She did not think it possible for her cheeks to burn any hotter, but they managed to exceed her expectations. To her horror a tear escaped and ran down one cheek, threatening to bring the rest pouring with it. She braced her spine and clutched her bag strap close and made her brisk way out of the building.

Winter pulled her car door shut, enclosing herself in silence and steel. Her breath sounded harsh in the confines of the cabin, coming too rapidly, and her teeth were beginning to chatter. Her hands shook so badly that when she gripped the steering wheel it translated into shuddering from her hands to her shoulders. She wrapped her arms around herself again and rested her forehead on the wheel. How was she going to get home like this?

Out of the corner of her eye she could see her faded-purple canvas bag. She turned her head and just looked at it. Her bag... The next thing she knew she was digging through it, shoving things aside with no regard for delicacy or order, mouth salivating, until her hand closed around cool glass. She pulled the long green bottle from the bag, clawed the stopper free, and drank down the foul-tasting potion with both hands clenched. Energy filled her, burned through her veins, driving away the violent shaking... and bringing a new violence of its own.

The nausea struck like a hammer. Winter scrabbled for the door handle, engaged it and rolled out of the car to her knees just as the body of the potion and what little else she had left in her stomach came up with crippling force. All she could do was kneel and dig at the asphalt with her fingertips. She had finally overdone it and she knew it. A part of her had known it even as she dug the potion from her bag and had not cared. She threw up long past the emptiness in her belly, past the burning bile, until it was the punishment of dry heaves wringing out the stolen energy from her muscles and bones, leaving her limp and clinging to the side of her car seat, gasping for breath in the moments between abdominal surges.

She heard male voices coming from the direction of the building. She had parked up against what few other cars were in the lot, clustered around one of the lights. Winter had lived in Seahaven her whole life and knew better than to park in the darkness. She did not know if the voices were office workers or security guards come to humiliate her further, but either way she did not wish to be found like this. She dragged herself back up into the driver's seat and pulled the door shut again. The exhaustion had returned like a living thing seeking to devour her, but there was nothing she could do except fight it and make her way home. By some miracle she did not drop her keys from her shaking fingers and got the Bug started. She turned the AC on full, blowing chilled air onto her flushed face, and backed the car out of the space to begin her long, defeated journey back to the Point.

Winter found herself again pausing to lean on the massive oak front door of her home, tracing her fingers over the elaborate carving. She turned the handle and pushed it open. The door was never locked. She was not entirely sure the door even had a lock and was far too tired to look for one, now. No one besides the family ever came down the mile-long drive to the House, anymore. The Mulcahy family owned the entire Point, all the way to their mailbox on the outer road. Besides that, the protections on the House itself were impenetrable. No one not invited in by a family member could get in. The House itself would not let them enter.

As usual, she was greeted with complete silence. Soft lights came up as she entered, lights she knew did not light for her father. She did not know if he had told the House to stop bringing them up for him, or if the House had forgotten he was here. The thought made her chest clench. She moved to the foot of the great staircase and slipped off her bag and coat, her third coat this week, leaving them on the last step. She gave the coat a small scowl. She had rubbed at it with a napkin in the car, but she was fairly sure she had gotten sick on it somewhere she could not see. Her dry-cleaning bill this week was going to be ugly.

She made her way through the library to where her father sat, unmoving. He had not touched the soup she had left for him before going to Moore Investments. "Papa, you need to eat," she murmured with more habit than force.

He kept his face turned toward the window, his hands unmoving.

Winter pulled up one of the ottomans and sat on it, facing her father. "Papa, I need your help. Jonathan Moore, the sidhe lord Midir, is doing something... I don't know what... but it's causing the instability we felt this morning." She watched his hands, his face. Nothing. "Papa, we have to do something. He's going to tear the city apart." She could hear the panic creeping into her own voice. She watched him. Nothing. She reached out and took his hands, giving him a small shake. "Listen to me, please! Papa, people are going to die. I know... I know you can't do anything, but you have to give me permission to do something. To make an alliance with Erik or..."

She felt his hands move against her own and pulled away to let him speak. He flexed his long fingers in slow, halting movements, like clearing his throat after his very long silence, and then he signed in sluggish, methodical words, *"Let him do what he wants."*

Winter felt her eyes widen as his meaning passed over her like cold water. "Papa?" She looked at his face, and his dull eyes were turned to face her.

His hands fluttered again. *"Let it burn."*

She gasped and stood, her heel barking painfully on the edge of the ottoman. She tripped backward, weariness and shock making her clumsy, but righted herself and faced him down. "How could you?" she asked in a whisper, afraid that if she said it too loudly that his horrible words would become true. "How could you say that?"

"They're all dead. We're dead, too. No one cares. To hell with this place. Let it burn."

His hands, his blasphemous hands kept moving. She had wanted him to say something, anything; now all she wanted was for him to shut up. "They died so this place can live," she replied, raising her voice. "While you hid away in the House for twenty years, they all died heroes, fighting for what they believed in." He turned his eyes away from her, back to the window. "Don't you look away from me! I know you can hear me. All you cared about was that mother left." Rage was rising up, fueled by her frustration, her humiliation, by a lifetime of grief. She choked on a harsh laugh. "How can I even call her 'mother?' Tersa never cared about us. The three of us were just byproducts of her marriage to you."

Winter paced away and back again. Colin was still looking out the window, his hands still, a new tear marking its way through the salt tracks on his cheek. She did not care. "You abandoned us, just like she did. You know who raised us? Grandma and Grandpa, and vampires. Papa, are you listening? You left us to be raised by vampires. You never cared enough to wonder if we were loved or being given good guidance—all you cared about was that your wife left you because you made a mistake, and you've spent twenty years wallowing in self-pity. You're negligent and self-indulgent."

Her father's eyes closed.

"Meanwhile, I'm giving everything for this city. My sanity, my health... look at me. Papa, look at me!"

He did not.

"Fine. You don't care about anything outside yourself. I understand that. But know I'm killing myself for the people of this city. A little bit more every day." She hesitated, because even in the midst of her rage she was afraid to say it out loud but pressed on. "I'm addicted to the energy potions, but I would rather be the one to burn."

He still would not look at her.

Winter shook her head in anger and disgust. "If you want to sit there in your dirty robe, that's your choice. But I refuse to have let everyone—my sisters, my cousins, Grandpa and Grandma—*everyone* to have died in vain. I will not dishonor their memories by sitting idly by and letting this city fall. So, to hell with you, Papa." She turned on her heel and stormed out, refusing to watch his hands anymore. If that was all he could say, then fine, let him talk to himself.

She found herself in the echoing expanse of the warm kitchen. Alone. She was shaking violently and did not know if she had begun again or simply had never stopped. She looked and saw Maria's Great Book still holding court on its stand. She had forgotten to put it up that morning. The shock of her carelessness was the last she could take. A choked sob escaped her mouth, and another. Winter tried clasping her hands over her mouth, but they kept coming, one after the other, until she was kneeling on the floor, tears of rage and humiliation warring with her need for self-control.

It was hours before she slept.

CHAPTER FIFTEEN

Aodhán and Midir stood in the Historical District in the cold rain. The back door of the clinic was protected by several wards, but Aodhán watched as Midir casually teased them aside. Breaking them would have alerted the caster—that was half the point of these types of wards, the other half being to destroy anything magical in nature inside the building in the event of a chance break-in—but she was young and inexperienced while the great prince had been practicing his art for longer than Aodhán knew. He did not know Midir's exact age; that was something no faerie knew about themselves, or really cared about, given the variable ways time flowed within the Faerie realms and the fact that most of them honestly did not care to be so precise with... well, anything. Time, borders, sexuality, names, sometimes even genders—it was all very flexible to the fae.

What he did know about Midir, though, was that he was one of the oldest of Dagda's sons. Dagda was High King of all Faerie and a most prolific breeder. His sons were numerous, and powerful, and most of them were kings of their own realms. Aodhán's own father was a son of Dagda, one of the middling ones. But with age came power, and Midir was so old it seemed he had always been one of the power players of Faerie.

But Midir was not a king. Had never been a king, as far as Aodhán knew. His brothers had seen to that.

Midir pushed open the door and they both stepped in out of the rain. It was dark and quiet, but the darkness did not matter to their sharp eyes. Aodhán closed the door behind them, careful to keep it from clicking shut, and strained his ears to listen for company. Midir was already moving into the room, apparently not caring if they were alone, but Aodhán did. It was not that Aodhán feared a confrontation—he simply wished to be prepared when it came. But no footfalls, no sounds of breathing other than his own or Midir's greeted his ears. Nothing but the sounds of music and cheerfully raised voices muffled by the thick, brick wall. It sounded like a party was in full swing next door. Aodhán relaxed.

Midir had sat down in the office chair and was opening and rifling through drawers in the desk that sat next to the thickly beaded curtain. Aodhán moved to the set of file cabinets beside it and opened one at random. "Finding anything interesting?" he asked.

Midir pulled out a thick leather book and opened it with interest, then closed it after a moment and tossed it back in the drawer. "She has no business acumen. That's full of expenditures for supplies and records of procedures, but no accounts receivable."

Aodhán pulled out a folder that proved to be a therian rabbit's medical record. His gut clenched at the extent of her injuries as he scanned the notes written in tight, neat handwriting. Wolves had brutalized her; the writer noted the rabbit was young, she had gotten too scared… He felt his jaw tighten because he knew what would come next. Rabbits, being prey animals, had very few ways to defend themselves from predatory therian. Their primary defense was to change their scent from fear, which made them smell tasty, to arousal, the theory being that it was better to survive a rape than to be eaten alive. But there were ways it could go wrong; excessive fear could flip the scent back over again and this little rabbit had found that out. She had not been sure how many wolves there had been. He felt his eyes widen. Had not been sure? How had she been able to talk? Aodhán flipped through the record, skipping past the horrors written there, and found the end—the rabbit had survived! He shook his head in wonder. "I think the wizard is treating them for free," he said.

"What makes you say that?"

Aodhán closed the file and waved it to make his point. "This is a rabbit. The local hutch is notoriously short on money, but this girl was treated for life-threatening injuries. That sort of surgery isn't cheap." He refiled the rabbit's folder. "Whatever this wizard child is, she's a good physician. I've seen therian die from lesser wounds than this rabbit suffered."

Midir made a dismissive noise. "Therian have so many varying levels of power—who's to say she isn't just very strong? They'll heal themselves without assistance if they can shift enough times."

Aodhán waved his hand in a gesture granting the great prince his point. But he knew he was right. He had not recognized the rabbit's name and he prided himself on knowing the power players in Seahaven. She was not one of the hutch's Matron's Assistants or Odd Bunnies, their alphas, which meant she was less able to heal herself of grievous wounds. No, the little rabbit should have died.

He looked around the small clinic. And if the wizard was performing these surgeries in this room, it was nothing short of miraculous. There were counters and cabinets, a double steel sink and an examination table, and what looked like a few pieces of medical equipment, but that was it. This was not a surgical suite. The floor was smooth concrete with a drain that reminded him of his lady's 'play' rooms, though he was willing to bet the wizard child did not play such bloody games.

However, the place also had the clean smell of disinfectant and the surfaces gleamed in the low light.

Aodhán moved past the large, heavy table in the center of the room, and a map that took up an entire wall caught his eye. It was covered with red marks and more tight, neat writing. "This is curious," he said.

"Indeed, it is."

It was not Midir.

Aodhán whirled to face the man who spoke with a clipped British accent, standing framed in the now-open doorway. Midir rose from the office chair, apparently as surprised by the man's appearance as he was which led Aodhán to wonder: who could sneak up on two sidhe? He looked the man over, from the cruel twist of his smile in the darkness to the rain drops that glittered in his dark hair and across his broad shoulders. He was mortal, a magician. From the way he held himself he was a man used to the power of his body, used to using it against others. Aodhán knew the type well. It reminded him of his older brother. He felt his gut harden in instant dislike and pushed the sensation away. Politics had little to do with personal feelings and he knew next to nothing about this stranger.

"I do not believe we have met, sorcerer," said Midir, his voice smooth.

Sorcerer. Aodhán looked more closely at the man, and now that he was looking for it could see the traces of the demonic interlaced with the man's own magic, strengthening him. Those traces trailed off and away from him to the source of his power, whatever item symbolized the pact he held with his greater demon. How could he have missed it? But he knew the answer to that question right away; his experience with sorcery was... unique.

The sorcerer moved a few feet into the room, black eyes gleaming as they shifted from Midir to Aodhán and back again. "No, indeed we have not," he replied. He looked at Aodhán and that smile widened. "'Curiouser and curiouser.'"

Midir gave him a blank look, but Aodhán frowned. "Quoting Lewis Carroll?"

The sorcerer looked about the room, including the other two men in the sweep of his eyes. "And doesn't being what we are make us all inhabitants of Wonderland? We *are* all mad here, you know." He kept his right hand in his coat pocket while his left held an eagle-headed cane. Aodhán was a betting man and his money said there was a focus object in there. It could be a gun, but this man did not strike him as the type who would want to finish his prey so quickly.

Midir looked annoyed. Aodhán knew he did not like missing cultural references. "In that case, whom do we have the pleasure of addressing?" He looked like that pleasure was dubious, at best.

The man waved the cane in a negligent fashion. "That is not important. All that really matters is that neither of you are supposed to be here."

Aodhán did not move his attention to Midir, nor did he feel the great prince's gaze on him. They were not children to share a guilty look. But he did move further away from both the wall and the central table to give himself more room to maneuver. This backroom clinic was not set up for a fight. Something occurred to him, and as he moved he spoke. "Interesting that you point that out, considering I didn't hear you using keys to get in here."

"Well, since you gentlemen so kindly left the door unlocked behind you, there was no need."

"And you knew that because…?" Aodhán let his question trail off.

"Because he was watching the clinic." Midir supplied. "Watching us."

"Well, now, that truly is curious." Aodhán's voice took on a slight mocking tone.

The sorcerer's smile slipped. Apparently, he could not take what he dished out. Aodhán filed that away in his mind. "I have a vested interest here, sidhe lords, which is more than I can say for you."

Aodhán turned his head to address Midir but kept his eyes on the big man. "In other words, he's not supposed to be here, either. The Mulcahys don't run with sorcerers, or their demons."

"Oh, what little you know," the sorcerer replied before the sidhe prince could. He looked to the wall above the desk, where personal pictures hung in a wild assortment of frames. "You have no idea the ties that bind me to this family." His voice was low, intense. He was no longer smiling. His eyes came back to Midir. "What do you want here?"

Midir was quiet a moment, and then, "The wizard child came to see me today. She performed a strange magic that I have never seen. Perhaps you can enlighten me."

The sorcerer smirked. "The Mulcahys are a muddled lot. There hasn't been a pure wizard in that line for generations. It could have been any-thing."

"This felt like she was looking inside me and rummaging around."

The man's dark brows twitched up. "You felt that?" His eyes moved back to the wall of photographs. "She's poorly trained," he muttered, then continued in fuller voice, "What she did is called 'soul reading.' It's a tal-ent she inherited from her paternal grandmother."

Aodhán kept control of his face. She was a soul reader? Fascinating. That was an ability he knew something about. He'd simply never felt it so strongly before.

Midir frowned. "What can she do with it?"

The man gave an elegant shrug. "It depends on how strong she is. She should see impressions made on your soul; images, intense memories, even intentions if you feel strongly enough about them." His smile widened. "She could read you like a book, or more correctly a well-annotated photo album, flipping through your sins in full color. She could even see things long forgotten, for the soul always remembers."

Midir frowned harder. Aodhán was not happy about the prospect, himself. He knew more than most how it might be used against them. "Where did you say she got this ability? Her grandmother? Where does it come from?" Midir demanded.

The sorcerer chuckled and shook his head. "Now, now, that's not how this game is played."

Midir's cheeks began to flush with rage. Aodhán jumped in, trying to avert disaster. "What are we playing, then? 'Show me yours, I'll show you mine?'"

"Close. We're playing 'Reciprocity.'"

"Fine. What the hell do you want?" Midir's voice was sharp with his rising anger.

Aodhán did not clap his hand over his eyes, but it was a close thing.

The man's eyes moved to Aodhán as if he was waiting for him to do just that, then went back to Midir after a moment. "What do I want?" he echoed. Aodhán wished the sorcerer would stop teasing Midir—it never ended well. "I want the two of you out of this clinic and to keep your hands off the Mulcahys." He stepped aside, giving them access to the open doorway and the rainy night beyond.

"What is your interest in the wizards?" asked Midir.

"That is my concern, not yours."

Midir frowned hard, sizing up the sorcerer with wary eyes, and Aodhán looked from man to man, his mind fretting as he tried to work out what each would do. He did not want to get into a fight in here—the space was limited and there was a small court of vampires having a party right next door who would be sure to hear the commotion and come running. And even though vampires and therian did not stand a chance against magicians, someone would be sure to run and tell the wizard child.

He had to swallow his own frustration that Midir's temper and this sorcerer were going to combine to lose him this opportunity to learn more about the players in this game, but he knew well how to bide his time. Even when it was not on his side.

Midir finally nodded. "Come along, Aodhán." He moved toward the door.

Aodhán nodded to the sorcerer as he moved past into the rain. After the darkness of the clinic the parking lot courtyard seemed bright under the streetlights. He watched as the man pulled the door closed behind them and locked it with keys he pulled from his pocket. The lights caught the silver wings that swept through his demon-black hair and the fine lines at the corners of his eyes. When the man pulled the wards back into place with apparent practiced ease and turned to face them, Aodhán realized with a start that his eyes were not black at all, but midnight blue. The color was unusual, even among the fae. He motioned to the wards on the door to cover his surprise. "Do that often?"

The sorcerer's eyes flickered in the direction he indicated and returned. His smile was cold, and he replied with silence.

"Now, tell me, what sort of magic is soul reading?"

The man turned his attention to Midir. "Soul reading is the province of demons and angels. Take what you will from that." He turned and began to walk away.

"Wait!" Midir moved after him. "How does this relate to her?"

The sorcerer looked over his shoulder. "That is another piece of information, and you have nothing more that I want. Good evening, gentlemen."

They watched the man disappear into the rain. Aodhán could hear the creak of Midir's teeth as he ground them together. "At least now we know what she was doing," he said.

"Yes," Midir ground out. "She was trying to discover my plans—and she may very well have succeeded." He headed out toward where they had left his driver, his long legs eating up ground with each stride.

Aodhán thought that over as he fell into step beside. "No, I don't think she did. She's too inexperienced and her poker face is complete shit. If she had seen anything worth seeing in you, it would have shown earlier."

"But she has the potential. She could ruin everything."

Aodhán had to grant half that point. He thought Midir's paranoia might be going a little far, though, to be honest. She was a little bottle-filler and by the look of her she was taking too many of her own potions. What could she do, really? "Well, what do we do, now? We just agreed—"

Midir stopped and turned. "We agreed to something?" he asked, his expression wry.

Aodhán thought for a moment and smirked.

Indeed.

CHAPTER SIXTEEN

"I thought you said the place would be deserted."

"It usually is."

Lana walked with Senán through the halls of Moore Investments and hoped the nervous whine in his voice wouldn't carry, but so far, so good. Three things struck her as strange... well, besides the crowd in the big office building late on a Saturday night. The first thing was that whenever they passed an office cluster or cube farm, very few people were actually working. They were mostly just hanging around, like a low-key office party, and none of them paid her and Senán any mind. Admittedly, she had never worked in an office, but shouldn't they be, well, doing what they were being paid to do? She knew if she just stood around at the club talking with the other strippers she would get fired.

The second was that very few of them were actually human.

Gathered around a snack machine were three people dressed in what she thought of as weekend office casual; jeans and button-down shirts. But she could see their true forms like after-images. The big, thick-set man crouched awkwardly as he tried to shove his arm through the dispenser slot had the ghost of his real self rising high above him—he was a jack-in-irons, gnashing his tusks in frustration and looking strangely naked without his chains of trophy heads. Lana guessed they weren't allowed in the office. The short man smacking the side of the machine was a redcap, and the thin-necked woman offering advice in a nasal tone was really a hag. Unseelie fae, all of them.

Being Unseelie herself she was neither alarmed nor uncomfortable, just wary. Midir the Proud was known to associate with both sides, Seelie and Unseelie, so had she seen them at his holdings in the Faerie Realm she would not have been surprised. But everywhere she looked there were Unseelie and wild fae that belonged to neither faction in human seeming—this kind of concentration in the Mortal Realm was just freakish.

Add to that the layers and layers of glamour surrounded by that iron fencing, and it all became highly suspicious. But of what?

And then there was the third thing. Like the ghost of a scent left after a lover has gone, or the fragment of a song half remembered, Lana felt a pull just at the edges of her perception. If she had not been looking so hard for anything out of the ordinary and finding it everywhere, she might have missed it. She knew what that pull meant. A rift, and it was coming from somewhere below her. She had followed just such a pull into the Mortal Realm in her search for Midir.

She followed Senán into the elevator and he swiped his key card. "Will that give us access to the basements?" she asked.

He pulled his hand back from the upper rank of buttons and gave her a curious look. "Yeah, sure, but I thought you wanted to get into his office?"

Lana pursed her lips and looked at the ranks of buttons as the elevator doors slid shut on their own with a whisper of air. She was operating on guesswork and instinct, and while her guess wanted to take her up to Midir's office on the off-chance of finding something useful there, instinct was pulling her down with the rift. She nodded to herself and reached over to push the lowest of the basement buttons. Her instincts had never let her down before.

"All that's down there are the servers and crap."

She passed him a sly smile as her mind churned and then she dug into her purse, pulling out a jump drive in the shape of a *neko* kitty. "And this bad boy will work better plugged directly into the servers instead of into your father's computer."

Senán's gray eyes lit up. "Awesome." He reached out and tried to take the drive, and she pulled it away. He gave her a petulant frown.

"I'll take care of this, babe," she said as she tucked it into her jeans pocket and leaned up to kiss his pout away. It was so hard to not bite the moron, but she resisted. All that was on the drive were some video clips for a porn audition tape one of the other girls at the strip club wanted her opinion on. Lana thought she needed some work.

Lana was also hungry, and it was shortening her temper. Saturday night was the busiest night of the week at the club and as a succubus Lana fed well on the sexual energy. But she had begged the night off for this chance to break into MI. She had planned on working last night and bringing someone home for a heavier feed to tide her over. But once decided on the plan Senán had become fucking nervous and clingy and had wanted to stay with her. Since he tended to be a possessive asshole when she stripped she could not take him to the club, so she had had to take off Friday night, too. Only her status as a top-earning dancer kept her employed this week.

Too bad it was doing nothing to feed her.

The elevator doors slid open and cold air rushed in, making Lana think there might really be servers down here as they stepped out. A long, blank hallway stretched out on either side, arcing away from them seemingly in a circle of naked concrete. The pull of the rift was no stronger—which was odd; if they had gotten closer it should have increased—but it had changed direction, coming from behind the elevator now.

Senán was looking up and down the hall. "So... which way?"

Lana turned right, figuring they only had the two directions, and strode with purpose down the featureless passage. She did not look behind her but smirked with satisfaction when she heard Senán's quick footsteps rushing to catch up.

The hall was lit at infrequent intervals by ugly fluorescent lights—apparently, they were on some sort of weekend power saving plan down here. She moved from pool to pool of yellow-green light in the concrete hallway and was reminded of the stone corridors of the Unseelie court she called home. With all the Unseelie fae in the building it was a comparison that did not make her comfortable, that made her painfully aware that she only had a moron ignorant of his true heritage to stand by her. If they chose to hunt her in these halls there was little he would do to protect her. She was pretty sure Senán would piss himself and run if he knew what was really upstairs.

No, her patron, her Unseelie prince, her protection in the corridors of the court, was gone. She mourned for her sense of safety, even though she did not mourn the man. She had only her cunning and her knives to protect her, now. She flexed her forearms slightly, feeling the reassuring grip of her wrist sheaths hidden under glamour and the sleeves of her jacket. It took some fancy maneuvering to keep Senán from noticing them—unlike her he was a full-blooded sidhe and would be able to feel by touch through her glamour, even if he could not see through it. If he felt them she would have to come up with a song and dance to explain them, but as the blades were sidhe steel and an iridescent, silvery-gold color not found in mortal metals, she did not want to mess with it. Oh, he would believe whatever bullshit she fed him—he was an idiot, after all. But he had smart friends, and she did not want them asking him smart questions when he talked to them about it, which he would because he was an idiot.

They came to a set of glass doors on their left and through them Lana could see row upon row of rectangular boxes with blinking lights and miles of cables streaming out behind it all in a river of plastic-coated color. Cold air leaked out, tickling her hands and cheeks. Senán swiped his card over the box beside the door and pulled the door open, letting the chill escape in a rush. Lana frowned. The pull of the rift was not coming from inside. She turned away and kept moving down the hall. It was coming from her right.

"Where are you going?"

"Trust me," she said over her shoulder.

"But the servers are in here."

She stopped and turned around. "Jeremy, would you just trust me?"

He looked confused but let the door fall closed and followed her. "What's this way?"

"Something good."

"Better be," he muttered.

She ignored him. The pull was getting no stronger. Very strange. But a few hundred more feet brought them to another door on the right, the interior wall. This door had no windows, was simply blank steel with a swipe box beside it. But when she stopped she could feel the weight of wards all around the door and shifted to her magical sight. They were wickedly complex and looked to her poorly trained eye like there may even have been more than one magician behind them. Shit. What was she going to…?

Senán reached past her while she was thinking, swiped his card and opened the door in one practiced motion.

"Fuck!" she yelped. The wards exploded, shooting like stars to their caster…

He flinched. "Jesus, what?"

Lana waited another moment, but nothing else happened. "Just get in," she said, pushing him ahead of her into the dark room. If there were going to be any more surprises she wanted them to blow up on his idiotic ass. They might only have minutes, now.

"What the fuck was that all about?" he demanded, the whine back in his voice.

She set her teeth against it. "Just feel for the light switch." She could have told him he tripped a silent alarm or something, but she did not want him freaking out. Not now. Because when they stepped into the room, the pull of the rift changed, and she knew why it had been so strange before.

It had been shielded.

The lights came up with a soft click and she moved past Senán's body, the pull overwhelming. Of course it was shielded—no fae could be in the building with a rift this strong and think straight if it had not been. The room was huge and circular, which explained the shape of the hallway, and looked like it took up most of the central footprint of the office tower. The floor was mostly just an outer walkway with a railing all around, and below that was exposed bedrock.

And like an open wound in the bedrock was the rift.

Lana stepped forward until the railing stopped her, silent in awe. She had heard tales of rifts like this, but never in her two centuries had she dreamed of seeing one. It was over a hundred feet long and close to thirty feet wide, an utterly massive tear in the veil. She stared past the licking flames into the darkness within and gasped when she saw the bedrock beneath it. The rift had not finished forming!

"Oh my god, what is that?"

This close, she guessed even Senán could not help but feel the pull of the nascent rift. But she ignored him. If it was still forming, that might explain the power flux this morning. She had convinced Senán he'd had the mother of all hangovers. But what could Midir need with a rift? What did it have to do with…?

"Lana?"

"Shut up, I need to think."

"But…"

Oh, what she would give for the ability to compel right now! "Jeremy, seriously. Shut. The. Fuck. Up." That whine could shatter her thoughts like glass.

He sulked, but it was in a panicked fashion. She had seconds to think, at most.

The rift. The fae. The iron. The glamour. Her mind churned, pulling out the puzzle pieces and trying desperately to put them into a picture she could see. What was Midir *doing*? Senán shifted beside her and prodded her memory to supply another piece. The princes.

Lana felt like her whole being was a bell that had just been rung. Two faerie courts, two ruling Sons of Dagda, two heirs removed; one by murder, the other by kidnapping. Two courts destabilized. She looked up at the ceiling, her thoughts moving to the fae above them, and her heart sped up as one more piece emerged in her mind.

Samhain was two nights away. The veil between the worlds would thin naturally. This rift would open on its own like a flower.

What was gathered upstairs was no office party.

It was an army.

"Lana, what's happen—" Senán began again.

"Babe, we have to get—"

The door swung open, and Midir the Proud burst in with another sidhe she did not know. She froze, afraid to breathe, but even in her fear something about the stranger struck her as familiar. His face, his eyes—but where did she know him from?

"Dad?" The whine had been replaced by a distinctive cracking tremble.

Lana glanced over at Senán. The whites showed all around his eyes, and his hands shook at his sides. He was breaking. Useless.

"Jeremy, what the hell are you doing down here?" Midir demanded, and then his eyes fell on her. His face flushed with rage. "You idiot! How dare you bring—"

And that was her cue to run. Her knives were useless against a prince as ancient and powerful as Midir, so she used the only other weapon she had at hand. Senán screamed as she gripped him by his right arm and whipped him through the air with every ounce of strength her half-blooded body possessed—which was still quite a bit, considering her mother was only a sweetheart faerie. His tall body flew sideways and crashed into both men, bringing all three down in a tangled heap. But Lana did not stay to enjoy the havoc she had caused, instead flitting out the door with Senán's pass key now firmly held in her hand.

She made it to the elevator running flat out in a blur of speed and sent out a prayer of thanks to whoever was listening that it was still in the basement, then swiped access to the lobby. Damn Senán for insisting on driving his own car! But that was a minor matter. First, she had to get out of this building. She had not seen a stairwell, but that meant nothing—they had only gone one way down the hall. Both sidhe lords were faster and stronger than she was. They could race up a stairwell and cut her off before the elevator made the lobby. If she could just make it out into the city she stood a chance.

The elevator doors opened onto the quiet lobby. She stepped out, keeping her demeanor casual, and walked with her heart hammering in her mouth past the rest of the elevator bays and toward the bank of glass doors. Just her and the two guards sitting encircled by the central desk. She relaxed with each step. Through the doors and down the drive, and she was certain she could coax a lift from a passing driver—all she needed was eye contact with someone who found her desirable and they would—

A door burst open behind her, and she ducked around the last corner before the doors. Expensive shoes crossed the polished stone of the lobby floor in rapid steps. "We have an intruder in the building," Midir's voice echoed in the tall space. "A woman, petite with long dark hair and a dark jacket…"

Lana did not catch any more with her sensitive hearing. She was walking just short of a run, putting as much distance between her and Midir as

she could, but her path was taking her deeper into the building. She needed... she needed... her mind whirled, trying to formulate a plan as she
peered into office doors. Nothing useful came to her sight. She needed...
she clipped her elbow on a pressure handle and bit back a curse. And then
she paused. It was a fire door to one of the stairwells.

She needed to be higher.

She pushed her way into the stairwell and ran at full speed up the stairs,
her footfalls blending into each other in wild echoes. If she was seen coming down from one of the upper floors it would raise less suspicion than if
she was spotted on the ground floor. She picked a floor at random and
came to a stop, pausing to catch her breath. She was not huffing and puff-
ing; stripping was an athletic job and she was in good shape. But she did
not want to attract any attention until she was ready.

Her next step needed to be to find a new appearance.

Lana moved out of the stairwell and looked around. The floor she
found herself on was well appointed, with a spacious reception area surrounded by office clusters. She began peering in door windows and only
found empty darkness behind each. Why was there never a man around
when you actually wanted one? As she moved deeper into the floor she
realized the name plates on many of the office doors were followed by the
title "attorney." She must be in the Legal Department. If Midir was forming an army of fae, none of them would be lawyers—the bulk of the
building's crowd must be on another floor. Shit. She began to backtrack.

Her sensitive ears caught the electronic sound of a voice over a speaker
mic and she opened the next door she came to and slipped inside. It was a
smaller reception area, or maybe just where a secretary sat. She was making guesses here, really. Four doors led off from there, and one had a light
on behind the glass. Lana perked up and looked inside. Empty, with a
purse on the desk. Damn. But the sound of the speaker mic drew closer.
Her heartbeat jumped, and she looked back at the lit office. An idea
formed, and she let herself in.

She emptied her jacket pockets of what little she had in them, set them
on the desk, and dropped her purse beside the little pile. She then stripped
off her jacket and laid it over the seat of the chair. This was not as easy as
finding a potential lover and enticing them into her thrall as she changed

her form to match their desires. She could do that instantly; it was her nature. She looked around the office and found several framed pictures, many of them featuring the same attractive blonde woman. So, a blonde... maybe. A calf-length tan coat hung on a coat stand in the corner. Lana found a long blonde hair on the coat and further searching turned up two more caught on the chair back.

She put her purse in the chair with her coat and spun it so its back faced the door. Then she positioned herself in the corner out of sight of the door window and wound the three hairs around her fingers. This kind of shape-changing took more focus and energy than her preferred method, but she was out of options. She closed her eyes and focused on the hairs, on the essence of the person whose body they came from. This was why magic using bits of hair and blood and nails was so potent—it all carried a direct connection to whoever had shed it. She felt the shiver pass over her body from her crown to her feet that told her she was changing. Her jeans became looser around the hips and her sweater tightened across the bust. And this was why she wore a body that was curvier than was normal for a sidhe; they did not make jeans in the stretchy material in smaller sizes.

Lana pulled a lock of hair forward. Blonde, all right. But, was it the right blonde for this office? The door opened, and a man looked in. Lana startled, and felt herself begin to shift in self-defense. She clamped down on her new form and smiled.

"Hey, Sandra," he said. "Everything okay in here?"

She nodded. She had to trust the voice. "Fine. Just stretching." It was high and chirpy. How could a woman with a voice like this be a lawyer?

The security guard grinned back in that slightly silly fashion Lana knew so well. He was a little pudgy in his security uniform but not hard on the eyes. This 'Sandra' had an admirer. "Great. Just checking." He paused for a moment, then looked a little embarrassed and closed the door.

Lana stayed smiling at the door until she heard his footsteps fade away and then set back into motion. She had to get out of this building.

She opened the woman's purse and dumped it into the bottom drawer, and then stuffed the contents of her own purse inside it without regard for order or organization. Dammit, she loved her purse, had paid three nights' worth of tips for it, but if it was a choice between it and a slow death, she could buy another fucking purse. She had seen firsthand what Midir was capable of doing just to make a point. She did not want to experience what he would do to an enemy at his mercy.

A thought occurred to her and she pulled up her sleeves and stripped off the glamour hiding her knives even as she stripped off the wrist sheaths. If she passed by Midir or his companion, they would not be able to sense her changed shape—that was a natural ability that left no magical signature. But they would be able to sense her glamour and it would get her killed. The knives and sheaths would not fit in the purse. Shit. She looked around, but no solution presented itself. She tucked both into the back of her jeans and pulled her belt a few notches tighter to keep them from falling down her pants.

She then stuffed her jacket and empty purse deep down between the woman's desk and the window and put on the long coat, grabbing the new purse on her way out the door. She had no idea how long the woman would be gone and needed to be out of the building before her theft was discovered.

Lana made it to the elevators without incident and pushed the down button. It did not light up. She frowned. She pushed it harder, then several times in rapid succession. Nothing. She saw a swipe box, pulled Senán's pass key out of her pocket and brushed it over the box. Again nothing. *Shit*. What was wrong? She didn't have time to figure it out. The stairwell, then.

She turned and stopped just short of hitting a large body. It was the security guard, again. Her chest clenched, but she put a smile on her face. Pleasantness was a survival trait for her kind. The light flashed on his name tag. Charles. But he looked like a "Chuck" or a "Charlie." Her life just could not be easy, could it? "Hey." Better to keep it simple.

He grinned. "Hey, Sandra. You leaving?"

"Trying to. But something's wrong with the elevator."

"Here, let me help." He swiped the box with his card and pressed the button. It obediently lit. "The building is on lockdown. There's an intruder."

She chose to look impressed. "Is it dangerous?"

He shrugged, straightened a bit. "Naw. They didn't say she was armed, but we need to be prepared for anything, you know. That's why we have security in a building this big."

Lana smiled, and the elevator opened. "Can you walk me out?" she asked, lowering her voice just a little and looking up at him through her lashes.

The guard flushed and looked conflicted, and Lana knew if she pushed it she could get him to do whatever she needed. "I have to stay on this floor," he said with a note of reluctance in his voice, as if he wanted to be talked out of it. "But Gary's at the desk—he'll swipe you out."

She smiled wider and released him. "Good night, then." She would have to take her chances with this 'Gary.' Manipulating this guard into assisting her would raise more suspicion than it was worth—she could be held up with questions she could not answer long enough for the real Sandra to return, and that would be her ruin.

The doors closed on his good night and his shining eyes and then the elevator was dropping to the lobby.

Lana clutched her stolen purse tight to her side and readied for when the doors opened again. Across the lobby and out the doors. Down the drive and into a car. She repeated the two phrases over and over in her head as she forced herself to relax. This was not the time to tense up and panic. She needed to focus.

The doors slid open, showing her nothing but the other bank of elevator doors facing her. She blew out a silent breath and stepped out like she had every right in the world to be there. There was more security at the central desk, now, and the slender form of the unknown sidhe lord was among them, bent over monitors with his spill of black hair hanging down over one shoulder. They were between her and the glass doors.

She kept walking, kept her eyes sweeping over the group as a whole. As she drew close she clamped down on her fear and said in a clear voice, "Gary?" The first man to look up won her full attention and smile. Please be him...

"Yeah?"

She did not show her relief. "Could you please swipe me out?" The sidhe glanced up in her direction, flickered his eyes over her, and looked back to his task. He still looked so familiar.

"Sure. Let me come around."

The guard walked with her to the doors and swiped his card. She heard the door click and reached out to push it open. "Thanks!"

"Anytime," he said, and brushed his hand over her back. It stopped at her knives. He frowned. "What's this?"

Lana put a little sheepishness into her smile as she turned her back away from him. "Seahaven defense system. A girl can't be too careful working late." She forced herself to not look in the direction of the desk. She could only hope the sidhe was too distracted to pay attention to their conversation.

"You know you're not supposed to have stuff like that in the building, Sandra."

She nodded and turned the wattage on her smile up just a little. "You're right. I'll leave it in the car." She pushed against the door. It had locked again.

Gary looked at her for a moment.

"Door?" She smiled. Her heart hammered.

He nodded and swiped his card. The door clicked again, and Lana pushed it open. "Have a good night, Sandra."

She waved with her free hand. "'Night!"

Lana watched through the glass as Gary turned away before she turned to make her brisk way down the drive. The rift, the army… she finally knew what Midir was planning and it threw her own desperately laid plan to the wind. She had been in over her head before.

Now she was drowning.

She needed help. Midir had to be stopped, and she knew of only one person she could turn to who had a connection to the courts, who might help her.

She had to find Etienne Queen's Son.

CHAPTER SEVENTEEN

Etienne threw his arm over his face, but the banging continued. Cian made a sound of sleepy protest beside him and rolled over onto his belly, pulling the pillow over his head. Etienne sat up and dragged his legs over the side of the bed, the remains of the wine making his head swim. Hadn't they just gone to bed? Winter had been right; Katherine was an excellent hostess. But it seemed that vampires were even worse than fae when it came to carousing all night and the hours had flown by in drink and music and conversation. Etienne found the clock on the nightstand and frowned.

They really had just gone to bed. What the hell? More infernal banging.

"What is it?" Cian asked from beneath the pillow.

Etienne stood up and snagged his jeans from the end of the bed. "I don't know. Maybe a patient for Winter. I'll find out."

"You want me to come down?"

Etienne buttoned his fly, pulled his t-shirt on, and clipped the semiautomatic's holster to the waistband at the small of his back. "No. At least one of us should get some sleep." He slipped Agmundr's rig over his arms and caught up his worn flannel shirt as he made his barefoot way out of the tiny bedroom.

"Be careful."

He gave a small smile despite his irritation. "I will. Now go back to sleep." He pulled the door shut behind him.

Etienne scratched the side of his scarred face and yawned as he pushed through the beaded curtain. He frowned even harder when he saw a short woman on the other side of the shop glass, knocking away at the door frame. She was looking over her shoulder as her hand worked, her long black hair in disarray, and did not see him emerge. Seemed like trouble was looking for Winter early today. He glanced at the night-black sky. Or late. Dawn was not far away, but still had yet to make an appearance.

As he reached the door she turned back and visibly startled as she saw him. Etienne ignored it. Even though the store was dark, this close to the glass the streetlights must have illuminated his scars. Some people, usually women, had stronger reactions to them than others. The ones on his face and neck were the most obvious, the ones he could not hide. Men also noticed them, of course, but tended to either tough out the reaction and ignore them entirely or take them as a signal to test out their own stupidity.

He flipped the deadbolt and pulled the door open just enough to talk comfortably through. "What?" Then he rethought that. Maybe he should be politer. She was probably looking for Winter. "Do you need something?"

She smiled at him. "Etienne Queen's Son?" She spoke in Faerie Gaelic. This couldn't be good. "We're closed." He shut the door and locked it.

"Wait!" Her voice was muffled by the glass. He moved away from the door and considered calling Winter... but she was exhausted as it was. She needed what sleep she could get. "Please! I need your help."

Etienne clenched his jaw. His gaze had never really left her, but he had stopped looking at her face—her hands and core would be more informative of what kind of threat she posed. Either casting or going for a weapon, the movements would involve her hands. Now he looked and wished he hadn't. Her eyes were glassy with fear and he saw the smile had been a façade. He wanted no part of whatever this was. Cian was just upstairs and though Etienne was indeed a knight, he was no hero. He did not need a damsel in distress.

He unlocked the door and opened it again. "How do you know my name?"

"Let me in and I'll tell you everything." She was bouncing in small motions with nerves. He looked at her more closely. Sidhe, but like himself, not pure. Though not human, either. Probably some sort of fae mix.

Etienne stepped back, and she moved past him into the store front. "Stop. That's as far as you go."

"But the streetlights…"

He scowled but moved and pushed aside the beaded curtain. "Fine, back here."

She ducked under his raised arm and rushed into the dark sanctuary of the clinic. "Thank you."

"Don't thank me, yet," he said as he followed her. "I haven't heard what you have to say. I'm not ruling out throwing you back outside."

She turned to face him as he glowered at her. "This is about Midir the Proud and Prince Senán. You're here looking for them, aren't you?"

"One of them." Etienne crossed his arms. "You seem to know a lot about my business for someone I don't know."

She tried the smile again. "My name is Lana." It was a good smile, full of vaguely worded promises, hints at what could be offered for the right price. It went well with her lush curves.

He wasn't in the mood to buy. "Tell me something more useful."

She gave him a pretty frown, which was even more impressive than the smile. "I see your reputation does you justice."

"Yeah, I'm an uncouth half-breed. Either start talking or stop wasting my time."

The girl—and as he studied her he decided she couldn't have more than two centuries on her at the most—took a breath and started talking. "Midir is opening a rift, an enormous rift, in the lowest sub-basement of his office tower. He's been gathering fae there, I think for weeks—Senán told me Midir has been 'hiring' for an 'expansion,'" she made a strange gesture in the air with her fingers as she placed emphasis on each word, "and now the building is packed with them."

"You've spoken to Senán?"

Lana nodded. "I'm his *girlfriend*." She said the last word in English and it took a moment for Etienne to parse it out. Faerie Gaelic did not have an equivalent term—there were lovers, casual and otherwise, or beloved in the bonds of True Love, or one had a mistress or concubine or other such power relationship. Marriage existed, and divorce did not, for once such vows were made they could not be foresworn. As a result, most who chose to be bound in marriage did not swear eternal fidelity.

"Fine, go on."

She blinked, her expression intense. "Don't you see what he's doing?"

"Enlighten me."

She rolled her eyes. "Midir deprived two kings, two of his brothers, of their heirs, one by kidnapping and one by murder. He destabilized two fae- rie realms and now he's building an army and opening a rift." She paused, watching his face. "He's planning to invade and take both realms for him- self."

Etienne furrowed his brows. "Why would he do that? He's never been interested in having a kingdom before."

Lana snorted. "Of course, he has. Where have you been?"

He gave her a wry look. "I'm not exactly welcome in the courts. Half- breed and all. How about you?"

"I don't have that problem."

"Oh, you're not a half-breed?"

"Ooh, nasty case of sarcasm you have there. No, I mean I'm more wel- come in the courts than you. And Midir has always wanted his own kingdom, which everybody in the courts knows, but he let his brothers talk him out of it in exchange for fostering their heirs."

"Except I know of one king who didn't do that."

"And I know of another. And guess who lost their heirs?"

"King Anluan is the only one I've heard of who had a child in the re- cent past. The prince Midir murdered was pushing nine-hundred-years-old. His father didn't foster him to Midir?"

Lana nodded. "Him *and* his younger brother."

"Why didn't he kill the younger prince, too, then?"

"Someone else got to him, first. About five hundred years ago."

"Huh. And everyone asks why I avoid the courts."

She tilted her head like a bird. "I thought you said you weren't wel- come."

"The feeling is mutual. So," he shifted before she could pursue the conversation worm, "you think Midir wants to invade the kingdoms of the princes he violated. Which would be King Anluan and what's the other one's name? Kal-something?" The one with the mad queen.

"King Ceallach."

"Midir's been sitting on his resentment for a long time, if the younger prince has been dead for five centuries." He thought for a moment and then shrugged. "You know, I can have sympathy for this Ceallach, but I don't give a rat's ass what happens to Anluan."

Lana's eyes widened. "How could you not?"

"Etienne!"

Etienne looked to see Cian standing at the bottom of the stairs, fully dressed and looking upset. "Cian, go back to bed."

"I heard her say Senán's name."

"Is that The Glorious Dawn?" Her voice was breathy with shock.

Etienne turned and gripped her arm, leaning into the enchantments on the rig to squeeze just short of crushing the long bone. Her knees buckled, and she cried out in pain, but he held her weight. "If that name leaves this room, no hole in any realm will be deep enough to hide you from me."

Cian crossed the room, alarm painted across his face. "Etienne, stop!"

Lana had begun to nod in a frantic manner, her breathing shallow and fast. Etienne took her other arm and lifted a little, settling her securely on her feet as he released her. She backed away from him until she hit the desk, her hand clasped protectively over her hurt arm. "I can't let Midir know Cian is here," he said to her. He was not apologizing. He would do worse to keep Cian safe. "I'm only here for Senán. Nothing more. Anluan is a big king, he can take care of himself." Etienne felt his mouth twist. It wasn't a smile. "And if he should fall, I'll be the first to celebrate."

"Etienne!"

"Cian, you know how I feel about this."

Her eyes darted about as she thought. "Well, you'll have to face Midir if you want to get Senán back…"

"How's that? He's spending time with you, screwing you if he's anything like his father—obviously he's been free to move about on his own. It doesn't look to me like he's much of a prisoner."

"But if that's true," Cian asked, a worried look on his pretty face, "then why hasn't he gone home?"

"You've met his parents."

Cian frowned at Etienne.

"Because he doesn't know who and what he is," Lana answered. "He thinks he's human, that he really is Jeremy Moore."

"We have to tell him the truth!" said Cian. "We have to take him home."

"Is it an enchantment?" Etienne asked.

Lana held up her hands. "I haven't found a magical signature on him to indicate it might be, but I'm not much of a magician. Most of my magic is inherent."

Etienne narrowed his eyes. "What is your other half?" The inviting smile, the curves too lush for any sidhe woman… he had a suspicion.

She hesitated, and then raised her chin. "Lhiannon sidhe."

"Fucking wonderful," he said with full disgust.

"What?" asked Cian.

"It's great to see *racism* is alive and well among the half-breeds," she spat.

Etienne sneered at her. "At least the Seelie don't hunt the weak among us along the corridors of our courts."

"Oh?" Lana replied, taking a mocking tone. "Scarred yourself then, did you?"

Etienne flipped an obscene gesture at her and said to Cian. "She's Unseelie. Lhiannon sidhe, sweetheart faeries, are succubae."

"What's *racism*?" Cian asked, repeating the English word.

Etienne waved his hand, not wanting to get into it. It was a new word for him, too, and as a human concept he really did not understand it. Human was human, as far as he knew. But the various races of fae were different. Those aligned with the evil Unseelie were untrustworthy and dangerous. He glared at her and got back on topic. "Fine, Senán doesn't know who he is. Why does this have anything to do with Midir if he's moving freely about the city? Bring him here and we'll deal with it." Unless she was trying to cover up what damage she had already done to him, of course. Could she feed on Senán without Midir knowing? Would Midir care? He had no idea. He knew some things about succubae, but not everything.

"Because Midir's very angry with him right now, so I don't think he'll be going anywhere freely anytime soon. Besides, Samhain is coming right up, and that rift will open. He'll be back in Faerie at the head of an army. You're running out of time."

Etienne frowned. Well… shit. He drummed his fingers over his bicep, thinking for a long moment, and then shook his head. "Then that's that. I'm not risking Cian's safety for Senán. It's done."

"Etienne, we can't leave him!"

"He's your brother!"

Etienne gritted his teeth against both voices of protest and raised his hand. "Cian, no, we can. You're much more important to me. And you," he pointed at Lana. "I've never even met him and the blood I share with him is through a viper of a woman, so how can I be that invested in the boy? What do you want with him? Are you in love with him?" Part of him wanted her to be. Wanted to know that he had not uprooted Cian and brought him this close to danger for nothing. Wanted Senán to be someone worthwhile of a woman's love and not just the son of Anluan.

The laugh that escaped was sudden and harsh. Her eyes widened a bit and then narrowed with anger. "No. He's a self-indulgent little prick who's only interested in his own pleasure. And when a succubus doesn't like fucking you, that's saying something. He uses glamour to rape mortal women, and not only does he not even realize it, I don't think realizing it would make him stop."

"So, he takes after his father." Of course, he did.

"Etienne, how can you say that?" Cian looked appalled.

"Because I've known Anluan longer than you have."

"But Senán's my friend. He's not like that."

"Cian, you haven't seen him since you were barely an adolescent. You can't—"

"Yes! Yes, I can! You never knew him." He looked from Etienne to Lana and back, and shook his head, his face flushed with anger. "He's not like that. He wouldn't do that."

Etienne uncrossed his arms and reached a hand out to Cian. "Do you mean Senán or Anluan?" he asked in a gentler voice. Cian shivered a little under his fingers. He glanced at Lana and squeezed Cian's arm. "We'll talk about this later."

Cian pulled away, frowning. "I'm going outside." He said it with no question in his tone, no request for permission. He just turned and headed out the back door.

Etienne sighed. "Stay in the courtyard."

The door slammed.

"What was that all about?"

Etienne scowled at her. "If you don't want Senán, what do you want?" Cian's trauma was none of her damn business.

That pert chin went up again. "I want Midir."

He couldn't help it. He laughed at her. "You?" he gasped out between chuckles. "Want Midir the Proud? Elder Son of Dagda?"

She remained silent.

He wiped his eyes as the last of the laughter left him. "You do realize you're a half-breed. Maybe you're a stronger one than I am, but you still don't stand a chance up against a full sidhe."

A small smirk pulled at the corner of her mouth. "I have the named blade, Keeper. Even Midir can't stand against it."

That brought Etienne up short. He had heard of Keeper. It was an ancient sword, incapable of delivering a mortal wound but it rendered its victims completely helpless. "How did you get it? By which I'm asking, 'Who did you piss off?' Because you didn't come by it honestly."

She could give great blank face, he had to give her some credit. "Ceallach is its caretaker. He won't be sorry to see Midir spitted on its blade and brought before him on his knees."

Etienne had to admit to himself that that was a very tempting image. After what Midir had done to Cian, after years of sitting through nightmare-filled nights with the boy, after finding the ruin and horror of what the great prince had done to a boy who had been little more than a child— Etienne wanted to be the one to drive the blade home, himself. Ceallach was an Unseelie king, and he had heard tales of the tortures the Unseelie could inflict.

He fleetingly wondered if this Ceallach would let him watch.

He pulled himself from his little daydream and riveted his gaze on the succubus. "You've gone to great lengths to capture him. Why?"

She looked away. "That's my concern. Suffice it to say I have a vested interest."

"Look, tempting as it might be that you have Keeper, you also have no plan and, according to you, there's an army in that building standing between just the two of us and Midir."

"Your reputation says you're crazy enough to do it." Lana raised her brows with just a hint of invitation.

Etienne was still not interested. "No, my reputation just says I'm crazy."

"You're a knight. Where's your honor?"

He gave her a sour look. "If you know so much about my reputation, you know I have none."

"You've fought and killed the last four sidhe lords to challenge you. If not for honor—"

He cut her off with a wave of his hand. "Listen, I'm only going to say this once. I'm not a duelist. I'm a killer. I fight for one reason and one reason only—to make everyone leave me the fuck alone."

"What about the wizard that's usually here?"

He shook his head. "She's not that kind of wizard."

"How about the little fat one? She looks feisty."

Etienne scowled. "So what if she's fat? And she's only half-trained. Winter won't let her go."

"She's really fat," Lana muttered.

But Etienne had turned his attention away, uneasy. He had heard something.

Cian stalked around the small courtyard before the parking lot, the soggy grass squelching under his boots. He did not want to cry, but tears of anger and fear welled up of their own accord. He dashed them away with the back of his hand and wanted to kick the door, but that would only bring Etienne out here. He did not want to see him right now.

Etienne hated Anluan. He knew that, had known that for years. But Uncle Anluan had raised Cian after his parents died and had always been kind to him. He had chosen Cian to be Senán's companion, even though his father Eoin had been the youngest of Dagda's sons and little more than a faerie knight, a prince in name only. Etienne said Anluan was using him, that he had been holding him back—and Cian did not like admitting it, but it was true that his education had focused on music and poetry while Senán had gone to study with the weapons trainers. But he was also younger than Senán! Maybe Anluan just hadn't found the right trainer for him, yet. Though Senán had been studying war and tactics and the princely arts since he was old enough to sit at table... But Etienne always said awful things about Anluan! He always let his prejudices against his step-father make him petty.

And on the rare occasion he spoke about his mother, Anluan's Queen Niamh, his comments were short and venomous. Cian had not had much occasion to see his Aunt Niamh, but what little he had seen of her she had not seemed so bad. Remote, maybe, but not the woman Etienne described. Cian could not imagine talking about his own mother like that. Even though he had no memory of her, Éibhleann of the Waters was celebrated in so many songs and poems that he felt she had always been part of his childhood. She had chosen to fade to mist and memory when his father was killed in battle, rather than live without her love. Etienne said he had never met her, but Cian could tell by the way he said it that Etienne did not think highly of her.

And then this Unseelie woman came along and said horrible things about Senán, accused him of awful things, and Etienne just agreed with her! Like there was no doubt in his mind that his own brother would... would do those things, be that way! Cian kicked a stick. It was wet and rotted and broke apart rather than fly from his anger. Very unsatisfying.

How could Etienne do that? Senán was Cian's friend, his only real friend until Etienne had rescued him after... Cian's mind automatically flinched away from the memories. He remembered how much Etienne had looked like Senán, how much it had grieved him for so long, thinking Senán was dead. He thought Midir had killed him, like he himself had been left for dead. Etienne had refused to return to look for the body. He had said it was too dangerous and that they had to keep putting distance between themselves and Midir, but by then they had been miles away. After they had found the picture, Cian knew he had made a horrible mistake, that he should have somehow made Etienne go back. He had left his friend to that monster.

That had to be it; the reason Senán was hurting those women. It was Midir. He was making him do it, somehow. Yes, that had to be it. Cian's stomach churned, and his mind turned away again; it hurt to think of his friend doing what Midir had done to him.

How could Etienne not care about Senán? Even though Etienne had never met him, they had the same mother. "What's wrong with him?" he muttered, shooting a glare at the door.

"What, indeed?"

Cian froze at the voice behind him that came straight from his nightmares. He wanted to cry out, to move, but he couldn't catch a breath. His frantic heartbeat thundered in his ears—surely Etienne would hear it.

"I had so hoped to find you again, Cian." Midir's voice was low and smooth, taunting. "I thought you were dead. Imagine my surprise at seeing you alive and well, sitting on that *motorcycle*."

Cian felt as if he had been dunked in ice. The helmet. Etienne had told him…

"Come along, now, we've not much time." Midir's hand was hot on the chilled skin of his neck.

The touch shocked Cian out of his freeze. He jerked away from Midir and ran for the door. "Et—!"

Midir's hand clamped down over his mouth, stifling his cry, and his fingers dug with bruising force into Cian's face. His other hand gripped Cian's left arm, finding a pressure point at the joint and grinding down as Cian made helpless pain noises. Then Cian felt a flash of magic course from his head down his spine and he was pulled into darkness.

Etienne pushed open the door. "Cian?"

But the courtyard was empty.

Unease began to border on panic and Etienne moved outside. "Cian!" There was just the strip of wet grass and the cars in the parking lot. If he was sulking down between the parked cars Etienne would throttle the boy. But why would he do that? Being that close to that much steel would be uncomfortable for him. It was the reason for the motorcycle. Riding the bike was preferable to being enclosed for long periods. Etienne started for the parking lot, anyway. Adolescents sometimes did not make smart choices, and even though Cian was particularly sensible he had started talking back and rolling his eyes...

But a quick walk through the small lot soon proved Cian was not there. Etienne felt himself becoming more frantic. Cian knew better than to wander off. When he told the boy to stay in a place, he stayed. What would be different about today? That he was angry at him? Cian had never been angry at him before. Etienne looked up at the second story windows that were the only eyes looking down on the courtyard. Even in the predawn, maybe someone had seen where Cian had stalked off to. Maybe he had just gone back over to Katherine's. The thought both relaxed and annoyed him. The boy should know better than to impose.

Lana had emerged into the courtyard, edging away from the doorway. In her hand she held a small pink card. As he neared she smiled at him and held it out. "I'll let you go find the kid. Here's my number..."

But Etienne was caught by something about her. It was the way she was shifting her body subtly away from him, the way her eyes flickered past him once, twice, as if looking for a way out. He was moving before the thought finished, his left hand around her neck as he shoved her back against the brick wall. "What did you do?" he demanded.

"I didn't do anything to your friend!" She had her smaller hands wrapped around his wrist, trying to pry him off her with remarkable strength. It hurt where her fingers ground against his bones, tearing the shirt under her nails. She could probably succeed, if given enough time. But Etienne was angry.

He pulled back and shoved her against the wall again with teeth-rattling force. "I didn't ask what you didn't do. I know you can't lie. I asked what you did."

She responded by going still under his hand. Etienne felt something shivery pass through him and as he watched her black hair lightened to a buttery brown, her eyes softened and brightened as she looked up at him. Her face became sweeter and her body became even smaller and rounder.

His breath caught as he realized what he was seeing. "Bess." The face he had forgotten, her beloved face, was forming right before his eyes. His vision swam with tears and he blinked, desperate to see clearly. To see her face again.

She smiled as she changed, tried to slip his hand from her neck… and it was wrong. His rage flared higher, and he reached under his arm for his weapon. Panic and recognition filled her bright colored eyes. "Agmundr," she gasped, pressing herself against the bricks.

"How dare you try to take my wife's form, succubus!"

"How?" Terror was causing her to bleed from one form to another, shifting under Etienne's hand, her eyes riveted on Agmundr's barrel. "You shouldn't have seen that."

Etienne cocked the revolver's hammer. "That's not my problem. You are. Now, answer my question—what did you do?" As enraged as he was about how she had tried to violate his wife's memory, he had to set it aside, too. For now. For Cian. He thought back to the way she had been dancing with anxiety at the shop door. "Who followed you?"

Lana seemed to wilt in his grasp. She shuddered, her eyes never leaving the revolver, and answered, "I'm not certain…" She was quiet for a long moment, and just as he tightened his grip to shake her she spoke again, her dark eyes dulling. "But Midir caught me as I discovered the rift in the basement of his building with Senán. I threw Senán at him and his companion to make my escape. Midir is more than capable of tracking me. It's why I came to you for help."

Horror washed over Etienne. Midir had Cian. Midir had Cian. The thought played over and over in his mind. He had to rescue him!

"I'm so sorry," her quiet voice intruded on his thoughts. "I didn't know your friend was The Glorious Dawn."

"Would that have changed anything?"

Lana looked away for a long moment and then met his eyes. "I don't know. I was scared, and Midir still needs to be stopped."

Etienne frowned at her, but finally let her go and holstered Agmundr. "What was that card?"

She blinked for a moment, and then the life began to seep back into her eyes as she seemed to realize he was not about to kill her. "It's my calling card." She bent and picked it up from the wet grass where she had dropped it, then thought better and dug a fresh one out of her purse.

Etienne took a glance at it before slipping it into his back pocket. It had her number on it and what looked like a pair of lips. "Not good enough. I want you and Keeper somewhere where I can find you in a hurry."

Her eyes lightened. "You'll help me?"

"I didn't say that. But if I need to engage Midir to get to Cian, I want every asset available."

Lana nodded, a little too quickly, the smile returning to her face. "Then what do you want?"

"First I want your cell phone. I need to make a call. And then we're going to your place to get Keeper. Both of you are staying where I can see you until this is over."

The smile slipped, but she made an assenting noise.

"And next you need to feed. You're young, so you don't know this, and fuck me for telling you, but I saw what you were doing because you were weakened and settled on my wife's form. Because I had True Love, once. If you were a lot older, stronger, or subtler it might have worked, but True Love grants some protection against succubae and incubi. If we're going into a fight you need to be at full strength." He let her see the full force of his displeasure. "Try it again and I'll kill you. Now give me that phone."

She paled and dug the phone out of her purse. "I live above Sweet Treats."

He jerked his head for her to lead the way and dialed Winter. He needed more help than a hungry half-breed sweetheart faerie could provide.

She picked up on the fifth ring. "'s Winter."

Her words were so slurred he barely understood her. "Are you alright?"

"'m fine. Gimme sec."

Etienne frowned as he walked. A suspicion was taking root in his mind. "Winter, did you take something?"

Lana looked back at him, interest lighting her face.

"'m fine." There was a ruffling noise that Etienne could not identify, perhaps fabric being dragged across the phone, and then her light, sharp breathing followed by swallowing.

Etienne scowled at Lana and turned away. He knew she could hear him no matter what he did, but he wanted at least an appearance of privacy. "What are you drinking?"

Her breathing came in short gasps. "Just something to help me wake up. Etienne, is this you?"

"I've been around a long time. Chasing potions like that isn't good for you." This could explain so much about her illness.

"I'm fine. I know what I'm doing. What do you need?"

Etienne wanted to argue with her, but the need to rescue Cian was more pressing. He would have to have it out with her later. "I think Cian has been kidnapped by Midir."

Winter gasped. "I'm on my way to you."

"Wait. I need something... strange, first. We've picked up an ally, a succubus, but she needs to feed."

There was a moment of quiet. "I can't let her kill anyone, Etienne."

Etienne slid his eyes to the young succubus. "She doesn't have to." His look turned to one of warning.

Lana quickly indicated her agreement.

"What do you need?" he mouthed at her.

She held up two fingers. "I'd prefer two female-centric men who don't mind sleeping Sunday away when I'm done with them. They're easiest to feed on."

Etienne passed along the request.

"I think I can ask Erik for volunteers easily enough. And if we need to get Cian out of that office tower, we'll need more than just the three of us. I need to ask Erik for help."

"Do you think he'll give it?"

"There's only one way to find out. I'll pick the two of you up at Curiosity's in thirty minutes."

Etienne heard the call end and handed the phone back to Lana. Thirty minutes before Winter arrived, and then who knew how long to talk to the Vampire King and feed the succubus. Time was not measured with such precision in Faerie and even while in the Mortal Realm he usually paid it no mind. But with Cian in Midir's hands he felt each second thrum through his bones. He closed his eyes and prayed Cian could hold on.

CHAPTER EIGHTEEN

Somebody was yelling.

Jessie was torn between curiosity and sinking further beneath the warm coverlet. She loved crashing at Erik's court. His guest rooms had awesome, old-fashioned beds with curtains and feather pillows and bed steps. Way cool. She also loved her little apartment above Curiosity's. It was her safe haven from her parent's particular brand of insanity. But when she couldn't be there, sleeping in the lap of luxury at the Theatre beat the hell out of couch surfing at her various friends' places under old blankets that smelled like cat pee and sour milk.

Another voice rose to meet the first. It sounded like Erik. Not surprising. She pulled her phone out from under the pillow and checked the time. Yeah, he couldn't be happy about being woken up this early. Vampires could move about during the day, the sun wouldn't hurt them, they just didn't like to. They were nocturnal hunters with perfect night vision and bright sunlight made it hard for them to see clearly. Jessie could hear doors opening in the corridor, vampires and court therian wondering what the commotion was about. Well, if Erik was pissed she didn't want any—

The next voice cut off Erik, apparently in mid-sentence. It was Winter! She felt prickles of shock run over her skin. Oh shit. Jessie had never heard her yell before. Not like this. She was out from under the covers and pulling on her clothes in the morning chill before she finished the thought.

Jessie rushed down the hall, passed people looking through their open doors and talking across the corridor. She made her way from the private floors down the long switchback stairs that ran along the brick back wall of the historic building. She was not the only one making the early morning trek—apparently this argument was becoming a happening. But for preternatural beings capable of blinding speed they moved so slow! She looked over the railing more than once, wishing not for the first time she was one of her video game characters. Granted, four years of judo had taught her to take a fall, but she didn't think this was what her sensei had in mind. The training had also taught her patience. Sort of.

The stairs let out onto the main floor and at last she had space to wedge her wide hips in between the lollygaggers, with a few rapid fire 'scuse me's,' and make a better pace through the main hallway.

"Here again, Jessie? When are you gonna get Marked?"

Jessie flipped off the therian who'd asked without breaking her stride and was met with laughter. It was a common joke directed at her at the Theatre. Court therian and what few humans who also lived here bore Marks behind their right ears identifying them as court property. But that was their business. As far as she was concerned, nobody was going to tag a 'Property of' label on her. Anyone who tried could go screw themselves.

The voices got louder.

"Erik, be reasonable!"

This time of year, with the Winter Concert Series getting underway, and any other time of year when the Theatre had a show running, Erik held court in the dining hall. Not his favorite place. Given any and every opportunity Erik held court on stage. So very Erik.

"Winter, forget this. He's not going to help us and we're running out of time." Was that Etienne? Why was the faerie knight here?

When he couldn't have his throne center stage, Erik had it up on a low dais against the back wall of the dining hall behind where the high table sat during meals. Jessie thought the dining hall was cooler for holding court, anyway. It was set up like a Viking mead hall. The long tables were brought out for meals and there were all sorts of weapons displayed on the walls that they couldn't put out on the stage walls because they were real historical artifacts and pretty delicate. Erik, however, loved the acoustics from the stage.

"The hell if you think I'm letting you take her out there alone with you!"

"You can't hold me here, Erik."

"Watch me, little girl!"

Given the way he could bellow, Jessie didn't see what difference the acoustics made.

Jessie pushed her way through the small crowd that had gathered loosely around the throne until she was standing at the edge of the argument between a therian she did not know well and Jason, Erik's personal assistant. She leaned into the Greek vampire who looked close to her own age but was actually older than Erik himself. "How long has this been going on?" She kept her voice very low. She did not want to attract the attention of any of the arguing adults.

Jason quirked a smirk. That it did not strike the usual spark in his light-green eyes told Jessie how concerned he was. "About fifteen minutes. Erik is trying to take this opportunity to press Winter for a formal alliance."

"What oppor—?"

"Dammit! Every minute we waste fucking around with you is one more minute Cian is held prisoner by his rapist!" Etienne's face was so flushed with anger that his scars stood out like white ink tattoos.

Cian? What had happened to Cian? He was her friend!

Erik paced in front of his throne, wearing only a pair of dudetastically faded jeans. The corded muscles in his arms flexed and shifted under his battle-scarred skin as he clenched and relaxed his big fists. "It's a shame about the boy. But if what your succubus says is true, there's an army in that building between us and him. Most of my people are not soldiers, and I am not committing any of them to possibly die for this without an alliance!"

Winter had her head down with one hand over her eyes, her bag strap dangling from her elbow. When she raised her head to speak Jessie saw how grayish she looked, how much thinner even than yesterday she seemed. Was it the lighting? What was going on with her? "I can't do that, Erik."

"Like hell—"

"*I* can't!" Winter beat her hand against her breast bone in emphasis, which made her drop her bag. She left it there. Her hand trembled before she balled it into a fist. "I want to, but I can't. If I was the Mulcahy I would do it, but I'm not."

"And I still say like hell you can't. You've been acting as the Mulcahy ever since it fell to your father, and I know Colin—he hasn't done shit, has he? Those few times you've said he'd made a decision, you've lied, haven't you?"

Winter shook her head. Her eyes moved over the crowd and her cheeks colored. But after a moment she pressed on. "He used to talk to me. I never lied to anyone, Erik. But after Kelley and Martina died..." she trailed off. She looked so sick. So lost.

"I'm sorry about your cousins, but he needs to grow a fucking spine and so do you."

Hurt blossomed across Winter's face and Jessie felt her own face flush with anger. What the fu—? She didn't realize she was moving forward until she felt Jason's hand fasten on her shoulder, keeping her at his side. The look he gave her was one of warning.

Etienne rounded on Erik. "That was uncalled for!"

"Mind your own business, faerie knight."

"I'm making it my business."

Jessie looked around and spotted Michael standing well behind Erik to the side of the throne. He seemed to be struggling to keep the worry off of his face as he stood there in silence. "Why isn't Michael doing anything?" she whispered to Jason.

"Because he can't. Erik might give lip service to disregarding politics when it comes to getting what he wants from Winter, but the truth is he's just as political an animal as any vampire. If Michael were to naysay him publicly, and this is a very public argument, then that could diminish Erik's authority. Erik may love him, but he can't afford to be called out by his own favorite."

"Then why aren't they doing this in private?"

"Because Erik wants this alliance. He also loves Winter like a daughter and he thinks this is the only way to save her."

Jason knew what he was talking about. He'd been by Erik's side even longer than Katherine and was one of his closest confidantes. "But Cian…"

Jason turned to face her fully. His eyes, usually bright with laughter, were filled with centuries of regret. "I'm sorry. He's making a choice—the girl he loves over a boy he doesn't know."

Jessie's eyes widened, and her heart began to race. Erik couldn't do that… wouldn't do that… would he? Not her new friend! Erik was a good guy!

"Erik, please, my father won't do it. He won't do anything!" Winter's eyes were reddening with unshed tears, and Jessie had never seen her look so angry before. "Just please help us."

"You know what I need."

"That's it. Winter, we're going. Send someone to fetch Lana—I don't care if she's done or not."

"I already told you, I won't let you put Winter in danger." Erik set his fists on his hips and seemed to take up twice as much space as he should.

Etienne looked unimpressed. "Fuck you and the ship that brought you here, Viking. She hired me to protect her, and that's what I'm going to do."

"One faerie knight against a whole army and an ancient sidhe magician. I don't like those odds, so no, you're not taking her."

"She's also still standing right here."

It wasn't just Erik—they were all going to keep arguing until who-knew-what horrible things happened to Cian. What the hell was wrong with adults? Jessie began to slip back into the crowd. Well, let them fight it out. Winter wasn't the only wizard in Seahaven.

"Where are you going?" Jason asked in a whisper.

"Back to my room. This is making me sick." She kept moving. The crowd was huge, now.

"Go get 'em, kid." His voice was so soft she wasn't sure she actually heard it. She wove her way through vampires and therian until she broke free of the press of bodies and could slip unnoticed from the dining hall.

Brian rolled over, groping for his buzzing phone. It had to be Jessie. She was the only one who texted him at all hours.

And there she was. *OMG shoot me if I turn stoopid at maturity*

He yawned and smiled, pushed his dreads out of his face, then tapped out, *lol what's up?*

Her response came so fast she must have been tapping even as he answered her. *Why do adults talk instead of act? what happend 2 helping ppl? srsly??? i may do something drastic*

Brian frowned. Jessie and drastic were never a good combination. *I'll be right there. Where are you?*

...

He sighed and kicked his legs up out of bed. Here she went with the secretive again.

Just at the theatre. No worries.

He stared at his phone and worried. Before coming to live with Norah, his life had been… well, ugly was a serviceable enough word for what had been done to him. What he had been forced to do. The nearly fatal beating from his 'daddy' when he was eleven had saved his life—it had gotten him off the streets and into this new, clean existence. He knew that this city held secrets and that the Theatre was full of them. Those secrets had teeth, and claws, and sometimes liked to eat street kids like he had been. So, yeah, he was going to worry.

Jessie had a secret. He was not sure what her secret was, exactly, just that she had one and that she ran with others like her. Jessie was going to have to come out of the magical closet some time.

Gotta run <3

Brian brushed his thumb over the little heart, wishing she meant it, and tapped out, *Be careful <3*

He meant every pixel.

CHAPTER NINETEEN

"Now, isn't this better? We can have a conversation in peace. We never got a chance to talk before, you and I."

"Is... is that all you want? To talk?"

Midir unfastened the last button on his suit jacket and fixed those cold, hard eyes on Cian's face. "Did I say that?"

Cian trembled harder.

Midir draped the rumpled jacket over the back of a chair near the expansive window and wasted a small grimace on its condition. He then turned back and looked Cian over, his expression a mixture of interest and speculation. "You've grown quite a bit. You're dressed like a vagrant, however. That simply won't do." He indicated one of the other chairs in the seating arrangement. "Come, sit with me."

Cian hesitated, but when Midir frowned at him he stepped forward, the memory of pain etched in his mind. He walked stiff-legged with terror past the sprawling bed—the bed he could not look at—his arms wrapped tightly around his body, and at last sat perched at the very edge of the seat Midir chose for him.

The older man smiled. "That's a good boy." He reached out with one hand and ran his long fingers through Cian's hair.

Cian did not think his heart could hammer any harder and fought against his panic to not throw up.

"You have grown so beautiful, Cian. They called you The Glorious Dawn even as a child, but I don't think they had any idea how much you would outshine your famous mother." He stroked down the side of Cian's face. "All of my brothers courted her, you know, even the married ones." His mouth twisted into a smirk. "She led them on a merry chase, playing them off each other, accepting gifts and songs and giving tokens. It went on for centuries."

Midir was so close Cian could see himself reflected in his eyes. He could see his own fear. He dug his fingers into his arms and tried to calm his breathing. He needed to keep Midir talking. Maybe if he was talking he would be too distracted to hurt him again. Maybe it would even buy Etienne time to rescue him. "Why did she choose my father?" His voice was weak and tremulous.

Midir looked as if he was remembering. "At first I thought it was spite or caprice. Éibhleann of the Waters was never actually stupid, but she could be foolish. I'm not sure you have enough experience to understand that distinction. Anluan wanted her more than any of the other Sons of Dagda and made many public declarations that he would forever love her above any others—which I heard angered and humiliated Niamh, his Queen." A smirk of pleasure crossed his face for a moment at that. "Your father, Eoin, was the youngest and least powerful of my brothers, and lived under Anluan's patronage as one of his knights. He had a reputation for gallantry and bravery but had so little power and magical ability it was rumored that he was evidence of Dagda's waning hold on the High King-ship of Faerie.

"And yet Éibhleann chose the least of Dagda's sons to be her love." Midir stayed quiet for a moment, lost in thought, his gaze turned toward the window overlooking the city. Finally, he spoke again. "It wasn't until your father died in battle and she chose to fade to mist and memory rather than live without him, that I knew she really did love him." He turned back to Cian. "Foolish and excessively dramatic, but still love."

Cian swallowed. He had to keep Midir talking. "You must all have been disappointed when she chose him."

Midir's smile turned bitter. "My brothers were certainly disappointed, but more significantly—with regard to Eoin's fate—they were angry. I would not be at all surprised to discover that one or more of them were behind his death."

Cian drew in a small gasp. "But, they were his brothers!"

Midir gave a graceful shrug. "Sidhe politics are a bloody affair, my boy. Anluan may have raised you by hand, swaddled in silk and poetry, but outside his shelter—or more accurately his blinders—we fight and gouge for every scrap we can get. We are simply very elegant as we go about it."

"But why would they want to kill him? She fell in love with him."

"Spite, maybe. Or the right opportunity emerged. Murder the husband and then comfort the widow is a classic, you know. But, no, that wasn't all there was to it. Your parents were together for decades before Eoin was slain. I would wager he was murdered because of you."

A wash of dread went through Cian that had nothing to do with his confinement. "Me?"

Midir's smile twisted with the same sadism that Cian remembered from his rape so many years before. It made his blood chill. "Children are precious to us. We live such long lives and produce very few offspring. Some of us never have children of our own." Pain flashed across his face. "And some of us lose them. So, when Éibhleann bore you, she suddenly became even more desirable than she was before, and there was talk that her fertility was wasted on Eoin. He died soon after."

Cian's breath was coming in short, sharp gasps. It was his fault? His parents had died because of him? But he looked back to Midir and again saw that smile. This time anger kindled in his belly, burning back the guilt and some of the fear. His hands dropped to his sides and balled into fists. "What did you have to do with it?"

The smile turned bitter again. "I had nothing to do with it. I did not court Éibhleann."

"Why not?" It was out of his mouth before he could stop it. But, as frightened as he was, this was a side of the story he had never heard before.

Midir stepped away, looking like he was trying to decide something as he gazed out the window. When he turned back he looked serious. Sad. "I could not love her."

Cian tilted his head. "I don't understand. How did you know that?"

Midir sat in the chair across from Cian's. "That will take some explaining. I want you to understand some things."

That surprised Cian. "Why?"

"Because I made mistakes with Senán that I do not want to make with you."

The quivering in Cian's belly travelled up into his chest. What did that mean? Eyes wide, he could only nod.

Midir laced his fingers together. "So long ago that all but the very oldest of us have forgotten, I ruled a kingdom of my own. It was when our two worlds, Faerie and the Mortal Realm, were so intertwined as to be nearly indistinguishable. I had two wives, and by my eldest wife I had a daughter, Bri." He paused, looking across the millennia to a vision only he could see. His voice lowered. "She was so gentle. I remember, when she was little, she would give me these sticky kisses that I couldn't stand. I tried to forbid her sweets because she was always sticky from them, but even my most hardened warriors would give in to her smiles and pleading." A smile that had nothing to do with sadism tugged at his mouth for a moment. "Bri grew into a beautiful girl, and one day she caught sight of a sidhe lord from the neighboring kingdom. She was very young, and her heart was untried, and she immediately fell in love with him. It seems he felt the same way. But she was my only child and he was not a Son of Dagda or even a descendant of one, and in my pride, I refused to let them be together. When he tried to meet with her I had soldiers run him and his men off—one of them died.

"Rumors jumble as they travel, and Bri and her ladies had watched my soldiers run the boys off and had seen one fall. The word that reached my daughter's ear confirmed her worst fear, that it was her young love that had been slain. She took to her chamber and within the hour died of a broken heart." Midir's face had become expressionless, but he could not keep the pain from his eyes. "It was because of me and my damnable pride. The rumor was wrong, it wasn't her young lord who died, but that didn't matter. All that mattered to me was that I would never get another sticky kiss." He glanced at Cian. "I took the name 'Midir the Proud' that day."

Cian was afraid of Midir, but he could not help but ache for him a little. "You never had more children?"

He shook his head. "I lost everything worth having. My eldest wife warred against my younger wife, and in the end Fate took them both from me. Without my family, my kingdom was worthless to me. I wandered for a long time, much like Dagda himself now wanders, a king in name only." His mouth twisted into the bitter smile. "Eventually, I even lost that."

"Is that why you didn't court my mother?"

"It is what led me there. You are still very young, so you do not have a frame of reference for this, but life is long and while we do not forget the past, the pain of loss eventually becomes something we can endure. Time passed, and I was ready to live again. To rule again. But by then Faerie had begun to withdraw from the Mortal Realm and was becoming the realm you know, where kingdoms are forged by force of will out of so much nothingness and gray mist. I now had many, many younger brothers with kingdoms of their own, thanks to Dagda's prolific ability to sire sons. Curiously, we have few sisters, but I digress. My brothers thought that any kingdom I could create from the raw stuff of Faerie would eclipse theirs and so they struck a deal with me. In exchange for not building my own realm within Faerie, I would be given generous holdings and the right to foster all of my brothers' sons.

"In a very real way, I could have children again—many children. I would raise and guide and mentor the next generation of kings, and the generations that followed. None of them could ever take the place of my Bri, but it was an offer that filled a need in me more than having a kingdom of my own did, so I agreed. For many centuries, I was happy."

Midir stood suddenly and began to pace, his steps measured, his right hand flexing, to the window and back again. "And then I met a woman. She was beautiful—but aren't all sidhe women? More than that, she was brilliant and powerful and intoxicating. She was a Queen of her own realm and not of Dagda's line, which is not common. I had taken other lovers before then. I even had a favored mistress when I first came to know her. I discarded the girl soon after." Rage colored Midir's face. "I lived for the moments I could be with my Summer Queen, and the hours without her crawled by like eternities. I was not the only one who courted her, but I was the most ardent and the most powerful." He turned toward Cian, his expression wild. Cian recoiled from his intensity. "I loved her! Finally, I swore to her that I would never love another." His breathing was ragged. "Just that. No stipulations, no prevarications. I gave her everything. And I won her heart." He gave a bitter laugh. "For a little while."

"A... a little while?"

Midir's smirk was twisted with rage and pain. "Her name is 'The Summer's Kiss,' after all. I just never thought I would be one to burn."

Cian's eyes widened. The Summer's Kiss? But... but that was Queen Niamh, Etienne and Senán's mother!

"No, Anluan, that viper, had learned the secret to courting her by watching his brothers try and fail, so when her passion for me began to cool he was there waiting, pretending disinterest, and enticed her to court him. They married and merged their realms." Midir sneered. "Of course, Niamh eventually tired of him, too, and their union is an unbreakable pantomime of misery—but *I* was the one left destroyed!" He brought his fist down on the back of the chair that held his jacket and the frame let out a resounding crack.

Cian flinched back with a whimper.

Midir gripped the chair back, his fingers turning white before tearing through the upholstery. The wood groaned. "Because of her, I cannot love *anyone* ever again. Lest I become foresworn, stripped of my power and rendered naked and vulnerable to my enemies." His eyes burned with intensity and his breath came fast and hard. "Do you understand? I've been trapped like this for over a thousand years!"

Cian shivered in terror. He tried to think through the fear, but he did not know what to say.

Midir turned away from Cian and the ruined chair. He stalked the short distance to the window and stood with both hands braced against the glass, glaring out at the city in the early morning sunlight. Tension sung across his shoulders like a bowstring pulled too tight.

Long moments passed in silence. Cian felt his shivering lessen, and his mind was able to work again. Questions began to pile up. He opened his mouth, but nothing came out. He nibbled on his lower lip, and then drew in a deep breath. "Is that why you kidnapped Senán and me? Is that why you're going to invade the realms? Revenge?" Midir turned to face him, an incredulous expression on his face, but Cian pressed on. "But you can't invade. You said it yourself. You'll be foresworn. You agreed you wouldn't have your own realm within Faerie…"

Midir held up his right hand, leaving the left pressed to the glass. "Stop. What are you talking…?" He stopped, his gaze turning inward for a moment, and then burst into laughter.

Cian frowned. "We know about the giant rift you're opening, and that you took Senán and killed that other prince to weaken the two courts, and that you're building an army of fae."

But Midir was still laughing. "Is that what she said?" His mirth rang through the bedroom and filled Cian with confusion. "Stupid bitch. I took Senán because he should have been my son, not Anluan's. And now he will always be mine. As for Prince Ciarán—let's just say that Ceallach is not the only brother of mine who should be wishing he had kept his promises. They thought they were clever, when only the eldest of them swore their sons to my care in exchange for my oath. They thought that meant they could just turn their backs on me. And now they have lost the sons they owed to my care." His grin could have drawn blood. "What I did to you… that was for revenge, too. Because Anluan would have you."

Cian shuddered, but kept to his plan to keep Midir talking. He just did not want to talk about that, specifically. "Then, you don't plan to invade Faerie?"

Midir snorted. "No. My brothers can keep their precious little realms." He turned back to the window and said, his voice quiet and intense, "I'm after something much better." Cian watched Midir's eyes as they scanned the skyline. At last he said in a voice so soft even Cian barely heard him, "The time of hiding is over."

Cian's brows knit together. "What—?"

A strange, warbling keen rose in the air, bringing with it an arcane resonance that set all the glass in the room vibrating. Midir backed away from the window, a frown turning his mouth. A ball of lavender energy burst through one of the inner walls and struck against his side, splattering color across his shields. Midir cursed and turned just as more colored balls flew through the same wall, shattering lamps and mirrors where they did not pass right through the next wall. Cian could hear the sounds of destruction in other rooms. The keen cut off and was replaced by a voice that screamed out words, ragged and breaking. "What's happening?"

Cian's heart stuttered with recognition. Even distorted, he knew that voice. "Senán!" He jumped to his feet. "I can hear you!"

There was a wail. "How can I understand you?"

Cian blinked, and then his eyes widened. He had still been speaking in Faerie Gaelic. He switched to English. "Senán! Jeremy? It's Ci—"

Midir struck Cian across the face. "Shut up!"

"Who am I?" The vibration intensified. Midir looked to the windows in alarm.

Cian took advantage of his distraction to shift further away. "You're Prince Senán of Seelie! You're my frie—"

"I said be silent, fool!" Midir backhanded Cian hard enough to take him off his feet, over the corner of the bed, and onto his side on the floor. "You're making it worse."

Senán had begun wailing again, repeating, "It's not true," over and over in rapid succession. Magic flew around the room with no pattern or direction. The windows shivered with increasing violence.

Midir strode halfway across the room, then turned back and pointed a threatening hand at Cian. "Stay. We're not finished." He held Cian's wide eyes a moment longer and then hurried away. He slammed the door shut behind him.

Cian collapsed to his side, quaking on the carpet. The whole side of his face throbbed with pain, he could taste blood in his mouth, and in his mind, he was again a young boy at Midir's mercy. The agony, the confusion, the smells; they all washed over him, threatening to drown him in horrific memory. He stared unblinking at the entwined leaf pattern of the bedspread. This time his blood would not soak the grass of that forest glade, but this blanket.

"Who *are* you? You're not my father!"

Cian jerked away from the hanging edge of the bedspread and raised himself up on his elbow to look in the direction of his friend's cry. Senán needed his help. But Midir's voice also carried through the wall, the words less clear but his anger unmistakable. Cian could not stop the whimper that rose to meet the blood in his mouth. He put his shaking hand on the edge of the bed and pulled himself to his knees. Compared to Midir he was nothing, an insect to be crushed without thought. Even Etienne was afraid of Midir, and Etienne wasn't afraid of anything.

There was a sharp pop to Cian's right. He looked and saw a map of cracks had formed in the window glass. Still it shivered from the magical vibrations.

Cian still shivered, too. He turned to the closed door. If he disobeyed Midir, he knew he would hurt him. And he did not want to leave Senán, not when he was so close. But, he had to be smart if he was going to save his friend. He didn't stand a chance against Midir. And what had Midir meant, '*I made mistakes with Senán that I do not want to make with you?*' Was he talking about tearing apart his mind like he had Senán's? The thought made Cian shake harder and he struggled against his fear. He had to think.

What would Etienne do? Cian's first thought was that Etienne wouldn't leave him and that thought filled him with warmth that eased the shaking. Etienne was coming for him; he knew he was—but he didn't want Etienne to get killed trying to rescue him. Etienne was smart. He would be looking for the right opportunity. Cian had to give it to him. And then they would get Winter and together they would save Senán.

Cian looked down at his hand against the patterned bedspread. He had to find his own way out of here.

He eased out the door and into the hall, to find himself face to face with a shattered mirror. The fragments of his reflection looked frightened and pale. He took another step—and jerked backwards as a blue streamer of magic blew past his face. He pulled the bedroom door shut behind him.

"Get away from me!"

"Damn it, boy, calm down!"

Cian could not help it. He was drawn to the open door just down the hall. He just wanted to see his friend.

Wild magic formed a maelstrom in the center of the room, a swirling storm of light and color that exploded randomly in all directions. It was the storm that was the source of the resonance. A huddled figure hunched down on the floor in the middle of it all. Midir had both arms raised as he tried to get closer and had to duck away when a ball of light spun toward his face.

Cian backed quickly away out of Midir's line of sight. There was nothing he could do here, and he needed to get out while Midir was distracted. He moved with rapid steps down the hall, trying to sense when the wild magic would start flying again and straining his hearing for the sound of anyone else. But all he could hear were Midir and Senán.

The hall let out into the large room that Midir had dragged him through before. It looked like a collection of smaller rooms without walls, each defined by its furnishing, with what he had come to recognize as a kitchen near a table and chairs, and then clusters of chairs and couches loosely arranged around the strange, featureless black hearth. But what he was looking for was displayed along the walls.

Weapons of every sort hung from racks and were exhibited on the walls in designs—some of varieties and uses Cian had never seen and could not imagine. But most of them he knew and not just from Etienne's tutelage. While they had lived among the therian wolves on their farm in Kentucky, their Wolf King had taken him as one of his squires and taught him many things about war and weapons of the Mortal Realm. Kendrick belonged to an order of knights called the 'Es Cee Ay.' Etienne thought the wolves were weird to always pretend it was still another time, but Cian thought it was wonderful.

His eye was drawn to one weapon in particular, one even he had heard of, holding court in isolated splendor against the glittering, black surface of the fireplace mantle. It was a war axe, a lethal work of exquisite art etched into silvery-gold sidhe steel. At a full four feet in length, each graceful, curved blade was capable of cutting a knight in half. A weeping sidhe maiden was engraved on each blade face, four different, elegant depictions of despair, and their tears trailed down the long handle to form the wickedly pointed teardrop-shaped hilt. It had slain thousands.

It was Grief.

Cian shivered and backed away from the named weapon. Etienne had taught him to never covet another's weapon, but Grief was one he wanted no part of, anyway. He needed something more mundane. Etienne had taught him to look for what he was most familiar with, and he looked, for a moment overwhelmed by the size of the collection and his need to hurry. Finally, he found a rapier resting on a display rack with others of a similar style. He drew it from its scabbard and nearly dropped it when an unpleasant sensation sizzled up his arm. It wasn't sidhe steel, but mortal steel.

Cian frowned in distaste. He did not often touch steel directly; Etienne did not let him. It was not unlike the time he touched the inside of that light socket, only less intense, but it still left him uncomfortable with a vague sense of nausea.

A bright ball of light struck one of the weapon displays, knocking the whole thing to the ground with a deafening metallic crash. Senán had been reduced to inarticulate screaming.

Cian looked around at the other sheathed swords but could not tell which ones might be sidhe steel and he did not have the time to check them all. He sheathed the rapier and gripped it by the scabbard. It would have to do.

Cian quickly made his way to Midir's front door and let himself out of the apartment. Out there were only the small entry chamber and the elevator door. He pushed the only button beside the door and waited. He remembered from being with Etienne that they had had to wait for these things. Even so, he looked frequently over his shoulder. Was it quieter in there, or were the walls just very thick? The soft chime of the elevator was loud in the silence and Cian stifled a small cry of alarm.

Alone inside, he was faced with a bank of buttons that crawled up the reflective surface. So many! Before on the way up he had been so afraid he had not noticed them. Which one should he push? He wanted down, down to the ground... His eyes traveled down the rows looking for a button with a large 'G' symbol. That was the first letter in the English word for ground. He had seen those on elevators before. But there was no 'G' button. The door slid shut and Cian's heart jumped. What was wrong? He looked at the lower buttons again. Etienne always pushed a lower button on an elevator to go down, but they had never been in one with so many buttons.

And then he saw a button with an 'L' symbol. He had seen Etienne push buttons with that one, too, to get to the ground. He pressed the button and it lit up. The elevator began to move down. Down and away from Midir. Cian sagged against one wall with relief.

Cian glanced up and caught his reflection. He looked exhausted and pale. One side of his face was swollen, and blood was drying between his lips. That would catch attention and he did not want anyone to notice him leaving. He dug into his pocket, pulled out a paper napkin and cleaned the blood, then cast a glamour over the injury. It was a small spell that even he could manage. He then cast a similar glamour of concealment over the rapier and settled in to watch the lights progress across the buttons.

Still the elevator carried him down.

CHAPTER TWENTY

"Seriously, who gets business deliveries from an herbal store first thing on a Sunday?"

"I don't know. This guy does. Just let me up."

The security guard rolled his eyes. "Fine, whatever. Give me his name and I'll call him."

Yeah, okay... so it wasn't Jessie's best plan ever. "Uh, sure. Gimme a sec." Why hadn't she thought about that? She made lots of business deliveries for Curiosity's, so the sneak-in-as-a-delivery-person idea had made perfect sense when she'd come up with it.

The only thing was she usually made those deliveries to the preternatural leaders and they were all people who knew her.

She turned her back on the big round desk and dug the receipt book out of her delivery bag while her mind spun at a frantic pace. She only knew the names of two people who worked here, and one was the guy who had kidnapped Cian. She really didn't want the guard to call him. Even if he let her up to his nefarious lair where he was holding her friend prisoner, she could just imagine how that conversation would go. *'Here, have some herbal lotion. I'm just going to grab this boy and run, now. Kthxbai.'*

Yeah, that would fly like a lead turkey.

The other one was Jeremy Moore, the walking, talking MacGuffin himself. Man, that would have to be a major mind fuck, knowing a knight was, like, on a quest to rescue you. Jessie wondered how much he could know about himself, to stay with a guy like Midir. Maybe nothing? Maybe everything and he was just really screwed up? Either way, she didn't know him and couldn't trust him, and she certainly couldn't have the guard call him.

"Well, kid? Who placed the order?"

"I'm looking." Shit! Jessie took her time flipping pages, but she knew she needed to make a choice. Fast. Her eyes slid to the elevator bank and her mind traveled up the floors of the office tower. Did she have the power and skill to fight her way through this building? Winter's cousins, Kelley and Martina, had taught her a lot about combat magic, but would it be enough? How many other magicians were in this building—besides the really big, scary one that had Cian? Once she made this choice, there was no turning back. She would have to fight her way up to Cian, who was only God knew where, and then fight to get them both back out. She had known that coming here.

She just hadn't known the tower was so freaking big.

The only other option was to turn back, admit that Winter was right, and she was just a half-grown wizard who'd bitten off more than she could chew. Leave Cian here. God, how could she do that?

"Look, if you don't have someone to deliver to, you're gonna have to leave."

Jessie looked up, her face heating in frustration, and out of the corner of her eye saw a tall man with red-gold hair step off the elevator. Her head snapped around in a double take. Cian? It was Cian! "Him," she said, her voice high with tension. She cleared her throat and pointed at Cian, trying to regain her cool. "I mean, that guy there. He's the one who came to the store yesterday." Was he okay? How had he gotten down here? But, questions had to wait. First, she had to get him to safety.

The guard gave her an irritated look and turned to face Cian. "Hey! Are you expecting a delivery?"

Cian froze, eyes wide.

Jessie raised her delivery bag to her chest to display the logo and wiggled it back and forth as she grinned at him.

Cian saw her, and a wide smile of relief spread across his face. Jessie's cheeks colored more. Nobody should be that gorgeous! There were laws. "Um, yes?"

The guard shook his head. "Well, come get it."

Cian skirted the tree in its big planter and crossed the lobby to Jessie. She tucked the receipt book in her bag. "I've got the rest of it in the car. Come on, I'll help you with it." She jerked her head toward the tall, glass doors.

The security guard muttered something under his breath and then answered his phone. Jessie pushed her glasses higher and decided to blow him off.

Cian fell into step close behind her.

"Stop him!" Jessie spun around to see a tall man with long, wavy, black hair striding toward them from the far side of the lobby. He was also impossibly hot, so he had to be another sidhe.

"Friend of yours?" she asked Cian. The guard was still talking on his phone but looked up at the commotion.

Cian shook his head with a worried frown and stepped away from her. She saw a shimmer and then he seemed to pull a sword, a rapier, out of thin air.

The black-haired sidhe stopped and a slow grin spread across his face. He also did the shimmering thing and a sword of a kind she did not recognize appeared in his hand. "Let's dance, little boy. Show me what you can do." And then he was moving too fast for Jessie to follow.

Cian made a small noise of panic, and he, too, was a blur.

"What the fuck?"

Jessie saw the guard standing up behind the desk, eyes wide in shock. But his hand lifted to his shoulder mic and he started talking. She surged forward. It was her turn.

As she moved she swung the delivery bag off her shoulder, around behind her and whipped it forward, clobbering the guard in the face with the full weight of a few pounds of herbal products. There was the crunch of cracking glass and the sudden scent of lotion filled the air, mixed with his muffled cry of surprise and pain. Jessie released the bag handle on impact and stretched over the counter, grabbing the guard's shoulder speaker mic, and with a Word of Command surged raw power into the line. A mind-splitting squeal erupted from the guard's earpiece and she heard cries of pain echo in the lobby behind her. She twisted, belly down on the counter, to see two more guards clawing at their ears. She forced more power into the communications line, bringing the tone to a fury's scream, until the whole system overloaded and cut out. There, no more talking for them. Jessie kicked back off the counter and palmed her focus object. The pink, rectangular eraser covered in glyphs was warm from her pocket. It was only her first one, her learning one, but it was one that she could take to school with her without question or hassle. She got off a quick stun spell on the guard she had struck with the bag and turned to the other two now recovering from the feedback.

Cian and the stranger moved past in a blur of singing steel, taking their fight to the far side of the lobby. Cian's voice reached her, broken and breathless, "Midir! Hurry!"

Jessie braced her feet, heart racing as the two men closed in on her. Yeah, no pressure. She caught the closest in the face with a stun spell, which Martina had liked to call the 'spectator special.' It was intended for use on human bystanders. It was fast, clean, kept a target down for about an hour and caused short-term memory loss. But she only had time for the one—the other man reached for her as his buddy fell.

This one wasn't clean, but it was fast. It was a lesson Kelley and Martina had hammered home hundreds of times. She side-stepped the man's grab and brought her knee up into his soft belly, driving hard for his spine. He folded, and she drilled her elbow into the back of his neck with all the force her young body could bring to bear.

The man dropped.

Jessie bounced backwards on the balls of her feet.

He did not move again.

Jessie waited, bouncing, a stun spell on the tip of her tongue. He still did not move. Dread crept cold into her blood. Why wasn't he moving? But she knew the answer, knew what the defensive move she had just done, in theory, was supposed to be able to do. It *should* knock a man out. It *could* kill. It was just that this wasn't a practice dummy, or the soft floor of the dojo. This was a strange man on cold marble, and he wasn't moving.

Jessie felt sick.

Behind her Cian cried out in pain. Jessie pulled her attention away from the guard to see Cian backed into a corner, a line of blood running down to his elbow and fear on his face.

The other sidhe laughed. "Come on, boy. Your girlfriend is watching. Pick up your game."

She forced herself to compartmentalize her emotions about the guard. She had to get Cian out of here.

But first a rhythmic chiming caught her attention. Jessie looked and saw the elevator numbers were all coming down from the upper floors. They could be bringing more guards—or worse, any one of them could carry Midir! She ran for the elevator bays, skidding to a stop on her denim-covered knees in front of the center set of buttons and slapped her right hand to the metal. She surged power into the elevator system, wasting her body's magic on brute force efficiency because she didn't know enough about the electrical system for finesse. She felt the drain even as she heard pops and a high-pitched whine and a series of dull graunching sounds that she prayed were the elevator breaks engaging. Two of the number lights exploded before the whole thing blanked out.

She waited a moment. No crashing. Good. But how long would the elevators be stalled? She turned, her breath coming in short pants, to see that the guard she had dropped was turning his head—thank God—but Cian was struggling. The black-haired sidhe was playing with him, flashing and dodging from side to side, leaving small cuts in his wake.

Jessie shot off a stun spell on the waking guard and got as close to the duel—if that was even the word for the ass-kicking Cian was getting—as she dared, one hand on the edge of the tree planter. They were so close and fast as they moved she could not risk throwing even a stun spell.

Cian cried out as the sidhe whipped his blade across the back of his sword hand once, twice, and the third time he dropped the rapier. The sidhe kicked Cian hard, forcing him to the floor, and held him at the point of his silvery-gold sword. "Time to end the fun, kid. I have no idea how you two got in here, but I know someone who's going to want to meet you."

Oh, bad, this was—Jessie looked at the pottery tree planter under her hand, and then at the profile of the standing sidhe.

This was her chance.

Clutching her focus object, she sketched glyphs in the air with more speed than she ever had in her life and watched them settle over the planter. She felt the pull of power as it was dragged from her body to encircle the planting, the tremendous weight of the thing as an abstract sensation that seemed to sink her into the cheap soles of her sneakers. And then she gathered every scrap of energy she could muster, pooled it—and used it to launch the tree, the soil, and the pot with violent force at the sidhe's upper body.

It took him off his feet and crushed him against the wall beside him.

"Run!" Jessie ran toward Cian and grabbed his arm. Dirt and debris were everywhere and only the sidhe's legs were visible sticking out from beneath the shattered remains of the huge pot.

Cian scrambled to his feet and ran with her.

They got exactly five steps before Jessie's knees buckled. Oh shit! She had forgotten this could happen.

"What's wrong?" Cian came skidding to a stop.

Jessie fell forward, tried to catch herself on her hands, but her arms went limp and she dropped.

Cian caught her before she smacked her face into the floor. Her glasses slipped down passed her nose and caught on her upper lip. "Jessie? Are you hurt? What's wrong?" His voice was high pitched with fear.

She tried to speak, to tell him, but no sound came out. She was utterly spent, her magic tapped, and she was left weak and helpless. Her fingers had no strength and she dropped her focus object. The eraser wobbled on the marble floor. Kelley and Martina had warned her against this so many times. Winter was going to kill her—if they got out of here alive.

There was a tinkling noise of broken shards of pottery shifting against one another. Cian looked over his shoulder and his eyes widened. He grabbed up her eraser, stuffed it in his pocket, and lifted her into his arms all in one, graceful, dizzying motion. She tried to object to a skinny guy like him picking her fat ass up, but she remembered him picking up that backpack; her weight would be nothing compared to that monster. Then he was running, the lobby a blur of motion, and they were at the glass doors. At least, she was pretty sure they were at the glass doors—her glasses were still in her mouth. Cian dropped her legs to work the pressure handle and they were out in the sunlight.

Which was awesome! Except that her legs still weren't working, and she was willing to bet Cian couldn't drive. The way she was, she couldn't even tell him that the blue compact in the circle drive was hers. How the fu—?

"What happened?"

Brian?

"I don't know. She just... um... I don't know the word. Fell down?"

Brian gently pulled her glasses off and tucked them back onto her face, and then scooped her up into his muscular arms. "C'mon."

Cian nodded, casting his attention behind them. "Yes, we need to go. Hurry, please."

Jessie's head rolled from side to side as Brian broke into a run, her face nestled against his warm shoulder. Her cheeks were heating up again and she was glad he couldn't see her, but God he smelled good. She didn't even care that her glasses dug against her nose with each bounce. As embarrassing as it was to have overextended her magic and done this to herself, it was almost worth it.

She just wished he wasn't too good for her.

They ran up along the passenger side of Brian's—well, the bookstore's—van, and Brian's voice rumbled against her cheek, "Can you get the door for me?" Cian figured out the handle and got the door open, and Brian lifted her inside.

He disappeared from her sight for a moment and she heard the side door slide open. The van dipped and rocked as Cian climbed in. Then Brian reappeared, stepped up on the running board and pulled her seatbelt around her, an activity that brought his face pleasantly, and blushingly, close to her breasts. It also made her think of something and gave her enough energy to get a question out. "How?" she breathed.

Brian looked up, his dark eyes questioning, his face inches from hers. "How?"

Jessie widened her eyes at him.

"Oh! Me." He gave her a little smile. "I followed you. The Theatre's only a few blocks from the bookstore, and you said you were going to do something drastic." His eyes twinkled, and he tapped the brim of her store cap. "Besides, you're not the only one who can pretend to be a delivery driver."

"They're coming! We have to go!"

Brian turned his head. "Pull that door closed, just like you opened it. Hard." He jumped into the van and crossed over Jessie as Cian slammed the sliding door home. She could hear running footsteps in syncopated rhythm getting closer. Brian turned the key and the big engine roared to life.

Something hit the side of the van and it rocked up on two wheels for a moment.

"Go! Go now!"

Jessie couldn't agree more.

Brian hit the gas. The van jerked and there was the sound of screaming metal, and then it jerked again, and they were speeding away. "What was that?" Brian asked, his eyes never leaving their path as he whipped around the circle drive.

Jessie turned her head and saw security guards running up to join a huge man in the security uniform and what had to be the sidhe, now filthy and looking the worse for wear, shaking his hand as if in pain. She thought again about the strength it took to lift that backpack and cringed at the thought of what the van looked like, now. Brian's mom, Norah, was going to be so pissed. How was she going to explain this to Brian?

Just as he passed out of sight from the window, the sidhe cast his hand out at the approaching pack of guards. They all dropped as one. Did he stun them? All at once? How did he do that? Why did he do—? And then the sidhe vanished behind a glamour. Oh, so not good! "Go faster." He did it to hide to what he was going to do next from the humans.

"What the… Is that guy *chasing* us?"

Jessie's heart sped up from both alarm and shock. Brian could see him? How? She couldn't see him, and she was a wizard. "Go," she whispered. "Go-go-go." She wanted to ask but couldn't. It would only draw attention to the fact that they were being chased by a guy who was supposed to be invisible.

Brian had floored the gas pedal even before her urging and Jessie imagined she could hear all eight cylinders of the engine roar. The van was empty of all but their weight, and it flew down the drive. The iron gates were wide open to let in the trickle of Sunday workers, but a barrier bar stood in their way. On the other side light weekend traffic moved back and forth. "Hold on!"

Jessie whimpered.

The van slammed into the barrier with a bang, twisting it backwards off its hinges and forcing it to an awkward angle. Brian dove into a natural break in traffic, crossing lanes and tipping onto two wheels for a moment with the force of their momentum, but only one car honked at them and they sped away from the office tower.

After a few minutes he slowed down. "Well, that was extremely dramatic. Good news is that guy's not chasing us anymore—and how he was able to do that, I guess we'll never know?" He took his eyes off the road for a second to glance at Jessie.

Jessie shrugged. But inside she was squirming with frustration. She wanted to tell him everything. He was smart, he was going to figure it out eventually. She wished it was possible to lie to Winter. Then she could tell Brian everything, then tell Winter he had guessed, but it wasn't happening. And the events of their get-away weren't wild enough to mandate full disclosure in Winter's book. Maybe Brian didn't want to know, anyway? Of course, that might change when he got a look at the side of his mom's van.

"Hey, you okay back there?" Brian was looking in the rearview mirror.

Cian! Jessie twisted in her seat as far as her weakness would allow and saw that he looked really sick. What was wrong? And then she remembered the way the strange sidhe had been shaking his hand and her eyes widened with understanding. It was the van. Norah had one of those old conversion vans from like a million years ago that was almost all steel. "Gotta get him back," she whispered. The sooner they got Cian out of the van, the better.

"Alright. Back where?"

"Theatre."

"How did I know you were going to say that?"

CHAPTER TWENTY-ONE

Winter emerged from the powder room, energy singing along her veins, an empty green bottle concealed in the bottom of her bag. She had had two before leaving the house in anticipation of this emergency, but they had burned right through her, and in the heat of the argument with Erik she could not drink coffee. She just needed it to get through the next few hours. She needed it to rescue Cian.

She needed it to keep Erik and Etienne from tearing each other apart.

"Have you lost your mind? There isn't time for breakfast."

The smell of eggs and sausage hit Winter and her stomach roiled in protest. She swallowed hard, clenching her jaw as she stretched her mouth in a parody of a smile in an attempt at controlling her sudden nausea. The energy potion and food did not mix. She had not eaten since... she cast her thoughts back, uncertain, and then shook her head. It wasn't important at the moment. "Erik, really, we need to—"

"Winter, sit down. You need to eat something." Erik indicated the seat that had materialized while she was sneaking the potion. One of his therian stood holding a steaming plate of food.

Oh... oh, no. The fake smile could not hold up. "I'm fine. I—"

"No, you are not fine. You look like death warmed over. And you are going to eat something."

"Erik, a boy's life is at stake! We don't have time for this." She gestured at the plate but meant the whole nonsense of the morning.

The Vampire King was standing in front of her, his movement so fast she had not seen it. He caught her wrist and held up her hand for inspection, then looked at her face. "Your hand isn't shaking anymore. But your eyes are glassy and though your cheeks are flushed bright your lips are white and your complexion is almost gray. What did you take?"

Winter tried to tug free, but he would not release her. There was no point in trying to lie outright. He had over eleven-hundred years of life experience. "I know what I'm doing, Erik. Let me go and let me do my job!"

"Jessie says she hasn't seen you eat in weeks and that she keeps finding your uneaten food in the trash. All anyone sees you drink are those coffees. You're sick and you're on something. Now, tell me what!" She watched fear and anger and worry chase each other across his face.

Winter stopped struggling and met his eyes. "I'll tell you if you help us get Cian back." It was a hope—a hope for help, a hope he would be distracted. A hope to buy her a little more time to hide her secret. She refused to look at Etienne. He suspected, he had said as much. All he had to do was keep quiet a little while longer and maybe she would have enough time left to help him.

She would have been surprised that Jessie had not jumped in with the accusations, but Erik in a full tirade was intimidating. Jessie's parents yelled at her too much, as it was. She was probably still hiding somewhere in the crowd.

Erik frowned, nodded, and let go of her wrist. "Agreed. But no more secrets. Now, you eat breakfast while I get what fighters I have together. You have a few minutes." He stepped away and made a summoning motion toward one of his lieutenants.

Her stomach twisted. "No, I should go on ahead and review Midir's protections, see what I can do to bypass—"

Erik silenced her with a look meant to quell warriors. "Winter. Sit. Down."

She stiffened her spine rod-straight and braced her knees. "Erik, I love you, but you do not tell me what to do."

He took a step toward her. "Do not think you're too big to spank, little girl. I'm already not happy with you."

Her face flushed an indignant shade of embarrassed. He had to say that in front of his court? Really?

"It's reasonable," said Etienne, watching her, his expression neutral. "You need food in you."

Winter had to fight to not look in desperation for a quick exit.

Erik looked at the faerie knight with curiosity but had to turn back to answer a question from his lieutenant.

Etienne held out his hand to Winter. She took it and let him lead her, her body stiff, to the chair beside the therian with the cooling plate of breakfast.

Lana emerged from the crowd, her color high and her lips swollen, a pleased smile on her face. She looked around with interest. "What did I miss?"

Etienne shot her a look of irritation.

Another therian produced a folding table for Winter and her breakfast was served on it with a glass of juice. She picked up her fork and took a breath, trying to ignore the savory, greasy smell of the sausage. Why was Erik trying to make her eat sausage? He hadn't eaten it in over a century, since the time he found that fingertip… She shuddered and shoved the visual out of her mind. She wasn't helping herself. Having been raised by Erik, she was not a fan of sausage, either.

This could be a good thing. Not eating really was very bad for her. If she could ride out the initial nausea, it would be good to have protein in her body. She stabbed at a bite of scrambled eggs and gave it the bare minimum of chewing to try to avoid tasting it before choking it down. Two more bites followed this pattern and then she had a sip of juice. She raised her brows in surprise. It was work—

She heard a scream and felt like a taloned fist ripped into her stomach. Winter was doubled over without remembering how, her throat buzzing, and realized she had been the one who cried out. She felt the food coming back up and tried to get out of the chair, but her legs tangled on the little table, knocking both it and her over. She got upright on her hands and one knee just as pain ripped again through her belly and the heaving took complete control. Alarmed voices swirled around her, and somewhere in the back of her mind she knew she would be utterly humiliated later. Hands rubbed her cold back, hot even through her coat, sweater, and dress. The green body of the potion mixed with a heavy stream of bright blood. She struggled to breathe through the clenching agony that rode her body, that forced tears from her eyes as she continued to vomit blood long past when she should have stopped. All she could do was clutch at the ornate carpet as if she were drowning.

Something was wrong.

At last the fist that crushed her released and Winter drew a gagging breath, her mouth tasting hot and metallic. It seemed to be over. All except for the pain. She felt torn inside and cried out when she tried to sit upright.

Erik pulled her away from the mess soaking into the rugs that covered his dais and wiped the blood from her mouth with a cloth. "What's wrong?" he asked her in a voice she had not heard since the last time she fell off her bike.

Winter's throat burned even more, and tears welled up. She had thought she had more time. She parted her lips... she had so much to tell him, but her vision spun, pulling her into darkness.

The pain found her. There were voices there, too.

"She's so thin. It's like she's made of bones. How did she get like this?"

"How did you miss it? Even sidhe women aren't this thin."

"With the clothes she wears, the loose sweaters and the long dresses, no one could tell. I mean, we saw something was wrong. The whole community is talking about it. We just didn't know how bad it was really getting."

Winter opened her eyes and found herself looking at the underside of a dark-blue bed canopy, embroidered with dragon-headed ships. She was in Erik's bed? How odd. She turned her head toward the voices. Etienne and Erik sat on either side of the hearth, leaning inward toward each other and speaking in low tones. A smile tugged at one corner of her mouth. They no longer seemed on the verge of violence.

Michael sat on the arm of Erik's chair. He turned to face her and smiled. "She's awake."

The men gathered at her bedside. Erik brushed his rough hand over her hair. His sea-blue eyes were dark with worry. "You gave us a scare, little girl."

She gave him a small grimace that was half pain, half apology. "I need my bag." Her voice was ragged. Michael nodded and moved away.

"What do you want?" Erik frowned with suspicion.

Winter looked at Etienne. He also frowned. They had spoken, it seemed. "I hurt." Talking was not helping, but she had to do it nonetheless. "I need the painkiller." She gasped and writhed a little, her arms wrapped tight around her belly as if to contain the tearing pain.

The mistrust vanished from Erik's face. "Michael, hurry!" He laid his hands over hers, as if trying to control her pain with his will.

Michael appeared at his side, eyes wide, and Etienne took the bag. He looked inside and scowled harder. "What the hell am I looking for? I thought my backpack was bad—your bag is a disaster." The contents rattled and clanked together as he shifted it around.

Winter gritted her teeth. "Upper pocket, nearest the strap. Small, blue bottle with a black, eye-dropper top." Her breathing came in short, shallow gasps, and sweat chilled her skin. Her bag was not a disaster—just because he didn't understand how she organized things, did not mean it was a mess.

Etienne dug around and came up with a bottle. "This?" His gray eyes were intense, but he exhibited none of the worry the two vampires did.

She appreciated his reserve and focused past the pain onto Etienne's hand. She nodded. "Three drops in a small glass of water."

Michael flashed away and returned, a shot glass in his hand. "Is this too small?"

Winter shook her head. Actually, a tumbler would be better, but given her earlier vomiting she did not trust herself to hold it all down. The shot glass would be fine.

Michael poured two fingers of water into the tiny glass and held it for Etienne to measure three drops of light-blue potion. Each one swirled in a dance of ghostly tendrils as it descended below the surface, suspended in place but never mixing completely. Etienne shifted forward and slid his free arm beneath Winter's back, cradling and lifting her into a sitting position.

Winter clenched her teeth against the pain, but whimpers escaped all the same.

Erik reached for her. "You're hurting her."

"Can't be helped." Etienne's tone was matter-of-fact, but only Winter could see his eyes. The strain of the morning was showing where the other men could not see. There was fear there. He must have been so worried for Cian. She needed to get back on her feet, so she could return his young friend to him. He held the shot glass steady to her lower lip, and then waited for her to bring her weak and shaking hand up to guide the mixture into her mouth.

It tasted like bright, metallic water turned too sharp, too intense. Winter downed it in one swallow and fought not to gag, convulsing once in Etienne's embrace. She had never taken this potion before but had administered it on hundreds of occasions. It flowed into her core and then swept outward, suppressing her pain with a suddenness that was itself a small agony. It took Winter's breath away and stiffened her spine. Etienne held her through it all.

Winter took her first deep breaths without pain and sagged against Etienne's arm in relief.

"Better?" he murmured against her hair.

She nodded and struggled to sit all the way up on her own. She didn't have time to rest. The painkiller would only work for a few hours and to be brutally honest with herself she was not sure how much longer she had to live. The painkiller would help her to function, but it would do nothing for the internal bleeding. Even the magic of her most potent potions could not stop the deterioration—not at this point. Etienne helped her swing her legs around and then stepped back.

Erik knelt down in front of her legs. "What happened? What's going on with you?"

She reached out and took the Vampire King's hands. Where to start? She wanted to push it off further away, after they got Cian back, but she knew Erik would not let her out of this room without an explanation, not now. She lowered her head. She did not want to hurt him. He had been the closest thing she had to a father, when her own refused to be there. Her lower lip trembled, and she bit down hard to still it. She was still so angry at her father—last night she had told him she was dying, and he had not cared. He still wouldn't care if she told him she had less time than she had thought. Erik, though... Erik would care.

But she couldn't do this in front of Jessie. She wouldn't understand. She was too young. Winter raised her head, looking around for the girl. Later. She would talk to her—Winter frowned, twisted to see around the bed curtains. "Erik, where's Jessie?" Maybe she was in the bathroom. After her collapse, there was no way Jessie would have stayed away.

"She's not here."

What? "No, she was right there..." Winter trailed off. She had seen Jessie earlier, standing by Jason, but that had been a while ago. With all the yelling and the fighting and going around and around, she had lost track of her. Where could she...? Her eyes widened in dawning comprehension and her heart began to hammer. "Oh, no. No-no-no-no-no," she whispered as horror swept through her.

"What?" Etienne gripped her shoulder and gave her a small shake. "What's wrong?"

She clenched Erik's hands. "We have to go get her. Erik, we have to go now!"

"Where? Wait... you don't mean... Winter, she wouldn't have."

Winter made a noise of exasperation. "Erik, have you *met* her?"

"What are you two talking about?" Etienne was looking back and forth between them in confusion.

"She's gone to Moore Investments. Erik, let me up. She's gone after Cian on her own." Winter stretched out to grab her bag. Her hands shook violently, and she had to twist the strap around her wrist to secure it. "Now we have both kids over there..." Her voice trailed off again, and she couldn't think. Her whole body was shaking. Now what was wrong with her?

Erik stood, towering over her. "Stay here. We'll go." His voice held tension.

"I can't lose her."

"That's not going to happen."

Winter grasped Erik's arm. He was still shirtless. "I've lost everyone else. Please, I can't lose Jessie, too." The faces of her family, in life—in death—flashed through her memory. She saw Jessie's sweet, round face the day she caught her shoplifting with magic, full of fear and anger; and then later, after she had not called the police and instead made Jessie sweep the store and put away stock, and then given her the items she had tried to steal and taught her a little magic. Jessie had been confused, suspicious... and had come back the next day, and the next. Not to steal, but to learn. To be accepted. Winter and her family had taken her in as if she had been born to them.

Her chest was tight with fear. She had already given her life to this city. What could she sacrifice for Jessie's safety? What more did she have to give? She would give it, if only she knew what it was.

All three men turned as one toward the bedroom door. Their hearing was so much more sensitive than hers. "What is it?"

"Hey, adult people!" Jessie's voice rang out into the silence. It sounded as if she was calling up the stairwell.

Winter did not realize she was running until she pushed her way through Erik's door.

Her legs buckled as she sprinted down the stairs, reminding her that she was still weak, and with the painkiller in her system she could seriously hurt herself without knowing. She clutched at the railing—but a strong arm caught her about the waist. She looked up and found herself with a face full of Etienne's hair as he kept racing down the stairs with her. He smelled like the herbal shampoo she made for the store and something else that she could not define. Something male. It smelled good, though.

But then they were at the bottom of the stairs and there were Jessie and Cian. Cian? Her knees nearly buckled again, this time with the intensity of her relief, and she pulled away from Etienne to run to Jessie, who stood grinning. Winter wrapped her arms around the younger girl and held her. She didn't care if Jessie tried to push her away; she needed to hold her, to know she was safe and whole. But Jessie suffered her mauling in silence.

Winter looked over to see Etienne embracing Cian, an arm tight around the boy's body while his other hand rested on the back of his head. He was saying something in Faerie Gaelic, and even though he bore several long lacerations, Cian blushed and beamed with pleasure. Winter smiled to see them, and then turned back to Jessie. "You worried me," she said, giving the girl's shoulders a small shake.

"I'm sorry," Jessie replied, sounding not at all contrite.

Winter pressed her lips tight and pulled back, preparing to scold her apprentice. She was safe, and Winter was profoundly grateful—but that did not excuse the fact that she had put herself in danger.

Jessie's eyes widened. "Why is there blood on your mouth?"

Winter wiped at her lips with her sweater sleeve. Cian was looking at her, now, too. "It's nothing." Her cheeks burned, but she refused to be derailed. She examined first one teen and then the other and her brows drew in. "Cian, please remove that glamour. Erik, I've left my bag upstairs and I need to tend Cian's cuts. And you," she fixed Jessie with narrowed eyes. "You're drained. How did you get back?"

Jessie crossed her arms. "I had it covered. I took out the communications system and the elevators, and I even creamed the sidhe that cut up Cian with this huge tree planter."

Winter raised one eyebrow. Etienne made an angry noise and she turned to see him brushing his fingers over the lurid purple swelling that covered half of Cian's face.

Jessie finally had the grace to look embarrassed. Her voice lowered nearly to a mumble. "And then I went down on my face in the lobby and Brian had to drive us back here."

Winter looked up past Jessie's shoulder to search the wide hallway in alarm. "You took Brian with you? Is he here?" The crowd from earlier had dispersed, but there was no sign of the strapping young man.

She rolled her eyes. "No and no. He followed me out there and then Erik's guys wouldn't let him in." She looked with irritation at the Vampire King. "He's not happy and he doesn't see why The Seahaven Opera House needs muscle, by the way."

Erik gave her a negligent wave of his hand in a manner closely resembling an obscene gesture and passed Winter's bag to her. "When I start to worry about the opinions of human teenage males, especially when it comes to the running of my Theatre, I'll make sure you're the first to know."

Jessie stuck her tongue out at him and turned back to Winter. "And here's another thing. The sidhe dude cast a glamour and Brian could see through it. How could he do that?"

Winter ignored the question. She knew the reason, but she didn't want to go into it with anyone. Not yet. Not ever, really. Instead she took Cian by his hand and led him to a chair. "Take off your shirts," she instructed quietly. As Cian's hands moved to his buttons she addressed her apprentice again. "We've talked about this, Jessie. You know better than to try to include him in our world." She helped Cian peel the blood-stiff fabric away from his wounds. "It only puts him in danger."

Jessie made a noise of frustration. "He's not stupid. How much longer do you really think it's going to be until he figures it out for himself?" She crouched down next to Cian's chair to better put herself near the center of Winter's attention. "Besides, you know just as well as the rest of us do that being ignorant is no protection in Seahaven. If it weren't for the fact that the monsters focus so much attention on the homeless who nobody tracks, the missing persons' rate would be astronomical."

Erik cleared his throat with a scowl. "Speaking as a 'Monster King,' I take offense to that. My people don't kill the sheep. It's too dangerous."

Winter wiped the dried blood from Cian's golden skin. His cuts were already showing signs of healing. "The two of you can argue about this after we figure out what to do about Midir's invasion of Faerie." Neither of them was wrong, but this was not the time…

"But he's not," said Cian. His green eyes kept flinching with pain under her ministrations, but he was looking at her intently. What was he seeing?

"Wait, what?" Etienne went down on one knee in front of Cian's chair. Winter felt the heat of his body radiating against her. It was getting a little crowded, but she kept working.

"He's not going to invade. That's what he said." Cian pulled his eyes from her to look to Etienne. "He said he would be foresworn if he did."

"Then what the hell is he up to?"

"That doesn't make any sense." It was the fae woman, Lana, emerging from the dining hall. "He's got the rift, the army, he destabilized the courts, he wants his own kingdom—what else could he be doing?"

"He said he wasn't trying to destabilize the courts," Cian said, his voice clear if a bit fearful. "He said he… did what he did out of revenge, because his brothers wouldn't foster their sons to him. And he said he did it to every brother who refused to foster a son, not just the two we knew about."

Winter opened a jar of pungent white cream and rubbed two fingers full into his bruised cheek with a gentle touch. Her mind worked furiously. "Cian, can you tell us exactly everything he said and did?"

Etienne frowned and gripped her arm. "I don't think that's a good idea."

Winter looked at Etienne's hand, and then raised her eyes until they met his. He did not release her.

"Hey!" Jessie's voice rose from beside Winter. "Let her go, Conan!"

Both Winter and Etienne ignored the teen. "Cian's stronger than you give him credit for," Winter said, her voice level. It was not the first time she had faced down someone who could crush her bones, and it would not be the last. Besides, he wasn't hurting her. "And even if he weren't, we need to know."

Etienne frowned harder.

"I'm fine." Cian drew Etienne's attention from her. "I'm really fine. I got away before he could hurt me."

The faerie knight still did not look happy, but he nodded and let go of Winter's arm.

Cian's eyes darted to the side as he gathered his thoughts and then he began talking. He started from when he was taken, the memory of fear seeming to make him stumble over his English words. Etienne or sometimes Winter would help get him over the bumps. But as he continued his story his confidence grew, and he began to gesture more with his hands as he spoke. It made it a little more challenging for Winter to see to his cuts, but she wanted him to focus on his storytelling more than she wanted him to hold still. Her hands moved of their own volition—she could treat minor injuries like this in her sleep and had come very close to doing just that in the past—while she listened intently to his every word, picking over each one for clues to Midir's intentions. When Cian said, "Then he said, 'The time of hiding is over,'" she heard Erik's shocked intake of breath behind her. Winter drew away and began to pace as she wiped her hands clean.

Her mind was whirling.

The others were talking around her, but she filtered them out. '*The time of hiding is over.*' The phrase played over in her head. It was insane. Preternaturals kept their existence a secret from the mass of humanity for a very good, very simple reason: humans dramatically outnumbered them. Of course, for centuries there had been debate among various factions who argued that the preternatural races should rule over the seemingly weaker humans, but those factions were always crushed by The Eldest. And even though preternaturals routinely preyed on humans when they were alone or in small groups, everyone sane understood that humans in large numbers were both paranoid and extremely dangerous. Even a single lucky human could slay a mighty dragon. As time passed into the modern era their weapons and technology made them even more deadly.

The annihilation of Hiroshima and Nagasaki had silenced even the insane.

What could Midir hope to accomplish? Winter ran her thumb over her lower lip. Cian had described him standing in front of his window as he spoke. *'I'm after something much better.'* She remembered him from the night before, standing before his office window staring out at the city lights as if he was king of all he surveyed. She blew out a breath in derision. King of all he surveyed, her... and then she froze. Her eyes widened. That was it!

"Winter, what is it?"

Winter raised her hand to Erik. She needed another moment to think. The black tower was a faerie building, like Mulcahy House. Mulcahy House was essentially a pocket faerie realm contained within what appeared on the outside to be a normal building. On the inside the House was semi-sentient—at full power it heeded simple requests, did routine housework and maintenance, rearranged the rooms according to perceived need, and would even borrow space from within Faerie. The inner space of the House was larger than the external footprint. And it did all that without sitting on a massive rift.

"I know what he's doing," she said. Midir could not forge a kingdom within Faerie without becoming foresworn. But he was still building an army, and he still had the power and desire to forge a faerie realm. She looked at her companions. "Midir is planning an invasion, but he's not invading Faerie. He's coming here."

Lana shook her head. "What would he have to gain from that? Our magic doesn't flow as powerfully in the Mortal Realm because of all the iron. He'd be forever weakened and his fae followers would eventually die off if they couldn't return to Faerie."

Winter nodded. "That's exactly what would happen if he planned to let things stay as they are. But like you said, Samhain is when the veil thins, and that rift will open. That's what's been causing the instability, and that's the key. The wild magic that we've seen will only be a fraction of what will come flooding through that rift when it blows open. You said on the way over that it would open like a flower? A closer description would be like a huge firework. It will be very fast and explosive. Midir is essentially making a new faerie realm right here in Seahaven," she paused, her mind working as she tried to calculate the scale of the damage an explosion of that magnitude would inflict. Fear dried out her mouth when she reached a conclusion. "And he's going to kill tens of thousands of people when he does it."

"How big could he make it?" asked Erik.

Winter shook her head. "It would depend on how much of Faerie he could pull through the rift. But judging by what I've seen of his tower and Lana's description of the rift, he could easily engulf the metro area, probably push out into the suburbs. Maybe he could even reach as far north as Seattle and as far south as Portland, I'm not sure."

"What the hell is with the iron, then?" asked Etienne, rubbing his thumb over the palm of his hand.

Lana rolled her eyes at him. "The building is full of untamed fae. Midir doesn't want his army getting loose and running around the city prematurely, bringing attention to his activities. Sidhe and half-breeds like you and me can get past it without any problems, but lesser fae can't."

"But none of this explains him wanting to end the 'time of hiding,'" said Erik. "Is he out of his mind? Plopping a faerie realm into the middle of the Pacific Northwest is going to draw a hell of a lot of attention from humans. He owns an investment company, for fuck's sake. He should know by now what humans are capable of."

"Unless he's counting on being able to keep the humans out." Winter thought back to Mulcahy House. "He may be able to lock his doors, as it were, and only let in or out who he chooses."

"Like your house," Erik said, understanding dawning.

Winter nodded, her expression grim. "I need to tell my father." If anything would compel him to action, this would.

She hoped.

"I'm going with you." Erik's tone was uncompromising. "He'll listen to me about this if I have to twist his arm."

Before last night Winter would have argued. Before last night she would have had more sympathy for her father. But she still burned with cold rage. So instead she nodded. It was time someone shook sense into him. If he refused to listen to her, maybe he would listen to the Vampire King.

He grinned. "Let me get some people together and we'll head over."

She hesitated. "Wait. Can we keep it to just us? You, me, Jessie, and our three sidhe friends?" She paused, and then continued. "I'm angry at my father, but I don't want to humiliate him. If we could keep it to family and immediate witnesses, I would be grateful."

Erik stroked her hair. "Then that's what we'll do. Let me go get dressed."

Jessie was talking in low tones to Cian and turned to Winter as Erik walked away. "Hey, how many banishing potions do you have? If we're fighting an army, we're going to need, like, all of them."

Winter thought about her stores. "A few dozen in bottles, but I have several large jars of potion and a few cases of empty bottles waiting for idle hands." Winter gave her apprentice a wry look. "Speaking of which, you owe me a frappe from that bet you made based on your silly TV show. Throwing potion bottles can be added to the list of things which do not work in real life."

Jessie blinked. "No! Really?"

"The glass didn't break when it hit fabric and flesh."

She pushed her glasses higher up the bridge of her nose. "Maybe something like a water balloon, then?"

"No, those are too big. It would be wasteful, and we're facing an army. Banishing potion really only needs a very small amount to work. I would think something like a slingshot, but I worry about the strength of the glass, and there is still the question about it breaking on contact with a soft target."

Jessie gasped and jumped up and down. "I've got it!" She stuck out her hand. "Gimme your card and let me borrow the Bug. I'll meet you guys out at the Point."

Winter reached into her bag, and then paused. "Wait... where is your car?"

"It's still at Moore Investments, but we can get it back after we save the world. Besides, you can't drive Cian around in yours, anyway. It's too old and has too much steel in the body. Brian's van made him sick." She wiggled her fingers. "Trust me, you're gonna love this."

Winter handed her the card and her keys. "Stay safe. Actually, talk to Jason about taking one or two of Erik's people with you. Midir probably knows what my car looks like and I don't want you out all by yourself."

Jessie sobered, but only a little. She saluted with the card and scampered off.

Winter met Etienne's eyes over Cian's head. He looked so serious, but so confident.

She wished she felt the same.

CHAPTER TWENTY-TWO

"There's no need to be nervous. Colin will see reason."

Winter stilled her fidgeting fingers and kept her face turned to the Pacific. The private lane down the length of the Point was roughly a mile long, but this morning it seemed too short. After last night she had no desire to see her father. "You didn't hear him. I just don't know what—"

"Shit!" Erik slammed on the breaks of his big SUV, throwing Winter forward against her seatbelt and making Lana exclaim in Faerie Gaelic from the backseat. Behind them Etienne swerved on his Harley to avoid a collision. Winter heard Cian's sharp cry of alarm. They had decided that it would be best for him to ride the bike, rather than take another trip in a vehicle with a large amount of steel in its construction. And Erik driving a plastic compact car was a punchline.

"What happened?" Winter asked, trying to see where Erik was looking, but her seatbelt had constricted just shy of strangulation.

"It was one of your damn cats."

"What? They know better than to run out in front of cars." Winter pushed back into the seat to relax the belt and reset the lock. She noted that they had stopped within a hundred yards of the circle drive. Her stomach clenched, from nerves or bleeding or both, she wasn't sure.

Erik hit the button to roll down his window and Winter could hear the approach of Etienne's Harley. "Maybe it was chasing something. Who knows? I've known the hairballs for over a hundred and fifty years and I couldn't tell you." He turned to assure Etienne that everything was all right.

Winter stared at the city side of Mulcahy House, covered in rose trellises. She didn't want to be here. She didn't want to argue with her father again. His betrayal of everything their family had lived for, that they had died for—that she was dying for even now—ate at her even more than the lethal deterioration of her organs. How could he throw it all away? But then Erik set the SUV rolling forward and they swung into the drive and into full view of the front of the house.

On the bench beside the ornately carved doors, sitting in the morning sunshine, was Colin.

Winter's brows shot up in shock. "Papa?" He was outside? Hope fluttered in her chest. Had he actually listened to her last night?

Her father stared down at his hands and ignored the vehicles as they pulled up to a stop.

Winter was first out, opening her door before Erik had shut off the engine. She hitched her bag up higher on her shoulder and made her swift way up the little stone footpath. She heard the others following at a slower pace behind her. "Papa, what are you doing out here?" He still wore only his brown robe. Even in the sunshine the October air was chill.

Colin's hands remained still, but she was used to that.

"Papa?" His stringy brown hair hung down, concealing most of his face. His jaw was slack, and his lips were parted. Had he fallen asleep?

"Wait…" Erik began.

Winter touched her father's shoulder and some delicate balance was disrupted. Colin toppled in a boneless heap on the ground. A tremor started in her belly and radiated out to her hands, her lips. Winter knew death. It wore her family's faces. She followed him down to the ground, to her knees. Her eyes were wide as she stared down at him. But she couldn't touch him. Her useless hands just hovered over his body and she was certain in some corner of her mind that if she touched him again, this time she would shatter him to dust.

Erik was behind her. "My God… Colin…?"

"Papa? Papa? Papa?" She kept hearing the word, over and over, the voice of a frantic little girl. With a start she realized it was her and clapped her hands over her mouth. Her heart pounded hard enough to make her rock with the rhythm. Not him... Why? "I need... I need to call..."

"Winter... little girl..." Erik touched her back.

"Please!" Winter shot to her feet, away from the Vampire King. "Please, don't... I need to make phone calls." The information was in the kitchen. Funeral home; the long, long list of relatives' phone numbers all crossed out. It was easier, after so very many deaths, to just keep it all near the phone.

She went to the front door. She needed to call the funeral home, and... and... She wrapped her arms tight about herself and pressed her forehead against the carvings. Nothing had changed since Kelley and Martina's funeral. Just as then, there was no one left to call. Erik was already here, so even the small torture of saying it aloud over the phone was spared her. Wait... there was Katherine. And there was Corinne. The Lion Queen was more Winter's personal friend than friend of the family, but she would... Winter stopped breathing as realization washed over her.

Corinne and her husband Santiago would be at Colin's funeral, but Winter wouldn't. It would take a couple of days to arrange the cremation and the service. She wouldn't live long enough.

"I don't see a wound. What happened?" Etienne's low voice carried to her. Every sound was so distinct. The crunch of sand against the stepping stones under their shoes. The waves slapping the rocks in hissing rhythm. The echo of each of her breaths against the door.

"Let's just get both of them inside and deal with it there," Erik replied. Winter heard movement, and then his voice came from right behind her, soft and gentle. "Little girl, you need to let us in."

Her hand rose to the handle of its own accord while her mind spun off in thought. Who would open the door when she was gone? Would the House shutter itself? Or would it stand open to the lashing winds and rain, an abandoned ruin—a home no longer? She pushed the door open and stepped into the grand foyer. Impetus carried her into the center of the room, to the big circular table that held the pictures of her immediate family, and she stopped, frozen by their beautiful smiles. Her sisters, her grandparents, her aunts and uncles, her sweet little niece.

Papa.

Her legs were carrying her down the hall, toward the back of the House, as grief tried to claw its burning way up her throat.

"Winter?" Etienne's voice chased after her.

"Let her go," she heard Erik say. "She won't go far."

Winter dropped her bag and broke into a run, one hand clamped over her mouth to stifle the sobs that tried to escape. She couldn't. She couldn't. She skidded to a stop in the kitchen, pushed open the sliding glass doors, and fled out to the garden. She ran up the gradual slope of the hill on familiar paths, ignoring both the overgrown plants that whipped at her body and the few pixies who had braved the October morning. She didn't stop until she reached the top of the cliff and the gazebo that crowned it. She stood there, eyes swimming with tears, and fought to keep her panting breaths from turning to... she gritted her teeth. Just thinking about it invited it, and she couldn't afford to break down. She couldn't. She had to hold together, and she had so little time left. Instead she stared without seeing at the sun sparking like embers on the waves and let the wind pick away at what was left of her loose bun.

Winter wrapped her arms around herself and gripped her shoulders tight, as if she would break apart if she let go. She didn't know... maybe she would. Her mind felt like it wasn't full of thoughts, but rather frantic little mice running around with no pattern or reason. One little mouse found its way to the front, and her eyes widened.

Was this her fault?

In her anger and bitterness at her father, through the worry about Cian, the circular arguing with Erik, her body finally breaking down, and the revelation about Midir's plot, she had completely forgotten that she had confronted the great sidhe prince last night. He had felt her attempt to soul read him and it had angered him. Angered him enough to frighten her. To hurt her. Had she angered Midir enough to bring him to her home?

Had he come looking for her, and found her father instead?

"Winter? Can you hear me?"

Cian's tenor voice cut into her horrified thoughts and she turned to face him. How long had he been there? She clung to her self-control by a fraying thread, so she only nodded to acknowledge his presence and dug her fingers more tightly into the fabric of her coat.

He approached her, worry plain on his beautiful face. "I… I don't know what to say. How to say it. I want to help."

Winter turned away. "No one can help," she whispered. "It's already over." She clapped her hand over her mouth and fought down the burn in her throat, the rising tears.

"I think… I want to help."

Winter could hear his frustration as he struggled to express himself in English, but right now she just did not have the room in her psyche for both patience and despair. "Go inside, Cian."

There was silence behind her for a moment. And then, "No." His voice was firm, determined, and then his hands were on her shoulders.

She twisted, startled. He was tall, taller than her. She was so used to Etienne calling him a boy that she had thought of him as a child, but he really wasn't. He was a man, simply a young one. She tried to pull herself away from his hands.

Cian shook his head. He pulled her gently against his chest and wrapped his arms around her.

"No… please, no…" But it was too late. His tenderness was her undoing. The burning tightness travelled up her throat, rushed into her mouth, and burst from her lips in a choked cry. Her knees buckled with the force of her sorrow and Cian followed her down, folding his body around hers as sob after racking sob tore through her, the despair of twenty years clawing its way free to howl into the morning air. This was no gentle mourning. She screamed her wordless grief for her family. For her father. For herself.

Cian held her against his body and rocked with her, his cheek against her hair, his thumb moving in slow circles over her arm.

Winter had no idea how much time passed as she cried, as he held her. An hour? An eternity? At last it ended, at least for now, and she hung limp in his embrace, her cheeks burned by wind and the salt of her own tears. Her hair had fallen from its bun at some point and long coils of it danced about the two of them, threatening to bind them together in tangles. She closed her eyes, and as she did she felt a sharp pain in her belly. She swallowed. She had been out here for longer than she thought. The painkiller was wearing off.

Cian lifted his cheek from her hair and a moment later he slipped one arm behind her knees and picked her up off the ground. She gasped, but it was from surprise. His movement was smooth, effortless, and did not jar her belly. He carried her into the gazebo out of the wind and sat in one of the corners, a foot propped on the bench, with her tucked in between his long legs.

Winter felt him wrap his arms around her again and was conflicted. On one hand, this should be awkward. Cian was younger than her. Exactly how much she wasn't sure, but somewhere around Brian's age she guessed, maybe a little older. And she didn't know him well. But on the other hand, as he tightened his embrace and she settled her head against his shoulder, she was so tired, and this was so comforting. And she had needed comfort for so long. His hand came up and stroked her tangled hair. His breath sounds rushed past her ear. She let her eyes close.

The pain stabbed through her belly and a whimper escaped. She shifted positions to try to escape it, but it found her a moment later.

"You're hurting." Cian's soft voice resonated under her ear. It wasn't a question.

She nodded, her cheek still pressed against him. "I'm dying."

He stilled under her for a moment. "Why?"

How to answer that? "For a long time, I've been in a position where I've had to do the work of many wizards, all by myself. I made a series of choices—maybe they were mistakes, it's too late now to really know— where I had to choose between my health and my responsibilities. My health lost. When I started I thought, 'I'll just do it today. It's safe every once in a while.' And then when I was using them more often it became, 'I know what I'm doing. I'll just use them for a while, just while I need to, and it will be safe.'" She sighed. "I stopped telling myself that weeks ago. I knew the energy potions were addictive and I knew that with extended use they cause organ degeneration and death…" She stopped. "I'm sorry. If I'm using words you don't know just stop me."

Cian had returned to stroking her hair. "I don't mind. I can figure it out from the other things you're saying." He was quiet for a moment. "Are you scared?"

Winter nodded. "Very."

His fingers caught in a tangle and he paused to tease it out.

If it wasn't for the increasing pain in her belly she could have stayed here forever. She wanted to fall asleep with him, just like this. She needed to go inside and take more of the painkilling potion, but that would mean bringing this moment of being comforted to an end. So instead she kept talking. "I'm afraid of the pain. That's a downside of being a physician, because my training and experience tell me that there is going to be a time, very soon, where the pain will become too extreme to control. And I'll have to choose..." She stopped again. Her choice was irrelevant. One would spare her from pain, the other would give her friends a few more hours to say goodbye. She would have to have this talk with Erik, later, but he would yell. Katherine would yell and cry. So would Corinne. She had worked so hard to be what they all needed, and she had failed them, anyway.

"What I fear the most is what will happen to the people I love after I'm gone." Pain lanced through her belly and between her shoulder blades. She turned her face further into the warmth of Cian's shirt as she struggled to breathe through it. If the pain was shifting to her shoulders how much blood was she holding in her abdomen, now? "I did this to myself because this city is on the verge of tearing itself apart." She spoke in a whisper, but she knew he would hear her. "My family used to be the ones who kept the peace, but now we're gone. Even without Midir's plans, the preternatural groups will war for dominance. The balance will be broken, and Seahaven will fall into chaos." And with Midir's plans, thousands would die and there was nothing she could do to save them. Not like this. "I just wish—"

Cian shifted his position and sat her upright against his bent leg. His hands went to the buttons of her coat and he started unfastening them.

The air was cool on her cheek, away from his shoulder, and Winter looked up at him. "What are you doing?" Her limbs felt heavy, and she noticed in some part of her mind that she was only vaguely curious about what Cian was doing. She felt floaty and numb, and wanted to return to being cuddled and comforted. She thought she might be in shock.

Cian finished unbuttoning her coat and spread it open. "I'm not sure. But I can feel that you hurt." He gave a small frustrated frown and met her eyes. Tucked against him like this he was very close. "I don't know how to say it right. Can I show you?"

Dazed, Winter nodded.

He reached into her coat and slid his hand up under her sweater to lay it with splayed fingers over her stomach. He was very gentle, so he caused her no additional pain. His eyes closed, and his red-gold brows knitted together in concentration.

His hair tickled against her nose. He smelled like the store shampoo, like Etienne... but also different. Spicy. Still good, though. Still male. What was he doing? She sat there for several long moments feeling the warmth of his palm on her skin through the fabric of her dress. His fingers were long, and his hand seemed to stretch over the whole of her abdomen. It was a new experience for her, and it wasn't unpleasant. She parted her lips to ask, and then gasped as sidhe magic began to flow from his hand into her body. Her eyes widened. It felt like warm water rushing into her belly, twisting around the pain and filling her up. Her spine bowed back over his knee with the strange mix of pleasure and agony, and she flailed with one arm, wrapping it around Cian's shoulders and digging her fingers into his shirt. She grasped at his wrist with her other hand, but she didn't try to pry him off of her.

She thought she knew what he was trying to do. The day she had met him and Etienne, Jessie had wrenched her shoulder trying to pick up that backpack. Winter had watched Cian heal the injury. It had been messy, but effective. Jessie had been too distracted by her pain to notice the magic, something Winter still needed to speak to the girl about. But what Cian had done with Jessie was a light touch compared to what he was attempting now.

His magic was still messy, but he had access to so much power! Winter had read about those who could heal by touch but had never met one. He had the ability and the desire, but she realized, as his magic moved through her damaged and failing body, that instinct alone wouldn't be enough for a healing this extensive. He needed guidance.

She slid her hand down over the back of his larger one. Her breathing had become labored, forcing spikes of agony through her belly again and again, and she struggled to find her voice. "Relax." She brought her other

hand up from his shoulder to the back of his neck and slipped her fingers
into his silky hair. "You're using too much energy. At this rate you'll use it
all up before you're done." She swallowed hard past the pain and felt the
flood of power begin to ebb. Her body relaxed. "Good. Good. Now, reach
down with your magic into the earth. Can you feel the energy there?" He
stretched out a tendril of power and using the magic from her own sidhe
heritage she followed with him to make sure he went far enough. He did,
and she felt him nod against her neck and shoulder. "Pull it into you. Slowly. Like you're drinking from a stream." She rested her cheek against his
fragrant hair and closed her eyes, the better to focus. If he drew power too
slowly he would deplete and fail, but if he did it too fast he could hurt
himself. It was even possible to die from too much power. But Cian apparently had excellent instincts. "Very good. A little more... yes. Just like
that. You need to maintain the flow while you work and use it to fuel your
magic."

"I feel... strange." His lips tickled her skin.

"The extra power is making you light-headed. Push it into me, now,
and I'll guide you." His hand pressed into her belly and Winter couldn't
catch the whimper of pain before it escaped. He tried to pull his hand back,
but she held him in place. "Don't. I don't know how this will feel, but right
now I'm in a lot of pain. You can't let it stop you." Besides, suddenly pulling away like that would only hurt her more, but he didn't need to know
right now.

Cian hesitated and then nodded. He let out a steadying breath and the
flow of magic into her body increased.

Winter felt her spine begin to bow again and she fought to keep her
breathing even. Here was hope. Given the destructive nature of the energy
potion she wasn't sure how much hope it was, but maybe he could buy her
just a few more days, long enough to stand against Midir. To serve her city
one last time. To attend her father's funeral. That was all she needed.

But first she had to be Cian's guide and teacher in this healing.

She shuddered under her body's onslaught and cast herself again into
the flow of his magic, following his magical senses into her own damaged
body. It was a strange experience, visualizing inside herself like this, and
seeing the systemic extent of the degeneration was shocking. And painful.

What was it about looking at an injury that made it hurt more? For a moment she was overwhelmed, but she shook it off. She had seen, and successfully operated on, guts that had been shredded by bullets, blades, and claws. Bellies that had been torn open and things both tender and foul, organs not meant to be seen that were exposed to the air, which pulsed with life and recoiled from touch.

It had simply never been her before. She had worked while exhausted, while shaking from pain and effort, while frightened—even while weeping. But she had never been the one on the table. This was a different kind of agony.

"Let's begin at the top of the abdominal cavity." Winter slid Cian's hand upward a few inches, bunching dress and sweater fabric over their joined wrists. "Here's the stomach, with the esophagus feeding down into it." Through his magic she could see the organ in its entirety, as clearly as if it were laid open to the light. Fascinating. "Do you see how the tissues are eaten away and bleeding? How it's swollen and raw?" She stopped and thought back to what she had said. Would he understand everything she needed to tell him? She had to remember that Cian's grasp of English wasn't strong, and she had to keep her explanations simple—not an easy task for a physician in her element.

Cian nodded and turned his face downwards against her chest as if he was trying to see it more closely. Maybe he was. "Yes. I can feel it's wrong. It's pulling at me to make it right again."

Interesting. She mentally shrugged. She really had no idea how magical healing was supposed to work, in practice. What did she have to lose by letting Cian's instincts be their guide? She was dying. "Follow that pull. I'm right here with you and I won't let you go too far."

The swirl of magic converged on her stomach, and as she watched the flesh was rebuilt, the bleeding stopped, and the standing blood reabsorbed. The swelling subsided leaving behind a healthy organ. Winter realized that she had stopped breathing and inhaled. It was amazing! "Perfect. How do you feel?" She checked to make sure he was maintaining his connection to the flow of power from the earth.

"I feel good."

"Then we can keep going. Don't stop pulling energy from the earth. We still have a long way to go." And with that she continued, guiding him organ by organ, structure by structure, through the intricacies of each system, performing repairs beyond her wildest dreams down to the daintiest of capillaries. She made him pause often, but he only forgot to maintain his power flow a couple of times and only showed minimal signs of tiring. The inflammation of her abdominal tissues caused by the degradation and internal bleeding dwindled to nothing as her body was restored, and the hurt faded away. Winter was limp with relief as Cian finished. "Thank you," she whispered into his hair. She closed her eyes and reveled in breathing without pain.

But Cian didn't shift away from her. He kept his hand on her abdomen and brushed his thumb once over her in a sweeping movement. Still traces of the magic swirled through her body.

"Cian, you're done. You can stop now." Winter could feel heat rising to her cheeks. Now that spikes of agony weren't lancing through her, the little movements of his hand and his magic were causing tiny shivers of pleasure—something very new for her. She knew what was happening, of course. She was a modern woman and a physician, not some ingénue in one of the Gothic romances Katherine used to write. Cian was turning her on.

She had just never had it happen before.

The reasons for it… were entirely beside the point. At just this moment she had a young man wrapped around her and she needed to figure out how to unwrap him. At the thought of "unwrapping" she blushed harder and then pushed the thought away. She wasn't afraid or exactly uncomfortable. The opposite, in fact, but as much as she felt the urge and curiosity to just stay here and be comforted and held—and maybe feel these lovely touches for a little while longer—her intellect was beginning to push through the numb feeling. She reminded herself that sexual arousal was perfectly normal in the wake of death, but there was still a sidhe prince out there who wanted to turn Seahaven into his personal faerie realm. She had a city to try to save.

Besides, she barely knew the young man in question, and Cian was quite a bit younger than her. He was heartbreakingly beautiful, yes. She was inexperienced, but she wasn't blind. And... she caught herself at the memory of the morning's events and her sudden pang of guilt was like slap. Cian had just been through what must have been a terrible ordeal. He was a rape survivor. In her daily life she worked with so many survivors like him—and not, because each was an individual who dealt with their experiences differently. What she knew was she didn't have the right or permission to be having any of these thoughts about him. What was she doing? She began to squirm away from him. "Cian? Cian, let me up."

He shifted his face higher and spoke against her throat, the sensation making her breath catch. "There's still something not right."

What? "You repaired everything. Pull the magic back, now."

"No. It's all breaking down again."

Winter's eyes widened just for a moment. The energy potion. It pervaded her system, her bloodstream, her cells, and would continue to kill her. But she had had no idea his ability was so sensitive. Maybe it was because he had continued to be, for lack of a better term, plugged in to her. "Yes, you were able to heal the damage, but the cause remains. Cian, sometimes in medicine that's all we can do. Sometimes we can only buy a little more time." Her throat tightened. "You've given me an amazing gift. You've given me time to do what I need to do for the people I love. I'll never be able to thank you—"

Cian lifted his head and looked at her from inches away. "I don't understand."

She stroked his cheek. "Sweetie, some things just can't be fixed."

His leaf-green eyes flickered back and forth as he thought hard. Then they fired with determination. "I can fix this." His arm tightened around her back and his hand pressed against her belly.

"Wait. I don't know how you can—"

"I know I can." And he increased the stream of his magic, again pouring it into her body.

Winter gasped. He had healed her, but with her guidance. She didn't know how to begin to lead the way through something like this. But this time he wasn't waiting for her to take him by the hand. His power swept through her, now more pleasure than pain, at first centered on her core and then it expanded outward to her extremities. Her fingertips and cheeks tingled, and a small moan escaped.

But it occurred to her that his magic was just continuing to fill her—and without an apparent purpose it was quickly becoming too much. Her cheeks were reddening, her breathing was becoming labored, and the sensation was crossing from pleasure completely to pain. This wasn't good. "Cian, you have to stop."

His brows knit together in concentration and he shook his head. Instead he amplified the flow even further.

Her mouth stretched open in a silent cry. It was all she could do to breathe. Drag in air. Feel the pressure force it out. And then again. His magic and his sidhe strength held her pinioned and helpless. Beads of sweat rose and rolled down her face. Her whole body was becoming soaked in it, her clothes clinging to her under her coat. Her heart felt like an insane bird battering itself against the bars to escape too small a cage. What was he doing? How much more could she take? Winter glanced down at her hand in Cian's hair. Maybe if she could poke him in the eye, she could—And she froze.

Tiny droplets of a poisonous green color dotted her skin. As she watched several coalesced and rolled off, to be replaced by new ones welling up from her pores. Was… was that the potion? Her heart beat even harder, if that was possible, and she drew fast, shallow breaths. He was doing it! He was really do—A pain noise escaped. Her every cell felt like it was being wrung out; it hurt worse than dying had. Her vision began to darken from the pressure behind her eyes.

"Winter?"

"Don't stop." She wasn't sure if she actually said the words or just breathed the hope of them. "Don't stop." Her heartbeat was so loud. Maybe she hadn't heard Cian speak at all. She wanted to rest her face against his hair again, but her head fell backwards, and she seemed to fall with it.

"Winter? Winter?"

"Don't stop." Her voice was raspy. Something was rubbing over her face. It was cold, and it felt good.

"It's all right. Wake up, little girl."

Winter opened her eyes. Erik smiled down at her and stroked a wet, white washcloth over her forehead. She noticed that it was tinted with green stains. She tried to talk and coughed instead.

"Here." Etienne brought a cup with a straw and Erik helped her sit upright to sip what turned out to be ice water.

Winter realized she was lying on towels on the kitchen table and pushed herself up to a sitting position, which was easier said than done because her hip-length hair was everywhere. Her eyebrows shot up once she was able to take stock of her situation. "Gentlemen, where are my clothes?"

She sat with her long, bare, skinny legs dangling off the edge of the table, her green-stained hair tangled around her right arm, dressed only in her camisole and panties. But she felt good. Her skin was sticky, and her underwear was wet and green, but inside she felt clean. The energy potion still pulled at her. She was still addicted—having it cleaned out of her system wouldn't change that. But like no longer screamed out for like; she no longer had a biological urge to maintain the level of potion in her body, so she felt perhaps she could resist. She took the thought and compartmentalized it for the time being. She would take it back out, later.

At her question, Erik only chuckled, and Etienne made himself busy taking the cup to the sink.

Lana snorted, pulling Winter's attention to the succubus. "You were covered in that green shit and your clothes were soaked with it. We figured it would be best to get you out of them and at least sponged off." She unfurled the bath sheet she was carrying and smirked. "Etienne wanted to get you down to your skin, but cooler heads prevailed."

Etienne turned around, angry. "Stop that. You'll embarrass her."

Lana raised an ebony eyebrow. "Embarrass who?" She slid her eyes toward Winter as she offered the towel. "I couldn't tell if he was being very sidhe about not thinking of nudity as exclusively sexual, or if he was acting like a dirty-minded human male." Her facial expression was innocent speculation, but her intonation was anything but.

The faerie knight shot Lana a venomous glare.

Winter's cheeks warmed. She wasn't sure why. She had been dodging sexual advances from men and some women since she was a teen. She normally took them in stride. This was just Lana teasing Etienne about her. She took the towel and wrapped it around her body, tucking it under her arms, and decided to ignore the whole thing. "Where's Cian?"

"He's taking a nap in the living room," Erik answered.

"Is he all right?"

"Oh, he's fine," Lana said, dropping into a kitchen chair. "When you passed out he got a bit scared. I was there, though—followed the magic—and talked him through the rest. But he stopped pulling power toward the end and tuckered himself out. Nothing a couple hours of sleep won't fix."

Winter let out a small sigh of relief.

Erik brushed his big hand over her hair. "Why don't you get cleaned up and get some sleep, too? Let me handle things."

She didn't need to ask what "things" he would handle. Erik knew who to call to make the funeral arrangements as well as she did. Her mind was still wrapped in an insulating layer of numbness that would let her function in the wake of her father's death. For a little while, at least. She would need time to process, to mourn. She knew, intimately, the stages of grief. And she knew that every time was just a little different. She had no time to waste. "Thank you, Erik. I need to go get cleaned up, but I'm the Mulcahy, now." She reached up and touched his hand. "We need to talk when I come back downstairs."

Winter turned toward the kitchen staircase. It was the Twenty-ninth. She might need time, but it was running out—for all of them.

"What now?" Aodhán's hand still burned from tearing a hole in that damn conversion van. He flexed his fingers and tried to keep from checking, yet again, to see how much the redness had faded. Looking at it just made it hurt more.

Midir had his attention riveted on the multiple monitors that had sprouted like mushrooms across his desk. "We've done what we can in that direction. Now we focus on Samhain."

"You don't think it's care—" Aodhán stopped himself, shocked at his indiscretion. He was only in minor pain. Had losing to children this morning turned him stupid?

Midir's intense, ice-blue gaze snapped to Aodhán's face. "Careless? To leave loose ends? Yes. And I despise it." He focused again on his monitors. "Samhain is tomorrow, at midnight. There are too many details that need my control and I need you here to supervise those things that I can't." He tensed his jaw. "It is a gamble. But I have no other choice. I am out of time."

Aodhán sat, brushing the pad of his thumb over his burned skin, and considered the face of a prince who would decimate a city.

CHAPTER TWENTY-THREE

"I don't understand. What happened?"

Jessie's voice, pitched high with distress, carried upstairs as Winter emerged from her bedroom, barefoot with her wet hair in a long, heavy braid down her back. She came to her father's door on the way down the hall and stopped, her fingers pressed to the wood. Erik had laid his body in there on his bed. It was the first time Colin had been in the room he had once shared with his wife in six months. Winter let her hand fall. She was so full of emotions behind the muffling numbness she didn't know which one to feel first—and right now she didn't have time for any of them.

Would she ever have the luxury to properly mourn?

Winter found Erik alone in the kitchen on his phone. He raised his sea-blue eyes to her and gave her a smile. "Hey, do something for me," he was saying. "Pack up and take Michael and the baby on the next plane to Rome." Winter could hear Katherine's faint voice. "Good news travels fast, doesn't it? No... no... Well, no shit, you need to take Giovanni." He looked at his phone in exasperation. "What good is he to me here without you? I want Giovanni in Rome annoying Marco. Why? Because one of these days my brother's going to make good on his promise to take a king-ship of his own and steal you from me, so I'll take every remaining chance to screw with him I can get." Erik grinned at Winter, who just shook her head. His rivalry with Marco over Katherine—or, more importantly to Erik, which of them would sire her prince—had lasted for the past five centuries. "And tell... did I just hear Michael? Why are you at the Theatre?" He listened, scowling. "Dammit, woman, why are we even having this conversation? Just make the fucking flight on time." He tapped the call off. "I miss slamming down the phone."

Winter raised her brows. "You used to break the phone every time you did that."

"So? It felt good."

"Katherine's already a few hours ahead of you, isn't she?"

He sighed and roughed his fingers through his short, black hair. Then he looked down. "I won't tell her about Colin until this is over with Midir. I can't risk her trying to stay to be with you."

Winter nodded. She hadn't thought about that. She hadn't thought about anything past making it though the next hour, and then the next. She needed to think past her grief. She was the Mulcahy, now. "I agree. Katherine needs to be in Rome with your father, Marcus, and with Marco. If this goes badly, they'll be able to protect her and little Mike." The little vampire prince couldn't survive without his mother's blood and milk, so sending him away without her wasn't possible.

A trio of large shopping bags sat on the floor next to the kitchen table. They hadn't been there before. The logo on the sides advertised that they came from Painted Warrior. "What are those?" Winter asked.

"Not a clue. Jessie brought them with her."

It probably had something to do with the reason Jessie had wanted her car and her credit card. "Where did she go? She sounded upset."

Erik jerked his head toward the sliding glass door. "She went outside to call her parents."

Winter looked out. Jessie was pacing around the garden courtyard, talking on her phone in an agitated fashion. Her face was flushed, and her eyes were red. Winter watched, feeling helpless. This was a familiar pattern and she knew where it was going. When Jessie became seriously distressed she looked to her parents for comfort. Coming out to the House to be met with the news of Colin's death must have been a shock. Seeing a friend lose a parent would make her reach for her own. Jessie's pacing came to an abrupt halt and she stared wide-eyed at her phone. Then she looked for a moment like she was going to throw it before stuffing it in her pocket and storming off deeper into the garden.

On cue the House phone rang. Winter stayed where she was.

"Do you want me to answer that?" asked Erik.

She shook her head. She did not want to speak with Darryl or Joanie St. James. Not today.

The voice mail answered in its robotic tones. There had been a time when they had recorded their own messages, but again and again the recordings had become the voices of the dead, so they had stopped. And then Darryl St. James' gravelly voice burst into her kitchen. "What shit are you trying to pull this time, bitch?"

Erik had the phone in hand before Jessie's father could draw breath to continue. "What the hell is wrong with you? This family is in mourning!" He carried the phone with him into the butler's pantry, where he continued to yell behind the closed door.

Winter sat down at the kitchen table and ran her fingers over the scuffs and dents that were so familiar. Marks that had been made by her, her sisters, her cousins... She wasn't sure exactly how old the big, sturdy table was; just that it had always been there for as long as she could remember. She wasn't dying anymore. That took some getting used to. If they lived through this plot of Midir's, if she lived through it, she had to face life alone in this House that had once been so full of love and family.

What a lonely thought.

The wineglass made a little noise as it was set down in front of her. Winter blinked and looked up to find Etienne standing at her elbow, two wine bottles in one hand and in the act of setting down a second glass. "Lana wants to move into your wine cellar."

A smile pulled at the corners of her mouth. "It's a nice collection."

Etienne snorted as he set down one of the bottles. "That's rather an understatement. Cian got lost down there."

"Only for a few minutes." Cian came up behind him carrying more glasses. His straight hair was tucked behind his ears and hung down loose past his shoulders. He gave Winter a smile as he set the glasses out on the table.

Winter felt her cheeks warm, remembering—and remembering. She returned his smile with a small one of her own, feeling strange and conflicted. He had somehow awakened a part of her that she hadn't known was even there, but with his past she couldn't help but feel as if she had wronged him. "How do you feel?"

He looked to the side as he seemed to search for the correct English words. "I'm a little tired, but I didn't want to sleep anymore." He looked down at her and reached for her hand. "I wanted to see that you are better."

Her smile widened, and she let him stroke his thumb over her knuckles. "I'm better than I've been in a long time. Words aren't enough to express how grateful I am but thank you." She squeezed his fingers and then looked up as Etienne uncorked a wine bottle. "What's all this for?"

"Shitty days and scheming are both occasions for drinking wine," said Lana as she emerged from the cellars, carrying another two bottles. Winter noticed the succubus was wearing a t-shirt that read, *"I Feel a Sin Coming On."*

"Scheming?" Winter couldn't argue with her assessment about the quality of the day so far.

"We need to figure out what we're going to do about Midir," said Etienne, pouring red wine into Winter's glass.

Winter nodded. She already had at least one thought in that direction.

Erik came back to the kitchen. "How often does this happen?" he demanded, holding up her landline phone.

Winter sighed. "Often enough."

"Well, this crap stops. You don't need—"

"Later." Winter saw Jessie crossing the garden courtyard behind Erik and cut him off. "We'll deal with it later."

He frowned and opened his mouth to argue, and she flickered her eyes to the girl coming up behind him. He didn't need to look to understand her meaning and went to hang up the phone.

Jessie pushed her way through the sliding glass door, her expression upset and distracted, but when she saw Winter she put on a smile. "Hey." Then she noticed all the wine and grimaced.

"I think there may still be Coke in the pantry," Winter suggested. Jessie had a strong aversion to alcohol in any form. She had explained once that watching her parents drink had killed any teenage attraction she might have had for it.

Jessie smiled again and went to investigate.

Etienne set down the wine bottle now that all the adults' glasses were full and reached out, caught Winter's hand in his own, and wrapped her fingers around the body of her glass. She looked up, startled at his gesture, and he held her eyes. "Just for once," he said in a soft voice, "just for a moment, you need to do something for you."

His thumb brushed over the pulse point on her wrist, sending a shiver of pleasure through her. Winter felt the heat rise to her face again.

Erik cleared his throat—theatrically.

Etienne gave her a small smile and took his seat.

Winter took a deep drink of her wine. It hit her empty stomach, reddening her cheeks even more.

Cian looked from one to the other with curiosity.

Jessie came out of the pantry, Coke in hand, and looked at the adults. "What did I miss?"

Lana laughed.

"Erik, I've been thinking," Winter said, jumping in before Lana could bring Jessie up to speed in whatever fashion most amused the succubus, "that it's time to revisit the discussion about an alliance."

Erik perked up. "This is a conversation I want to have."

She tapped her index finger on the stem of her glass, choosing her words. "Not that alliance. The original one. The one you proposed to Mahon Mulcahy."

"He reneged on it."

"That's neither here nor there. I'm talking about you and me. I'm talking about a preternatural coalition with every group having an equal voice."

"That sounds a lot like democracy, Miss Mulcahy," said Erik with a dry tone.

"Maybe. But what is the biggest complaint the groups have in my dealings with the other groups? That I show too much favor, that I give too much power when I lean one way or another. Fine then, let them all have power—equal power. We need every group in the city on the same page, working together, if we hope to have a prayer of defending it from Midir. And I also think a coalition might…" She took a breath and grimaced. "Or at least I *hope* that it would go a long way toward rectifying the political instability in the city."

"One step at a time, little girl." Erik looked thoughtful. "I can see a few problems with this right out of the gate. To begin with, getting the groups to work together is a lot like herding cats—literally, for some of them. And then there is the issue of fighting against Midir's fae army. The preternatural groups in Seahaven may be teetering on the edge of open conflict, but aside from my Court no one has what I would call an organized fighting force. And even I only have a few dozen warriors. The therian groups fight a lot, internally and against each other, but vampires rule cities because we're organized. Therian are basically animals that just happen to turn into people…"

"Erik, that's not fair…" Jessie broke in.

"Hey, they turn into some of my favorite people, but at the end of the day most of them don't have the ability to think past today's dominance fight, much less function within an army."

Jessie snorted. "How much brain power do you need to stand around in uniform?"

Erik gave her an irritated look. "There's a bit more to it than that. And not attacking your superiors at the first sign of weakness is also helpful to make an army function properly."

"How many eighteen-year-old boys do you know?" she asked under her breath.

But Erik ignored her. "My point is our therian can fight, and some of the bigger groups even have organized security for their businesses, but nothing like an actual standing army. The non-therian are just ordinary people living ordinary lives with a magical spark. I honestly don't want to even get them involved if we can avoid it. We'll have two days to try to make up for a hell of a steep learning curve with the therian groups alone."

"Less," said Lana before taking a sip of her wine.

Erik looked at the fae woman. "What?"

Winter sighed. "She's right. It's now early afternoon on the Twenty-ninth. The rift will explode at midnight tomorrow."

"I thought we had another day!" Jessie looked torn between being panicked and offended. "Midnight on Samhain night, Halloween night—that's another day, right?"

Winter shook her head. "That is the end of Samhain, not the beginning."

Erik cut off Jessie before she could continue. "Fine. We have less time than we thought." He looked at Jessie. "It happens. We deal." He sat back. "What most concerns me is Midir. From what you've said, he's a hell of a magician, and who knows how many others he has squirrelled away in that tower of his? All we have on our side of the board are you and Mighty Mite here," he jabbed his thumb at Jessie.

The table fell into grim silence.

Winter took a sip of her wine. What none of them needed to say aloud was that the majority of the preternatural community was essentially helpless against powerful magic. The spark within them allowed them sensitivity, but that only let them see the train coming—in most cases it did not even help them get off the tracks. It was why wizards were so feared by other preternaturals. It was why the Council of the Eldest ruled over all. There was simply no way for them to defend themselves.

"I think you need to bring in more wizards," Erik said, breaking her reverie.

Winter laughed. It was high-pitched with an edge of hysteria and she pressed her lips together, embarrassed by the sound. After a moment she said, "They won't come."

He held her gaze. He didn't look at Jessie, and for that she was grateful. The girl was sharp and wouldn't fail to miss the gesture, to question it. Erik knew a bit about wizard society and knew that Jessie was a wizard sport. He knew how dangerous it would be for her to be spotted by other wizards. He was trying to tell Winter it was time to tell Jessie the truth. She could see it in his eyes.

Winter shook her head. She couldn't. "Do you really think they care what happens to us? They've stood by for the past twenty years while my family has died..." she bit back a curse, "has been slaughtered! They've watched and had their parties and their politics and their weddings and left us—" Cian reached over and took her hand. She stopped. Her voice had been rising higher and higher in both pitch and volume. She took a deep drink of her wine. "They left us to die." Maybe, to save the city, to save the Mortal Realm, from Midir, she needed to risk Jessie, but it didn't matter. Wizard society had turned its back on the Mulcahys just as much as the Mulcahys had turned their backs on the rest of the wizards. They really wouldn't come. She didn't even know who to call.

Jessie tapped her fingernail on her soda can, making a hollow metallic noise, and looked at Cian with her lips pursed. "What about the sidhe?"

"What are you talking about?" Erik frowned at the teen.

Lana's brows rose in interest and Etienne glowered and began to shake his head. Cian, still holding Winter's hand, perked his attention and nodded with enthusiasm.

"Well, the guy who dueled with Cian was amazing. He was so fast, as fast as any vampire, and so good, too! It was like *The Princess Bride*! Cian didn't have a prayer. And to be honest, I think the only reason I was able to nail him with the planter was because he'd written me off as a kid and was too busy playing around." She shrugged. "I lucked out."

Lana smirked. "Sounds about right for a sidhe. They're arrogant as fuck."

"Anyway," Jessie continued, "that guy was awesome, and Etienne, you're like a real knight, right? So, could we find more of you guys to help us?"

"No." Etienne's voice rang with finality.

Cian drew in a startled breath. "But, we know where Senán is, now. We can—"

Etienne cut him off. "No, you don't know them like I do. I know you're thinking to run to Anluan with this, but even if he does decide to help, he'll only make matters worse. Besides, if Midir isn't actually planning to invade Faerie, then what does Anluan have to gain by committing his forces to a battle that isn't his? Knowing that shit, once he knows where Senán is, he'll be content to simply buy his freedom. Simple, practical… he has always preferred the diplomatic solution, when war didn't suit his ends."

"This *is* Anluan's battle." The humor was gone from Lana's face. "Whether he wishes to admit it or not, he is bound by honor to fight. Even ignoring the kidnapping of Senán, he is owed a blood *debt* by Midir for the rape of his ward," her eyes flicked up to Cian, "and he owes blood *guilt* for the crimes committed by Midir, his brother." She ran her finger around the rim of her empty glass. "And Anluan is not the only king of Faerie the great prince should fear. Midir has committed crimes against both our courts, Queen's Son."

Etienne narrowed his eyes at her. "Anluan's is no court of mine."

Winter glanced at Etienne. She had seen hints of this animosity earlier when she had read his soul, so seeing it expressed was no surprise. She turned her attention back to Lana. "What else has Midir done?" She remembered something Etienne had said the afternoon they met, something about a rumor of the murdered prince being turned into a cup or vessel of some sort. Was this it?

Lana continued to trace her fingertip around the rim of her glass until the crystal sang a soft, mournful note. "On Midir's final visit to Ceallach and Deirdre's court, he presented the Unseelie Queen with a golden chalice. It was exquisite, with bas-relief decorations of a prince in various entertainments; hunting, riding, dancing, dueling, and playing a lute. Around the edge were round jewels and cunningly carved bits of ivory. And the prince was modeled on Ceallach and Deirdre's son, Prince Ciarán. The likeness was perfect, as if Ciarán had sat for the artist. Queen Deirdre was charmed with the gift. Her sons were her life. After the loss of their younger son, Ciarán had become all the more precious."

She poured herself a little more wine and held the glass up to the light. "Midir also gifted the Queen with bottles of wine bearing labels that read, 'For Delight.' When the wine was poured into the chalice, the little figures sprang to life and played out their scenes. Prince Ciarán wasn't there to see it, though. He had responsibilities that had called him away from court." Lana frowned. "That was what King Ceallach told Midir. Ciarán actually never took his duties as Prince and Heir seriously. No, he had a new lover in a neighboring court and had been there for days. But Ceallach could dance around that without lying because he wanted an alliance with that court and Midir graciously accepted the story because he hadn't come to see Ciarán, anyway.

"And then Midir left Deirdre with her pretty new toy."

The group was silent as Lana spoke, letting her spin her tale. Her dark eyes were focused on what were now clearly her memories. She was quiet for several long moments, and when she spoke again her voice was thick with repressed emotion. "Days stretched into weeks, and Ciarán lingered at the other court. The Queen missed him and being fragile of mind she became melancholy. She would play with her new chalice and sip the wine, but it didn't soothe her. The King grew annoyed with his son's callousness, because this wasn't the first time—Ciarán only cared for Ciarán—and sent a messenger to fetch him home. When the messenger returned, she was alone. She told the King and Queen that the other court claimed Ciarán and his companions had never arrived."

Pain filled her eyes. "The Queen was in a panic. When her younger son disappeared centuries before, it was much the same. He went riding out on a visit and never returned. There were whispers, even in my time, that Ciarán had murdered his brother, but that was all they were—whispers. For her it was the same nightmare all over again. The King was ready to ride to war against the other court on any scrap of evidence that they were behind Ciarán's disappearance. He sent out war parties under the guise of search parties to comb every inch of territory between the shifting borders of the two courts. And the Queen carried that chalice with her everywhere and cried.

"Then a few days into this a wine bottle was delivered to the kitchens. No one remembered exactly where it had come from, just that it arrived. A sharp-eyed page noticed it and brought it to the King where he was meeting with his advisors. Its label read, 'For Truth.' He sent for his Queen's chalice, but she came with it and try as he might, she refused to be parted from it. Ceallach was torn, we could see it, but in the end, he had to know, so he set the chalice on the table and poured the wine."

Lana twisted the stem of her glass, swirling the liquid. "It was the exact color and consistency of freshly spilled blood." Etienne made a soft noise and she flashed a glare at him. "Say what you like about the Unseelie courts, there are some things that shouldn't pour from wine bottles. Not before the eyes of a frightened mother."

Etienne gave her a nod of apology.

Lana looked away from him, to her wineglass, and then pushed it away. "The thick liquid filled the chalice and just as before the little figures of Ciarán began to move, but then the scenes changed. Now in one scene the Prince laughed with his companions as they violated a helpless fae; in another he drove a sword through the body of a younger sidhe in princely dress, pinning him to an embankment; in another he writhed and screamed under torture horrific to even our eyes; and in the last one he was held fast in a vice, shrieking as a blade sawed at his head. When Ceallach saw the scenes change, he moved to shield Deirdre, but it was too late. She had seen too much. And to make things worse, where it had been silent before, now the chalice screamed. It screamed in Ciarán's voice. Within a few breaths the Queen joined in.

"Ceallach was desperate to make it stop. He splashed the liquid on the floor, but still the cup screamed. So, he dashed it against the table. Once. Twice. Three times." Lana's eyes had gotten wide. "It didn't crumple or bend like metal should. It cracked and split. We all knew the quality of that cracking sound. We were Unseelie. It was fresh bone—not dry, white bone, but bone still wet in the marrow.

"The screaming stopped, both from the chalice and from the Queen. Several of the jewels and ivory pieces had broken off, scattering over the tabletop, and the gold had stripped away from one of the shards. We knew, now, looking at the raw bone core of the chalice, what the little carved ivory bits really were. The Queen saw it and whispered, 'My sons,' over and over and over. It was all she said for days, until she gave over entirely to madness."

Lana's voice lowered to a hiss of anger. "It was widely known that Deirdre was fragile. She was called Deirdre of the Sorrows long before Ceallach took her as his wife. But Midir fashioned her son's skull into a cup, and gifted it to her to *drink* from, and then *taunted* her with it." She brought herself out of her memories and focused on the others at the table. "If he wanted some sort of revenge on Ceallach, then fine... but why punish her like that? It was cruel."

Etienne purposely did not look at Cian. "The older sidhe enjoy creativity when they send their messages. I think it's because they get bored." He narrowed his eyes at Lana with suspicion. "That was some story. Who are you to Ceallach and Deirdre?"

The succubus flashed him an angry look and took up her wineglass again, seeming to hesitate as she took a deep drink.

"'Some story?' What sort of cold-hearted bastard are you?" Jessie's eyes glittered with unshed tears.

Etienne's expression turned to wry irritation as he looked at the teen. "The sort of bastard who needs to know exactly what you and this succubus want to get us involved in. Remember, girl, calling on the sidhe courts is your idea. This is what the sidhe do." The corner of his mouth twisted with distaste as he spoke, pulling at the spell scars on his cheek. He turned back to Lana. "Now tell us."

She raised her chin just a little. "I am one of Queen Deirdre's handmaidens."

The faerie knight raised his eyebrow. "That's a rather prestigious position for a half-breed. Who put you there?"

"That's none of your fucking business."

"You're making it my business, succubus, by trying to drag your court into our problems."

His pronoun use caught Winter's attention, but she remained silent. She was still too numb to cope with more than the crisis at hand and analyzing Etienne's potentially shifting moods and motivations wasn't part of that.

Etienne was continuing. "So, enlighten us." His tone was uncompromising.

Lana looked away from the group, frowning and thinking. After a moment she spoke, her voice quiet. "Ciarán did. I was his primary mistress at court and his mother denied him nothing."

Winter's brows knitted with sympathy. "I'm so sorry."

Lana turned to her with a sharp expression and for an instant, harsh words seemed to be forming behind her eyes... but she looked at Winter and paused. Her gaze softened. "Don't be. I'm not." She returned to contemplating her wine. "Ciarán was a blight among the Darkling Throng. He had a reputation among the lesser fae as a fate worse than death. His companions did nothing to temper his behavior, even though they were technically supposed to. I heard that it had been a power struggle with his father for years. His father would choose a companion, Ciarán would get him killed or drive him off and pick a replacement of his own. Finally, the king had to give up and let him have his way." She took a drink. "I had some protection from the worst of his 'fun' because I held his favor, but I spent enough time with him and his boys that I knew exactly what would happen when he tired of me. So, I worked hard to hold his interest... but I worked harder to get away."

"Why didn't you just leave?" Jessie looked confused.

"Where would I go?" Lana gave a bitter laugh. "Kid, you've got a really nice place here. Civil rights. Laws 'by the people, for the people.' Fucking... streetlights and police who come when you call and services for the poor. And you don't even realize that it's an island, an anomaly in your own realm. I watch the news. Most of your world isn't like this. And even here, you don't 'just leave.' I work alongside women whose men terrorize them, who are makeup masters with a bruise or who have to grovel for gas money out of their own tips, but they can't leave for too damn many reasons to even start to get into with you. Stupid, simplistic question." She sat back in her chair and looked at Jessie like she was an idiot.

Jessie's cheeks colored.

"In our world there are three types of people; the strong, the protected, and victims. I'm not strong and I refuse to be a victim."

"'In our world,'" Etienne scoffed, repeating her words. "Speak for yourself. The Seelie aren't like that."

Lana turned to him and drew one fingertip slowly down the side of her face.

Etienne glared but said nothing more.

Winter looked in sympathy at both of them.

Lana sighed. "No, Ciarán was a nightmare, but he was a powerful protector. With him I at least knew... I knew I could walk the halls in safety. I knew who was going to hurt me, and that he would, for the sake of pride and honor, punish anyone else who tried." A look of shame flashed across her face. "...without his permission." She emptied a wine bottle into her glass. "But when he was killed I lost even that. I don't mourn the man. I mourn for my security and wellbeing." She took a deep drink.

"If you are a handmaiden of the Queen, doesn't that help you?" Winter asked, wanting to understand her distress. Wanting to soothe it.

Lana shook her head. "Not unless I never want to leave her quarters again. And I'm a succubus. I need to feed. The other handmaidens aren't game for being on my menu, which is unfortunate. I do love pure sidhe when I can get it." Her eyes fell on Cian and an inviting grin pulled at the corners of her mouth.

Etienne frowned hard.

Winter also frowned and shifted to hold Cian's larger hand protectively in her own.

Cian looked around at the three of them, his red-gold brows raised in mild confusion.

"Well, since you stole Keeper from Ceallach, I can't imagine you're even a handmaiden anymore," Etienne pointed out, his tone unfriendly. "He's not going to greet your return with open arms—more likely an open torture cell."

Lana tossed her hair back. "Ceallach will want vengeance more than he'll want to punish me. I was counting on that when I took the blade. Maybe I won't be able to present Midir to him on a spit like I had originally planned..." she paused, thinking, "But if I can point and say to him, 'Your son's murderer is in that black tower,' that will be close enough. Then he'll bring his army."

"And when your Unseelie army is here among us, what then?" Etienne's voice dripped with suspicion.

Lana's eyes widened. "Are you serious? You, racist bastard."

"You really love throwing that word around, don't you?"

Jessie looked from one to the other. "Wait... what?"

Etienne glared at Lana. "I'm not acting this 'racist' you accuse me of."

Lana raised an ebony brow. "Fine, then. Why don't you tell these nice people how 'racist' translates into our language?"

"It doesn't, and you know that."

Jessie's face showed her confusion. "Then what word do you use?"

"Common sense," he snapped.

The teen's eyes widened. She scooted her chair away from his, closer to Lana's. "Wow. I'm going to sit on the bigot-free side of the table, now."

Lana laughed.

He scowled at her and then turned to Jessie. "This concept, your racism, is stupid among mortals. You base it on appearance, on differences in cultures, when all of you are at heart the same. You're all human."

"But you're all fae, aren't you?"

Etienne barked a laugh. "That word covers hundreds of sp... sp... what is the word? Kinds of creatures. Some are harmless. Some will rip off your leg and eat it before your eyes. Humans don't do that." He looked pointedly at Lana. "Creatures like that are dangerous, treacherous, and sadistic. Creatures like that are Unseelie."

Lana gave him a spiteful smile. "Oh, and the Shining Ones never betray? Never rape? Never plot the downfall of their rivals?" She stroked her cheek again. "Never prey on the helpless?"

Etienne's lip curled. "All the more reason to not call on any of the bastards for help."

Erik drummed his fingers on the tabletop. "I know you don't like it, but if she can bring us an army, I'll take it. Not dying tomorrow while facing down insurmountable odds is rather high on my priority list."

Lana flashed Etienne a look of triumph. "I can do it."

Etienne sat back, angry, and looked at Erik. "Fine, but they're your problem when they get out of hand."

The Vampire King nodded, thoughtful.

"I need to tell Anluan where Senán is."

Etienne jerked as if he'd been burned. He turned to Cian. "Dammit, I said no!"

Cian dropped his eyes, but then looked at Winter for a moment. He raised his chin. "Yes. This is my re... re..."

"Responsibility," Winter supplied.

Etienne pushed away from the table and stood over them. "No. I don't want you anywhere near his court. We are not having this discussion."

Cian's eyes widened for an instant. Then he dropped his eyes again, beginning to wilt under the force of Etienne's dominance.

Winter turned to face Cian and squeezed his hand. She probably shouldn't get in the middle of this, she knew it, but Cian wasn't a child. Etienne needed to stop treating him like one.

Cian looked up, meeting her gaze, and she smiled encouragement. He had saved her life and she let that fill her eyes, let him see her faith in his determination, his compassion, and his strength.

Cian returned her smile. His eyes darkened, taking on the shade of the deep forest, and he straightened his shoulders.

Etienne watched their silent exchange with a frown, and he focused on Winter, his tone harsh. "Don't encourage him."

Cian rose up from the table, taller than Etienne. "Don't snap at her. This is between us."

Etienne turned away, began to pace. He shook his head.

Cian moved around Winter's chair to intercept him. "Etienne, it's my duty. I'm Senán's companion."

"Bullshit. You're just a boy. You don't have a duty to anyone."

"I have a duty to my king and my kin."

Etienne brushed his hand over his cheek, his arm. A nervous flutter of movement like Winter hadn't seen from him before. He only did it once, but in that moment, she knew—Anluan was the one who had scarred him. If not personally, then the king was responsible. But what Etienne said was, "That king tried to rob you of being a prince. He tried to make you a plaything." He turned to face Cian, rage making the scars on his cheeks stand out. "He betrayed your father—my friend—for the sake of the memory of your dead mother's beauty and to reduce the princely competition for power by one."

Cian frowned. "I know you think that, but that's not—"

"Yes, it is!" Etienne roared, making Winter's eyes widen and Jessie flinch. "When I found you, you couldn't dress yourself. But you could dance. You played the lute beautifully. But you couldn't comb your own hair. You couldn't mount a horse without assistance. And you, an adolescent prince, *a grandson of Dagda*, had never held a blade, or a bow, or learned even the most rudimentary of magics." Etienne turned to Erik. "What say you, Viking? Was that training as befit a prince's son, a king's nephew and ward?"

Erik raised an eyebrow. "No…"

"Maybe he just hadn't found the right tutors yet," Cian protested.

"Oh, and Senán's weren't good enough, then?" Etienne asked with derision.

"You weren't there. You don't know. Anluan was always good to me."

"I imagine he was, boy," said Erik. "It was in his best interests to be."

Cian turned toward Erik, a hopeful light in his eyes, but when he saw the vampire's speculative expression he seemed to realize he would find no ally there. Frustration and confusion played across his face. "It wasn't... it wasn't like that. Anluan isn't like that. You're twisting things." He frowned, determination tightening his jaw, and he turned toward Etienne again. "And even if it was, it wouldn't matter. Midir is my uncle. I have blood guilt and I'm honor-bound to help make him pay for his crimes."

Etienne rolled his eyes. "Damn Sons of Dagda. Boy, Anluan is your uncle. Ceallach is also your uncle. The only male sidhe of rank you've ever met who isn't related to you is *me*. I'm not a Son of Dagda because by some miracle no one in my mother's line ever spread her legs for him. It's said Dagda's sons are numbered among the stars. You know why? Because there are so damn many scattered through the realms that nobody has ever gotten an accurate count! The one and only reason your father, Eoin, was acknowledged as the youngest was because Dagda wandered off or died or whatever the hell happened to him right after he was born, and no others have turned up." Etienne shook his head in disgust. "Blood guilt? In my opinion the only one who has blood guilt is Midir. Don't saddle yourself with his stain."

"That's just your opinion. I'm still honor-bound, Etienne." Cian took a breath. "I'll go alone if I have to."

Etienne paced away. "You can't. You don't know the way."

"Lana, do you—?"

Etienne moved back across the kitchen faster than Winter could track and stopped just in front of Cian. He reached up and clasped one hand around the back of the youth's neck. Winter could see the fear in his gray eyes as he spoke from just inches away from Cian's face. "Don't you understand? If you go back, he'll try to keep you." Etienne's voice trembled. "I can't stand against him. Not in his court, surrounded by his knights." His grip tightened. "I won't be able to stop him."

Cian's cheeks colored, and he reached up to lay his hands on Etienne's shoulders. His smile was earnest and his voice gentle. "It won't be like that. You'll see."

Etienne's eyes widened for a moment. He pulled Cian down and pressed his forehead to his... and then broke away, turned on his heel, and pushed his way out the sliding glass doors to the garden.

Cian stood where Etienne had left him, his breath shaking, and his face flushed.

Erik cast a sympathetic look at the boy while Lana drank her wine with a smirk of amusement. Jessie watched Etienne disappear around an overgrown berry bush in confusion.

Winter stood up from the table to follow the faerie knight. She brushed her fingers over Cian's hand as she passed, giving him what she hoped was a touch of reassurance.

The paving stones were chill under her bare feet. Winter hesitated for a moment in the courtyard, thinking of the shoes left behind in her bedroom, and then shook her head and forged onward, the dusting of sand gritty against her soles. She was needed.

Finding Etienne was fairly simple. Even though the gardens were extensive, all she had to do was follow the trail of stressed pixies. Apparently, he hadn't been patient with their curious nature. Four-inches-tall, they fluttered about her hands, eager to tell her of their rude intruder. Winter soothed them as best she could and continued on her search.

She finally found him in one of the many grottos, the plantings run riot and intertwined with the enthusiastic care the pixies provided. He paced, stalking from one side to the other with a killer's grace, his auburn hair now loose around his shoulders. He ran one hand through it in a gesture of agitation, and Winter knew how it had come undone. She looked, saw where his hair tie had fallen, and stepped forward to pick it up.

Etienne turned at her approach and anger filled his eyes.

Winter did not pause. She lived her life facing down the rages of people who could tear her to pieces. She let it wash over her and bent at her knees to pick up the elastic ring. She then held it in her hand and stood there, waiting patiently for him to speak.

She did not wait long. "Why the hell did you encourage him?"

She turned her answer over in her mind. Etienne was angry, but more than that, he was afraid... and she sensed he was afraid on more than one level. "He needed encouragement."

"Not in this, dammit."

She looked at him with an open expression. "Yes, in this, and in the next thing and the next. Cian's ready to stand on his own."

"He's only a child."

Winter stopped and responded with silence. Arguing with him would do him no good right now.

Etienne turned and started pacing again. "No... I can't let him go back to Anluan. Cian has this fantasy memory of what he's like. He doesn't understand the truth of the bastard, of what he's capable of." He shook his head. "I should take Cian and keep running," he muttered.

"If we fall here, there may not be anywhere left to run to. We may need Anluan's army to save this realm from Midir."

Etienne stopped, looked at her. "Would you risk Jessie?"

She had just had to entertain this very thought. To bring other wizards to the city would place Jessie very much in harm's way. "To save our city... our realm. Yes." It would kill something inside her, but she would do it. However, she also didn't feel about Jessie the way Etienne seemed to feel for Cian.

He frowned and spun away. "It doesn't have to be here. I can take him back to Faerie, back to wandering the borderlands." He stopped pacing. "That's what I'll do."

Winter's breath caught. He meant it. "But I won't see you again." It was out of her mouth before she could catch it.

Etienne turned back, brows raised.

Her cheeks warmed. She kept talking, the words continuing to tumble out. "If you go back to Faerie, I'll have no way to contact the two of you." She would lose both him and Cian at once. The thought set her lip to quivering, and she fought to still it. When had they come to mean so much to her?

Etienne's eyes flickered toward the House and back to her, and then he turned away with a soft curse. After a moment he turned back, his expression softer. He approached, reached out, and cupped the side of her face with his rough hand. "I'd ask you to come with us, but I know the answer."

Winter closed her eyes against his next words. Against her next loss. She nodded. "You do."

He was quiet for several long moments, his hand warm on her cheek. Then, "What sort of a mercenary would I be, if I abandoned my lady on the eve of battle?"

She gasped, and her eyes snapped open.

Etienne wore a smile. Fear still lurked in the depths of his eyes, as well as something else she couldn't identify, but determination had tightened his jaw and straightened his shoulders.

She covered his hand with her own. "You're not a mercenary. You're a knight."

He snorted. "I'm a pathetic excuse for a knight."

She smiled. "Not to me."

His eyes warmed and he stroked his thumb over her skin. He shook his head and grinned. "Come on. Let's go finish planning this debacle."

"Well, as long as we're being optimistic..."

Etienne chuckled and led Winter by the hand back to the House.

CHAPTER TWENTY-FOUR

"They'll really listen to a teenager?" Lana asked.

Winter pulled into the merchant parking lot behind Curiosity's. Etienne's old Harley growled an aggressive rhythm as he followed her with Cian. Lana had been quiet most of the way, thinking about her return to Ceallach's court, Winter had imagined. The question about Jessie surprised her, but it was a fair one. "Some of them will. She's easy to talk to—when she'll hold still. And many of them speak to her rather frequently." An affectionate smile spread across her face. "The rest of the leadership is familiar with her by name, at least. She's not an unknown quantity." They had decided that Erik would contact the leadership of the other preternatural groups and invite them to gather at Mulcahy House that afternoon. Jessie would speak for Winter at the meeting.

Winter wouldn't be there because she was going to Faerie.

Her belly quivered with nerves again at the thought. Faerie, where her mother, Tersa, had come from and presumably returned to. Would... would she see her there? There were countless realms within Faerie. Statistically speaking the odds of encountering her mother were remote, at best. Would she even recognize Tersa if she saw her? Winter only had a few pictures of her and her own childhood memories of eyes and hair like flame.

Which brought her to the question of whether or not she wanted to find her mother at all. She had been four-years-old when her mother had left. As a child, she had thought that with the conditions of the binding broken her mother was somehow banished from the Mortal Realm. But as she got older and became more educated she had learned that wasn't the case at all. The break had only banished her from contact with Colin. There were many stories of faerie wives returning to care for their children. But Tersa never had. She had only cared about Colin.

… toppled in a boneless heap on the ground…

"Are you coming?"

Winter jerked herself from the memory, sharp as a freshly broken bone. Lana was looking at her with impatience, the passenger-side door open. The Bug was parked, the ignition off, and the keys were warm in her hand. "Yes." Her voice rasped, and she cleared her tightened throat. "Yes," she repeated, and busied herself with putting away her keys and getting out of the car to cover the few moments she needed to recover.

Lana either didn't notice or didn't care—or maybe she understood all too well. Winter didn't know. Lana simply shut the car door without a backward glance and left Winter to it.

Winter led the way around the century-and-a-half-old brick buildings and crossed the pedestrian-only street, to come to a pause before the locked wooden gate that guarded the wide gap between East Meets West and Otherworld Books. The merchants' kids played in the grassy courtyard beyond. It was a small, green oasis with a couple of trees and some newish playground equipment that she could hear whining and sighing in time with young voices. She remembered watching her sisters climb those trees. How Sorcha and Mirilyn's coppery hair had shone in the sunlight as they dared each other to clamber ever higher. Winter had never been a tree climber, but their cousins, Kelley and Martina, and the rest, all of them had been so adventurous.

She stopped, her hand on the lock, and closed her eyes as pain knifed through her chest. She needed to stop this. If she survived the coming confrontation she would take time to grieve. And if she died, then she would join them. Either way, she needed to focus on getting through this crisis.

Just like she had to every single day.

Winter stuffed that thought down harder than the rest, that self-indulgent, self-pitying thought, and opened her eyes, her mouth tight. An unlocking cantrip made swift work of the lock, faster than digging the key from her cavernous bag, and she let the three fae through the gate, pulling it shut and locking it behind her.

Tucked in the cool shadow between the two brick buildings, out of sight—hopefully—of the playing children, Winter dug out her felt tip pen and drew misdirection glyphs on the backs of all their hands. She felt the corners of her mouth pull into a small smile as she remembered the last time she had done this. She had been alone and had come to reinforce the seals on the Gate below the bookstore. One of the children had spotted her drawing 'pictures' on herself and she ended up spending the next twenty minutes decorating the whole gaggle in spell chalk with made-up designs. But luck was with her today as she spoke the Words of Command and each ward glowed bright for a moment in turn without pint-sized interference.

Etienne took a step forward and Winter held up a staying hand. "One more moment, please." He nodded, and she shifted to her magical sight. And then sighed as it seemed her luck had come to an end. There was Brian, glowing bright and moving around the storefront. She had hoped that he would be away, working at one of his many side jobs. This was going to make getting into the bookstore basement a bit more difficult. She reverted to normal sight. "We'll need to be as quiet as possible. Brian is working in the store." She hitched her purple canvas bag higher on her shoulder and moved in the direction of the bookstore's backroom door.

"Who's Brian?" Lana asked with a note of mild interest.

"He's my cousin." Which was an accurate enough description. Norah and toddler Justin were very distant cousins, and Brian was adopted, but they were all the family Winter had left and she would protect them. Somehow. If only she could come up with a pretense for getting them out of the city and away from their business on such short notice.

"Brian is Jessie's friend," Cian added as they followed Winter. "He could see through the glamour that the black-haired sidhe lord cast over himself, when we were getting away."

"What?" Etienne sounded shocked. "How?" He had apparently not overheard Jessie mention it at the Theatre, earlier.

Winter held up her hand for silence. They were close to the door and she had no desire to answer the question, anyway.

The children continued to play without as much as a curious glance in their direction. None of them had the spark of magic needed to see past the wards. Winter shifted again to her magical sight, making sure that Brian was still in the storefront, not in the backroom which would really make things difficult, and then listened hard for Norah's voice. She was greeted with silence—which really only meant that there was no one making noise. She pressed her finger to her lips, and touched the knob for the unlock—

"Be vewy, vewy qwiet," Lana whispered.

Winter raised an eyebrow at her.

Lana grinned and shrugged, clearly amused with herself.

Etienne frowned for an instant, and then rolled his eyes as he made the connection.

Cian looked at all three of them with an expression of mild confusion.

Winter performed the unlocking cantrip and pushed the door open just enough to see that the backroom was, indeed, empty. Some of the tension released from her shoulders and she eased it open further, her attention now on the playing children, on the alert for any who might be looking too closely at a door that seemed to be opening all by itself. But they busied themselves with their games as the fae slipped in past her, and Winter followed them, closing the door again.

The backroom was long and narrow, with the staircase leading up to the family apartment on the wall to their left. The basement stairs were tucked underneath, facing the swinging door to the store front. As they rounded the tight corner she saw the basement door was closed, the baby gate pulled shut in front of it. Winter's brows knit in concentration as she lifted the latch on the little plastic gate...

"I saw one on the shelf back here." Brian pushed through the swinging door as he spoke and turned just in time to see Winter. His dark brows shot up and he looked at the three strangers behind her with confusion. "What—?"

"Hello, hottie," Lana murmured with enthusiasm behind Winter.

Winter didn't swat the succubus, but it was a close thing.

"Brian?" Norah pushed open the swinging door and leaned through, her dark, curly hair in a messy bun. "Could you snag another box of register tape while you're back here?"

There was nothing for Winter to do but point at Norah and shake her head. *"She can't see us,"* she mouthed. Blast it! She didn't want Brian involved.

Brian blinked, his back to his mother, and then exasperation flashed across his handsome face.

Not the response Winter was expecting.

Brian schooled his expression as he crossed to the long line of shelves. "Sure, no problem."

Norah smiled and ducked back into the store front.

Brian waited for his mother to disappear for his expression to turn wry and he faced Winter again. "So… are you finally coming out of the broom closet, then?" he whispered. He glanced past her and offered a smile and his hand in greeting to her fae companions. "I'm Brian MacDowell. Pleased to meet you."

Winter watched Etienne take Brian's hand, her mind racing as the three fae introduced themselves. She needed to lie, but what could she say? She'd been lying to Brian for years and now it seemed he knew something, after all. But how? "What did Jessie tell you?"

Brian shook his head. "She didn't tell me anything. But street kids see a lot of things other people don't." He shrugged. "I saw some strange stuff before Norah and Jake adopted me." He glanced back at the fae behind her. "But why are you here?"

Winter reached into her bag for a tube of forgetting powder, but the moment it touched her hand Brian changed. The spark of magic within him, before like a candle's flame, burst into golden, glorious life, brighter than anything she'd ever seen.

Lana and Cian gasped, and Etienne swore. "He's a fucking *Hero*?"

Winter dropped the forgetting powder and bowed her head, defeated by Fate. Brian's Hero's Journey had begun.

Brian frowned. "What are you talking about?"

Winter gave him a sad smile. "I'll explain down in your basement. There's something I need to show you there."

Brian gave Winter a skeptical look, but at last he nodded. "Okay." He thought it was about time. He brought Norah the requested box of register tape, told her he was running upstairs for a few minutes, and then led Winter and her three friends downstairs.

The basement was fairly uncluttered, given its dirt floor and tendency to leak during hard rains, which in the Pacific Northwest they had with frequency. It took up the entire length of the bookstore building, about a third of the block. The ceiling was rather high for an old basement, the walls were stone, and there were weight-bearing stone pillars at regular intervals. Toward the far end was the Gap, the large space where stones had fallen in at some point, leaving a huge hole in the wall. Someone, at some point, had covered it with an iron grate—to keep kids out of it Brian had always supposed. He'd always been curious about what was back there, but the lock had proven to be frozen shut, and with Justin being so little, Brian hadn't wanted to risk breaking it just to explore.

Brian paused for a moment at the bottom of the stairs and then turned to face Winter. "Does this have anything to do with me not being allowed into the Theatre this morning?"

Winter nodded. "It does, but some secrets aren't mine to tell."

Brian didn't like that, with Jessie spending so much time there, but he'd have to accept it for now. "Okay... so what *can* you tell me?"

Winter steepled her hands and touched her index fingers to her lower lip. He knew that expression well. It was her thinking face. Finally, she said, "I can tell you that I'm a wizard." She thought for another moment. "And so is Jessie."

"A wizard? Not a witch?"

"It's not a gendered term. A witch is something else, a blanket term for something more spiritual."

Brian nodded, adding that to his shifting worldview. He glanced at Winter's friends, curious now.

"I'm a sidhe," Etienne said.

Brian blinked.

Etienne scowled. "Why the hell does English have to be so damn difficult?" He pointed at himself. "I'm a faerie knight. A male one."

Brian's brows rose as understanding dawned. "Oh!" He thought about that for a moment. "I thought fairies were little with wings."

Cian smiled brightly. "We're like Legolas!"

"From *The Lord of the Rings*?"

"Yep."

Brian looked at Cian a little more closely. "But you don't have pointed ears."

Lana made an irritated noise. "That's because we're not Tolkien elves. We're fae." She looked from boy to boy and finally rolled her eyes. "But it's close enough for government work. The whole explanation would take too long and none of us has that kind of time."

Winter laid a hand on Cian's shoulder. "Which brings me to the reason we're here." She proceeded to spin a story of kidnapped faerie princes and a would-be king who sought to turn Seahaven into his very own fairyland. She finally stopped, giving him a curious look. "You're taking this very well."

Brian's gaze flickered to the three fae and back to her before he shrugged. "I was on the streets until I was eleven. Street kids see a lot of weird in this city and I saw my share. People turning into animals and... things happening." He still sometimes woke up to the memory of the screaming. "So, it's not a big stretch that there's magic in the world. I'm assuming a wizard has something to do with magic?"

Winter nodded.

"I've figured Jessie was mixed up with something like that for years. She hangs out at the Theatre and everyone on the streets knows that there's something going on there. Not, 'kids go in, but they don't come out' something, but still something." That sort of horror happened in South City and the Warehouse District. Unfortunately, the bus station was located in the Warehouse District, so new arrivals to the homeless scene had to survive a gauntlet to make it to the relative safety of the Historical District, assuming they knew to even try.

"Fair enough." Winter gave him a small smile and it went all the way to her eyes. Brian's breath caught. When had that happened? She still looked exhausted and sad, but there was life to her again, like watching Norah come back from depression. He smiled in return.

The thought of his mom brought him to another question. "Why can I see you, but Norah can't?" It reminded him somehow of the guy who trashed the side of the van that morning, the one who'd actually chased them up the drive.

Come to think of it, he was having a really weird day.

Winter held out her hand, which had a complex design drawn on the back. "This is a misdirection ward. It's magic." She moved her hand and sure enough the glyph had a barely perceptible shimmer to it. "What it does is encourages human eyes to scan past whoever or whatever it's cast on, and whatever we're engaged with. It makes working near humans— those without a magical spark—easier and safer."

"It's pretty." Brian's brows twitched at the word "human." What did that make him? "So, do I have a 'magical spark,' then? And what does that mean?"

Winter looked like she was gathering her thoughts. Was this part of the *'some secrets weren't hers to tell'* thing? "You do. You always have, ever since I first met you."

"But why? I'm just me."

She looked pained. Why? "You're something very special, Brian. You're a Hero."

He could practically hear the capitalization. He glanced at Etienne, re-membering what the faerie knight had said before. He'd made it sound like it wasn't a good thing. "What's a Hero? And why do we need to be in the basement?"

Winter looked past him. "Well, your basement question is a bit easier to answer." She made her way across the dimly lit space toward the wrought iron gate. "This is what we're here for."

"The Gap?" Brian followed her, the three fae trailing behind him.

Winter nodded and hitched her bag higher on her shoulder. "It's much more than just a hole in the wall. It's a stable gateway to the realm of Fae-rie, and we need to travel through it." She pulled out a ring on a silver chain around her neck and began fiddling with the broken lock.

Brian tilted his head just to one side, his dreads shifting against his cheek, trying to figure out what she was doing. "Why do you need to go there?"

"Because we're looking for help," Etienne said while Winter was working. "This Midir that Winter told you about has an army of fae standing between us and the rift he's creating. We need an army of our own."

Brian's brows rose. "You know where to find one?"

Lana smirked. "Damn skippy, we do. My king has a fine army and a strong desire to see Midir on a spit." She glanced at Cian. "And his king is owed a blood debt. Midir kidnapped his son."

Brian took a long look at the wrought iron gate, watching Winter as she drew symbols in the air. She might seem happier, but she was still thin and sick, and he didn't know these other people, yet. "Can I help?" The question fell out of his mouth, but it felt right. Winter needed him.

"No." Winter and Etienne answered in unison and shared a look before Winter freed the lock with a loud clang and pulled the door open. "You're not ready," she explained. "To answer your other ques—"

Etienne's head jerked around toward the opening, frowning. "What's that noise?"

A grunting, rustling sound filtered through the hole and a moment later a gray blur of movement exploded out the opening as a massive... thing entered the basement. It slammed the iron gate further open, knocking Winter backwards with a cry, and bellowed, its huge hand smoking.

The creature crouched for a moment, its head brushing the basement ceiling, and looked at them with small, hungry, yellow eyes. Its lumpy, stocky body was studded with what looked like stones and its broad shoulders were easily as wide as Brian was tall.

Etienne pointed at the gateway with his sword and spoke in a lilting language, seeming to order the creature through it, while Cian eased toward Winter, who lay on her side behind the creature.

The creature bellowed again, cutting off Etienne's demands, and lunged forward, grabbing for the faerie knight. Etienne stabbed at the creature's hand, his dark-edged blade sliding in a smoking trail over the rocky skin. The creature punched at Etienne with its other hand and the faerie knight danced away, but not fast enough and the creature clipped him with its stone-covered knuckles. Etienne spun, his sword flying from suddenly limp fingers, and smacked against the wall hard enough that Brian heard the crack of bone against rock.

The faerie knight fell to the dirt, stunned.

Cian ducked behind the creature and picked Winter up into his arms, just in time to keep her from being trampled.

Brian charged forward without a second thought and caught up Etienne's sword, brandishing it at the creature. He had to hold its attention long enough to give Cian a chance to get Winter away. He had to figure out how to stop something covered in stone.

He had no idea what he was doing.

"Stab it with the pointy end!" Lana had a dagger in each hand and was circling around to the back of the creature.

Brian dodged a swipe of the thing's fist. "Where?"

"Anywhere between the stones!"

What was she talking about? The thing was entirely covered. And then he saw it, a small gap where a stone had broken away. It was his only chance. He dove for it, sword at the ready.

The stone creature grabbed the blade and punched Brian hard enough to send him flying nearly to the staircase. He landed in the dirt with a cough, trying to remember how to breathe. He lay there for a moment, taking stock, expecting the once-familiar feeling of broken ribs. Maybe a punctured lung. But once he regained his wind he was… fine? He sat up, slightly dazed by the realization, and saw that Lana was on top of the creature, trying to stab its eyes. To no avail. It grabbed her and threw her against a wall, where she slid down into a still heap.

Cian and Winter were still trapped behind the thing.

Brian rolled onto his feet and charged the creature again, this time not bothering with the sword. He had to keep the creature off them. The creature bellowed and swung its fist at Brian, who dove inside its guard and punched it in its rocky face with all his strength.

The creature staggered sideways.

Brian blinked, startled, and looked down at his unblemished fist. It hadn't even hurt that much.

Cian darted out from behind the creature, pulling a now-standing Winter by her hand.

"Break its neck!" Etienne was up on one elbow, blood streaming over half his face. "You're a *Hero*. You can do it."

Was that what was happening? This Hero thing? Brian's stomach churned at the thought of intentionally killing something, but he'd lived on the streets for years. It had taught him practicality. He pulled a rubber band from his pocket and tied his dreadlocks up out of his way into a thick tail. He could handle this. His mother and baby brother were upstairs, and this thing would slaughter them if it got loose. If killing it was the only way—

And then the thing charged him and took away his choices.

Brian did all he could do in the limited space he had. He braced and caught the monster's hands, his feet sliding backwards as he tried to gain a foothold on the hard-packed dirt floor. His legs pumped hard and his feet found purchase, and slowly the stone-covered creature was pushed back.

"Good," Etienne called over the creature's grunts. "Now get up behind it and get a grip on its neck."

Brian grimaced, still pushing. How the hell was he supposed to do that? And then the creature put in added effort and he remembered Jessie's judo classes. She talked about it as the art of using an opponent's momentum against them.

He could do that.

Brian dropped to one knee and let go of one of the creature's hands, sending its massive body tumbling over his head. He held on to the other arm and used it as a fulcrum to flip himself over the thing's back, the rough stones tearing at his jeans, and scrambled along its spine to its misshapen head. "What now?"

"Twist, like you're twisting it off!"

Brian wrapped his arms around its neck, locked his hand around his wrist, and twisted with all his might. The creature's head turned, its hands scrabbling for purchase, trying to pry Brian loose. Brian dropped down low over one of its shoulders and twisted harder, the head turning impossibly far, until finally he felt a dull, resonant crack against his chest.

The creature collapsed beneath him and lay still.

"Oh my god…"

Brian looked up to see Norah standing on the stairs, the blood drained from her face, staring at him and the creature beneath him. She must have been drawn by the bellowing. He heard Etienne mutter, "*Merde*."

Winter limped across the basement, a hand digging in her bag. "Norah, it's all right."

Norah's eyes were too wide. "What is that? What just happened?"

Cian was helping Lana stand, her nose bleeding profusely.

Winter pulled a small tube out of her bag just as she reached Norah's side. "Nothing happened." She blew a yellow, powdery substance right in his mother's face.

Norah sighed, and her expression went slack.

Brian jumped off the creature's back. "What did you do?"

Winter was looking closely at Norah and nodded with satisfaction. "It's called forgetting powder. It's basically enspelled pollen. She won't remember anything about this, or about an hour or two on either side." She turned toward Brian. "It keeps her safe. We have to keep our world secret from humans behind the Veil of Secrecy, at all costs. There are those who would kill Norah or make her one of us simply for seeing what she did. This method is gentler."

Looking at Norah, Brian wasn't so sure, but he'd trusted Winter for years. He made the choice to continue trusting her. "Can she take care of Justin like this?"

"As soon as I release her, she'll be fine." Winter turned to Norah and her voice took on a strange resonance. "Norah, hear me. You heard a box fall over and Brian was already picking it up. There is nothing to worry about in the basement. Now go back to the storefront and go about your business. You will avoid the basement for the rest of the day."

Norah's full attention was on Winter as she spoke and finally she nodded and turned around, leaving the basement.

Brian watched his mother disappear up the stairs and sighed. He hoped Winter was right and that she would be okay.

Behind him the creature let out a heavy breath.

Brian spun, ready for another attack, but it remained still. "It's alive!"

Etienne snorted, mopping at his bleeding face with a bandana. "Of course, it's alive. It's a stone ogre. Takes more than breaking its neck to kill it."

"Then why did you tell me to do it?"

"Because it's the fastest way to stop it and you were perfectly capable of it."

Brian nodded. Okay, that made a weird sort of sense. "Now what do we do with it?"

Winter patted his shoulder as she limped past. "We banish it back to where it came from." She was now holding a small, round, bright-blue bottle in her hand, which she uncorked and upended on the ogre's head. The ogre vanished in a cloud of stinking smoke.

Brian coughed and fanned the smoke away, watching as Winter limped over to Etienne, whose head was still bleeding. The ogre had come through the gateway. Winter was going through it. "I'm going with you."

"No," they said, again in unison.

Lana squawked in alarm. "Would you two stop doing that? Fate wants him to go, haven't you two idiots figured that out yet? We would have been crushed to jelly if not for Brian."

Etienne submitted to Winter dabbing some green gel stuff on his forehead but flashed an obscene gesture at Lana.

Winter gave Brian a glance over her shoulder as she worked. "Fine." He could tell she was less than enthusiastic. "Come with Lana and me."

Etienne frowned. "I don't want you going. It's not safe."

Winter let him touch her on the arm—when had she started doing that? She'd been shrinking away from touch for months—and gave him a small smile. "Etienne, I don't know what we have, here. But no matter where it's going, you don't get to tell me what to do." She laid her hand over his, a gentle touch, and finished cleaning up the blood on his face.

Brian looked at the frustrated faerie knight with curiosity. What was he to Winter? He watched Etienne pick up his sword from the dirt and clean it with the sleeve of his shirt before sliding it home in its scabbard, and then looked toward the gateway. "Do I need a sword, too?" he asked, thinking about the safety of the two women he would travel with.

Etienne glanced up at him. "Do you know how to use one?"

Brian shook his head. "No, but I can learn."

One corner of Etienne's mouth twitched up. "Not in twenty minutes, you can't." Brian opened his mouth and Etienne raised a hand to quiet him. "I can teach you to kill someone in twenty minutes, but I can't teach you to defend yourself or them, which is what you're asking me. I'm not saying I won't teach you, just not today. Listen, boy. Where we are going, warriors have been perfecting the art of death for hundreds, if not thousands of years. A blade, or any weapon, immediately makes you a target. It marks you as ready to fight. The bigger you are, the bigger the target, and you're pretty damn big as it is."

Brian looked over to where Lana was holding still for Winter's ministrations. "But how can I keep them safe?" he asked quietly.

Etienne followed his gaze to Lana. "Her? Don't let that pretty face fool you. She's survived an Unseelie court for over two centuries. Granted, she had a patron, but so do most in the courts."

Brian wasn't sure he was following all this, but he packed away his mental notes for further review. However, one word caught his attention. "Unseelie?"

This time, Etienne's small smile was distinctly grim. "Unseelie is where the nightmares live."

CHAPTER TWENTY-FIVE

Winter was content to let Etienne lead the way. They moved in utter darkness for what seemed to be mere minutes, the dirt beneath their feet giving way to unyielding and uneven stone and the tunnel walls to what felt like branches and leaves. Finally, a strange moon's light broke through the gloom and they found themselves standing at a crossroads. All around were crowded night-dark trees, the only sign of the group's passage the ravaged greenery the stone ogre must have left behind as it was drawn to the open Gate.

"How long have we been walking?" Brian asked, looking around in confusion. Winter couldn't blame him. It had only been early afternoon when they left.

"Time flows differently in Faerie," said Etienne. "And just because it's night here doesn't mean it will be night where we're going." He glanced at Lana and snorted under his breath. "Well, where Cian and I are going, anyway."

Lana gave Etienne a dirty look. "There is as much light among the Unseelie courts as among the Seelie."

"The Seelie don't shun the light, unlike the Darkling Throng."

Lana flipped the faerie knight off.

"If we're done…" Winter gave the two fae a sardonic look and hitched her bag higher on her thin shoulder. Her hurt knee was making her cross and the bickering was getting old. "For the record, I don't know if I'm Seelie or Unseelie."

"How?" Cian asked.

"It was one of two conditions my mother demanded when my grand-parents bound her to the Mortal Realm. If she could not take my father back to Faerie with her, then no one in my family could ask her about her lineage. That one's pretty common. But it was broken when I was four. I think my father did it."

"What makes you think that?"

"He never spoke of it, and he grieved so much after she was gone—I think he blamed himself. I'm sure it was an innocent question, but that's really all it takes, isn't it?"

"Are you sure it wasn't the other condition that was broken?" Brian asked, curious.

Winter shook her head and smiled. "No, that one would not have been possible."

"What was it?"

"That any then present—and that day it was only my grandparents and my father in the garden when Tersa came to claim him—that any then pre-sent would not kill an innocent." Lana opened her mouth, but Winter cut her off, knowing she would only be argumentative. "Enough about me. Which way are we going?"

Etienne took a good look at the forest paths presented to them. "It doesn't really matter. You navigate Faerie by force of will."

Lana gave Winter a mildly hostile expression and then rolled her eyes. "Basically, we each pick a path and we focus on where we want to go. The three of us to Ceallach's court and those two to Anluan's."

Brian peered down one of the paths. "The light doesn't penetrate very far. How easy is it to get lost?"

"Very," Etienne said, looking at Winter. "It's possible to wander the paths for a lifetime, to wander the borders between realms and never find what you're looking for."

Winter nodded, brisk. "Then we'll focus extra hard." She was not about to let him frighten her back home.

Etienne reached out and took her hand in his. His gray eyes softened. "Be careful," he said in a low voice. "It's dangerous out here and even more so in the courts." He stepped in closer and murmured, "And I don't trust Lana to keep you safe."

Winter gave his hand a squeeze. To be honest, neither did she. "You be careful, too." As much as he worried about her, she wasn't returning from exile to the court of the man who'd had her tortured and scarred. She then turned to Cian and returned his warm smile with one of her own. "And you. Both of you. Take care of each other and we'll meet back up at Mulcahy House when we're done." Come back to me. The intensity of the thought caught Winter off guard. What was she going to do when this was all over, and Etienne and Cian left?

Assuming they all survived, of course.

Etienne kissed her hand. "As my lady bids." He pulled back slowly, sliding his fingers along hers, until they were finally parted. "We will find you an army."

Winter's hand was cool in the sudden absence of his lips and her skin tingled. What would they feel like pressed warm against her own? She smiled and knew it was a bit of a silly smile.

Etienne led Cian away down one of the paths and in a few short minutes they disappeared into darkness.

"This way," said Lana, her tone curt, and she led the way down another path, not looking back. Brian and Winter followed, lest they be left behind at the crossroads.

Winter hobbled along, wishing the ointment she'd rubbed into her knee would work more quickly. But the fact of the matter was she healed at a human rate and chasing Lana down the path made her wish for elevation and an icepack.

Brian watched her for several long minutes with worry etched into his terracotta face. "Winter, should I carry you?"

Winter shook her head. "I'm fine." Her knee throbbed.

Brian turned to Lana. "Excuse me, can we stop for a minute?"

Lana looked annoyed, but she slowed to a stop. "What's wrong?"

"I just need a moment." With that Brian walked down the path a bit and slipped into a gap between the bushes that had not been there before.

Lana's brows rose. "Either he's already gotten the hang of this or Faerie is about to eat your cousin."

Worry churned in Winter's belly and she limped forward to go after him. He was her responsibility.

Before she reached the gap, Brian slipped back through onto the path, now carrying a branch of a length to make a good walking stick.

Lana grinned and looked Brian over as if she liked what she saw. "Faerie likes you, Hero."

Brian handed the walking stick to Winter. "This should help."

Winter smiled, relief and gratitude mingling in her eyes. "Thank you."

Lana set out again and the two mortals followed, and while Winter still struggled her progress was made easier.

Brian looked thoughtful. "Can you tell me about this Hero thing?"

Beside the fact that Winter wished it would just go away? But it wouldn't. She knew, now, that there was no hope of that. Brian's Hero's Journey had begun.

And it would end in his death.

But Winter didn't want to frighten Brian. There would come time to talk about that, later. "Everyone experiences Fate, the endless network of choices that shapes the course of our lives. But Heroes are selected by the Universe and born into the world each with a singular Destiny. Each Hero's Destiny is different, but even so their lives all follow a similar general path." She looked up at the moon, so strange here, yet still following a path across the sky. "During the early part of their lives, Heroes will go through a period of tempering where they face great trials and hardships and come out the stronger for them." Such as Brian's time on the streets. "They will often gain and lose an early mentor." The loss of his adopted father, Jake. "And then they will begin their Hero's Journey which will lead them irrevocably toward their final Destiny. Once they meet that Destiny, triumph or fail, their service to the Universe is done."

"And then what happens?"

"They die," said Lana, tart.

Winter gave her a withering look but was ignored.

"Die?" Brian's tone was even but his brows were raised.

"Yup, they go out in a blaze of—"

"Would you stop?" Winter wanted to brain the fae with her walking stick.

Brian blew out a breath. "No, it's okay. I need to know this." He looked at Winter. "Is it true?"

For once, Winter told the truth. "Yes, most Heroes die in service to their Destinies."

Brian was quiet for several minutes, watching the woods as they walked. Finally, he gave Winter a small smile. "Everyone dies. I know I'll get to die doing the right thing, right?"

Winter returned his smile. "Heroes can serve both the darkness and the light. I don't have any doubts about which side you're on."

Brian's smile widened with her praise.

"We're here." Lana's voice cut through their warm moment and Winter looked around to see they were approaching a massive, moss-covered stone wall, its extremes lost to darkness and mist.

Light poured through a gate at the end of the path; cool light, with the curious quality of moonlight. And stationed at the gate were three guards playing a dice game.

Lana put more swing into her step as they got closer, her hips moving in an eye-catching rhythm. The guards looked up at their approach, for a moment eyes riveted on Lana. And then one frowned and smacked his fellows, speaking in Faerie Gaelic. Winter could make out a single possible word: Lanadrielle.

Lana stopped, muttering, "Shit," under her breath. She then smiled brightly and began to speak in rapid Faerie Gaelic.

Brian murmured in Winter's ear. "What's going on?"

"I don't know, but it can't be good."

Whatever Lana was saying did not impress the guards, because a moment later one grabbed her.

"Lana!" Brian stepped forward, ready to defend her.

"No!" Lana gritted her teeth against the guard's grip. "I'm just under arrest. They're taking us to King Ceallach."

"Why?" Winter sensed they had not been told everything.

Lana sighed. "I stole something when I left."

"What?"

"Keeper."

Winter frowned for a moment, confused… and then her brows shot up. "Keeper? You stole a named blade?" Was that what Etienne had been talking about in the kitchen? Even she had heard of Keeper.

"It's the only way I can catch Midir."

The guards murmured among themselves at the mention of that name.

"I need to plead my case before the king." For once Lana seemed earnest.

Winter glanced at the other two guards. "Then by all means, let us proceed."

They were taken through the stone doorway into a cool, moonlit corridor, barely wide enough for two to walk abreast, the walls meeting in a peaked ceiling arcing high overhead. Water dripped slowly down the mossy walls and mist swirled about their feet, concealing the slick stone beneath. Here and there eyestalks sprouted from the moss and watched them pass in mouthless silence and Brian's eyes widened a bit to see them.

Lana hissed back at him. "Don't do that."

Brian studiously looked away. "Can they hurt us?"

Lana looked at him like he was a truly special sort of idiot. "No. They're only moss." She turned back to minding her footing. "It's just creepy to stare back."

The halls went on for an eternity… for those who did not know the way. Lana had been born in these misty corridors, protected only by her sweetheart fairy mother and forgotten by the sidhe lord who had sired her. Looking for him after her mother's death had proven fruitless and she had ended up with Ciarán.

Music, wild and free, nothing like the staid, set human melodies Lana had had to listen to for the past year-and-a-half, greeted them with a burst of moonlight and then they were in the heart of Ceallach's Unseelie court.

Ladies and lords gathered around, dressed in finery of spider silk and bone and glimmering stone. Humans and fae in artfully torn livery moved among them with trays of treats and sweet wine. Wearing blood-spattered mortal weave, Lana felt like the ugly duckling and wished for a chance to change. But no, time had run out, and she was brought before her king.

King Ceallach was tall, even for a sidhe, and his long, black curls were dressed tonight in blood-red stones. He sat on his raised throne watching

Lana and her company approach with dark, curious eyes. The guards forced Lana to her knees on the stone floor, the force resonating up her thighs and wrenching a small sound from her lips, and Ceallach leaned forward, regarding her like an interesting bug. "So, you've returned, my child's mistress." He glanced at her companions who could not understand the Faerie tongue, his eyes resting on Brian for a long moment, and then her guards, and then back at her. "But something is missing. Where is my property?"

Familiar faces stared at her with the same expressions of curiosity and contempt. The half-breed consort was again in their midst. But, no, she would never again be on Prince Ciarán's arm. She had to make her own way, now. Lana raised her head at the acknowledgement and refused to cower. At least he did not name her a common thief and have her tossed down an oubliette. "I have, my dread lord, and the blade, Keeper, is safe." Time to play her card. "I bring you news of the great Prince Midir." No mention of Midir as Ceallach's brother. Let Ceallach draw attention to the association himself, if he so wished.

Ceallach raised an eyebrow, but she could see the rage kindle in his dark eyes. "Tell me."

"I know where he is and what he plans." Lana paused for dramatic effect, the storyteller's art appreciated by all fae, and launched into her tale. "I admit, I took Keeper, but my intentions were pure." She ignored the soft scoffing noises from several in the crowd. Ciarán had not helped her make many friends. "My beloved prince had been murdered and I craved vengeance."

"As did we all." Ceallach's voice held a thread of threat.

Lana bowed her head. "But in my breast, it burned bright, until on my own I devised a plan. I would take Keeper, get close to the great prince, and use the blade to capture him." Lana looked up.

Laughter broke out all around her... but it died down as courtiers realized that their king had not joined them. Instead he watched her with a calculating expression. At last he asked, "And how close did you get?"

Here was her chance. "Prince Senán, son of Anluan, son of Niamh, yet lives. Midir has destroyed his memories and recreated him as his own son. I got close to Senán and learned much about Midir's plans."

"Close?"

"I am his lover." At least she had been, before she pitched him into Midir. She wasn't lying.

Ceallach looked amused and waved for Lana to continue.

Lana's knees on the stone floor were beginning to burn but she ignored it out of long practice. "The great prince is tearing a hole in the veil between realms and wishes to create his own Faerie kingdom within the Mortal Realm. He has an army of fae and plans to invade tomorrow night."

Ceallach sat back, thinking. He looked at Lana's companions again. "And why do you bring mortals among us?"

Lana glanced at Winter. Here was another opportunity. "The whitehaired woman is half fae and a great healer. I brought her—"

"They don't understand us. What language do they speak?"

Lana bowed her head again. "The mortal language of English, my king."

Ceallach stood and the gathered courtiers bowed before him, leaving Winter and Brian standing above them all for a moment, looking confused, before Winter bowed and pulled Brian down into a bow with her. He chuckled. "And what is your name, little healer?"

Winter raised her head, a jolt of surprise moving through her to hear the king speak English. "My name is Winter Mulcahy, your majesty. I apologize that I do not speak Faerie Gaelic. I was never taught."

Ceallach stepped down from his dais and approached, each step casual. He was indeed lord of all he surveyed. "I will forgive you if you introduce me to your companion, Winter."

"This is Brian MacDowell. He is my cousin."

Ceallach paused for a moment, and then smiled, amused. "I think we both know he's more than that." He swept his arm out. "I think we all know, for who among the sidhe does not know a Hero when we see one?"

Winter felt the color drain from her already pale lips. "Please, your majesty, he's untrained. His Hero's Journey only began today."

Ceallach raised an eyebrow. "You don't seem to have a high opinion of your young Hero, do you?"

"I have a very high opinion of him, your majesty. He's the finest young man I've ever met." Which was entirely true, and the Faerie king would taste the truth in her voice.

"Then let him meet my challenge. I must know what quality of Hero I am dealing with."

Brian looked up. "I don't know that, myself, but I'll meet your challenge, your majesty."

Winter closed her eyes for a moment, unsure of who to pray to. No one was listening, anyway.

Ceallach smiled and spoke to the crowd. "It should be a challenge worthy of a true Hero…" his nod to Winter was slightly mocking, "but not too onerous." His courtiers shouted out suggestions, ranging from trial by combat which made Winter's breath shiver with fear to games of skill and chance the names of which Winter had never heard. The stakes were high, of that Winter had no doubt. Finally, Ceallach's smile widened as an idea seemed to occur to him, and he drew a courtier close to whisper in her ear. She grinned at Brian and slipped away to carry out her master's bidding.

Apprehension made Winter shiver.

Ceallach turned back to his courtiers, a showman's smile on his face. "Our young Hero is lacking something." He made a show of looking Brian over. "It's not strapping good looks. Those he has in abundance."

Brian's cheeks darkened and the fae around him laughed.

Ceallach raised a hand. "No, no, it is good he is modest. A vain Hero is insufferable." He walked around Brian, the two men of a height even if the muscular Brian was much broader. "No, he is modest, he is handsome, I dare say he is hardworking?" He looked to Winter for that, and she nodded agreement. "So, what is he missing?"

"Experience?" Winter suggested, hoping to get Brian out of this.

Ceallach waved her off. "We all start somewhere. He starts here. Today."

"A weapon?"

The suggestion came from a small sidhe girl who tugged her king's tunic and his smile changed to one of tenderness and indulgence. He stroked her dark hair with a gentle hand. "Yes, my clever pet. A Hero needs a weapon."

The little girl beamed up at him.

Ceallach waved his arm toward a doorway. "And here we have a weapon fit for a Hero!"

The courtier returned with a brace of guards who between them carried a loaded weapons rack that trailed thick cobwebs like streamers. The guards set the rack down in the clear space before their king and bowed low before stepping back.

Something about this struck Brian as strangely familiar, but he couldn't put his finger on what. He looked up to find the Faerie king watching him closely. What was he looking for? "What sort of challenge is this?"

"A simple one," Ceallach spread his arms. "For our neophyte Hero, a choice." He looked to Brian again. "Choose wisely."

Brian looked at the rack and hesitated. "Or what?" The way Lana talked this place wasn't far off from being like the streets. There would always be a catch.

Ceallach chuckled and dropped his arm around Winter's shoulders. "Else you forfeit your fair maiden."

"What?" Winter tried to squirm away, but Ceallach held her close.

Brian reached for Winter but Ceallach's guards, bristling with weapons, stepped in between them. He'd have to choose one of the cobweb-covered weapons from the rack if he wanted a hope of not getting cut to ribbons getting her back. He turned back to the king. "Choose a weapon. That's all?"

"Choose wisely."

Wisely. Okay, so he needed to choose a particular weapon. Fine. Brian turned back to the rack.

Seven weapons rested there. Two elaborately carved bows, a spear-looking thing, and four swords of various sizes from a monster nearly the size of the spear to a dainty blade barely the length of his forearm. But it was a middle-size sword with a lion's head on her crossbar that arrested his attention.

Her?

Brian crouched down and gently tore away the cobwebs, revealing a fairly simple sword with minimal decoration outside the elegant lion's head which he could now see graced both sides of the pommel. The metal was strange, all silvery-gold and shimmery under the moonlight, and Brian felt a strong urge to feel her weight in his hand. He looked up at Ceallach. "Can I draw her?"

Ceallach looked pleased. "Her, is it?"

Brian flushed again. "It seems right to me."

Ceallach grinned. "Then her it is. Draw her, let's see what happens."

Brian swallowed and stood, suddenly nervous. What if he was wrong? He looked over the other weapons, just in case... but no, none of them affected him the way she did. So, he picked the lion-headed sword up by her scabbard... sheath...? and brought her blade out into the air with a ringing hiss of steel.

"Greetings, Hero. Long have I awaited your touch."

Brian gasped and looked around, only to realize the voice was in his head. "I... Hello. It's nice to meet you."

"Is she speaking to you, young Hero?"

"Yes."

Ceallach looked delighted. "Ask her name. She has refused to tell all who asked, even they who forged her."

"May I ask your name?" It felt rather strange, speaking to an inanimate object... and also very right, as if he'd been waiting for this his whole life.

"I am Courage. I have been waiting for you."

"My name is Brian. May I tell these people your name?"

"As you wish. I am yours."

And he was hers. He knew that on a visceral level. But out loud he said, "Her name is Courage."

Ceallach removed his arm from Winter's shoulders and his guards stepped aside. "Well done, my boy! Well done." He motioned toward a liveried servant. "Get our young Hero a fine sword belt. He must be able to bear his companion with pride."

Brian finally smiled, looking in wonder at Courage for a few moments before sheathing her. He couldn't wait to show her to Jessie when they got home. He nearly pulled out his phone to text her and then stopped. It was a pretty safe bet that his phone wouldn't work, here. As soon as they reemerged, then.

Ceallach ascended the dais, passing Lana who remained on her knees on the stone where her king had left her. He drummed his fingers on the arm of his throne, watching Lana, and finally said, "A Hero and a healer. You keep interesting company, Lanadrielle." He glanced at Winter with renewed curiosity. "And you make a lovely maiden, young Winter."

Winter bowed her head. "Thank you, your majesty." Her heart still fluttered from her scare.

"Why are you here?"

Winter looked up at him. "I'm the wizard of the city Prince Midir is going to invade. Tens of thousands of my people will die if he succeeds."

Ceallach nodded, thinking. "You have much at stake."

Was Lana wrong about his commitment to Midir's destruction? Winter drew breath to speak.

"Winter Mulcahy is a great healer. She can cure Queen Deirdre, your majesty." Lana held her head high, even on her knees. "In exchange for your help."

Ceallach's brows knit.

Winter's eyes widened. That was too much and too cruel. But now that it was said she couldn't walk it back without either appearing weak in front of an unknown ruler who had just used her as a hostage, or potentially getting Lana hurt. On the other hand, she couldn't make any promises, especially not in this place where to be foresworn could mean death. "Lana may be promising more than I can deliver." Lana shot her a dirty look. "If I may see the queen, your majesty, I can give you a better idea of what treatment options are available."

Ceallach gave Lana an unfriendly expression, but he stood. "Fine. Come with me, little healer. Let us see what your skills will trade for."

CHAPTER TWENTY-SIX

Winter followed Ceallach through a door behind the dais and into a narrow hallway. Gone was the wide-eyed moss and the dripping moisture, replaced by smooth, dry stone and soft tapestries. They passed open doorways revealing opulent private rooms until they arrived at the heart of Ceallach's kingly quarters.

Through a sequence of offices and sitting rooms decorated in a delicate, elaborate style for which Winter had no name was a closed door. Ceallach rapped on the carved wood and waited a moment before a light, feminine voice carried from within. He smiled at Winter, his expression tired. "My queen's favorite handmaiden," he said, and opened the door. Dismay stole over his handsome face.

The golden chamber was a disaster. Furniture pieces were overturned, and clothing strewn about as if a fancy-dress ball had collapsed inside the room. Embroidery and thread hung from the ceiling fixtures like wildly colorful cobwebs. Only a chaise in the center of the room remained standing and two sidhe women sat there, one upright, the other laying with her head in her companion's lap. Her cheeks were sunken and pale, her thin nightgown torn and hanging off one shoulder. Her companion stroked her long, tangled hair with a gentle hand, making soft, soothing sounds.

Ceallach looked around the room. "This happens from time to time. Normally, my queen..." he covered his eyes and whispered what may have been a prayer in Faerie Gaelic. "Can you help her?"

Winter ached for him. She knew his pain intimately. "I won't make any promises, but I hope I can. May I ask you some questions about her, your majesty?"

"Yes, yes. Whatever you need." Ceallach turned the table closest to him to rights. "I'll answer anything."

"Do you know what happened in here?" Start small and work outwards like a ripple. What had happened in this room was a symptom of the larger condition.

Ceallach spoke to the sitting woman, who replied in Faerie Gaelic. "This is Musette, my queen's favorite. She says that Deirdre lost one of our younger son's toys and can't find it." He picked up an upturned embroidery basket and looked beneath. "It's a palm-sized toy horse, a painted blood bay. It was here this morning when I left her."

Winter looked around and joined in the search, setting furniture and ornaments to rights as she looked beneath. "So, she panicked and tore the room apart looking for it." She looked at Queen Deirdre, laying silent on the chaise, her eyes half-lidded. "Will she speak to me?"

Pain flashed across Ceallach's face. "She won't speak to *me*." He shook his head. "She speaks to no one."

Winter nodded, thinking. "How much sleep does she get a night. Some? None? Does she nap during the day?"

"She rarely sleeps, and when she does she has nightmares. She often naps for short periods, usually like this with Musette petting her to soothe her."

"And how often does she eat?"

"She often refuses to. I can usually get her to drink watered wine, though."

Winter nodded again, relieved. That was their way in. If Deirdre drank wine every day, she could get potions into her. Now to figure out what kind.

Ceallach watched her closely. "You've had a thought, little healer."

Winter smiled. "The potions I use to treat conditions like your queen suffers from need to be mixed with food or drink and taken daily. If you can get her to drink wine every day, then I think we stand a good chance of treating her."

"Then, she's not the only one who suffers madness like this?"

Winter shook her head. "Far from it. Hers is simply rather severe." She set a chair with a broken leg against the wall. "My father suffered from something similar. He refused to speak or eat or take his medications. He gave up on the world, on our city, on life, and because he wouldn't take his medications there was little I could do to comfort him."

Ceallach paused with a tangle of embroidery floss in his hands. "When did he pass?"

Winter's hand went to the sudden agony under her sternum. "This morning. Midir murdered him." She swallowed back the tears, but what came tumbling out were words. "The last things I said to him were horrible, angry things. But the worst part is... I'm still so angry. I'll never get to see my father again, but right now I'm not sorry for what I said. And I don't know what sort of person that makes me."

Ceallach crossed the room and took her lightly by her shoulders. "We share the same pain, Winter Mulcahy. The last things I said to Ciarán were in anger and I am forced to live with the knowledge that I did not love my son as I should have. As my wife did. But the fact was he was not easy to love, unlike our younger son. He did horrible things, even by our standards." He gave her shoulders a gentle squeeze and Winter nearly began to cry. "Do not fear that you are a bad person, little healer. I would not let a bad person this close to my Deirdre."

Winter sniffed back her tears. "Thank you, your majesty. You are very kind."

Ceallach chuckled. "Don't tell anyone out there that. This can be our secret."

With thoughts of her father came thoughts of her mother, and Winter's curiosity flared. "Your majesty, may I ask a question for myself?"

Ceallach nodded. "I will grant it to you, though you may not like the answer."

She was prepared for that. "My mother was a sidhe mix of some sort and disappeared when I was four. We think she returned to Faerie. Her name was Tersa and she had eyes and hair like flame." She hesitated. "Have you heard of her?"

Ceallach shook his head. "I am sorry, but I have not. I know many fae in many courts and I have never encountered one such as she. But I'm sure you must have her look about you. You have all the grace and light of one of our own women."

She wiped her eyes on her sweater cuff and smiled, trying to sort out her disappointment... and then tipped her head further to one side as the angle revealed a tiny hoof poking out from behind the bulk of a large embroidery basket. She crossed the room with slow, careful strides so as to not startle the queen and retrieved the small, elegant horse from beneath.

Ceallach cast a broad smile on her like a benediction. "Well done, little healer. Well done." He took the offered toy and knelt before his queen. "Deirdre, my love," he said in soothing tones. "The healer has found the blood bay stallion. Do you want to see it?"

Deirdre's eyelids slowly opened as if from a long sleep, revealing beautiful eyes of cornflower blue with gold flecks. She remained unfocused for several long moments until finally settling on the toy horse. She reached her hand out and folded her long fingers about the toy, bringing it to her breast... and then brushed her fingers across the back of Ceallach's hand as her eyes closed again.

Ceallach's eyes teared and he stood, crossing the room away from the three women to gather himself. Winter waited patiently, and after several long minutes he returned, his dark eyes a bit red. "I miss her," he said, his voice barely above a whisper.

"How long has she been like this?"

Ceallach looked at his wife. "This is the worst she's ever been, and this has lasted since our older son's death. But Deirdre has always been frail. She led a tragic life before I met her, when she earned the name Deirdre of the Sorrows, and I am not her first love. I am simply the one she has not lost. But losing one son and then the other, combined with my brother Midir's cruelty, were the hammer blows that truly drove her to madness."

Winter nodded. "I believe that your queen is suffering from several different maladies." An entire alphabet soup of them, but she did not think that Ceallach would understand the list moving through her mind. "It's not unusual, considering her history. I won't use the word 'cure' but I do think

I can alleviate some of her symptoms and make the illness easier for her to deal with."

"Why can't you cure her?"

Winter steepled her fingers and pressed them to her lower lip for a moment as she gathered her words. "Mental health is very complicated and even I can't make a potion that will simply fix it. It involves dealing with past trauma, with stabilizing her brain chemistry—what's going on with her mind—so she can develop resilience again and be able to interact with others somewhat normally, so she can overcome her melancholy, and her anxiety, and so she can get restful sleep."

Ceallach listened and nodded. "So, what can you do for her, then?"

Now came the hard part. "I'm going to have to ask you to trust me. I'll need a small vial of her blood every month—and to do that you'll need to tie your realm more firmly to the Mortal Realm, so our time syncs up. I'll use her blood to make a powerful potion that she must take every day to be effective." Winter glanced at the queen. "A missed day once in a while is okay, but more than that and it simply won't build up in her system. After a week or two of compliance, you should start seeing some improvement and it will become more marked as time goes on and the potion builds up in her body."

"All this in exchange for my help," Ceallach said, his tone turned sardonic.

Winter blinked and shook her head. She'd forgotten all about that. "No, that was Lana. I would never leave anyone like this if I could help them. I'm a surgeon, not a therapist, but I'll do my best by your wife."

Ceallach's expression softened and his gaze found his queen. "If you can offer my Deirdre hope, I will gladly ride into battle for you."

CHAPTER TWENTY-SEVEN

Cian couldn't get Winter's smile out of his head. The way her mouth curved just so and the way her gentle eyes warmed at his touch filled him with a desire to return to the gazebo at Mulcahy House and cover her with kisses.

Etienne touched his shoulder. "Hey, try to focus before we get lost."

Cian flushed. Speaking of someone he wanted to cover with kisses...

Etienne glanced back. "I'm thinking of her, too. But concentrate on Anluan's court and finding her an army. We need to succeed because there isn't a chance that Unseelie will help us."

Cian nodded, trying to do as he was told, but he couldn't help but wonder... were the Unseelie really so bad? If Winter was one of them, he doubted it. How could someone like her be evil? And Lana might be a little odd, but she wasn't so bad, really. Prickly and contrary, maybe, but not evil like Etienne seemed to think she was.

Fortunately for the two of them, only one person was needed to navigate the paths of Faerie. Soon enough the light got bright beneath the trees and they crested a hill, coming in view of a glittering, glorious palace sitting atop a rise like a jewel in the forested setting. Cian's lips parted, and he let out a soft breath.

They were home.

He turned to say as much to Etienne and stopped. Emotions danced across the faerie knight's normally stoic face, some Cian recognized and some he didn't. Anger. Pain. Longing. His tanned cheeks were flushed, making his spell scars stand out in stark relief. In all their years of travelling together, Cian had never seen his companion—his protector—in such a state of distress.

Was returning such a good idea, after all?

Cian reached out and slid his fingers down the shorter man's wrist, slipping his hand into his, offering comfort and touch.

Etienne took a deep breath and gave Cian's hand a squeeze. "I'm... fine. I... Dammit, now I sound like Winter." His expression turned sardonic for a moment and then he sighed, his gray eyes open and honest in their pain. "No, I'm not fine, but I'll be okay. We need to do this for her." He let go of Cian's hand and they began walking again.

They made the short trip in silence, passing farms where lesser fae labored to bring in the summer wheat. King Anluan and Queen Niamh tolerated no chill kiss of winter's cold in their realm. Here it was eternal summer, eternal daylight.

Four guards stood at the closed gates. No more were needed. The great king knew all who passed through his realm and could warn his soldiers in times of invasion. The guards were whispering among themselves and one word carried.

Agmundr.

"Great," Etienne muttered. "This should be fun."

Two of the guards crossed their spears as Cian and Etienne approached. A third stepped forward and bowed. The leaves embossed into her armor shifted with her movements as if alive. "Etienne Queen's Son, greetings," she said, her words at opposition with the rest of the guards' body language. "May I ask the reason for your return from exile?" None of the guards gave Cian a second glance. Had it really been so long?

Etienne's jaw tightened enough that the scars on his cheek moved and Cian had traveled with the faerie knight long enough to know the next words to fall from his lips would be, *'None of your fucking business.'* But instead, he released a breath of tension and nodded in the courtliest fashion Cian had ever seen from him. "I have come to visit with my mother and her husband. Long have I wandered, and I wish to look again upon their shining faces." He even managed to keep a straight face. Etienne's gaze fell on the crossed spears. "May we pass?"

"The last time you passed through these gates, death followed in your wake." The fourth guard looked out from behind the spears, one hand flexing on the hilt of his sword.

And that was when Etienne's patience wore out. He looked from the guard's hand to his face. "I remember the sidhe lord in question. Thought he'd duel me and kill me for Anluan. Thing is... I don't duel." Etienne held the guard's gaze. "Friend of yours?"

Cian stepped away, giving Etienne room to fight, and his hand moved to his own sword, for all the good it would do him. After his fight—if he could call it that—with the black-haired sidhe lord, he knew he was severely outclassed.

The first guard noticed him move and held out her hand. "Who are you?"

Etienne shook his head and Cian hesitated... and then spoke. "I am Cian, son of Eoin and Éibh—"

"He is Prince Cian, the Glorious Dawn! My beloved nephew, returned to me from the dead." Framed by the open gates stood King Anluan, golden and glorious as his palace. He stood with arms spread wide, his leonine mane of shining hair held off his face by his crown, this one a simple twist of leaves and small flowers in shaped silvery-gold sidhe steel which set off his brilliant, blue tunic and summer-sky eyes.

Anluan's guards each dropped to one knee on their king's arrival, opening the way between him and Cian. The king strode forward and took Cian into a tight embrace. "My boy... my shining boy of spring... how I mourned you."

Cian's lip quivered with emotion. Etienne had always said he couldn't return, but here they were, being welcomed with open arms. Etienne had been wrong; his uncle wasn't some horrible monster. He was a king. "I missed you, too, Uncle." He pulled back as he remembered why they were here. "I have news—"

Anluan kept an arm around Cian's shoulders and guided him through the gates. "Of course, of course. Come inside and we shall feast your return!"

"King Anluan, it is urgent that we beg audience," Etienne said from behind them. But Anluan did not so much as twitch in his direction. Instead he pulled Cian along with him through the brightly lit hallways, past kneeling guards and bowing courtiers who whispered after they were gone, until finally they reached his great dining hall with its graceful, curling staircases and glittering chandeliers lit by faerie fire.

Cian devoured everything with his eyes, remembering the lavish feasts and dazzling balls of the past. He had not seen this, any of this, since he was half grown, a boy just entering manhood. Living in the wilderness with Etienne, he had forgotten how beautiful his uncle's court was. A trio of pixies flew from the table, bearing a goblet of wine for Cian. It was just as sweet and delicious as he remembered.

"All right, we're here." Etienne still stood behind them, fighting a battle against the irritated expression on his face and losing badly. There was no wine goblet in his hand. "My lord, will you hear me? I bear—"

"What's this?" Anluan bumped against the sword on Cian's hip and frowned.

"It's my sword," Cian replied, not sure why his uncle would be displeased. "I'm still learning, though. Etienne is teaching me."

Anluan motioned for a page to approach. It was a beautiful human boy on the cusp of puberty with bright, yellow hair. "Here, take this. There is no need for it here."

The page reached for Cian's belt and he gently pushed the boy's hands away. "No, thank you, my lord. I would prefer to keep it." He looked around as he spoke. Other pages and servants wandered the hall in Anluan and Niamh's livery, serving the gathered sidhe lords, but all of them were human or lesser fae. No sidhe served at table.

How had he missed that, before?

"My lord, we beg an audience with you."

Anluan continued to studiously ignore Etienne. Why? They were trying to tell him about Senán. Finally, he could no longer stand it. "Uncle. My lord. We bear news of Prince Senán."

Anluan graced Cian with a magnanimous smile. "You have my attention."

Cian let out a breath of relief.

The king accepted a lute from another liveried servant and handed it to Cian. "But play for me as we walk and talk. As you used to do to please me."

Cian felt his own jaw beginning to tighten and a growing desire to smack Anluan with the lute. Why wouldn't he just listen? This was about his son! His only son, returned from the dead! But instead he ran his fingers over the strings and began to play one of the king's old favorites. "We found him, my lord. We found Senán. Prince Midir has taken him and keeps him in a tower in the Mortal Realm." Cian hesitated. "Midir has performed unknown magic on him, though, and driven him mad. He doesn't know who he is. He doesn't even know he's sidhe."

Anluan's golden brows rose with shock and he stopped walking beneath the grand staircase. "What are you saying?"

From the top of the stairs carried a voice like honey. "My son bleats for your attention like a goat, but it is your catamite nephew who catches your ear."

Catamite?

Queen Niamh made her slow way down, watching the men below her with calculating gray eyes. Her auburn hair was piled high upon her head, a dainty pixie perched atop it like an ornament to keep it in place.

Etienne froze, as if waiting for something. "Mother."

Niamh raked him over with her gaze. "Etienne. I see you have returned to us from your self-imposed exile."

His eyes hardened with anger. "You know why I left."

"Indeed." She just as quickly dismissed him, turning to her husband and Cian without a second glance. "And now you have your young nephew back, Anluan. Joy must be bursting from your heart." Her words were pretty, but her tone was venomous. She held out her hand and a goblet of wine was placed in it.

"Niamh, stifle your barbed tongue and listen to the boy." Anluan did not look amused. "And who are you to speak of catamites when you stand before me with your human minstrel's get?"

Etienne ground his teeth but remained silent.

Niamh peered at her husband from over the brim of her goblet. "Chretien was able to accomplish what you were not. It's not my fault you—"

Anluan bellowed with rage and dashed a flower arrangement to the ground, scattering petals and pixies into the air. One pixie lay on the marble floor in the ruins of the vase, whimpering in pain, and her fellows gathered her up before she could be trampled. "I sired a son! I sired Senán! You cannot deny me that!"

Niamh threw down her goblet, chipping the floor and destroying the vessel. "Senán is dead, and it's your fault. You sent him riding with your catamite and brigands fell upon them." She pointed an elegant hand at Anluan. "You killed my son."

"Dammit, Niamh, listen to me! Cian comes bearing news of Senán. He is not dead. Midir took him and holds him prisoner in the Mortal Realm."

Niamh was taken aback. Then she slapped Cian across the mouth. "You liar! You shall be foresworn; I will see to it myself."

Etienne stepped forward, putting himself between Cian and his mother, his face flushed with rage. Guards all around reached for their weapons but Etienne did not give them so much as a glance. "And we're done. We've brought you truthful news. You know where your precious son is and hopefully Ceallach's thirst for vengeance is greater than your desire for petty squabbling. Midir is planning to invade the Mortal Realm tomorrow night, in the city of Seahaven, if you care to make an appearance." He dropped his volume, his voice for their small company alone. "I don't care how you felt about Éibhleann, I don't care how jealous you were, but I will not allow you to abuse Cian. Ever. We're finished, here." He turned and walked away, pulling Cian along behind him.

Anluan followed. "Cian, wait, don't go."

Cian turned back, disturbed by what he had seen, his mouth still stinging from Niamh's slap. "My lord, I must go."

"But why? You only just arrived."

Cian looked at Anluan in his golden crown and only felt disappointment. "Because my honor demands that I help my kinsman. I hope you remember your own sense of honor before it is too late." He turned on his heel and followed Etienne, leaving Anluan to stare after him with an open mouth.

CHAPTER TWENTY-EIGHT

At Mulcahy House, Jessie had barely brought the last of the chairs to the dining room table when the first fight broke out.

"You're in my seat."

Jessie looked up to see Basil, the deer Harem Master, standing over Brooks, the bachelor deer buck, with his arms crossed. Jessie liked Brooks. When the harem masters threw out young bucks at puberty, he was the one who took them in and saved them from the streets. Brooks was strong enough to be a harem master in his own right, but instead he was raising the abandoned sons of other bucks. Brooks gestured at the other places at the table. "Seriously? There are a lot of seats."

Basil sneered. "But these are for leaders."

Brooks flushed in anger beneath his short beard. "Then why do you want one?"

"What did you say to me, bachelor? I'm the Harem Master of Seahaven."

At that, Seahaven's other two Harem Masters, Gordon and Spencer, shared a look. Basil's dairy may have been the most successful business of the harem masters, and he may have had the most does, but Gordon and Spencer were brothers who shared. Together they could challenge him for power.

Today simply was not that day.

Instead the challenge came from another source. "For now," growled the teenage buck standing behind Brooks' chair. Jessie knew him in passing. Kelsey or something.

Basil glared at the boy. "Who the fuck do you think you are? You look like a future grease stain."

In the seat beside Brooks, Logan of the orca looked up at the commotion and motioned to Octavia and Cole, his daughter and son. The three Native American therian moved further down the long table, away from the developing cervid fight.

Brooks grimaced at their departure but scowled at the other deer. "Fuck off, Basil. Kelsey is your own son. Leave him alone. He's with me."

"And you aren't shit to me. Neither of you should be here."

"We were invited."

"By someone who doesn't know a buck from a doe."

Brooks stood, teeth bared. "Take the fucking chair. This is supposed to be about saving the city."

Basil did not give an inch, his voice dripping with contempt. "Then you should let the men do that. Don't you have little boys to mind?"

Brooks' hand tightened into a fist.

Jessie met the gaze of a tall, gangly boy on the other side of Basil and saw her tension mirrored in his dark brown eyes. She didn't know his name, just that he was here with his father, some moose stag down from Mount Sarah. She saw him struggling to cover his fear and knew he would fight if pushed.

They would all fight if pushed.

Brooks turned with a soft curse and walked away, young Kelsey behind him guarding his back.

Jessie blew out a breath of relief and sat down at the table with her shopping bags from Painted Warrior, two syringes with needles, and a full jar of blue banishing potion. As the therian leaders made their way into the Mulcahy dining room, she got to work, sucking paint from each colorful sphere and replacing it with charged potion.

She grinned to herself. This was really going to work! No more little bottles. All Winter had to do was point and shoot and poof! Bye-bye baddies.

"You seem pleased with yourself."

Jessie looked up to see Corinne standing beside her. "Hey!" she cried out with delight, drawing stares. She jumped up and hugged the pregnant Lion Queen, earning a kick in the hip from tiny Bella. She grinned down at her friend's belly, accentuated rather than hidden by her chic, silk business suit. "Hey, little soccer player. Anyone tell you kicking isn't nice?"

Corinne rolled her eyes and smiled. "Welcome to my life." The red-headed Lion Queen looked gorgeous, as always, and reminded Jessie of a 1940s movie star.

Santiago slipped his arm around his Queen's waist. "Soon, *mi corazón.*" Jessie swallowed a girly sigh. Santiago had a voice to roll around in. And the way he looked at Corinne was magical.

From behind them came the sounds of gagging, followed by a laugh designed to turn heads—which it did. Vivaine, the Wolf Queen, was only three years older than Jessie, but she ruled the second largest group in the city—and they might have been the biggest. Vivaine and her King, Darian, kept many secrets, the true size of their pack one of them. She stood there in her gladiator heels and leather skirt, with the kind of dusky beauty that only came with a global pedigree, smirking just like the mean girls at Jessie's school.

Darian stood with his arm across his young Queen's shoulders and just let her do her thing—as usual—steel-blue eyes dancing with amusement.

Instead of rolling her eyes, Jessie schooled her face like Winter had taught her. "It's a pleasure to see you both. Can I show you to your seats?"

Vivaine cast a languid look at the table. "I think we can seat ourselves." Mischief played at her painted lips and she led Darian toward the head of the table.

Corinne and Santiago went to find their seats on the opposite side of the table near the dolphins and the selkies, leaving Jessie alone for a breather. Parvati, the solitary alpha tigress and custom leather clothing designer, was flirting with the sea otters' eldest son while his parents chatted with the river otters.

The ravens arrived, and Jessie saw that their leader, Gaubert, was another to come with offspring in tow. For him it was his twelve-year-old daughter, Colette. Jessie smiled and approached. Gaubert always reminded her of a pleasantly Goth-looking David Bowie. "Can I help you find seats?"

Gaubert inclined his head toward her. "Thank you, but I'll let Colette choose, if I may."

Colette smiled at her father and then surveyed the table with serious, black eyes. "Erik sits at the head. Vivaine and Corinne are sitting close and eyeing each other, but the Shark King has not yet arrived to tip the balance... The bucks are bickering already. Joel and Amara of the coyotes are up and coming, though, and they chose to sit in the middle." She turned to her father. "I would sit on the opposite side of the coyotes."

"Why is that?"

"It's close enough to power to contribute to the conversation, but on the door side of the room in case violence breaks out." Ravens, like rabbits, were not physically strong and shied away from direct confrontations.

Gaubert patted her hair. "Well reasoned, my cautious girl. Then we sit in the middle." He gave Jessie another little nod and moved to sit.

Three men in crisp suits arrived and three... less-than-crisp individuals entered with them. It had started to rain, and droplets glittered like diamonds on their coats under the bright chandelier lights.

John Donovan was a tall, elegant black man, the controlling partner at the law firm of Donovan and Associates. He also happened to be a great white shark and the Shark King of Seahaven. He smiled at Jessie, a flash of white against mahogany, and said, "Please accept our apologies for being late."

The pretty brunette woman at his side with kind, tired eyes nodded. "Our car broke down. Donovan was kind enough to stop for us." Rachel was the Matron of the rabbits and being in charge of over three hundred bunnies took its toll.

Jessie's brows rose with concern. "The station wagon? Are you guys okay?" The old car was the only hutch vehicle not up on blocks for various reasons. If it died, the rabbits would be limited to public transportation, limited to what they could carry, food-wise. That wasn't a lot of calories for the physical effort, especially for people who needed thousands of calories a day just to live.

Donovan gave a graceful nod and excused himself to go sit down, his two sharks following him. Jessie was grateful. With the car thing, she was hoping to talk to Rachel and her two Matron's Assistants, and it would be better if it was done in a semblance of privacy. Maybe Winter could give them a car, like she'd given her for her birthday? But a thought gave her pause. Would that look too much like favoritism if it came from the Mulcahy garage, politically? Something used, not, like, new or anything. Jessie didn't know.

"We're fine," said Miles, Rachel's Matron's Assistant and hutch jack. "We're going to get it towed in the morning, and I'll work on it at the hutch." The vast majority of rabbits were female and called bunnies or does, but usually bunnies. The few males fell into two categories: breeding jacks, which were highly territorial and could not live near each other, and hutch jacks, who did live in the hutches because, while they could be aggressive, they weren't ruled by their hormones.

Miles shifted his shoulders, subtly adjusting his binder. "I think it's the alternator ag—"

"It's all great for you half-form furbies, but what about the rest of us?" Cole's voice had risen to fill the room, cutting Miles off. The orca stood leaning over the table, his long, glossy braids swinging. "If *we* shift on land, all we'll do is suffocate under our own weight."

Emmett of the dolphins glared and tossed his long, black hair back, his copper cheeks flushed with anger. "It's called a Smith & Wesson, asshole. We fight in human form."

Octavia played with the large, elaborately beaded clasp of her long, black braid. She always did the most beautiful beadwork and this piece was no exception. The stylized blue orca on a white background set off her copper skin. "Either way, we're putting our lives at risk."

"Hey! We're all going to die if we sit and do nothing." Jessie crossed back to the table and put the lid on her potion jar before Cole's table-pounding knocked it over.

Beside her Vivaine stretched, showing herself to advantage, Darian's arm still draped across her shoulders. "What's the point? I say let this Midir turn it all into Faerie. It's all the same. Meet the new boss, same as the old boss."

Jessie stared, incredulous. "Are you crazy? Tens of thousands of people will die."

Vivaine quirked an eyebrow. "Humans. Humans will die."

Jessie snorted. "How do you get that? Are you explosion proof, now? Because he's going to blow up everything from here to fucking Seattle."

Vivaine's smile wasn't pleasant. "He has to have some plan for his own tower not being blown up. Maybe I take my wolves there? Meet the new boss myself. We all know Winter Mulcahy can't hold this city together. It's been every wolf for herself for years, now. Why should I waste my time with the losers when my wolves could be on the winning team?"

Jessie's hands clenched into fists and she felt power pooling there. "You're out of your fucking mind. Winter can hold it, if we *help* her! We just have to get along." This drew more than one derisive look from around the table.

Vivaine laughed. "Grow the fuck up, you cheap special effect. Your wizard has an expiration date, and everyone knows it. Maybe it's finally here."

Jessie's hands ignited. "I'll show you fucking special effects!"

Vivaine's hand elongated in response to Jessie's challenge, her painted nails disappearing into scythe-like claws. "Let's see how tough you are without your magic, butterball!" And she lunged forward, slashing at Jessie before Erik could get out of his chair.

Jessie squealed with fright just as a blur of movement caught her eye. There was a pain sound and tearing fabric, and Jason stood between her and the enraged Wolf Queen as the claw marks on his back began to bleed.

Vivaine was up out of her seat. "Step out of the way, pretty boy. I don't like to cut up the yummy ones."

Jason's green eyes glittered as he tilted his head just so. "You and I are gonna dance, you crazy bitch."

Corinne broke free from Santiago's restraining arms and leapt over the table, her suit shredding away as she shifted into a lioness the size of a horse. She barreled into Vivaine, roaring and slashing with teeth and claws. The two queens tumbled away from the table.

Jason watched them roll away like a cartoon dustup. "Looks like your dance card is full."

Darian moved to follow them, reaching to pull Corinne off Vivaine.

Santiago shoved him away. "Touch my Queen and Seahaven won't have a wolf problem anymore."

Darian narrowed his steel-blue eyes. "What are you gonna do about it?"

Santiago's lips twisted into a grin and his hands began to shift. "Take out the trash. It's time for some city beautification."

Darian sneered. "You don't have the balls or the men to take on my wolves."

"I do if they don't have a King." And it was on.

Juan, Santiago's second, leapt over the table. "*¡Mierda!* Here we go."

Erik jumped up to help Juan, knocking his chair over in his rush to break up the two kings, and was knocked over in turn by two deer in half-form as Basil and Brooks finally turned their fight physical.

Jessie turned back to watch the queens fight, looking for an opening to jump in… and squeaked as Jason picked her up, squishing her plump waist a bit as he did so. Blood coated his arms, smearing all over her clothes. "Put me down!"

"No way in hell," he said as he carried her away from the fights. "Winter would never forgive me if you got killed or changed. Being therian would destroy your magic and you know it, and Vivaine's gonna aim toward making you furry."

"I'm gonna kill her! I'm not a child." Jessie tried kicking her legs in the air, but against the vampire's strength all it did was make her look stupid.

"Then act like it. I'm not going to argue with you, Jessie." He bumped against the edge of the china cabinet and turned to look up. "Parvati?"

Jessie could see the Indian tigress and the sea otters' son—was his name Journey? She blinked. Were they *making out* up there?

Parvati smiled down at them, her lips swollen from kissing, her long, black hair hanging in a shining rope like Rapunzel's braid. "Hello, Jason. Lovely meeting we're having."

Something shattered against the wall behind them. Jessie felt glass pepper her hair.

Jason looked exasperated. "Are you gonna help?"

Parvati surveyed the expanding anarchy. "Everyone seems to be doing about normal. No one seems to need my help. Except Journey here, who is small and fragile and needs a nice tiger to make it all okay."

Journey didn't seem so sure of that sentiment, but as her hand was currently in his pants...

Jason sighed. "For fuck's sake. At least take Jessie up there with you."

Parvati's grin was toothy and wicked. "Gladly."

Jessie shook her head. "Oh *hell* no. You're *not* leaving me here with these two."

Jason handed her up to Parvati, who used both hands to pull the young wizard up beside her. "If she gets loose I'm getting a stripy new rug."

Parvati purred. "I do like a man who plays with knives."

Jason returned her grin with a fierce one of his own and left Jessie with the alpha tigress.

Jessie knew jumping down from the china cabinet would only end in being chased around the room, which would be rather embarrassing in front of the entire therian leadership of the city. So instead she was forced to watch the chaos. Jason didn't get far before he went down, dropped near the head of the table by one of the cowering rabbits who had apparently not seen who it was. Rabbits weren't preternaturally strong like most other therian, but they had a defensive kick that could put an attacker through a wall. Jessie heard Jason cry out and then the three rabbits pulled him under the table to shelter with them, apologizing profusely.

The ravens were making their careful way out of the room, guns drawn, Colette hidden behind a wall of adults.

The orca and the dolphins were going flat out, now, on the other side of the table. Jessie let out a low whistle as Octavia knocked Emmett flat with a wicked left hook and thanked whoever was listening that neither therian species had fang or claw on land, like a wolf or a lion. Otherwise that fight would have gotten truly bloody.

Donovan looked like he was fighting the urge to get involved in the melee, which wasn't surprising. Sharks were renowned for their love of violence in the water. But this was on land and he was wading into the king fight, looking for all the world like he was trying to help Juan.

Juan wasn't having it. He roared at Donovan. "Get your cold fish ass away from my King!"

Donovan stepped back a single pace and shook his head. "I'm trying to help!"

"Try to help elsewhere, shark."

"What's wrong with you? This isn't the time."

Juan drew his gun and pointed it at Donovan's head and said in measured syllables, "Get the *fuck* away from my King."

Donovan glanced up at Jessie on the china cabinet, gestured to his sharks to stay back, and backed away. "Fine. I'll leave you to it, lion."

Erik was in the middle of the fight between the two stags, doling out beatings to both of them in equal measure. Jessie couldn't tell if he was genuinely pissed or having fun. Or both. Knowing the Viking it was both. Until Basil gored his shoulder. Then fun time was over. Erik roared in pain and jerked the antler from his shoulder, breaking the entire thing off near the base with a vicious twist that nearly broke the Harem Master's neck. Brooks had the good sense to back off, but Basil attacked again, and Erik grabbed him by his hide, throwing him through the large, stained-glass window.

Winter entered the room, one hand over her mouth, blue eyes wide in astonishment. At her side was a tall, slender man in elaborate matte-black armor, his long, curly hair falling about his shoulders and a black circlet on his brow. Was this the faerie king Winter had gone after? He looked... vaguely familiar. Weird.

A vase flew at Winter and his hand snapped out, catching it before it could hit her. Okay, that was hot. The king set the vase down on the small table beside the door and looked at Winter as if she'd brought him to an asylum, which Jessie had to admit was fair. He held out his hand and shouted, "Stop!" with the same lilting accent Etienne and Cian had. The faerie house responded. Vines shot out of the floor, wrapping around everyone fighting and pulling them apart, holding them steady. "*What* is going on here?"

Everyone started talking all at once, with varying degrees of outrage at being handled by a magical stranger.

The faerie king swept his hand out, silencing the combatants. He turned to Winter. "I believe these are your people. Pick one."

Winter, cheeks flushed with embarrassment, looked around and her eyes started to settle on Erik... until she caught sight of Jessie on the china cabinet, complete with Jason's blood all over her shirt. "Jessie!" she cried out with alarm and ran to the base of the cabinet.

"All right." The faerie king seemed to misunderstand. Vines grew up from the floor and wrapped around Jessie, gently lifting her down from the cabinet and setting her on the ground at his feet. "What is going on here, child?" he asked as he lifted the spell from her.

By the broken window Erik floundered in the silencing spell rather like a landed marlin.

Jessie looked away from Erik, to Winter, who nodded encouragement, and then up at the faerie king, who was even taller than Erik. "We were figuring out how to help."

He blinked. Once. "I see." He looked at Winter as if he might bail, but then he seemed to reconsider. "Then everyone sit down and we will come up with a plan." He lifted the spell of silence and the vines receded.

Vivaine stood naked and pissed in all her brown-skinned glory while ignoring Darian who was trying to hand her his shirt. "And who the hell are you?"

The faerie king rose to his full, considerable height and met her fierce gaze. "I am Ceallach, the King who is going to help you misfits save your city." He turned away, summarily dismissing her, and addressed the entire room. "Time is not our friend. We have only tonight to make our plans. Samhain begins tomorrow night. We have to stop Midir and close the rift before midnight or forfeit your city to him. We have less than twenty-six of your hours." He turned to his soldiers in the hallway. "If you can separate the injured from the able-bodied, we can begin."

CHAPTER TWENTY-NINE

Had they been fighting for an hour or an eternity? Cian was sweating beneath his borrowed helm in the cool night, rain running in rivulets over the
matte-black metal. Etienne had threatened to lock him up in Mulcahy
House unless he promised to stay away from the fighting and so here he
was, in the back of the battle with the magicians and the healers. Watching
Etienne weave through the battlefield with his insertion team toward the
tower's side door.

Watching with his frantically beating heart in his mouth.

Winter's team was already out of sight, their goal the utility access tunnel leading in from the edge of the corporate reserve to the subbasement
where the rift lay. Not being able to see them only served to feed his anxiety, though, filling his mind with frightening visions. He wished she could
be back here with him, fulfilling her role as healer, but she was needed
more as a wizard tonight. She was needed to seal Midir's rift. Jessie had
never sealed a rift by herself before, and they needed Winter's expertise
down there in case something went wrong.

On the battlefield, knight clashed with knight and lesser fae fought in
packs to bring the mighty sidhe lords down. On their own side, Erik's
vampires fought with blade and gun, while therian of all shapes and sizes
fought in bodies both furred and clothed. Vivaine and Darian had finally
made the joint decision to bring their wolves in on Seahaven's side, single-
handedly swelling the army's numbers by well over two hundred bodies.

Etienne dove into the gap between combatants and made for the tower's glass doors, trusting his party to follow. He could hear Lana's soft cursing just behind him and the rhythmic, metallic steps of Scoithín, King Ceallach's champion in his heavy armor, who now bore Keeper at his lord's order. Unseelie, both. Wonderful. Behind them were nine warriors comprised of therian, vampire, and more Unseelie sidhe. Twelve in all.

An auspicious number to take down a great prince, or so Ceallach thought.

Etienne would have liked to have been anywhere else.

But no, here they were with two missions: find Senán and draw Midir away from the rift so Winter could seal it before it blew open at midnight. They knew based on Cian's brief time here that Senán was probably being kept somewhere in the penthouse.

Midir, however, could be anywhere in the building.

The glass front of the building was in sight as they ran, and through the glass, armed guards. Which was to be expected. Perhaps not so many, though. Midir had prepared.

But it was too late, and they had been seen. Bullets created spider web patterns in the glass and one of the wolves yipped in pain, his steps only faltering for a moment, the wound already healing. It took more than a single bullet to the body to stop a therian in full charge. Etienne, on the other hand, was not a therian.

Not for the first time, Etienne wished he did not have to wear Agmundr's rig to have access to his full strength and speed. To access its magic, he needed it in contact with his body through no more than fabric, so he was unable to wear it over armor. As a result, his torso was protected only by his clothing and brown leather jacket, while his legs, arms, groin, head, and shoulders sported light, sidhe steel protection.

There was no point in pulling the bullet-damaged doors open. Etienne leapt at full speed, curling and twisting sideways to protect himself from broken glass, shattered the door with his body, and landed lightly on his feet on the other side as he skidded a bit on shards, Glock already drawn. A bullet caught him in the shoulder, sparking off his armor and spinning him to one side, numbing his arm for a moment. Someone was sporting something high caliber.

But so was he.

Ambidextrous as any sidhe, he switched hands and took aim. Thirteen rounds in the magazine. One in the chamber. Whole lot of guards. Each bullet needed to count. His targets were human security guards, paid to be here he imagined, but he had neither time nor inclination to sympathy. They were trying to kill him.

He would return the favor.

It was impossibly loud within the echoing confines of the marble and glass lobby, gunshots rendering all other sound useless. Lana slid into position on Etienne's numbed side and raised her own gun, a .45 just barely small enough for her hands. The vampire who landed at Etienne's other side took a bullet to the head before the glass hit the floor, blood spraying Etienne's exposed cheek as she dropped like a stone. Time seemed to slow down as Etienne leaned further into the gun rig's magics, drawing on all the power it had to offer, and his first victim was the vampire's killer.

These humans were firing out of fear, not training. They were not soldiers. They stood in a ragtag line to keep from hitting each other but neglected to use the central desk as cover to protect themselves. Using the preternatural speed of the sidhe, Etienne shot them without mercy, without pity, as the rest of his team came through the glass. He knew there would be no reasoning with them, no talking them down. There was only death.

Scoithín burst through a window, glass shards exploding around him and pattering against Etienne's jacket and helm like rain. His longsword was drawn, a named blade Etienne had not been introduced to, Keeper still sheathed on his back. Keeper was not a blade for this sort of fight.

The Unseelie champion landed with one foot on the floor and with the other launched into his sword dance, heedless of the gunfire, bullets striking his sidhe steel armor with little more than scorch marks. Even as Etienne was calling for their side to cease firing, Scoithín reached the unarmored guards with preternatural speed and what amounted to a three-foot-long razor blade.

It was over in seconds.

They left the vampire where she lay and headed for the stairs. The time to gather the dead would come after the battle's end. The main power to the building had been cut, which rendered the elevators useless, but it did the same to the door locks. The building was wide open to them.

Etienne's ears rang like cathedral bells as he looked up the stairwell, lit only by emergency lights. The remaining two vampires, both soldiers before their transformations, moved past him, their eyes infinitely better in the near-dark than his. They slipped by in what Etienne had to assume was silence up the twilit stairs a level before one of them made some sort of hand signal Etienne did not recognize. His mouth tightened with irritation. Those signals hadn't made any sense during the war, either, when Arthur and his fellow soldiers had used them. He'd simply mimicked their movements.

Scoithín hooked his thumb into his sword belt and looked up the stairs at the two vampires. Etienne was unable to make out his expression through the champion's heavy helm, but his dark eyes glittered through the eye slits. "What in Dagda's name are they doing?" he asked with bullet-deafened volume.

Etienne winced. It was loud even to his deafened ears. Idiot Unseelie.

The vampires and therian with their highly sensitive hearing flinched and looked up the stairs, guns drawn.

But there was nothing there.

Sighs of relief went all around, and Etienne scowled up at the Unseelie champion. "Perhaps next time you should think before bellowing like a cow in heat."

Scoithín narrowed his eyes at Etienne. "You are beneath me, half-breed." And with that he began to climb.

Lana made a face at the champion's back. "Pleasant, isn't he?" she said to Etienne in soft English. She was difficult to understand with his returning hearing.

Etienne wanted to forcibly bounce a bullet off the back of Scoithín's helm, but it would be a waste of good ammunition. "A joy."

As they climbed the stairs he ejected the empty magazine from his Glock and pulled a fresh one from his jacket pocket, sliding it home, grateful to Erik for providing replacements. He had loaded the six-shooter Agmundr with six of its remaining seven companion bullets, each a small, lethal work of dwarven art and magic designed to bring death to the sidhe.

Seven remaining, representing four dead sidhe lords and one bullet lost under... ignominious circumstances.

Just then sound erupted into the stairwell from two floors up and through the ringing in his ears Etienne heard raised voices. He kicked open the closest door and pushed the therian nearest him through it, funneling their team out of the stairwell.

They found themselves in a huge, open space, broken up only by low, fabric-covered walls forming endless squares. It reminded Etienne of some sort of simple labyrinth. Across the space from them a red sign glowed in the darkness: Exit. There was another stairwell. Etienne jerked his head that way and dropped low, using the fabric walls for what little cover they offered. The team followed suit, following the faerie knight along the narrow path toward the other stairs.

The door behind them opened and Etienne looked back to see more human guards pouring out into the fabric labyrinth. A hue and cry went up and bullets chased them across the space, Etienne cursing vehemently. They could not risk returning fire without giving up their position.

The squawk of shoulder speaker mics announced the return of Etienne's hearing as well as another group of guards bursting through the stairwell door on the other side of the office space. They were being boxed in! Now they had no other choice than to shoot their way out of a crossfire with minimal cover. Etienne crouched low and turned to his own shoulder mic. "Etienne here. Erik, can you hear me?"

"Loud and clear. What's your situation?"

"We're pinned down on the fourteenth floor. Could use a little assistance if you can spare it."

"I'll send someone right away. Hold on."

Etienne blew out a breath. Hold on. Assuming the lobby was still clear, and there really was no assuming that given the guards on this floor, it could take another team maybe fifteen minutes to cross the battlefield, and another five to get up the stairs. Twenty minutes, if all went smoothly.

It was a fucking eternity.

Etienne checked the slide on his Glock and nodded to his team.

Someone screamed.

Etienne whipped his head around. It hadn't been one of his people, but rather a human guard. What the fuck…?

"Summer's Get!" The voices were thick with mucus and gave Etienne a terrible urge to clear his throat. "My dread lord, Midir, desires your presence."

Fuck. Etienne raised his head to look. He couldn't not.

Tall enough to brush the ceiling with its head—the humanoid one—a nuckalevee advanced toward them. An unholy, skinless nightmare of horse and rider fused together at the rider's naked, legless hips, the veins across its crimson, glistening shoulders were open to view and pulsing with effort. Exposed muscles flexed and contracted over white bone and tendon and each skeletal, eyeless face spoke in unison. Drying seaweed and slime dropped from its haunches to leave a trail behind it. What the hell was it doing here? Waiting to be turned loose in the Pacific?

The human guards were scrambling away from the Unseelie horror and converging on their position. Scoithín drew his sword.

Etienne laid a hand on the champion's wrist and earned a dirty look for his trouble. "Wait. We can always shoot them in a minute."

"I'd rather kill them now, half-breed."

Etienne watched the humans approach. "I'm in charge here, by your king's command, Unseelie. I'm responsible for your, and everyone else's, life. My charge is to get you to Midir, so you can skewer him… and keep you alive until then. I say stand down."

Scoithín frowned but lowered the tip of his blade.

Etienne figured it was as good as he was going to get and did not argue the details. The other three Unseelie would follow their champion's lead and that was what mattered.

The first of the human guards came close, gun drawn but pointed at the nuckalevee. He took in their team, the three therian in fur form, the two remaining vampires, and the Unseelie in their matte-black armor, his eyes showing white around the edges. "What the hell is that thing?"

Etienne took a calculated risk and put his gun up. "Your boss has interesting pets. That's one of them. It's a nuckalevee."

"A nut-what?" The human looked from the approaching fae with horror and confusion back to Etienne. "What are you doing here?"

Etienne's mouth pulled into a reckless grin. "We're here to kill that thing, and then your boss. And then save the city. Maybe the world."

"Save the city? From… from things like that?"

"That's it exactly."

The human nodded, perhaps a little too fast, but he nodded all the same. "All right, then. I'm Chuck—"

"Summer's Get!"

Chuck crouched low at the nuckalevee's bellow, as did his fellow guards. "Who's that supposed to be?"

Etienne reached for his sword hilt. "That would be me." Much as he hated that name, he hated 'Queen's Son' more. If Midir wanted to needle him he'd have to get to know him better. He put one hand on the fabric wall and prepared to leap over.

"How can we help?"

Etienne looked over his shoulder. "Shoot it, not us. Don't die."

Chuck smiled for the first time. "Deal."

Etienne's grin widened. "Then let's kill a monster." With that he leapt over the low wall, drawing his sword as he cleared the partition, flickers of movement on either side telling him that his team was moving with him.

The nuckalevee was ready for them. The rider snapped a webbed hand out and a wickedly barbed trident appeared in its grip, the spreading tendons of its double skeletal grin drawing Etienne and his companions up short. This was no average nuckalevee. "You will come with me now, Summer's Get," it said in its strange double voice.

Etienne narrowed his eyes. "Not a chance." He drew the new handgun that Jessie had acquired, this potion-shooting paintball thing, and pointed it at the Unseelie monstrosity. Time to—

The stairwell door opened and this time a handful of fae soldiers came spilling out. "Scoithín, keep that thing busy! Stay out of my line of fire! Watch that trident!" Etienne shouted orders to his team, pointed the paintball gun, and fired at the oncoming fae. A small surprise of bright blue exploded across the point man's breastplate and with a billow of smoke he was gone. Etienne grinned and shot down the others, watching the clear tube on top of the gun empty until he had only a few potion balls left. That was fine. He just needed one to send the nuckalevee back to whatever hole in Faerie it had crawled out of.

Scoithín was toe-to-hoof with the creature, dodging the horse head's vicious, pointed teeth, his longsword locked with the trident. The nuckalevee landed a bite on the champion's arm, denting his heavy armor before he was able to wrest himself free.

A dagger in each hand, Lana vaulted over the back of one of the wolves as he bit at the thing's legs. She landed on the horse's neck, sinking blades deep into flesh. The nuckalevee screamed with both voices and grabbed Lana by her hair, throwing her hard into the cubes.

The nuckalevee reared up and kicked Scoithín back.

Etienne brought the paintball gun up, aiming for the bulk of the creature's body. It didn't have to be a killing shot, just a sure one. He pulled the trigger.

Click.

What the fuck? Etienne frowned and had just enough time to notice the slight offset of the gas canister before the nuckalevee's hoof dealt him a glancing blow to the hand, crushing the barrel and numbing Etienne's arm. He dashed backwards, cradling his useless limb.

Lana came crawling out from the cubes, looking a bit worse for wear but carrying some sort of small cylinder. She came to a crouch and then darted between snapping wolves, slashing blades, and flashing hooves, only stopping when she was directly beneath the belly of the beast. Between her teeth she held a lighter. What was she going to do with—?

Lana leaned back on her knees, flicked the lighter, held up the cylinder, and engulfed the drying, skinless nuckalevee in flames.

It shrieked and shrieked and tried to get away, but the rest of the team held it in reach, its flesh crisping and curling away, until it was clawing at itself to escape the pain of its charring bones. Scoithín hacked at the burning body with his longsword, until the trident lay on the carpet beside its twitching arm, and first the rider and then the horse were deprived of their heads.

Silence descended on the fabric labyrinth, broken only by the dull popping of flames.

Chuck appeared with another canister, this one red, and used it to spit white foam all over the nuckalevee's remains. The security guard shrugged when he realized everyone was looking at him. "No reason to burn down the building with us inside, right?"

Lana smiled at him, looking pleased for some reason.

And then fae soldiers came pouring through the stairwell doors.

Perfect.

Etienne drew his gun and began firing.

CHAPTER THIRTY

Cian overheard Etienne on Erik's shoulder speaker mic and his heart tried to leap from his chest. He needed to help! But how? He rounded on the Vampire King. "Send me to Etienne with that team."

Erik's eyes never left the battlefield. "Boy, even if I were to risk getting shot by that crazy ass faerie knight for sending you in, I can't get a team through, yet."

"But you just said—"

"I know what I said, and I have all intentions of sending a team up the instant I'm able. But our forces are barely holding on to what ground we currently have. The only way I can get a team in that tower is if we punch a fresh hole through their lines and that's going to take time and energy."

"Isn't that the entire reason we're here? To push through their lines and take the rift?"

"No, we're here to distract. Without Midir, that army will fall apart." Erik sighed. "Etienne's pinned down. I'm not going to tell him no. Nothing kills like hopelessness. If he can hold out for a little while I can get people up to him… it'll just take longer than I'd like."

That sounded insane, but Cian could not think of a counter argument besides the single frantic thought scrambling through his mind: Etienne needed him!

He turned back to the battlefield, the soft grass ground down into blood and mud, a wall of struggling bodies between him and the sleek, black tower. Movement caught his frantic attention and he saw Corinne, the Lion

Queen, pacing in sleek-furred half-form among the wounded, guarding her healers, the lions' Doc included, with her fierce amber-eyed gaze on the battle. If her Santiago was pinned down in there, would she stay put?

Cian didn't think so.

Brian's voice carried from Erik's speaker mic to Cian's sensitive ears. "We're nearly through the utility door. According to the planning commission, we're about to break into the subbasement."

"Great. Keep us informed and Godspeed."

Cian felt some of the knot in his chest loosen. Winter's team was still okay. Now all he had to do was—

Brilliant light pierced the night, brighter than any dawn, and knights in glittering golden armor poured forth riding gleaming white horses. They crashed fresh against the tiring tide of Midir's forces and pushed them back, greeted by cheers from Ceallach's Darkling Throng.

Cian cheered with them, one eye still on the black tower. Anluan had finally come.

He watched as his uncle arrived, meeting up with the Unseelie king, his golden armor glowing softly in the darkness. Erik moved to join them. Anluan's helmed head turned and briefly took in Cian standing there, and then motioned for a small coterie of knights in his retinue to move forward. The Shining King spoke in low tones to one of the knights and then they bowed and broke away as a unit to approach Cian. They dismounted and bowed as one. "Our liege entrusts you to our care," said the tallest of them. "How may we serve you, my Prince?"

Cian froze... and then glanced at Erik, who was deep in conversation with the two faerie kings. "You're here to protect me? I need inside the tower." He turned and ran for one of the new breaks, hoping... praying... not particularly caring that the knights were behind him. He needed to get to Etienne and this was his only chance.

The tall knight caught up with him, looking pained. "My Prince, this was not our King's intent."

Cian moved faster. "That break there, and then through those broken doors."

The knight cursed softly and drew his weapon. "As you wish, my lord."

Cian heard another knight mutter, "Well, we're not going to be bored," just as they broke through the small gap, weapons striking at them from both sides—and then they were through and crossing the threshold of the tower. He looked up. The fourteenth floor. Etienne just needed to hold on, just for a few more minutes.

Just hold on.

Where the fuck was Erik's backup?

Etienne crouched by the bathroom door listening hard for the final attack on their position. The nuckalevee's dying screams had brought a torrent of Midir's forces down on their heads and the fighting had been brutal, leaving what was left of their team wounded, exhausted, caked in blood, and pinned down in a bathroom mere yards from the nuckalevee's remains and the stairwell door.

"I don't want to die here." Rocio, their last vampire, coughed blood. He'd bled out so badly he no longer had control of his fangs and his deep brown eyes were glazed with shock and pain.

Lana finished a neat line of stitching, closing the last of the wounds that had laid his belly open. "You won't die here. You're going to die over there, in the stairwell, fighting for honor and glory."

"And saving the world." Chuck held the blood-soaked remains of Lana's sleeve to his face, trying to staunch the flow from the ruin of his right eye. "Can't forget saving the world."

Etienne gave him a small smile. "Hell yeah, we're saving the world." Just as soon as Erik kept his promise.

Scoithín sat apart from the small group, cradling his longsword. Blood glittered against the matte-black of the Unseelie's armor and he glowered from beneath his heavy helm. On his back Keeper still rested, and Etienne knew the truth. Their only hope lay in delivering this champion to Midir's presence. Not with Erik. Erik was good and honorable, but the battle raged between them. The second team wasn't coming.

They were on their own.

Sounds carried from outside the bathroom and Etienne tensed. They were getting ready to attack. He met Lana's gaze and gave her a miniscule nod. It was time. They would fight for the stairwell. The stairwell gave them options that dying in the bathroom did not. "Scoithín, you take point. Chuck, I'm going to need you to help Rocio to the stairs. Lana and I will bring up the sides and cover the two of you."

Scoithín gave the human and the vampire a scathing look. "Leave them. They are of no further use to us."

"Not happening." Etienne's tone left no room for argument.

"I'm not carrying them."

The look Etienne turned on the champion was a thing of pure ice. "I didn't ask you to. Do your job. Take point. Use Keeper on Midir. That's all."

Scoithín stood to his full height, towering over Etienne in his crouch, his gauntleted hands trembling with rage around the hilt of his sword.

Etienne raised an auburn brow but did not rise. "Take it up with your king, champion."

Scoithín's jaw tightened, but he stepped back. "When this is over, you and I will have a reckoning."

"I daresay we will." Etienne rose, then, and straightened his jacket over Agmundr. Seven bullets, and one now had Scoithín's name written on it.

But for the moment they had other problems. Lana helped Rocio and Chuck lean on each other before checking her weapons one last time. Scoithín held his sword and stared at the door as if he could see through it. Etienne crouched low and opened it a crack...

Heading toward them was a blood-spattered company of golden knights in heavy armor, swords drawn and blooded, led by a tall knight in matte-black. This lot were new, and alone. No others remained on the floor.

He, Lana, and Scoithín against an entire coterie of sidhe knights... Etienne was hard pressed to see how they were going to get to the stairwell alive. Maybe they could sneak past through the fabric labyrinth?

One of the golden knights stopped to deliver a death blow to one of Midir's fae soldiers and Etienne's heart skipped. Were these Anluan's knights? If he was mistaken they were all dead.

The one in black turned and seemed to look right at Etienne and his heart skipped again, this time with fear... until the knight removed his helmet, revealing a tumble of loosely braided red-gold hair.

Cian.

Etienne surged through the bathroom door, relief and anger warring through his chest.

Cian looked about ready to cry as tension drained from his beautiful face. "Etienne!"

Etienne clasped his hand over the back of Cian's neck and hugged him as tightly as he could in armor, holding the boy close for several long moments, realizing that he had not known if he would ever see him again. He turned his head a little, their breath mingling for a moment... and then he took Cian by the shoulders and gave him a small shake. "What the hell are you doing here?"

Cian shivered under his hands, his cheeks flushed, but after a moment he found his voice. "Saving you?"

Etienne frowned and looked to the golden knights. "Get him out of here. Now!"

The tallest of the knights shook his head. "We don't work for you, Queen's Son."

Lana made an exasperated noise. "For fuck's sake, Etienne. We need them. We still have a job to do, dipshit."

One of the other knights looked amused. "Nice company you're keeping there, Summer's Get."

Lana put a hand on her hip. "Blow me, Goldenrod."

"Maybe later, Darkling."

She snorted. "In your dreams."

"The good ones, may—"

"*Seriously?*" Cian broke into their banter. "We have to find Senán and Midir. We don't have time to screw around."

Etienne crossed his arms. "You're not going any—"

"Stuff it. I am rescuing my friend, by myself if I have to." With that Cian stalked toward the stairwell.

Chuck grinned. "I like him."

Lana smirked. "So does Etienne. That's the problem."

"Less talking, more killing," Etienne snarled.

Lana laughed. "Who's a testy bastard?"

Etienne flipped her off and made to catch up with Cian and his knights.

CHAPTER THIRTY-ONE

Winter studied the wards on the door to the rift room, a small frown on her face. They were works of art, but looking closely, she could see that they had been cast in a hasty fashion. They adhered to the door, and only the door.

This she could handle.

She dug into her overstuffed bag and pulled out a squirt bottle with two chambers. "Everyone step back. This potion is highly corrosive." Brian, Jessie, and the two sidhe knights Ceallach had sent to accompany them, moved back down the curved hallway. Winter held up the bottle and paused before turning to the knights. "Gentlemen, would you please move back to the entrance? I don't want to risk this spray coming anywhere near those magical explosives."

The two knights gave her a small bow and moved as one around the curve of the wall and out of sight.

Winter cast a protective barrier in between herself and the door and felt Jessie do the same for herself and Brian behind her. She then poked a small hole and pushed the nozzle of the bottle through it and squeezed the handle. The two halves of the potion, inert in their separate chambers, combined in a fine, orange mist and coated the wards and the door beneath, dripping along the lines of the matrix like dew on a spider's web.

Dew that dissolved whatever it touched.

The wards softened and buckled, the potion negating the magic within the strands and melting them into nothing. A hole opened in the door itself, the potion eating through paint and steel, until at last the corrosive potion was exhausted and Winter could have slipped through the steaming hole that remained. Instead she turned the doorknob, confident now that there were no remaining wards.

On the other side, waiting in the rift-lit twilight, was the sidhe lord with the beautiful eyes, his sword drawn, his expression both puzzled and amused.

The color drained from her lips.

A smirk pulled at the corner of his mouth. "Lady Mulcahy, so nice of you to come to my lord's coronation."

Winter rallied. "I'm afraid you are mistaken. There will be no coronation today." She glanced at the rift, so close to exploding, and back to him. Nine glyphs in the seal... They had some time, yet, before midnight, before the rift blew, they had planned this insertion with time in mind, but still, it was possible he could hold them in a stalemate until it was too late. If he was down here alone to guard it, he must be either truly powerful or truly cunning. Either way, they had to get him out of the way. "I don't believe we were properly introduced."

"My apologies, my lady. I am Aodhán. Ah, nice to see you again, miss." His cornflower-blue eyes, so familiar, were looking past Winter to Jessie, now in the doorway. "That was a clever trick with the pot, before. You'll notice there are none down here."

Brian came to stand behind Winter and Jessie in the wide doorway, watching Aodhán carefully.

The sidhe lord returned his look with one of keen interest. "And who might you be, Hero?"

Brian settled his hand on Courage's hilt, more as a warning than as a gesture of aggression. "Just Brian MacDowell."

Those lovely eyes fell to the sword, gold flecks catching the light from their faerie lanterns. "Where did you get your friend, Brian MacDowell?"

"She was a gift from King Ceallach."

Aodhán arched one black eyebrow. "Really? What do you know of Ceallach?"

Jessie pushed herself a step into the room. "He's the guy who's gonna mess up your boss's big day."

Aodhán turned, looking in the direction of the battle, suddenly, subtly, rattled. "Ceallach is here?"

Jessie grinned. "Yep. Kicking invading army ass right now. I'm sure he'd love to meet you. We should totally introduce you." She leaned backwards and called down the hall. "Hey, Legolas, Thranduil, come meet the guy I was telling you about!"

Jessie had been calling the knights Tolkien names all night and Winter was grateful the two had been playing along. The one dubbed 'Legolas' arrived at the door first. "The sidhe lord?" He took a look at Aodhán and gasped before looking to his counterpart and dropping to one knee. "My Prince?"

Thranduil was on his knee a rabbit's heartbeat behind him. "Prince Aodhán. Son of Ceallach, Son of Deirdre."

Winter's heart leapt to her throat. Was this the Unseelie betrayal that Etienne had worried about? If this was indeed the dead prince, what did that mean for her, Jessie, and Brian? What did it mean for the entire city? Surely Ceallach could be convinced to change sides on the word of his missing son.

Brian stepped in front of Winter and Jessie and drew Courage. "Excuse me, guys, you're supposed to be guarding Winter *from* him, not handing her *to* him, remember?"

Thranduil looked briefly at Legolas and then turned to Aodhán. "My Prince, how did you come to be here? You have long been feared dead."

Aodhán's cornflower-blue eyes, now that Winter could see the connection—so like his mother's—flickered from side to side as he thought furiously. "And… I'd like to stay that way. For a bit longer."

Legolas looked scandalized. "But, my lord, your father…"

"Has mourned me for five hundred years. Another few won't lessen his grief. Besides, he seems to have his hands full tonight. I think I should leave him to his work and bid you all a good evening." He moved backwards toward the door on the other side of the room. "Lady Mulcahy, it has proved interesting to meet you. Miss, I'd concentrate your charges on the pillars along the railing. They're load bearing. Brian MacDowell, I will see you, and your new friend, another time." With that he pulled the door open and jumped through, slamming it shut behind him.

Legolas rushed to reopen the door, but by the time he opened it and looked up and down the curved hallway there was nothing to be seen.

Jessie looked from the door to Winter, shaking her head in confusion. "Okay. Didn't see that one coming."

Brian still stood with Courage bare in his hand, but she was pointed at the floor. "So, are we still good? Your king's instructions would override a prince's, right?"

Thranduil nodded, ignoring the bared blade. "Indeed. Let's get these explosives set."

Jessie giggled with destructive glee and helped him with his pack. "Let's do this thing!"

Winter watched the door Aodhán had disappeared through for a long moment, half expecting him to reappear, but when that did not happen she pulled out a large chunk of spell chalk and finally turned to the massive rift.

Nine glyphs in the seal.

CHAPTER THIRTY-TWO

They made it to the penthouse apartment with little resistance, Midir's remaining forces seemingly called to deal with the new threat Anluan's army presented. Cian had used some of his healing magic to make Rocio and Chuck more comfortable, but without Winter's expert guidance, a full repair would have to wait.

The large, open space was decorated in sleek black and metal, with racks of weapons lining the walls, all of it looking the worse for wear. The October wind whistled through multiple cracks in the windows. The floor was littered with weapons and broken housewares. Etienne briefly noted the empty brackets above the stark, black fireplace and knew that Midir was carrying Grief tonight.

A ball of wild magic hurtled toward them, forcing them all to dive out of the way. "Go away!" The voice was ragged and high-pitched, hanging by a fraying thread of madness.

Lana peered up from behind the couch, looking both exasperated and alarmed. "And that would be Senán."

Cian crouched beneath the table with two of the knights. "Midir did this to him," he said, defending his friend. "He's been throwing magic since I was here last."

Rocio had his arm wrapped around his waist. The dive to the floor had not done him any favors. "Shouldn't he be running out of juice, by now, then?"

Etienne shook his head, kneeling on the floor. "He's a sidhe prince and will someday be capable of creating an entire faerie realm from his will alone." As would Cian, Etienne believed, no matter how weak his father, Eoin, may have been thought. "He has a lot of 'juice.'"

"Get out!"

Cian crept out from under the table. "Senán! It's me, Cian!"

The voice developed a distinctive whine. "I don't know you!" A yellow sphere of magic shot through the wall and shattered the dish cabinet behind them.

Lana's jaw clenched, and Etienne heard her mutter, "God, I hate that sound." She stood up, checked her dagger sheaths, and stepped out from behind the couch. "I've got this shit." She walked toward the hallway. "Jeremy, babe? It's Lana. Can you hear me?"

"L... Lana?" The door at the end of the hall opened and what must have been Senán emerged, hunched over, the whites of his gray eyes showing. Etienne could not help but stare. They really did look alike, but for the differences of a thousand years and nearly a foot of height. They both favored their mother.

Lana held her arms out to Senán. "It's me, babe. I'm here to help you."

The boy's face crumpled, and he crept toward Lana like a frightened child. "I don't know what's happening to me. I think I'm going crazy."

Lana made soothing noises and coaxing gestures. "It'll be okay."

"How? I have all these memories, and they're filling up my head and swirling around... How will this be okay? Tell me how this will be okay." He folded himself around the much shorter Lana and pressed his head to her shoulder.

"Just trust me, babe. I'll take care of everything."

Senán stiffened. "Trust you..." He looked up, rage distorting his face, and gripped her by her arm.

"You're hurting me, Jeremy!"

"Trust you?! You said that before, and then you threw me into father and his flunky. You left me!" He shook her like a terrier. "This is your fault!"

Etienne lunged forward, the others a step behind him.

"Oh, fuck this!" Lana jerked one of her daggers free as her body was being whipped back and forth and hammered Senán in the temple with the pommel. The prince dropped like a stone, taking her to the floor with him.

Cian helped Etienne pry Senán's fingers off her swelling arm and then checked his friend. "His skull is cracked."

Lana snorted, sliding her dagger back into its sheath. "Hard as his head is, it won't do him any lasting harm."

Etienne glanced down at the boy... at his brother... and nodded. "He'll be fine, Cian. He's sidhe."

Lana put her hands on her hips. "So, who carries nutters here out?"

Etienne looked pointedly at Cian.

Cian was staring with worried compassion at Senán but scowled at Etienne as soon as he felt his gaze and turned to his coterie of knights. "Can two of you please escort Prince Senán, Rocio, and Chuck back to the healers?"

Etienne pointed at the apartment door. "You go with them."

Cian shook his head, stubborn and defiant. "I stay here. You're down a few people."

Etienne turned to the tall knight. "Take him with you."

The tall knight gestured for two of his number to pick up Senán and gave Etienne a level stare. "If I do I withdraw my coterie. Our job is to protect the young prince, not you and the Darkling half-breed."

Cian lifted his chin a little, his green eyes challenging even as they kept flickering toward his mad, injured friend. Senán. The entire reason they'd come here to begin with.

Etienne wanted to tie him up and toss his skinny little sidhe butt in the elevator, but he was out of choices. "Fine," he said, his voice on the edge of a growl. "You and your knights stay. You, take these three down. No need to get them killed."

Chuck looked disappointed. "I thought we were gonna save the world."

Etienne clasped the security guard's good shoulder. "You already did. You saved our lives. Now let us return the favor."

Chuck smiled at that and nodded. "Good luck up there. He's got a roof access through that door there. Only place left for him to go."

Scoithín sheathed his longsword, drew Keeper, and gave Etienne a grim nod. It was time.

Etienne waited until the elevator door closed on their wounded before turning to Cian. "Stay in the back. I don't want you hurt."

Cian nodded. "I don't want you hurt, either."

Etienne's expression softened, and he gave Cian a small smile. He was going to get hurt, there was no avoiding it. He was just a half-breed with a gun. But maybe having a coterie of sidhe knights and a champion would make a difference in the long run. He took Cian's shoulders. "For Winter."

Cian smiled. "For Winter."

CHAPTER THIRTY-THREE

Etienne was right behind Scoithín as they emerged onto the building's roof. Standing on the very edge of the knee-high overhang was a tall sidhe lord with short, ice-blond hair, bearing a large great axe and wearing a dark-gray suit. He did not look happy as he watched the battle play out below, his grip on the elaborately wrapped haft white-knuckled with stress.

Prince Midir and Grief.

Midir turned his head as their party slipped from the roof access doorway, immediately schooling his features to bland boredom... and then his ice-blue eyes lit with genuine pleasure to see Cian, arriving last. "Have you come to watch my triumph, sweet prince?" He stepped backwards away from the edge, dropping gracefully down to the graveled roof. "Come and watch with me."

Etienne looked down. "Not much to watch. Looks like you've already lost."

Midir tapped his leg with the side of the axe. "I don't lose." He held his hand out to Cian. "Come, boy."

The coterie of knights shifted positions, ranging out to give themselves room to fight. The tall one drew his sword, a signal for the others. "You cannot have him."

Midir's mouth twisted into a cruel grin. "I've already had him." Grief gleamed in Midir's hand and then the ancient prince was moving in a lethal dance too fast for Etienne's half-mortal eyes to see, too fast for him to lean into the gun rig's magic. Metal screamed with men as they were carved open, heavy sidhe steel no match for Grief. A weight knocked into his side, driving him down to the rough gravel of the roof and he smelled Lana's shampoo in his face. Was she okay?

From his back, Etienne watched Scoithín leap over him, Keeper in hand, and lunge at Midir as the great prince hacked at one of the knights. As blade parted suit fabric, Midir spun, parrying the champion's strike. On the backswing he severed Scoithín's head and kicked the body from the roof, leaving Keeper where the faerie champion had dropped it. He stomped the head, crushing the skull, and then strode forward and grabbed Cian, pulling the boy by his arm to his side. "I told you to come here."

The tall knight found his feet again, blood pouring in a torrent from his many wounds, and held his sword in his shaking hand. "And I said you cannot have him."

Cian's eyes widened.

Midir sneered at Cian. "You do pick rather pathetic guardians, boy." He spun Grief once.

The tall knight nodded and flickered his eyes within his helm toward Keeper once, then saluted with his sword.

Midir moved in a blur of motion.

Lana was off Etienne in an instant, Keeper in hand.

Metal screamed as the knight was dismembered.

So did Cian. "*Anraí!*" Etienne realized it was the knight's name. He hadn't bothered to learn it.

Lana moved to spear Midir, but he was already in motion, dancing past her thrust and snatching Cian back into his arms with a grin. "Well, well, we do seem to be at an impasse, here."

Etienne rocked to his feet, Agmundr in hand. He hated witty banter, so he remained silent, looking for the opportunity to shoot. Ceallach wanted the great prince alive. Etienne wanted Cian safe. He would do anything to make that happen, including angering the Unseelie king.

Midir pulled Cian closer and brushed his thumb along the boy's armored arm. "You want me dead. I want the same of you. None of us really have an interest in killing the child. I don't suppose I could tempt you both. I'm sure my new kingdom would have room for a couple of junkyard dogs. What do you think, boy? Shall we keep them as pets?"

Cian stilled. "The problem with junkyard dogs is they bite." He lashed out with his teeth, biting through the suit jacket sleeve and into the meat of Midir's arm, savagely biting down with all his considerable strength until fabric and flesh ripped free.

Midir roared with pain and rage and flung Cian away with enough force to fold the corner of one of the great metal structures on the roof around his slender body, knocking the boy senseless. Midir dove after him with Grief, but Lana parried the swing with Keeper, the sound of impact ringing like an angelic chime. Lana cried out and Etienne watched Keeper's blade drop as her arms went numb from the force of Grief's blow. Midir caught Keeper with the hook of the right axe blade and neatly disarmed her, flipping the great blade off the roof. Grief rose again. Etienne raised Agmundr and fired.

Midir jerked backwards, a crimson wound blossoming above his collarbone. Damn. He would heal like a human, but that was not a lethal blow, and now he had the prince's full attention. He aimed again, determined... and barely heard Lana's cry of warning before Grief came whipping around, Midir again moving too fast to be seen. He jerked back, the rig giving him speed, and watched as if through thick water as the axe cut through where his hand had been.

Right through Agmundr.

Etienne's chest clenched. Bullets and powder rained to the gravel. Keeper was gone. Scoithín had fallen. Agmundr was destroyed. All they had left were two half-breeds and an unconscious prince.

They were going to die up here.

Midir stabbed at Etienne with the wicked, tear-shaped pommel and he jumped back and away. He might die, but he wasn't going to make it easy. The longer he stayed alive, the more chances Cian had to get away. To get back to Winter.

Lana rushed Midir and leapt high, wrapping her legs around his neck and knocking him off balance. The great prince staggered and pulled her off, holding her out at arm's length and squeezing until her face turned purple. "I'll teach you to jump on people, you rabid little weasel."

Etienne drew his Glock from the back of his pants and fired.

Midir's head jerked back.

Etienne rolled his eyes. Of course, *now* he scored a head shot.

Midir threw Lana across the roof to come to a skidding halt next to a groggy Cian and turned on Etienne, his forehead bleeding but the bullet already sliding out as the wound closed. "It is about time you learned the difference between a Son of Dagda and a minstrel's bastard." He spun Grief.

Etienne backed away and emptied the rest of his magazine into the approaching prince, to no effect.

Midir swung Grief back and brought it down to take Etienne's head... just as Lana barreled into the ancient prince again, daggers out, and hit him with her full weight. The blow went wide, missing his neck and sparing his head but punching through armor and flesh and chewing through collarbone, ribs, and lung until Grief's entire head was buried in his chest. It was strangely painless.

Etienne watched them stagger backwards over the edge, his and Lana's combined weight tearing Grief from the great prince's hand, Midir's leg catching on the low ledge as Lana stabbed him over and over. He wanted to grab her, to snatch her out of the air, but all he could do was grip the hilt as the weight of Grief dragged him to his suddenly weak knees on the rooftop. And then they were gone.

CHAPTER THIRTY-FOUR

Just as they emerged from the utility tunnel Brian saw the black-armored body fall, impacting with the thick mud with a dull splat. His legs carried him forward past Legolas and Thranduil before they could call him back, before thought could fully engage. He rushed to the knight's side, only to find the body flailing about without a head.

Where was their head?

The two Unseelie knights joined him. "Scoithín," Legolas murmured. He looked around. "We have to find his head. He may yet survive."

Brian searched as well, the ground slick and littered with debris and discarded bodies. The battle had been here and gone and all that seemed left of it were black and golden knights mopping up pockets of resistance. "I didn't see it fall with him."

After several minutes of frantic searching they all three looked up. "It's still on the roof," Thranduil said, sounding lost.

Scoithín's body kicked once more and lay still.

As they watched, another object flew from the rooftop and plummeted toward them. Brian's eyes widened, and he pushed Legolas out of the way just as a sword drove itself into the mud at their feet. It was long, straight, and had a curious, reverse curve to the blade. He reached out and pulled it from the thick, black goop and a shiver ran up his arm.

It was another named weapon.

"It is Keeper, Hero."

Brian's mind turned to Courage, riding his hip. Keeper. This was the blade Scoithín had been tasked with carrying. "Is it okay that I'm holding it?" They must have been fighting Midir up on the roof and were losing.

"*Yes. It has chosen you for a reason, my Hero.*"

Brian's blood ran cold. Was this his Destiny, then? He was only eighteen and had been a Hero for a single day. He blew out a breath. If it was, he would face it.

"*Fear not, Hero.*" Courage sounded somewhat amused. "*I did not choose you for such a short journey. Heroes are capable of many acts before their ultimate Destinies.*"

He looked at the sword. Then what did he need to do? He looked up. Get this back up to the roof where it could be put to use? Yes, that must be it. He looked for the building entrance…

"Look out!" Jessie cried.

Bodies pitched over the roof edge and plummeted down, forcing Brian and the knights to dive out of the way. It was Lana and a strange man, landing in a tangle of limbs, daggers, and blood.

Lana lay limp, but the man seemed barely phased. He rolled to his knees with a roar of rage and wrapped both hands around Lana's throat, squeezing down with all his strength. "I'll rip your head off, half-breed!"

"*Now!*"

Brian rushed forward and drove Keeper through the man's back, jerking to a stop before he pierced Lana. The man cried out in pain, blood spraying Lana's unconscious face, and without warning the blade sprouted chains that latched onto the man's wrists and ankles and pulled up short, prying his hands from Lana and binding him painfully to the blade.

Brian blinked. That was different. He moved around the coughing man and knelt beside Lana, her throat swelling and purpling with bruises. "Winter! We need you."

Winter rushed forward, stepping carefully around the bound man, and knelt in the mud beside Lana. "She's not breathing," she muttered and palpated Lana's throat. "Her hyoid is broken, and her trachea feels crushed. She's suffocating." Winter dug in her bag, pulling out a bottle of rubbing alcohol, a scalpel, and a pen.

Jessie's eyebrows rose, and she moved to hold the bag open for her mistress.

Brian looked from wizard to wizard. "What are you doing?"

Midir scowled, blood trickling from his lips. "Ruining a perfectly good murder."

Winter gave him an unfriendly look and doused the scalpel with the rubbing alcohol, handing the bottle to Jessie, who doused Lana's neck from chin to chest. "She needs to be intubated. She needs help to breathe until her body can heal the damage he caused. So, I'm making an alternate access point for the air. Jessie, fish out the water bottle and get me a dose of the painkiller, please."

"With... a pen?"

Winter took the pen apart and threw the innards into the purse, creating a tube. She cleaned out the inside with the alcohol and nodded. "Yes." She then took up the scalpel and made a precise cut just above the meeting of Lana's clavicles, just below the swelling, blood welling up around her fingers, and neatly popped the pen casing into place. Immediately air whistled through the tube and Lana's chest rose, greedy for oxygen. Winter began taping it in place.

Brian breathed a sigh of relief. "Okay, that was one of the cooler—"

Lana's eyes snapped open and she came up swinging.

Brian caught her hands before she could batter Winter, and Lana began coughing while Winter held her tube in place.

Winter stroked Lana's dark hair and murmured soothing things while Lana coughed and shook. After a moment the succubus tried to say something around the swelling, but nothing came. She then looked up at the roof, and then back at Winter and pointed, lips parted with wonder.

It looked as if the sun was rising up there.

Etienne did not feel the gravel dig into his knees. All he could feel was a warm, numb sensation. He knew somewhere that he could not breathe. That blood flowed hot from his mouth and tickled his neck, his chest.

He knew he was dying.

But before his eyes was his mother's glittering court. His father Chretien, alive once more, playing at her feet. He saw himself in great regard, the favored son... and then he saw himself suddenly cast out of the light to be anyone's meat. His mind turned to the dwarves, to the years of sweat and pain that he had traded for Agmundr, for peace of mind.

Agmundr was gone.

He saw the years he had wandered alone and lonely along the borderlands, a hunted thing. Hungry. Outcast. Exiled.

But there was one shining light in all that time, and he felt her draw near.

Bess.

She shone through the light that surrounded him, and finally—*finally*—he could see her beautiful face. Her round cheeks and her full lips. Her bright eyes, so full of love. She smiled at him and held out her hands.

He did not feel the roof smack him in the back, knocking Grief loose from his chest. Instead he smiled as warm hands touched his chest and through the brightening light he could hear a voice... but it was not the one he expected. Instead of Bess's deep, earthy voice welcoming him home, the voice he heard was light, anguished, and begging him to stay.

Etienne blinked hard, past the light and the blood loss, and saw Cian kneeling beside him, incandescent with the power that he was pouring into Etienne's body. Etienne opened his mouth to tell him to stop, that he was too hurt, that Bess was here to take him home, but his mouth was full of blood and his lungs would not work. The power only grew, filling Etienne's body with growing agony and ecstasy, until his spine bowed with it, digging his heels and head into the gravel. Etienne saw a twin glow and raised his hand, his own flesh radiant with magic. A shuddering breath filled his lungs and he coughed a spray of blood.

The power grew until it drew an undulating scream from Etienne, his heels beating against the rooftop... and then it stopped as if someone had blown out the candle. Etienne collapsed, weak and sweating, just as Cian fell sideways, limp.

Cian! Etienne rolled up on his armored elbow, bracing for pain even as he tried to get to Cian… but it did not come. He looked down to see his jacket and shirt tattered, Agmundr's rig split in two, but beneath the blood and torn fabric he was smooth and whole. Unblemished. His brows knit. Unblemished? He flipped the fabric back to reveal unscarred skin. No burns, no glyphs, no old injuries. His heart clenched. How much had Cian given for this?

Etienne sat up and rolled Cian onto his back, terrified of the answer. Cian was new to his abilities and Winter was still training him. But the boy took a deep breath and Etienne's eyes teared with relief. One hand found red-gold hair and stroked it back from his face with tender fingers. Dear boy.

Then he went up on his knees and picked Cian up in his arms. They still had business to attend to. Midir needed to be dealt with, and the rift needed to be closed. He carried Cian down from the roof.

Etienne came out carrying Cian just as Winter was trying to talk her way onto the team headed back into the building. He looked up and gave Winter a weary smile and her heart squeezed with happiness even as her eyes took in his blood-covered clothes and Cian's unconscious form. What had happened up there?

Etienne brought Cian to her where she stood with Erik, Brian, Jessie, Lana, and Ceallach's knights. "Winter, he's breathing but not moving."

Lana looked astonished and mouthed, "How?"

Etienne's expression as he looked down at Cian mingled pride, love, and loss. "He's a grandson of Dagda."

Ceallach arrived without fanfare and walked right up to Midir, kicking the bound prince in the face. "Hello, brother. I have some games for us to play together." He gestured to his guards. "Take him."

"Wait." Midir's voice was choked with blood. "Wizard."

Winter turned toward the rasping voice. Midir the Proud was on his knees between two of Ceallach's sidhe, Keeper still binding him. She pulled her eyes from the grisly sight of the blade erupting from his shuddering chest, wrists bound at its tip, and looked instead at the blood running freely from one corner of his mouth, at his pain glazed eyes. She looked inside herself for pity and found none. "My lord?" she questioned, her voice cold.

"I told you that opposing me would be a mistake."

She looked to where Etienne was standing strong, holding Cian. "Etienne is going to live." She looked back, meeting those ice-blue eyes, arrogant even in the face of defeat. "Senán has been returned to his parents' care. And you are going to enjoy your brother's hospitality. Your plan has failed. I fail to see my mistake."

Midir opened his mouth to speak and choked on his blood. Agony tore across his elegant face as the coughing took him, leaving him gasping for air.

Winter waited while he struggled, then lost patience. She wanted to see the sealed rift buried and was in no mood to indulge her fallen enemy. She looked at Ceallach's soldiers and motioned for them to take him.

"Wait," he croaked. The knights hesitated at the word of such a mighty prince, even with their king present, and he again met Winter's eyes. "Your world is doomed. I was the only hope you had of salvation, and you squandered it." Anger flared in his eyes. "Enjoy your precious realm, for however long you have it."

The memory of her father's body falling boneless to the ground flashed through her mind, her guilt at leaving him like she had, and she met Midir's anger with her cold rage. She was exhausted and in no mood to believe the lies of her father's murderer, so she bent closer to his face. "And you... you enjoy the full depth of your failure. Your years of preparation, of building, of slaughtering my family to clear the way for your conquest of my city... it was all for *nothing*."

Confusion flashed through Midir's eyes. "What are you talking about?"

His response stoked the icy fire of her rage, and she shook with the force of it. She spoke through clenched teeth. "You murdered my father."

He frowned… and then his eyes widened. A grin spread across his face. He barked a laugh that turned into a spasm of choked coughing.

"What? What are you laughing at?" Winter stepped back as droplets of blood speckled her face.

The great prince got his breathing back under control, blood running down his chin, cruel mirth filling his eyes. "You, wizard child." He turned to the knights. "Now, you may take me away." He gave her a courtly, mocking nod as Ceallach's sidhe hauled him away.

Winter stood there, wide-eyed, her heart pounding, her whole body shaking, and watched them. The rain began to fall again, cold on her flushed cheeks. She didn't understand. What did that mean?

Erik found her standing there and wrapped his bandaged and bloody arms around her. "I've got you, little girl. I've got you."

She pressed her face against his shirt and let her tears join the raindrops.

Ceallach watched for several long moments, ignoring the rain, and then cleared his throat as Anluan approached. "I am sorry to break into your mourning, but we still have business to attend."

Winter nodded and stepped away from Erik, letting him brush the tears from her face. "I understand. I'm sorry."

Ceallach reached out and laid a gentle hand on her shoulder. "Don't be. You have much to mourn. And the time for it is fast approaching."

Winter nodded again and turned to where Etienne waited patiently with Cian.

"Can you rouse him?"

Winter laid her hand on Cian's forehead. "He's exhausted his energy. Honestly, he's not in real danger." Thank goodness. He really could have hurt himself, but she could feel no magical injuries. "He may sleep for a few days, but what he needs is magic."

Ceallach stepped forward. "Perhaps I can help."

Anluan frowned. "Don't touch my nephew, Darkling Brother."

Ceallach looked annoyed. "He's my nephew, too, and he needs my help."

Anluan gestured grandly. "I'm all the help he needs. Stand aside, Etienne."

Etienne's hold on Cian tightened. "That's never going to happen. Nice of you to finally show up, by the way."

Anluan drew his sword. "I was tired of you long ago, *Queen's Son.*"

Ceallach blocked Anluan's sword with his own. "Etienne Knight is under my protection, brother. You will not have him or the boy." He reached back with his free hand and let power flow into Cian.

Cian took on a soft glow for a moment and his eyes opened. He glanced at Ceallach and Anluan, but a radiant smile spread across his face as his gaze fell on Etienne. "You're alive!"

Etienne set Cian on his feet but kept his hands on his shoulders. "Thanks to you."

Anluan made a rude noise, and Winter had to fight the urge to hit him with her bag. "This is all very touching, but dawn is coming and we all need to be gone before it does, the better to avoid human eyes. Cian, you are coming home."

Cian backed away slightly behind Etienne. "No, I'm not."

"You are of my house and you will obey."

Ceallach smirked. "I'm not sure you have the right to command a faerie king, brother."

"He's not a king."

"He is, just a young one. Do you want to go home with your uncle, Cian?"

Cian looked from Etienne to Winter, and her heart soared. "That's not my home. This is."

Ceallach made a mocking version of Anluan's grand gesture. "Sorry, Anluan. Looks like you'll need a new ornament."

The golden king snarled and stalked off.

Ceallach watched him go, pleasure plain on his face, and then he turned to Lana. "You betrayed my wife's trust and stole my sword. I'm not sure Deirdre will have you back."

Lana, still voiceless, bowed low.

He smiled. "But I will. Come along, Lana. Let's discuss you and my guard. I could use a rebel with more courage than brains."

Lana rose from her bow, beaming, and followed her lord.

Jessie watched them go, a bit wistful. "I'm glad you're staying and all. You *are* staying, right? But can we *please* blow up this building and go home?"

Cian looked from Winter to Etienne again. "*Are* we staying?"

Winter could not help the bright smile that took over her face. "Yes. Please."

Etienne brushed his hand over Winter's and gave Cian a one-armed hug. "Yes, we're staying."

Jessie whooped, hugging Brian. "Awesome! Boom now?"

They got out of range and Winter triggered the magical explosives in the basement, the building coming down in an impressive display of magic and pyrotechnics. Winter watched with a certain degree of pleasure that was a balm to even her exhausted body. She smiled at Etienne and Cian as the last of the dust settled. "Let's go home."

Jessie grinned at the three of them. "I'll drive." She looked toward the remains of the building where she had left her car in the circle drive. It was empty. She blinked. She knew exactly where she left it. "Um… guys… where's my car?"

EPILOGUES

"Midir lost his bid for power." Aodhán stepped through the bedroom doorway in socked feet, loosening his collar. A thin wail rose from the nursery, rising and falling in a weak rhythm. He started moving that way.

"I do not smell the blood of your enemies."

He turned to face the bed. Perched atop and swathed in a luxurious red kimono sat a dainty, sweet-faced girl. Her legs peeked out, flashing tiny bare feet and calves, and hair like a black, silken river flowed thick to pool at last on the bamboo floor beside the tall bed. One side of the kimono was open to breastfeed the robust baby boy who clutched at her with a little fist. She smiled down at him indulgently, her delicate hand brushing over his thick mop of black curls. A perfect vision of a Japanese Madonna and Child. Then, Himiko raised her dark, phoenix eyes to Aodhán, and arched one raven brow. He felt the weight of millennia in her gaze, but after five centuries he was used to it. "No, you don't." He shrugged out of his shirt and continued toward the crying in the nursery.

"Since when does Aodhán of Unseelie flee the field of battle?" she asked, her tone mocking. The large gray wolf curled up at the foot of the bed woke at her taunt and turned curious blue eyes toward Aodhán.

Aodhán sighed. Why did she have to make everything a pissing contest? But, he knew the answer to that. It was just part of her charm. "When his father suddenly takes the field." He turned to face her again. "I'm not ready to reveal myself, yet."

She rolled her eyes and tucked her finger into the baby's mouth to try to get him to detach. "And what of Carrick? What of your son's future kingdom?" The boy released, leaving four tiny holes around her dainty nipple which sealed up before she finished switching sides. "That was the plan. Help that megalomaniac, and then snatch his new kingdom out from under him."

"Plans change. You taught me that, my love."

She made a small, thoughtful noise.

He started moving again.

"So, then, with your brother dead, why won't you reveal yourself to your father?"

His eyes widened a bit in exasperation, but he was faced away from her. When he turned back, his expression was bland. "Midir complicated things for me. Had he succeeded in carving out his faerie realm here, I could have claimed to my father that I was taking vengeance for Ciarán's murder, in spite of Ciarán's role in my supposed demise."

She nodded. She had been the one to save his life, after all.

"However, with Midir defeated by other hands, I cannot afford to be associated with him. Though I was well within rights to exact vengeance on my brother for my attempted murder, Midir's cruelty to my mother is unforgivable. I have to distance myself from him and bide my time, now." He kept moving, the crying pulling him forward.

The nursery was entirely blue and green. A boy's place. Rich wooden furniture was crowded with stuffed animals and small toy weapons that Carrick was still too little to play with. Soon, though. He was a big boy and growing fast. Two cribs sat in the room—one in the center of the room, the place with the best flow of energy, and one shoved off to the side and out of the way. Aodhán gritted his teeth and made his way over to the second crib, the source of the pitiful cries. No matter how many times he rearranged the nursery, she just put it back like this while he was gone. In the crib lay a much smaller baby, arms and legs thin and frail, black hair wispy, eyes swollen red from crying and huge in her thin face. While Carrick would have been standing in his wobbly fashion, clinging to the side of his crib to demand his infant due, Keiko lacked the strength to sit up. Aodhán reached down and picked up the delicate baby, Carrick's twin, and cradled her close to the bare skin of his chest. He rocked her and gently stroked her back, but her distress would not be soothed.

She was starving.

He emerged from the nursery with Keiko tucked tight against him. "Himiko, how long has she been crying?" he asked, keeping his voice as neutral as possible.

Himiko looked up in irritation at the increased noise level and waved a negligent hand. "It woke poor Carrick up. He was very distressed." She cast an annoyed look at the frail girl and returned to stroking her son's back as he fed.

Aodhán hesitated, but Keiko's cries and failure to thrive pushed him yet again to desperation. "Himiko... my love... please, just this once..."

Himiko looked at him quizzically and then her eyes widened slightly as she understood his meaning. Her face hardened, her dark eyes turned to ice. "You wanted her. You feed her," she said, her voice deepening with cold warning.

Aodhán stepped back and bowed slightly, his starving daughter wailing in his arms. In her mortal life, Himiko had prided herself on only bearing boys. When she had realized last year that she was carrying twins, she had told everyone who would listen she was bearing twin princes. After all, vampire queens only bore princes. Carrick had been born first and she had exalted. And then the midwife had presented her with Keiko. Himiko had taken the newborn and thrown her across the room in disgust. Only Aodhán's sidhe reflexes had saved her. Then Himiko had refused to feed her.

He left the bedroom he shared with Himiko, carrying his tiny daughter, frustration and fear grinding away at him. A vampire child needed the milk and blood of his... or her... mother for the first few years to survive. Himiko refused to touch the child, had barely named her. Keiko basically meant 'girl child.' He had chosen the kanji to mean 'blessing,' but she would not know that for many years to come—if she survived to learn to write her own name.

Feeding her was one of the few things they came close to fighting about—close, because Aodhán feared Himiko taking her legendary temper out on the baby. Himiko could kill her in anger and then blame him for enflaming her. He had no doubt she would. Only love for him kept her from killing the girl in cold blood—Himiko in a rage was capable of anything. In cold blood, Himiko had already abandoned Keiko to an orphanage once. Fortunately, Aodhán found out and had been able to retrieve her.

He carried the wailing baby through the large, traditionally Japanese-style house, bouncing her slightly in a futile attempt at soothing her. Keiko cried most of the time she did not sleep, and Aodhán could not blame her. Fortunately for the little girl's survival, Himiko tended to tune out the constant thin cries. Carrick, however, found it distressing when his twin was unhappy. Sometimes Aodhán thought the boy fed and grew for the two of them.

"Aodhán."

Aodhán stopped at the sound of the voice like soft thunder. In the doorway was easily the largest mortal he had ever had occasion to know, and the man may have some jack-in-irons out massed. Grizzly Mountain stood well over seven-feet-tall, a wall of solid copper-skinned muscle peering down at him from behind the frame of his bedroom door. "Good morning, Mountain." Originally from the Tanana people of Alaska, Mountain had found his way into Himiko's household the century before.

Mountain nodded, his dark eyes solemn, as usual. "The little girl is hungry." He reached out a massive hand and brushed his fingers over her thin hair. Aodhán let him. Mountain may be a ferocious warrior, but he would never harm Keiko. "May I help?"

Aodhán nearly closed his eyes with relief. He had hoped Mountain would offer, but he could not ask. The bear king belonged to Himiko. It was not the first time Mountain would feed Keiko, rich feedings which Aodhán knew helped his daughter, though even the blood of a king could not come close to taking the place of her mother. But it was something they did in secret—if Himiko found out one of her kings was feeding her unwanted child she would forbid it. He nodded, a grateful smile on his face, and glanced up and down the hallway before stepping into Mountain's room.

◗

What had she just seen? Lelia crouched near the wall as the black tower fell, her eyes wide. The occasional car... the occasional *police car* drove by, and no one else seemed to notice the battle. The knights in armor. The... monsters! A building fell! People were hurt, dead, and no one seemed to care.

Why?

She wasn't crazy. She wasn't crazy! Lelia felt tears pooling yet again. All she knew for certain was that she was in trouble and it was Jeremy Moore's fault. She had come here to see his father, to tell him what Jeremy had done to her, to settle this once and for all, but there he was, being dragged away. She rested her hand on her pregnant belly. She needed help but forced herself to walk away into the dark night before they dragged her away, too.

What was she going to do now?

◗

In the dark of his makeshift shelter tucked against the base of one of the wharves, Stephen suddenly stopped strumming his guitar and looked skyward. Ever so slightly, fates were shifting, realigning... Winter Mulcahy had made the first binding, forging the ties of her new family. Good. It was one step closer and just in time, too. For one such as he who faced eternity, time was becoming frighteningly short. Smiling grimly, Stephen returned to his music, picking up the tune where he had left off.

Frighteningly short, indeed.

(Coming 2018)

The headlights carved out his path through the moonlit night up the I-5 through Washington State, the tires gripping the road remarkably well at a hundred and thirty miles per hour. Alerich came up behind a truck and a semi just as one was moving to pass the other and floored the gas, darting between the other vehicles like they were standing still. His passenger gripped the bar and made a small squeaking noise. All he had to remember was to stay on the right and the wide median helped with that.

Bloody Americans. Madness.

Moments later another sports car shot around the slower truck, engine screaming, and a voice sounded through Alerich's speaker phone. "Rick, suicide is not going to get you out of marrying Celia."

Alerich laughed at Thomas, his best friend and best man, sweet adrenaline coursing through his body. "I didn't know that was even an option."

Elspeth let out an elegant snort. "Thomas is right. I don't think even killing yourself would save you."

He glanced at his twin as she unwound her fingers from the passenger door's grab bar, her short, chic, black hair barely brushing her ears. "I think you two are envisioning a zombie version of myself shuffling down the aisle."

Thomas chuckled. "Yes, I wouldn't put necromancy past her."

Alerich chuckled, thinking of himself gray and green, flesh decaying, his black leather jacket the only thing keeping him intact… All right, that was disgusting. But anything to keep his mind off the wedding.

Off Celia Carralond.

He felt the smile slide from his face. Celia was everything a wizard could want in a wife. She was both politically and magically powerful, being the only child of the Archwizard of the Wizards' Council. She was brilliant. She was beautiful. But beauty wasn't everything. "'Sweetest things turn sourest by their deeds,'" he said with a bitter edge to his tongue.

Celia was also a raging, unrepentant bitch.

"Alerich, man, what was that, now? I can barely hear you."

Fitz, ironic as always, raised his voice just a bit louder than was needed to be heard through Thomas's earpiece from the passenger seat of the other car and still sounded vaguely intoxicated, the words enunciated with the razor's edge his father had beaten into him. Of course, that was Fitz pretty much at any given time. He avoided hangovers by staying piss drunk and was also profoundly deaf.

Elspeth leaned towards Alerich's phone mic, knowing her voice would translate to Fitz's phone's talk-to-text app. "He's quoting Shakespeare again, Fitz."

"Ah yes, the Bard." Fitz sounded like he was pulling out his flask, his magical focus object and scotch transportation device all-in-one. He had it enchanted to refill from a source at Thomas's family estate, so that it was never empty. An impressive piece of magic, indeed. They could hear the small, squeaky noise of the top being unscrewed. "To dear Will. May he always endeavor to inspire us." The sarcasm in his voice carried loud and clear.

"'O God, that men should put an enemy in their mouths to steal away their brains!'" Thomas intoned, his voice filled with amusement.

"'In vino veritas,'" Fitz retorted as his app provided. Alerich knew Thomas would not be able to turn his head for his lips to be read at these speeds, and the interiors of the cars were dark, anyway.

"Will never wrote that, Fitz," Alerich said with a grin and changed lanes.

"Oh really? The only thing the Romans ever wrote he never cribbed, then."

Elspeth burst into harsh laughter.

Thomas and Alerich groaned. "No, no. No more about Shakespeare and Plautus from you."

"You're ruining a perfectly good car chase."

"Have you two heathens ever read Plautus? Your *Will was a bloody plagiarist. Now Kit Marlowe, there was an original writer for you!" He cleared his throat. "'Was this the face that launch'd a thousand ships, and burnt the topmost towers of Ilium? Sweet Helen, make me immortal with a kiss. Her lips—'"

Cries of derision rang out from both cars, drowning out Fitz's recitation and likely filling up his phone's screen. "No, no, not that. Anything but that." Alerich drummed his fingers on the steering wheel in time to his racing thoughts.

"Do me better, then."

Alerich passed a sedan in a blur and rose to the drunken challenge. "'I'm armed with more than complete steel—The justice of my quarrel.'"

Elspeth cast her gaze at the overhead signs, navigating as they blew past. "'I am Envy. I cannot read and therefore wish all books burned.'" Her voice was half-soft, half-defiant.

Alerich glanced at his twin. Unlike the three of them she had not had the opportunity to go away to school. The reasons did not bear dwelling upon. Instead he said, "'Honour is purchas'd by the deeds we do.'"

"How about some advice for the ladies?" Elspeth turned to face the mic again, a crafty look in her midnight-blue eyes. "'You must be proud, bold, pleasant, resolute, and now and then stab, when occasion serves.'"

Alerich grinned, approving, as Fitz made sputtering noises, and added, "'Fornication: but that was in another country; and besides, the wench is dead.'"

Thomas's voice sounded eloquent in Alerich's earpiece. "'Till swollen with cunning, of a self-conceit, his waxen wings did mount above his reach, and melting, Heavens conspir'd his overthrow.'"

Fitz sighed melodramatically. "'Accursed be he that first invented war.'"

Alerich and Thomas cheered their victory.

Elspeth rolled her eyes and smirked. "*Si hoc legere scis nimium eruditionis habes.*"

The three men laughed, and Fitz made a mock scoffing noise. "Keep your modern jokes out of my quote battle, wench. You're confusing my phone app with your terrible pronunciation. Next it'll be '*semper ubi sub ubi*.'"

Thomas chuckled. "Our lives are not like other people's lives…"

There was a moment of companionable silence broken only by road noise and then Fitz said, "I hear John Heathrow is getting married, too."

Alerich's hands tightened on the steering wheel and he floored it.

"For fuck's sake, Fitz!" Elspeth snapped as she reached for the grab bar. "Seriously?"

"Well, I'm just saying that since I'm not invited to Rick's wedding that maybe I'll go to old John's instead. Or maybe someone else's. Seems to be a veritable plague of them going around this season."

Alerich's mouth pulled into a small smile. Maybe he could get himself uninvited from his own wedding and go with Fitz somewhere else.

"Our exit is coming up… quite soon in fact. Perhaps the breaks?" Elspeth held the grab bar with one hand and her phone with its GPS application in the other.

Alerich finally allowed himself to slow down and took the lazy angle of the off ramp as he looked out over the horizon. Somewhere out there in the darkness was the coast and the Pacific Ocean. He'd seen it in L.A. but never this far north. Would it be cold? Would he see whales?

Would he care?

He glanced at the highway sign and picked up speed again, trusting in the misdirection wards to save them from human notice.

Forty-nine miles to Seahaven.

ABOUT THE AUTHOR

A. E. Lowan is the pseudonym of three authors who collectively create the dark urban fantasy series, *The Books of Binding*. Born in Texas, Jessica Smith is a college student who brings a passion for science to tame the physics of Seahaven. Hailing from Missouri, Jennifer Vinck is a former bookseller who brings a love of theatre and linguistics to breathe life into the characters. A Navy brat, raised in Washington, California, and Missouri, Kristin Vinck is a recovering medievalist who brings an obsession with history and folklore to paint a detailed cultural canvas for *The Books of Binding*.

We would be honored to have you follow us online. You can find more of A. E. Lowan and *The Books of Binding* at:

https://www.aelowan.com
https://www.facebook.com/aelowan
https://www.amazon.com/author/aelowan
https://www.goodreads.com/aelowan
https://aelowan.tumblr.com
https://twitter.com/AELowan

CPSIA information can be obtained
at www.ICGtesting.com
Printed in the USA
LVHW08s1518290718
585289LV00001BA/143/P

9 781732 316409